A GOOD VENGEANCE

LOUISA LO

TIN CAN
PRESS

Cover Design: Jacqueline Sweet

Cover Photo: Sara Eirew

Beta Reading: Melissa Bleier

Concept, Line and Copy Editing: Help Me Edit

A Good Vengeance/Louisa Lo—1st edition

ISBN: 978-0-9952302-2-4

To Al,

For being so wonderful to my sister all those years. You are missed.

ACKNOWLEDGMENT

To Dr. S. Raheb and Dr. D. Costello, thanks for taking care of my baby so I could find the mental strength to keep on editing.

❧ I ❧
A VENGEANCE FREE-FOR-ALL

❧ I ❧

PRINCE WHO?

I MUST HAVE HAD an old people theme going when it came to vengeance assignments.

"Hi, I'm Megan. I'm here to see Sandra Hogan, room one twelve." I pasted on a sad smile, hoping for some sympathy to get me in, and leaned over the oversized reception booth. With my hair pulled back in a ponytail and my face sprinkled with a dash of de-aging fairy dust, I looked about sixteen. A regular human girl here to see a sick loved one, not a vengeance-demon-in-training dishing out comeuppance to dying wrongdoers in order to earn good grades.

The receptionist smiled back. "And Ms. Hogan is your...?"

"Aunt. I'm late because I had softball practice. You know, I should've just skipped it." I bit my lip, my voice caught with regret I wasn't actually feeling. The visiting hours ended at four thirty today, and it was already four twenty-eight. I needed to see Ms. Hogan today if I could, as my work schedule was rather packed this week.

The receptionist looked around as if checking if her boss or other visitors were within hearing range, then she winked at me and tilted her head toward the hall. "Go on in, hon.

Visiting hours are pretty much over now, but I don't see why you can't go in and see your auntie real quick. Don't tell anyone I let you in, though, or I'll be in trouble."

"Thank you *so* much." My gratitude was heartfelt, but not in the way the receptionist might think. I could've waltzed right through the reception during all hours of the day using a bit of compulsion, but I was on conservation mode having just exchanged most of my magical credits into human currency for this month's rent. Living on the human plane while going to university on the demon side carried some additional expenses compared to other students.

Independence was expensive, but acting was cheap. This way I could save my magic for direct interaction with the target only.

I walked down the hall to find room one twelve, excited to get started. Now that I wasn't so green anymore, the prospect of cracking open a fresh case of vengeance and seeing bad people getting theirs filled me with a sense of happy anticipation.

For the first vengeance assignment of my second co-op work term at University of Demonic Studies, Faculty of Arts and Vengeance, I found myself with yet another senior citizen on my work order. I certainly hoped this new assignment would go smoother. Considering I almost got fried alive the last time I tried performing vengeance at a retirement home, that shouldn't be too hard.

But this wasn't a retirement home; it was a hospice, hence the lax security. It was a place for the terminally ill. A place for making peace with one's life and family members before moving on to the next world.

Or, a place for wrongdoers to get served some overdue vengeance, and in addressing the injustice they caused in this lifetime, give their victims the peace and balance that had long eluded *them*.

The prospect of facilitating this healing process was what made me want to become a licensed vengeance demon in the first place. Anyone could be *born* a vengeance demon, but being *licensed* as one was a deliberate choice. It was like the difference between being born a native English speaker and getting a master in English Literature. Beyond social acceptance and prestige of the vengeance license, I really wanted to help bring forth that kind of peace for the victims.

Well, getting paid doing it wasn't so bad, either.

I found the room stated on my work order with no problem at all. My new mentor for the co-op program, who happened to be my grandmother, had provided me with a detailed layout of the building, along with the target's profile.

Sandra Hogan, retired nurse at the triage desk of a local ER. Petty. Power-tripping. Purposefully unhelpful.

A classic case of minor bureaucrat syndrome. I'd seen *those* types before.

I walked into the room and closed the door behind me, making sure to place a muting spell over the immediate area. My target's pension must have been pretty good, if having a private room and nurses making rounds at the top of every hour was anything to go by. A small-framed woman lay in the bed, facing away from me and looking toward the window. Outside, the ground was covered in snow; a Toronto streetcar could be heard but not seen.

"Finally. Give me more of those damn shots." She turned to me. Either she didn't notice I wasn't dressed as a nurse, or she didn't care.

"Hello, I'm Megan Aequitas," I began. Not everything I'd told the receptionist was a lie. My name *was* Megan. "Are you Sandra Marlena Elizabeth Hogan, of Hamilton, Ontario, born to Ann and Michael Hogan?" I asked as I walked over to the window and drew the heavy blinds.

"What about it?" Seventy-seven years' worth of spite

showed as she snapped at me. Her eyes were clouded with pain, but nevertheless shrewd. No age, discomfort, or late-stage cancer was going to soften this old gal up. "You people know perfectly well who I am. I pay good money to make sure you do. Now get me that morphine or your supervisor will hear about this."

I tightened my jaw. I didn't understand how people, super-natural or otherwise, could do bad things and simply assume that what goes around would never come around. "Don't you think it's ironic to demand excellent medical care, when you devoted your entire life to being crappy in attending other people's needs?"

"I have no idea what you're talking about." In contrary to her harsh denial, the faintest hint of fear crossed her face.

I took out her file, enchanted to be small enough to fit in the pocket of my jacket. I expanded and opened it, and started reading aloud. "Samuel Robertson. Visited the ER on July 2, 1974 with an inflamed appendix. He was six years old. You didn't like the way his mother talked to you. She was worried about her little boy so she kept asking you if he was next. To retaliate, you moved him all the way to the back of the queue when he should have been next to see the doctor. His appendix burst while he was waiting for help, infecting the abdominal cavity's lining. The boy lived, but you caused him a great deal of pain."

Sandra sat up from her bed. "What the hell?"

"Jenny Weston. Middle-aged." I tried to keep the anger from my voice, my fingers bunching up the file from my effort. Vengeance demons were supposed to be the instru-ment of justice, but unaffected by the grievances themselves. I guess being a half-blood meant I might never be aloof like the rest of them. "May 5, 1991. Mrs. Weston came in because she was experiencing the symptoms that her eye specialist had told her to go straight to the ER if they ever appeared.

You informed her—without consulting the eye resident—that she was just fine and had imagined the whole thing. You sent her home without care. She ended up with a detached retina and vision loss."

"This is crazy talk." Sandra's face told me she knew exactly what I was talking about. She might not remember the specific names and faces of the people she'd hurt through the years, but the modus operandi should sound very familiar to her.

As I read out a selection of her crimes spanning over four decades, I had to will my hands to un-clutch the file, longing as I was to wrap them around my target's neck. Her negligence had resulted in everything from unnecessary agony to three preventable deaths. What a witch. And I'd met some real ones in my day.

She had always been super clever about making sure there wasn't any hard evidence that could later link back to her. She never got caught—hence the cushy retirement with a full pension. After all this time, she probably thought she'd gotten away with murder, or murders, in this case.

"Sandra Hogan, it is time to pay for your sins." I closed the file after I finished reading ten cases out of it at random. I'd be here all night if I was to read out all of her crimes. "By the power vested in me by the Concord Council, you're hereby sentenced to Vengeance. May you endure it with grace and contemplation."

Now that the proper wordings had been recited, the real work could begin.

Just then a nurse came in, so I quickly activated an invisibility spell over myself with a snap of my fingers.

"Good afternoon, Ms. Hogan. It's snack time. How are you doing?" The nurse put a tray of food on the table over Sandra's bed. There was a bowl of Jell-O, a cup of fruit, and a glass of orange juice on the tray. Sandra stared at the space in the room where I had been visible to her just seconds ago; her mouth opened and then closed. I was still physically there —she just couldn't see me anymore.

Sandra pointed toward where I stood with a mixture of horror, relief, and puzzlement on her face. Horror of having seen me, relief that I was no longer there, and puzzlement as to whether or not I was merely a fragment of her imagination.

"What is it?" The nurse frowned, glanced at my direction, seeing nothing but an empty room. "What are you looking at?"

"Noth...nothing." Sandra shook her head and seemed to come to a conclusion. "My mind must be playing tricks on me."

Probably unsure how to respond to that, the nurse asked instead, "How's your pain been?"

"The pain. Right. Of course," Sandra murmured. Self-centered to the bone, having her pain mentioned seemed to have snapped her out of the shock she'd been experiencing from her interaction with me. She set her jaw firm and reverted back to her good old charming self. "About that. Give me the morphine, girl. I know people on the board who can make your life miserable if you don't take good care of me."

"No need to use that kind of language, Sandra. You're due another shot anyway." The nurse sighed and turned to get whatever medical instrument might be required to dispense the morphine. I cast a freezing spell on her.

With the nurse rigid and motionless, I reappeared to Sandra. She hissed at the sight of me.

"Yes, I'm real," I assured her, "and so is the punishment you're about to receive."

"Go to hell!" she bellowed, making me glad of my fore-sight to envelope the room in a muting spell upon entrance. I so didn't need anyone to come running because of the noise she was making.

"I won't be going to Hell with a capital H, but you will be. Well, not until *after* I'm done with you." It was the vengeance demon's job to "soften up" the wrongdoers before they moved on to eternal damnation. And damnation was what Sandra totally deserved, for all the patients she'd hurt, people who came to her in their hour of need. "Do you remember what you told little Samuel Robertson's mother when she unintentionally offended you?"

"I don't remember," she snarled. "That was a long time ago. Who the heck cares?"

"You *should* care, because as your punishment, the cruel words and excuses you used on those patients to deny them care are now going to be thrown back at you."

I snapped my fingers, and the nurse woke from her trance at the same moment I became invisible again. She straightened her spine and faced Sandra. "I'm sorry, but I will not be talked to in this manner. If you're going to disrespect me, then you can stand to wait a bit more."

The nurse walked out without administering the morphine.

An hour passed as I watched Sandra sweat and shake with pain. Had a vengeance demon been assigned to her earlier, her punishment would've been a lot more active. Like getting her into a heart surgery and have her lungs replaced, or something like that. But since she was already in pain, my job involved preventing the relief of it, which in a way was harder to do because my instinct was to comfort upon seeing an old lady in distress.

While vengeance laws demanded that I be physically present during her punishment, I was no sadist. Witnessing her suffering wasn't fun for me. I longed for the clinical detachment that came so easily for my classmates.

At the end of the hour, another nurse showed up and checked in on Sandra. Again the latter asked for the morphine.

I froze Nurse Number Two before she reached for the painkiller.

"Do you remember what you said to Mrs. Jenny Weston when she begged for your help?" I asked, remembering the details from the file and getting angry at my target all over again. Okay, so maybe I could get some manner of satisfaction out of this, after all.

Sandra just glared at me with sheer hatred.

I snapped my fingers. The nurse could talk again, but she didn't see me. "The pain is all in your head. Geez, people complain about everything these days. My time is too valuable for this."

The nurse turned and left.

I settled down in the chair beside the bed. This was going to be a long day, and it would last well into the night. Sandra had a lot of victims that needed avenging, and she had used many classic lines on them, such as "Calm down. I'm looking into it as fast as I can," "You're not the center of the universe, you know," and "Cry me a river, the hospital is full of people like you."

I pulled out a pocket novel from my backpack and started reading, but couldn't concentrate. To sit around and hear the wheezing and moaning of the old lady as waves of pain rocked through her wasn't easy, especially since I had a grandmother of my own—albeit a near immortal and powerful one. I kept reciting the various crimes Sandra had committed to remind myself that my job had a healthy function for the Cosmic Balance.

But really, couldn't the Council have gotten to her sooner? Punishing someone this old and frail was really not a fun task, and over two-thirds of her victims had passed on already.

When a vengeance was served, the anger and bitterness that festered in the victims' hearts would magically dissolve, replaced with a great sense of peace and relief—but only if those hearts were still beating to begin with.

As it was, almost all the victims carried the burden of the injustice to their graves. How was that for being fair?

Sometimes the inefficiencies of the Council could drive a girl mad. I knew what I said before about justice comes slowly but surely. But really, this was super-slow. Molasses-in-January slow. If they had punished Sandra sooner there might not have been so many victims; knowing that there were nasty consequences to their actions had a wonderful way of scaring people straight. And what was up with just a single day and night of pain for a lifetime of sins? Vengeance heavily discounted due to her age, that was what it was.

It reminded me of those catchy human pizza delivery commercials that I used to watch. If it took over forty minutes you could have it for free. In this case, if a vengeance was not delivered to the target in a timely manner, it was discounted.

That just didn't sit well with me. At all.

"If this was left to us mercenaries, this target would've been punished a long time ago," a voice said from across the other side of the bed, as though someone had read my mind.

I dropped my novel and jumped out of the chair, realizing a beat too late that there were now more than two people in the room. Damn, I hated it when people teleported in without any forewarning.

There was Gregory, looking sinfully delicious in a tight black sweatshirt and dark jeans, filling them out in all the right places. Muscular build, long limbs, graceful movement... he reminded me of a lithe jungle cat. The Earl Grey aftertaste of his power signature was rich and potent. His brown hair was shorter than when I had last seen him; it was cut just above his chiseled cheekbones. His lips were arrogant and sensuous. I always had a heck of a time pinning down his age. His measured manners and self-assurance bespoke experiences that outmatched people in their late twenties, yet I got a feeling he was in fact a lot closer to me in age.

Look at that pair of annoyingly proud wings of his. Midnight blue. Uncamouflaged. We didn't have the kind of relationship for him to pop by unannounced and let his wings spread out across half the room. It was considered rude in vengeance society to do so, unless it was between family members, or lovers, which we were neither. Mercenaries obviously worked with a very different set of rules, and he was flaunting it.

It had been over three months since I'd seen Gregory. A school semester ago, to be exact; funny how my life was measured in semesters now. Co-op work term, school term, then co-op work term again.

I was a little busy when I last dealt with him, saving Esme and the world and all, but not so busy that I forgot that I'd promised him a boon—who even used that word these days, let alone asked for one? I was forced to give him a stupid, unspecific boon like I was some lame-ass, wish-granting genie. Worse, the bastard hadn't even bothered to come collect yet. I hated being indebted to someone.

Yeah, that's the story I'm sticking with. No way was I going to admit to missing the jerk.

"What the hell are you doing here?" I snapped. Better to show annoyance than drool over the jerk face. Gregory wasn't exactly the world's most trustworthy guy. He'd withheld information from me that almost cost my half-sister, Esme, her life.

"Well, hello to you, too." Gregory smiled ruefully. "I was just commenting on the inefficient and dreadfully slow process of your governing body."

There was no need for him to know that I was thinking the exact same thing just before he popped up. "Yeah, and the mercenaries do it so much better."

"Of course." He didn't seem to get my sarcasm. Asshole. "We're hired by the victims. For the victims. None of that bureaucratic crap that drags on forever."

"And what if there's a misunderstanding, or your client is just being vindictive? You'll end up with a miscarriage of justice." *Ha, take that!*

"We vet all the clients carefully, often more so than licensed vengeance demons. We vet the target thoroughly, too." He smirked. "Too bad the same couldn't be said about the homework that was done on Dan Pillar, or the lack of it."

I glared at him at the mention of the target from my last work term. The supposedly harmless human turned out to be in possession of dark magic and he had almost killed me with it. And yes, it was an agent of the Council who had vetted him and sent me to him.

I could've told Gregory that the same agent later turned out to be a fanatic from a secret society. I didn't think it would've helped my case in his argument about the low vetting quality of the Council.

But I wasn't about to admit he had a point, either. So instead, I went on the offense. "You didn't answer me the first time. What are you doing here?"

"Can I not just come by and say hi?" Gregory's lips curved into a smile that was sexy if not for the hint of sarcasm in it. "You know, from one professional to another?"

I was a vengeance demon in the process of being properly licensed by the governing body of my race in order to become a guardian for the Cosmic Balance. He was a vengeance demon exploiting his mama-given ability for profit, and only employed civility in his speech and appearance for the purpose of mockery. We. Were. Not. Both. Professionals.

When I just crossed my arms and stared at Gregory, he dropped his devil-may-care attitude, his expression turned serious. "Alright, the truth is, I came here to confess. I haven't been entirely truthful with you. In fact, I might've misled you somewhat, and I'm sorry."

Sorry, my butt. Whatever he claimed to have lied to me about.

I snorted. "You've been untruthful to me? Really? *You*, of all people? And the surprise here is...what?"

Gregory's eyes narrowed. "You might not believe it, but we mercenaries have our own code of conduct."

"Whatever happened to 'no honor among thieves'?"

From the muscle that jumped in his jaw, I knew I'd just crossed the line. I reminded myself that there was probably a heck of a backstory behind someone of highborn vengeance blood who resorted to this shady manner of earning a livelihood. Maybe my criticism regarding his chosen career hit a sore spot.

Right. Insult the man, not his job.

"What do you want? As you can see, I'm in the middle of an assignment." I made my tone as professional as I could, courtesy of a course I took last semester called *Business Communication 207: Before, During and After the Punishment.*

Gregory blinked, and then he was back. His jaw loosened and his shoulders, which I didn't even realize were tense, relaxed. Vengeance demons, being a race that systematically managed the Cosmic Balance, tended to respond best to official sounding stuff. Looked like even a rogue and mercenary like him was no exception. I made a mental note of that. "I would like to call in my boon, of course. But as I tried to explain, in the process of obtaining it, I might've created some misunderstanding between us."

"Which part of it was misunderstood? It sounded pretty clear to me." I reminded him, "You said that the job is going to be legal for both vengeance and human laws, doesn't involve trickery, and got my grandmother's stamp of approval."

I knew the parameters he'd set for the boon well because I'd spent many sleepless nights in the past few months thinking about them. I'd granted the boon in desperation to save Esme's life, and only afterward did I ponder what Gregory would try to trick me into doing. There must've been some kind of legal technicality he was counting on. It was like that old human movie *Bedazzled*—the devil would always find some loophole.

Sandra groaned, reminding me that we were not alone. I really hated having this conversation with Gregory in front of her, but it wasn't like she was going to tell anyone else. At least my target was still in discomfort, and still going without her painkiller, so it wasn't like the vengeance stopped while I was forced to deal with Gregory. There was that.

"All of those conditions are still true," he confirmed.

"Then which part did you lie about?"

He straightened. "Now, *lying* is such a harsh word—"

"Tomato. Tomahto. Which. Part. Did. You. Lie. About?"

"I'm simply trying to point out that I might have given you the impression that I needed your help for an assignment I'd already obtained, when in fact it was more like I was—"

"Fishing," I said simply.

He swallowed his unfinished sentence, seemingly surprised at my lack of reaction, so I continued. "Let me guess. You have a certain instinct about where a freelance job might be, and you wanted to secure my help before soliciting the potential client."

"And you knew this?"

"Yep." I shrugged. "I did a bit of freelancing, remember? I understand sometimes you have to create your own jobs. So hit me with the next lie already. Don't deny it. You threw that bit at me to test the water. Consider it tested. Get to what you're really here to confess."

He smiled. "I sometimes forget you can be refreshingly practical."

Practical. Right. In this matter, yes. But I wasn't entirely practical when it came to thinking about him. But he needn't know that. I made a great show of checking on Sandra's suffering progress, checking her pulse and pupils and all that, when there was really nothing new, passive vengeance that it was. "Go on."

"Alright." This time he swallowed. Seeing someone who was usually arrogant looking nervous was making *me* nervous. "I also mentioned that your help would make your changeling friend happy. Truth is, it might cause her as much pain as it would joy."

I walked around the bed toward him, barely containing my temper at his suggestion of possibly hurting Serafina. How dare he think I would even consider causing grief for one of my closest friends? If that's what he expected me to do to repay him, we'd see how badly he wanted his damn boon after I shrank his nuts.

No, Megan.

I'd recently started to learn meditation from Grandma Aequitas, and I'd been practicing letting my trickster tendencies run wild in a controlled environment. But this was no controlled environment. Serafina was one of mine and just thinking about what Gregory wanted from me made my blood boil.

I kept walking until we were mere inches apart.

My pearl pendant grew bright, signaling the gearing up of my power.

"Even if it hurts her, she would still want you to help, you know," Gregory said quietly. He stood his ground, not powering up in response. Somehow, his not rising to my challenge was pissing me off even more. "Look, I just want you to tell her what's going on. And we'll go from there. She'll never forgive you if you don't tell her what I know."

That gave me pause. "Just what is this really about?"

His eyes were so close to mine, I could see the white parts of them. He didn't blink. "Prince Eldon."

"Prince who?"

"Crown Prince Eldon. Of Fae. She'll know who I'm talking about. He's in trouble. Can you tell her that? She's the only one who can locate him."

"And this benefits you how?" I spit out. Gregory wouldn't be doing this if there weren't something in it for him. He was a mercenary, for Hades's sake.

"I would rather not say at this point. Let's just say that I've been keeping my ears on the ground, and an opportunity to curry favor from someone has just presented itself."

"Currying favors? Like from someone who's going to be king one day? By helping a certain crown prince out of a spot of trouble?" I pressed.

"Something like that. Look, I'll explain later. You better hurry. My source told me this is urgent."

Was it really urgent, or was Gregory trying to shut me up until I was in too deep? My gut feeling was that this guy was totally bullshitting me about his role in all this.

I pointed at Sandra. She was keeping quiet, but I could sense her hope rising. She'd heard every word between me and Gregory, and she thought she might be able to get off easy after all. "So you're expecting me to leave my target in the middle of a vengeance assignment to do this? What if she, like, died in the meanwhile or something? You know how much trouble I could be in?"

Without my interference, Sandra would be relieved by a shot of morphine at the top of the next hour and at regular intervals after that. She could pass on to the beyond in relative comfort, her vengeance unserved. Did Gregory not know the backlog down at the underworld? If Sandra got there without at least some of her sins abated, it would be an administrative nightmare to process her.

"I assure you this can't wait," Gregory insisted.

"Alright. On the off chance that you're telling the truth, I'll go talk to her. But if she refuses to help," I warned, "I'm not going to push her."

"Agreed," he said quickly. Too quickly. His tone was curt, his eyes confident. He seemed very sure that Serafina would say yes.

Huh.

"And I'll speak to her alone."

"Of course. You don't even have to bring me along to find the prince if you don't want to."

"I don't." The less Gregory could be a part of this, the better. I needed to see what was really going on first.

"Not a problem."

Again, he agreed too easily.

"Alright, then." I started for the door, stopped, turning to point at Sandra, who had a look of triumph on her face. "You. Don't die on me."

"Don't worry." Gregory grinned like a cat that ate a canary. "I already checked with my contact at Hades. This lady is not due to die for another two weeks. It's going to be a long and drawn-out death. She'll be right here when you come back."

Sandra's curses filled the room as I exited it. The anticipation of pain—to be inflicted by me or otherwise—was a punishment all on its own.

Gregory followed me out, winking at me. "A freebie off the books. I must be getting soft."

❧ 2 ❧

SCENIC PAINTING

GUESSING where Serafina was located wasn't hard at all. But the getting there part was a pain.

Thanks to Grandma Aequitas, Serafina had failed her first year at Demon U—for her own good. Being kidnapped at birth by the changelings, she had barely returned to the vengeance plane before being enrolled in school by her powerful family. She had an entire new way of life to adjust to, and the result of rushing the process was disastrous. Her grades were terrible; she was constantly bullied by everyone. Anyone who thought bullying ended after high school had never experienced Demon U, with its small classroom size and deep-rooted elitist culture. Serafina and I were in the same year together, so I'd seen her hardship firsthand.

Grandma eventually stepped in and put her on a one-year hiatus. From what I understood, her family backed off, too, allowing her some much needed time to immerse herself in the vengeance culture, however begrudgingly.

Serafina's family home was on the vengeance plane. Though vengeance demons were responsible for addressing the injustices for *all* the planes in the Cosmic Balance, the human one was considered a special case. That was due to the mortal's lack of magic, and the fact that the vengeance and human planes were parallel universes.

There were thousands of planes in the Cosmic Balance. Well, technically there was an infinite number of them out there, but those who had life intelligent enough to be active participants were in the thousands, with the ones holding the most powers in the double digits. Some planes were similar to one another, though not exactly identical, and some were drastically different. The difficulties in teleporting through the barriers between planes varied, and depended on the traveler's skill level.

The ease of cross-dimensional traveling and the low difficulty in handling the targets made the human plane the perfect practice grounds for vengeance trainees such as myself. That was why I was assigned to work on Ms. Hogan.

Yet there was a different reason why human movies and smartphones made their way into many supernaturals' households, and became a counter-culture of sorts throughout the Cosmic Balance. Granted, the wide availability of the mortals' handiwork was a factor, but that was not all.

Many, including myself, actually found the humans fascinating. In the relatively short time since progressing from near savages, humans had come up with quite a lot of technologies that were almost indistinguishable from magic. Of course, Hades forbid if the snobbish vengeance demons would ever openly consider the mortals their equals, let alone living among them. Nope, especially not Serafina's family, with an ancestry illustrious enough to fill a medical textbook.

Due to the supposed urgent nature of the visit, I didn't bother to save magic by finding pre-existing portals to the vengeance plane. So it took me mere seconds to teleport to the outer boundary of Serafina's home. Like all vengeance families, big or small, a protection spell was placed around the perimeter of the twenty-bedroom Advocatus family estate. The Bridle Path neighborhood of Toronto, with large mansions on two to four acre lots, was no less affluent than its counterpart on the human side. The teleporting part was easy, but the walk to get to the actual front door of the property took me almost twenty minutes.

The contemptuous butler told me that Serafina was out back. He didn't, however, offer to let me walk *through* the mansion, though it would've saved me much time and energy. Instead, he made it very clear my path was to go *around* it. Dear old Andre and I had interacted with each other whenever I was here to visit my friend, and the experience had not endeared us to each other. He could smell the trickster in me, and I could smell the classist asshole in him. Funny how some people could really get behind a system that would put them in a servant's rank, if it meant there were others considered even lower ranking than them.

I turned to start the long trek around the mansion when a disapproving voice boomed behind Andre, "What exactly are you doing here, Miss Megan Aequitas?"

In the past months since I'd gotten closer to Serafina, I'd always been lucky enough to visit her when no one else in her family was home. But just the way my day was going, High Judge Edbert Llewellyn Advocatus was there. Serafina's uncle played a pretty heavy hand in my suspension during the last work term, and he was also a powerful member of the Council. He wasn't someone I could afford to offend.

But that didn't mean I was happy to see him.

"High Judge Advocatus." I bowed to him in accordance to vengeance etiquette. "I'm here to see Serafina."

"And what's the purpose of this visit?"

"With all due respect, that's between Serafina and me."
Then I added, "Your Honor."

Buzz off, jerk. If Gregory is telling the truth, then I'm on a time-line here.

"I fail to see the benefits of my niece hanging out with the likes of you." The high judge huffed. "That defeats the entire purpose of the hiatus."

I guess when they gave their consent for Serafina to take the hiatus, they were hoping that she would use this free time to job shadow a few of her many accomplished relatives and in doing so, realize her incredible fortune in being born into such a privileged family. There was the high judge's court she could sit in, and one of her twin aunts was the chief liaison with the four major witches' unions, while the other was an arch vengeance demon just like my dad.

To the family's disappointment, Serafina simply chose to stay home. Reading, doing art, and contemplating the changes in her life.

I thought it was the healthiest thing she could've done.

With Serafina's uncle looking at me like I was a bug and costing me precious time I didn't have, I knew I had to get out of the high judge's presence fast. Without looking like I was trying to.

"Maybe seeing my difficulties being accepted into the vengeance society will, er, reiterate to her the importance of having a proper place in it?" I offered helpfully, my eyes 100 percent sarcasm-free.

Take that, creepy dude.

High Judge Advocatus studied me for a long moment but couldn't call me out on my bullshit when it was done with just enough politeness and pretend sincerity. "Perhaps," he murmured.

That was all the cue I needed to take off.

I found Serafina by a small clearing facing a frozen pond

on the edge of the Advocatus family estate. The waning rays from twilight reflected on the iced-over body of water, dried twigs of pussy willows poked out from the snow covering the surrounding marsh. I pulled the sleeves of my jacket farther down. I had no idea why anybody would want to be outside when they didn't have to.

Serafina stood by a propped up canvas on the clearing with an easel and paintbrush in hand, her eyebrows knitted in concentration as she added a careful stroke on what looked to be a landscape painting, yet she wasn't painting the wintery nature scene before her at all.

Rectangular midnight blue strips, depicting skyscrapers, filled the background with tiny yellow dots over them representing fluorescent lights. A bird of prey, glowing as if on fire, swooped down from above, heading straight for the roof of a building on the foreground. There was a person standing on the roof, and with a splash of flesh-colored paint, Serafina was in the middle of adding details to her face. The character's body was clad in black. Skin tight.

Classic vengeance demon outfit.

"Hey," I called out.

Serafina jumped and dropped the paintbrush. It disappeared in the snow surrounding her.

"Sorry." I hurried over. "I thought you already knew I was here and were playing the cool-artist-being-in-the-zone thing."

That wasn't entirely true. In the past months we'd hung out a lot, and I knew her enough to know she wasn't the pretentious type. I figured she was probably too distracted to notice me, but I felt like I had to talk about something, anything more trivial before broaching on the real reason I was there. After all, how do you tell someone that a mercenary you'd met from an old crisis wanted to drag the both of you into a new one?

Serafina turned those soulful brown eyes on me. "You're here about something." Dammit, she was so quiet most of the time I always forgot how perceptive she was. Well, better get on with the explanation then. I swallowed and told her about my encounter with Gregory.

"You have no idea what he's talking about, right?" I asked her anxiously. "I mean, the guy is a jerk. A total jerk. In fact, forget the whole thing. It's probably some sort of false lead he cooked up anyway."

"I know exactly *who* he's talking about. Though I never expected to hear that name ever again," she whispered in a shaky voice, and the rest of her started trembling, too. She reached out to steady herself, suddenly gripping my arm like an anaconda. Ouch, I didn't even know her grip could be that firm. "This Gregory, he said Eldon is in trouble?"

"Yeah, that's what he said." I eyed her curiously, wondering at her referring to this Crown Prince Eldon on a first name basis. Just who the heck was he? And what was he to her? "What's this all about?"

I was already speaking to her back. She dragged me toward the Advocatus mansion. When I started following her lead, she broke into a dead run. It was a ten-minute trek crossing half the estate, but we did it in under two. Once inside, Serafina raced up the grand staircase, perfectly suited to *Gone with the Wind*, and took me to an enormous bedroom in a private wing. Before I could even admire the fine cream silk décor—or catch my breath, for that matter—she drew the heavy curtains, effectively cutting off the last ray of sunlight and plunging the entire room into darkness.

"Whoa. These are some top quality black out curtains; I can't even see my fingers. Can you wait until I get the light?"

"Don't." There was urgency to her voice. "I can't make this work if there are lights around."

"Alright." I gingerly felt my way around, using the flash

mental map of the room in my head, making sure I didn't bump into any sharp objects. I sat down on what felt like a shaggy armchair. It could be the back of a very patient—or very pissed off—hellhound for all I knew. Big families like Serafina's were known to keep these creatures of the underworld as pets. The little buggers were adept at blending in— how else were they supposed to collect souls if they made their presence known a mile away?

On the high vaulted ceiling, dozens of maps made of neon green lights exploded into my vision, overlapping one another. They reminded me a bit of the laser shows humans liked to put on.

"What is this?" I asked, already forming a theory in my head. I remembered how handy Serafina's tracking ability was when Esme, my half-sister, was kidnapped. An ability Serafina picked up from her changeling captors, and the maps seemed to be a physical manifestation of it.

"Bird's eye view of all the known planes. Hopefully Eldon is on here somewhere," Serafina replied.

"Hey, don't you need an anchor to do the locating spell?"

Last time, Serafina required something of Esme's to properly identify her location. Luckily, Esme had donated some of her life force to charge me up before the kidnapping, and we used that as the anchor to find her. I had no idea who this Prince Eldon was to Serafina—though there was no doubt she knew him from the way she spoke of him—much less what she might have of his that could serve as an anchor.

"I already have a magical baseline to go by." Her voice sounded incredibly sad.

He's in trouble and she's the only one who can locate him.

Huh. I'd been friends with Serafina for months now; she never even mentioned an Eldon, prince or no prince.

By the eerie glow of the juxtaposition maps, I could see Serafina standing in the middle of the bedroom, her hands waving as if conducting an orchestra. With each movement there were fewer maps on the ceiling, until only one remained. With a last wave, she brought the map down from the ceiling onto the space just above our heads. She magnified it and made it three dimensional, with bright lines indicating the X, Y, and Z axis.

Large clusters of tall buildings. Narrow streets. Moving rectangular boxes representing what must be cars. It could be either the vengeance plane or the human plane.

"Human plane," Serafina said, as if reading my mind.

"How could you tell?"

She magnified even farther and pointed at the scattered dots in the alleyways. They weren't moving like the dots on the main streets. "The homeless."

"Okay, but there are homeless on both planes."

"It's spring break for the University of Vampiric Studies."

"Oh."

The vampire plane was on a different time rotation than us, so our mid-winter was their spring break, and nobody on the vengeance plane—homeless or otherwise—would be dumb enough to be caught outside when the streets were flooded with waves of raucous, fanged frat boys. Humans, on the other hand, either denied the existence of the supernatural or believed they were tormented romantic heroes. Hence the lack of self-preservation.

Drunken college kids from any planes could be trouble. Those with fangs, especially.

"Alright, so this Prince Eldon is on the human plane. You have any idea which city he's in?"

"It doesn't matter. I can take us there." Serafina's voice was firm, her hand reaching for mine and I grasped it. Then she froze, and she said with great hesitation, "Actually, I can go on from here. I don't want to trouble you."

"Don't you dare. You're my friend and I'm going. Who knows what might be there?"

I was the one who brought Prince Eldon—whoever the heck he was—back into her life. I did it because of Gregory, though I was still unsure of his motive. That made me responsible, and no way was I going to let her go in alone.

❧ 3 ❧

A PLACE TO HIDE

WE TELEPORTED into the downtown core of whatever city we were at, right by a garbage bin behind a convenience store. Based on the sign saying "Private Parking" in English, we were in, well, some English-speaking country and city, anyway.

Great help there, Megan.

Shut up.

I wished I could bring Esme with me. A full-blooded vengeance demon with the sweetest heart and the mightiest ass-kicking ability would be a great asset in the face of danger, but she wasn't back from a vacation with her birth mother yet.

Her birthmother—my dad's ex-wife—was a vengeance demon who specialized in unfaithful men. Thank Hades he never cheated on her, or I would've never been born; her reputation for male organ mutilation was legendary. With so many cheaters finding partners-in-crime on the Internet in the modern age, Esme's mom would disappear for weeks and even months on end, immersing herself in the cyber world. She kept busy with everything from ensuring flirtatious emails were "accidentally" forwarded to spouses, to encouraging asthma attacks during over-stimulated online naughty chats.

Esme had been really looking forward to spending quality time with her mom, and she'd been saving up for this vacation by working part-time for some undersecretary at the Council. I wasn't going to spoil that. Serafina and I were on our own.

"This way." Serafina gestured me to follow her to the main street. The lights were brighter there, with more foot traffic. "I think he's in the next alley."

I was expecting, I don't know, maybe a fair-haired prince with a unicorn by his side or something. I'd never met a prince. Vengeance demons had done away with their monarchy a long time ago. Many of the old families had some traces of royal blood in them in one form or another, but now people measured success based on their position in the Concord Council, the governing body for all things vengeance, not some illusion of power through the randomness of birth.

So I was curious, to say the least. I should've known that a dirty alleyway was hardly a suitable place for unicorns and rainbows.

What we found instead was a figure slumped over by a puddle of rusty water, with his back to us. His outfit might've been white at some point, but now it was covered in grime. His body was tall and slender; I could tell that even with him lying on the ground. I wouldn't call the weird angles the limbs stuck out graceful, though.

With a gasp, Serafina ran to the figure that must be Prince Eldon. She kneeled over him, her hands turning him over and gently pushing his grimy hair off his forehead. He opened his eyes and tried to focus them on her.

"Fi-Finny?" he croaked.

"Eldon, what happened?"

"Deirdre...she jumped me. Took most of my power away and exiled me from Dualsing." Prince Eldon moaned and slipped back into a semi-conscious state.

Serafina looked up at me. "We have to get him out of here."

I had tons of questions, including where the heck was Dualsing and why had I never heard of it before? But I held them back for later.

"Let's go to the University hospital." The University of Demonic Studies had a teaching hospital for magical healing and it was nearby. "I'm sure they'll be able to help even if he's from a species they're not familiar with."

"No!" Serafina said. "We can't go there. Do you have somewhere private we can take him? Somewhere vengeance demons generally won't go?"

———

There *was* one place regular vengeance demons would never be caught dead in—my parents' house.

The home of my father, a high-ranking arch vengeance demon, should have been a place everybody wanted to visit. By all rights, he should have lived in an estate home befitting of his station, with his underlings coming over for dinner parties and trying to suck up to the boss. But my dad married a trickster, which was unheard of and socially frowned upon.

With a tremendous wealth of love, my parents accepted the children from each other's previous relationships, and formed a *mine, yours, and ours* kind of family. I was the *ours* part of the equation, their only biological child together. Between the boss's wife being a trickster, a household full of rambunctious children, and the household itself being established in a *common folks* neighborhood, it was scandalous enough to scare off even the most career-minded underlings.

Serafina and I teleported onto the pavement in front of my parents' house. We were stopped outside the boundary, landing as close as their safeguard allowed. While my parents hardly had any unexpected visitors, the standard safeguard was still employed. Nobody wanted people popping in and out of their houses unannounced.

I loved the middle-class, suburban neighborhood my parents chose to raise me in. It was considered a "mixed" neighborhood, and by that it meant the area was on the vengeance plane, but consisted mostly of non-vengeance-demon immigrants. Due to war, de-forestation, and lack of job prospects, many magical folks couldn't stay on their own planes anymore. What better place to go to live than on the vengeance plane, among the guardians of the Cosmic Balance? It was like the peace of mind of living right next to a police station, perceived or otherwise.

Here the neighbors ranged from displaced woodland nymphs from the human plane, to paid-by-the-wail banshee who relied on payday loans, to retired hags brewing love potions on the side to supplement their income. Not exactly the supernatural upper crust. But growing up I got to play hide and seek with the Invisible Kid, and draw hangman with zombies. No complaints there.

So as I said, I love my old hood. It didn't matter that I'd already moved out and couldn't be happier with my human roommate and personal space; this area would always hold a special place in my heart. But that being said, carrying a semi-conscious guy fireman-style and hurrying toward my parents' house wasn't exactly what I'd call a regular visit, especially with Miss Neringa, our nosy giantess neighbor right out on her lawn. I did a quick wave to her, yanked open my parents' side door and dashed in, neatly avoiding her attempt to grill some juicy gossip out of me. Serafina followed right at my heels and closed the door.

"This way." I gestured to her to follow me down to the basement.

Now, when I thought of eventually bringing a guy home to meet my parents, this wasn't what I had in mind. For one, he wasn't my type—I preferred a guy free of grime and back alley stench. Two, as I said, the guy in question wasn't entirely conscious. Three, my parents weren't even home. Dad was on an off-plane assignment. Top secret. So of course Mom went with him.

I tramped down the stairs and placed Prince Eldon on the floor at the back of the family room. On the other side of the room was a large TV screen, and planted firmly in front of it was my trickster half-brother, Fir.

Just one more thing about tricksters that vengeance demons looked down upon: they didn't have a plane of their own like most supernatural did. Tricksters had little use for that, as they needed a constant supply of fresh victims. Unlike many of her kind, Mom didn't abandon my half-brothers at birth. Still, if my vengeance dad hadn't married my trickster mom and formed a stable household, my half-brothers would've left home by the age of seven.

Instead, they now embodied the worst of both worlds—failure-to-launch tricksters in their early to late twenties who were addicted to video games and beer.

Fir was totally into the fight currently displayed on the screen. It was some kind of alien battle game. He was surrounded and losing. Badly.

"Hey, Clef," Fir yelled, not taking his eyes off the battle at hand while calling for my second trickster half-brother. His ginger hair, which used to be spiky, grew so long that his bangs were now partially blocking his vision. He shook his head impatiently to get them out of the way. "Man, you came at the right time. Get your ass over here. I can't fend off these bastards on my own."

I ignored Fir, yanking open the futon sofa so it became a bed, and put Prince Eldon on it.

Fir let out a frustrated groan, and I glanced at the screen. His avatar was dead. Game over.

Fir threw his console onto the floor and turned toward me. "Why didn't you come help me—oh, hey, Megan. I thought you were Clef."

"You between gigs?" Fir was home instead of being out making mischief like my other three half-brothers. A trickster without a job was never a good thing for those around him. I remembered the fiasco at Grandma Aequitas's vengeance ball and shuddered.

Fir crossed his arms just a little too defensively. His body held the stubborn hunch of a mule. "I just finished one. Didn't you see that cosmetic-surgery-gone-bad debacle on the news? The one with patients accidently getting half a denture implanted on each of their butt cheeks then the two sides kept wanting to get back together? That was me."

"That was three weeks ago." Too long. Uh-oh. He must be itching for trouble by now.

"Said the girl who's got no trickster cred to her name." Fir snorted, then his gaze shifted to the futon. "Um. Megan, why is there a changeling on my bed?"

"Because I have to hide him somewhere. It's not even really your bed. You've got a room upstairs and only sleep down here when you're too drunk on junk food to climb a few steps. Besides, in a real trickster family you wouldn't even *have* a bed because our kind doesn't usually raise their young, let alone let them live in the house long after they come of age." I rumbled off the reasoning I rehearsed in my head before coming here until I realized that I totally missed the most important part of Fir's words. "Wait, what do you mean by 'why is there a *changeling* on my bed'?"

Fir just gave me a coy look and said nothing.

"It means Eldon is a changeling." Serafina stepped closer. "Megan, meet His Royal Highness, Crown Prince Eldon of Dualsing, the plane of the changelings. We grew up together."

Eldon, however, wasn't up for any formal introduction. His eyes were closed on his ashen face, his breathing shallow. "We have to get him some medical help. Are you sure we can't go to a hospital?"

"Yes," Serafina said, her refusal was gentler but no less determined this time. "We can't. We can't afford to let anyone know he's here. I'll see to him. He doesn't have any outward injury that I can see, and I learned a bit of healing in the past year. Let's see if I can tell what's happening."

"Well, I'm out of here," Fir huffed as Serafina settled next to Eldon. "My game is lost and my refuge is taken over. I need to find a place for a nice cold beer."

"Fir, you're not going to tell anyone what you saw here, right?" I wasn't sure why Serafina wanted the secrecy, but I could find that out later. Right now I needed Fir's word that he wouldn't bring further chaos into this situation. Tricksters were known for their big mouths.

"By Fleur's name, I won't tell anyone," Fir promised. The use of the name of the most celebrated trickster in all history should've made me feel assured, but with Fir you just never knew.

No time to think about that now. Serafina was kneeling by Eldon, her eyes shut tight. I knew that she was sending her spirit out of her body, hovering above in order to "see" his medical state of being. I understood how healing worked, but I never had any real experience with it. The healing art passed down through the generations, and it was never a strong suit in my own family. It was in Serafina's clan, though.

Moments later, Serafina took a shaky breath and opened her eyes. "He'll be fine. He has some superficial wounds, and most of his magic was drained out of him. But he isn't injured in any way that a visit to the doctor would've helped. He needs to rest, more than anything."

I waited while Serafina washed as much grime off Eldon as she could with a sponge, then finished the rest with magic. Then she changed him into one of Fir's multi-layered outfits —with magic again, with her face turned away in modesty. I bit my tongue until she gently closed the door to the basement and we sat down upstairs by the breakfast bar in the kitchen. Then I couldn't hold back anymore. "What the hell is going on? Why are we hiding this guy? Why can't we go seek medical help for him?"

Serafina hesitated.

"Come on, you owe me, girlfriend," I pressed. "Geez, I put Mr. Prince in my parents' basement for you."

She stared at me for a long time, and then finally started talking. "You know I was raised by the Dualsingians—I mean, the changelings."

"I know the changelings are like a type of fae, but I had no idea until today that they called themselves a different name." I pursed my lips. "I would've used names like Scumbags of the Universe or the Big Fat Baby Robbers."

Serafina sighed. "A lot of people in the Concord share that sentiment, and who could blame them? The stealing of children offends all of us at the basest level. The Dualsingians are generational baby-switchers, and they have done this since the beginning of time. It's in the very identity of their culture. They're like the cuckoo birds. Brood parasites, the humans called it. But what nobody talks about is the *why*."

"I wondered about that. I mean, they're missing their own kids' childhood, too. What's in it for them?"

"When a changeling child returns home, they reveal to

their real family all the secrets they learned while masquerading as a valued member of another race's household. It could be anything from ancient spells passed from father to son, knowledge of secret political alliances, or cutting edge product formulas. All that information gets sold to black marketeers, who in turn sell them to political spies, the host family's enemies, and even corporations eager for a competitive advantage. That's how the changelings as a race have made their living since time eternal. Stealing secrets by planting their young to be nurtured and cherished by other races."

"Those bastards!" I slapped my thigh, and then lowered my voice as I glanced at the basement door. "And this guy is the prince of people like that? And you're helping him?"

"He's...important to me." Serafina's face was solemn. "And his being here, on the vengeance plane, is very dangerous for him. The location of the changeling plane is a well-guarded secret. Nobody knows where they live; otherwise the victims of their crimes would have torn that plane apart a long time ago. If they ever find out who Eldon is, there's going to be a lot of supernaturals out there who want to claim him as their prisoner. They'll try to force Eldon to tell them how to get on the changeling plane in order to have their revenge. He will be hunted for the rest of his life."

Oh, crap. And he was in my parents' basement. What kind of trouble had I just brought onto their doorstep? "Can't he just go back?"

"He's in no shape to travel. Even if he was, there's only so much inter-dimensional crossing a changeling's body can take. I think he has almost used up his by now."

"So he's stuck on this plane." A growing sense of dread gnawed at my insides.

"More or less. Eldon really has nowhere to go." Serafina, too, glanced at the basement door. With sympathy, and something else. Something that was close to—could it be?—guilt-laced joy?

There was something else that had been bothering me since the alleyway.

"You keep dropping his title when you say his name," I accused. In the vengeance demon society, it was considered polite to address a stranger by their full name when possible. If today was the first day I met Serafina, I would be calling her Serafina Anastassia Advocatus. I've been calling this guy Eldon in my head since I found out whom he was a prince of, but that was because his royal title kinda got neutralized by the whole coming-from-a-scumbag-race thing. But what about Serafina? Why wasn't she more deferent to a royalty she was probably conditioned to respect and fear from her former life? "You said you grew up with him."

"Yes. For every child that the changelings took, they left behind a child of their own to be raised by their unsuspecting host family. Eldon's sister, Deirdre, was my imposter on the vengeance plane. I grew up living in the Mirage Palace with him."

"Wait." I was beginning to put two and two together. I knew Serafina had an older cousin, a certified vengeance demon by the name of Gabriella Bethany Advocatus. She was murdered by the changeling who impersonated Serafina. In other words, the queen who was now residing on the throne of the changelings had a blood debt with the house of Advocatus.

And she was the sister of the dude who was currently in my parents' basement. Great.

"Look, Megan, I'm aware of the difficult position I put you in—"

"You like him," I dared to guess. I'd never seen Serafina into a guy in all the time I knew her, but there was no mistaking the tenderness that she had shown toward Eldon.

"It's...complicated." Serafina avoided my eyes.

"Huh. Does that connection tie into the whole I-already-got-a-magical-baseline-to-find-him thing?"

Rather than answering that, she touched my forearm, her eyes pleading. "Please try to help him. I know we don't have a lot of information yet, but what we do know, it's not good. I don't think Deirdre understands the trouble she's inviting by simply dumping Eldon somewhere away from Dualsing. She's let her arrogance blind her, but she might just realize her mistake tomorrow and come and finish him off. One of Eldon's legs is impaired since birth, so he couldn't even run in a fight, and now he has no magic to protect himself."

I didn't know about Eldon's impaired leg. But then again, ever since I met him he was in one unconscious state or another, and he certainly hadn't really stood on his own for me to get a good look.

"Megan, I need your help in this. I-I can't go to my family."

No kidding.

The mighty Advocatus family was utterly humiliated by the switching of one family member and the murder of another. They would be the first out for the changeling prince's blood.

With Serafina's hand on my forearm, I was much more in tune with her mood than usual. I could feel the anxiety and distress rolling off her, and right then I made up my mind to help.

She obviously cared about Eldon a great deal. And I cared about her. Besides, I seriously didn't believe Eldon deserved to be punished for the misdeed of an entire race. I would be a hypocrite if I thought that way.

Besides, I watched TV. Human interrogations, in the event of being captured, were never pretty. I could only imagine that the supernatural version of it would be worse.

There had always been rumors whispering of the Council's brutality. Not that vengeance demons usually paid it much heed, it was the whole "they're evil, but they're *our* evil" mentality.

Not so much for Eldon, though.

I gave Serafina a hug. "It'll be alright. Nobody knows that he's here, and this house gives off some really confusing energy signatures—a cocktail mix of vengeance demons, tricksters, and hybrid. Most supernaturals are used to the weirdness and just dismiss it as white noise. It'll most likely mask Eldon's changeling signature."

I took out my cell phone and called my parents and grandma. When they didn't answer, I left each of them messages with a brief rundown of the situation. I felt no shame in enlisting my family's help in these circumstances.

I'd outgrown it.

Toddlers ran to their families for protection. Young adults refused do the same in a bid to be grownups. True adults call for help real fast when there's genuine trouble because they know they could use all the help they could get.

Grandma Aequitas was my grandmother from the vengeance side of the family. More importantly, she was a longtime influential member of the Concord Council. In fact, she served there for so many decades that she didn't get her hands dirty with the daily operational stuff anymore. With her honorary seat on the Council and my dad being an arch vengeance demon, I would be stupid to allow pride to dismiss the value of their help.

See, I felt so much more mature already. What could possibly go wrong?

❧ 4 ❧

SUI-LING

SOMETHING WAS VERY WRONG.

I was raiding the pantry for some of Mom's truly awesome chocolate chip cookies when I felt it—the first sign that something was amiss. The air felt...heavier. Like the low rumbling of thunder right before a storm. Then the wall itself vibrated, and a woman's voice was nowhere and everywhere at the same time, both inside and outside the house. "I, Sui-Ling, from the house of Gong, would like to request an audience with the head of the Aequitas household."

Something about the speaker's family name tickled at my mind, but I couldn't place it. I exchanged a puzzled look with Serafina. This kind of formal pronouncement would be more suitable in front of a vast mansion on estate grounds, not a modest bungalow with a birdbath and a pink plastic flamingo on the lawn.

Miss Neringa the nosy giantess was going to have a field day.

"Head of the Aequitas household, please respond." The voice repeated the request, which really wasn't a request at all.

Well, my parents weren't home. Fir wasn't home. The rest of my trickster older half-siblings weren't home. I guess that made me the head of the household.

I squared my shoulders and headed for the door, gesturing for Serafina to stay put.

"No." Her lips formed a tight line. "I want to come and see who's there. I got you into this mess to begin with."

"Actually, it's more like Gregory got me into this mess..." I trailed off. One look at Serafina's face and I knew there would be no arguing with her. She might appear meek and sweet to the world, but through the last few months I'd come to see that under all that gentleness was a deep reservoir of steadfast will and quiet determination.

I pushed open the door and let Serafina pass before closing it. The night had settled in, but the street lamps basked everything with an orange glow.

Waiting on the front lawn of my parents' house, next to the silly pink plastic flamingo, was a long-limbed Asian woman with sleek waist-length hair and a nasty looking sword in her hands. The sword had the same intricate carving of the ceremonial dagger every vengeance demon got upon being professionally certified, but the way the woman was holding it, it was obvious that she was trained to use it for more than decorative purpose.

The woman's power signature held the note of fragrant tea that was typical of our kind, but it wasn't the bitter Earl Grey flavor. I breathed in through my mouth and rolled the flavor around my taste buds.

Longjing tea. That was what my summoner reminded me of. Rich, pan-roasted Chinese green tea.

She lowered the sword upon seeing us.

"Where are your elders, younglings?" The woman looked us up and down.

Now that just grated on my nerves. For one, who the heck

used the word "younglings" anymore? Two, while the woman appeared to be in her mid-twenties, she wasn't that much older than us.

"I'm fifty-four," the woman said.

Wow. I knew that vengeance demons' aging process slowed in our twenties, allowing us to live over two hundred years while never looking much older than late middle age, but the woman on the lawn still looked pretty darn good for a fifty-four year old. Not a single wrinkle marked the corners of her almond-shaped eyes.

Wait.

"You can read minds?" For vengeance demons, being sensitive to mental impressions and emotional disturbance was common, but true mind reading was pretty rare. Grandma could do it with me, but it was because we were kin, and she still had to be relatively close by.

The woman sighed. "No, I can't read your mind, but the question about my age was all over your face. Being assumed to be a lot younger is an Asian woman thing, vengeance demon or not. I just want to get that out and over with."

Okay, so this lady was like Agent May from *Agents of S.H.I.E.L.D.* A little older yet super agile. With that matching abrasive attitude to go with it, too.

"Er, hi." I had no idea what to say to her. She couldn't be here for Eldon, could she? Nobody knew he was here. Best to play dumb. "Who did you say you are again?"

"I'm Sui-Ling. My family, the Gongs, is loyal to the Condor League."

From behind me, Serafina gasped. I took it that wasn't a good thing, whatever this Condor League was.

Then I realized why the newcomer's family name triggered something in my memory. It was in a textbook from a first-year university course called *Vengeance: A History*. Gong was the Chinese word for justice, very much like Aequitas was the Latin equivalent.

This lady in front of us came from a *very* old vengeance family.

"I'm Megan Aequitas." I enunciated each word, hoping that she would demand to know why I hadn't mentioned a middle name in my introduction, giving me an opening to drag this out by launching into my life story. It wasn't entirely impossible, given her oh-so-proper family lineage. And that would give me a few more moments to figure her out. But she just looked at me, refusing to take the bait.

Damn.

"So, what brings you here, Ms. Gong?" I attempted to work up a smile.

As Sui-Ling started talking, she shifted her weight between her two feet. While at first glance her outfit was the typical, head-to-toe black, with movement I could see gleams of reflective glow from it. It caught the light from the street lamp and turned into something more. The material looked like it was covered with countless slick dark green scales, and it had a phosphorescent quality to it. It was gorgeous and mesmerizing at the same time. The more I stared at it, the more I felt myself relaxing, and I could tell Sui-Ling just about anything, as long as she kept making her outfit glow in that wonderful way.

Serafina elbowed me. Hard. Ouch, the girl sure had bony elbows.

"Stop looking at her clothes," Serafina whispered in my ear. "Her outfit is made of dragonhide. That itself is a weapon, a means to hypnotize her target to obtain information and prevent escape. The woman is in the Condor League, Megan. A secret ancient order. I heard one of my tutors mention them once."

A secret ancient order, like the Greys. That woke me up from my trance real fast.

"My apologies. Ms. Gong." I shook the cobwebs out of my head and did a little curtsey to Sui-Ling. It might seem a bit overdone, but I had a big fat reason in my parents' basement to play nice—and dumb. "I missed what you just said, can you repeat the answer to my question?"

"I'm here for the changeling. If you would be kind enough to fetch him, we'll be on our way."

Oh, so much for niceness and playing dumb.

I thought about denial, and then promptly decided against it. A person who tracked Eldon all the way here wasn't going away with a simple "He's not here." Might as well go for a bit more information while the going was good. Besides, for all I knew Dad could be on his way as we spoke. "How do you know the changeling is here?"

Sui-Ling's mouth curved up. She seemed to find my lack of denial refreshing, and that put her in the mood for sharing. "One of the Condor League's founding mandates is to stop the abominable practice of switching and to finally bring the changelings to justice. We've been working on a detection system for thousands of years. Normally the changelings who get onto our plane have spells planted on them that mask their presence, making it very hard to identify them. But not in the case of the one currently residing in your house."

Well, considering Eldon was kicked out of his plane by his own sister, I doubted she cared much about wrapping him up in protective spells.

Hoping that Sui-Ling's chatty mood continued, I asked, "So, this Condor League. You're like their muscle girl with a sword?"

"I'm sworn to serve my order," she said simply. "Now, I've answered enough of your questions. Move out of the way, younglings. I've got orders to take the changeling in."

"For questioning and torture," Serafina added quietly. She'd been silent this whole time, but I knew that just because she appeared quiet and unassuming, it didn't mean she wouldn't stand up and defend what she set her mind to. And now she was very determined to prevent Eldon from being captured.

And we were so screwed. Though it was set to be a two-against-one fight, Sui-Ling was older and no doubt had a lot more battle experience. The very atmosphere was saturated with her enriched magic. Serafina and I were university-aged. We weren't even close to being in her league.

I sorely missed Esme at that moment. My half-sister would have been a welcome addition for the upcoming fight. Even if she was by the book and wouldn't support the act of hiding a royal from a criminal race, she'd still have my back.

I could feel Serafina gearing up her power beside me, just as I knew she was fully aware of how hopeless this was. I sighed and started gearing up mine as well. In for a penny, in for a pound.

Sui-Ling smiled, flexed her sword, and waited for us to finish pulling our powers around us. That was how confident she was that she would kick our asses.

Someone teleported nearby and immediately inserted herself between us and Sui-Ling. It happened so fast it took my brain a few seconds to realize who it was.

Grandma Aequitas.

I was so relieved to see Gran I could have kissed her, but she was in her tough-ass mode right now and that might just ruin the image she wanted to project.

"Stop." The single word from her sounded more authoritative and intimidating than anything I could've come up with.

Sui-Ling narrowed her eyes at Grandma. She flared her nostrils in a clear attempt to suss out Grandma's power.

Aware now that she was in the presence of someone far more powerful than Serafina and me—I resisted the urge to stick out my tongue and say "Ha-ha"—Sui-Ling gave Grandma a deep, respectful bow. "You must be Lady Aequitas."

"I am. And you're a Condor." Grandma nodded toward the sword in Sui-Ling's hand. "I suppose you're here for the changeling my granddaughter mentioned in her message."

Even months after discovering Grandma's love for me, hearing her referring to me as her granddaughter still sent thrills through my heart. But I really needed to focus on the conversation at hand, as Grandma asked Sui-Ling to stay put while she discussed the matter with the Council. There was a whole lot of *blah, blah, blah* about jurisdiction, first right to vengeance, and ensuring that the proper protocol and procedures were followed, which was silly considering there wasn't actually a precedent for this. Like, ever.

One thing was certain. Grandma might be able to delay Sui-ling for a while, but in the end it was inevitable that either Sui-Ling or the Council would get their hands on Eldon.

Damn.

❦ 5 ❦

THE POLITICS OF IT

SUI-LING SETTLED in at the parkette across the street a few houses down the block, waiting to hear what the Council might say about the current dilemma. I would've enjoyed the look of her leaning on a rocking horse and stabbing her sword into the dirt around her in frustration if Grandma hadn't pulled me and Serafina into my parents' house with brisk efficiency.

Might as well be indoor. Sui-Ling's ever-watchful eyes were getting a bit unsettling.

"Miss Advocatus, can you give me a moment to speak to my granddaughter?" Grandma asked Serafina.

With a glance at me that spoke volumes, Serafina nodded and went down to the basement, closing the door behind her. That look told me that she had made up her mind to protect Eldon and she would follow through with it, no matter what Grandma had to say to me in private.

"Before I call the Council," Grandma said as soon as she weaved a privacy spell around the entire house, "tell me everything."

So I did. Except the part where I believed Serafina was in

love with Eldon, but Grandma would figure that out on her own anyway. After I finished talking, Grandma paced around the living room then turned to look at me.

"That Gregory." Grandma's lips thinned. "I have to have a chat with him. I would hardly call this whole business as having my stamp of approval. I wouldn't normally object to a Good Samaritan act, and I agree that Miss Advocatus has to confront her past at some point, but, Megan, do you realize the potential fallout from this situation, at this specific point in time? We can't afford to offend the Condor League."

My glee at the thought of Gregory having a tongue-lashing from Grandma was doused by the agitated tone of her voice.

"I don't understand." I frowned. Hadn't the Council been trying to smoke out the Greys with the information provided by Dan Pillar? What was one more secret society to take care of? "No matter how sneaky and influential this Condor League is, the Council is still the Council. It's still the most powerful organization in the Cosmic Balance."

"Except the Council isn't trying to *overpower* them. They're trying to earn their trust and support."

"What?"

"Look at it this way, Megan." Grandma sighed. "Dan Pillar told us there are six remaining sects of the Greys out there. The Council has its hands full trying to find them. What is the best way to investigate a secret society? Get another secret society to help. They have networks and resources that intersect with one another. We need the Condor League."

This wasn't going the way I expected. The little girl in me who previously hadn't been aware of her grandma's love had a fantasy that she would just ride in and make everything all right. But the reality was, even a loving grandparent could only work within certain parameters, and mine wasn't without her own enemies.

"But you do agree that we *should* help Eldon, right?" I asked anxiously. That, at the very least, I wanted to be absolutely certain of, whether or not Gran was actually *able* to help.

"Of course. He doesn't deserve to be punished for the misdeeds of an entire race of people through all of history. But his presence on our plane is the last thing we need during this delicate time. The Council can't afford to alienate the Condors. Other groups will use it as an excuse not to co-operate with us."

"And adding to that, there might be fracture within the Council itself." Serafina's voice rang from the doorway to the basement. Her face was pale. "I'm sorry to be listening in, but I have to know. My family is going to put pressure on the Council, aren't they?"

"Once they're aware of Prince Eldon, yes." Grandma nodded. "The house of Advocatus will demand justice for your cousin. We cannot have a divided Council, so my power to sway them would be limited."

"Then what are we going to do?" I asked, trying not to let the frustration I felt slide into my voice.

"It's a question of what you're willing to do, dear. The basement is no longer safe. If Sui-Ling could find you, others will surely follow. You can stand by and let the Council, or whoever else, take Prince Eldon, or you can do something about it. I cannot advise you either way. My position on the Council demands me to be neutral in this matter."

But she *wasn't* being neutral. Otherwise she would've called the Council already. And she *was* trying to advise me, without advising me.

She was telling me that I had a choice. Escape with Eldon and Serafina while I still could, or allow him to be a political pawn in a game that every fiber in my being was telling me he would be sacrificed.

Would I dare to do that?

The Council hadn't officially declared Eldon a fugitive of the vengeance laws yet—but that was only because Grandma hadn't made them aware of his existence for them to do so. Technically it wouldn't be a crime to run off with him right now, but that was just splitting hairs. I knew it. And they would know it, too.

It would be the closest I'd ever come to openly defying them. And damn, I'd just managed to fade from their radar after getting myself out of suspension at Demon U. I could even argue that I'd earned a few brownie points by delivering them Dan Pillar. All that goodwill would evaporate if I stole a prize this big from right under their noses.

"Thanks for your, er, neutrality." I gave Grandma a grave smile. "I'll think everything over."

"You do that. In the meanwhile, I suggest you refrain from contacting your other trickster siblings, and I'll hire a technician from the Gremlin Group Inc. to erase the voice-mail you sent to your parents. The less people involved, the better. Your dad's off-plane assignment isn't due to wrap up for another half a week anyway." Grandma approached Serafina. "Do you think I can speak to His Royal Highness for a moment?"

"He's awake," Serafina confirmed.

The fact that Grandma had addressed Eldon by his title was surprising. She glanced at me. "A prince of thieves is still a prince, dear, and should be shown the respect that he's due."

Eldon struggled to stand up as Grandma led the way down to the basement. As he made a few steps toward us and I saw him moving on his own for the first time, I could see what Serafina meant about his impaired leg. His right leg was definitely weaker than his left one, causing a heavy reliance on the latter in a noticeable limp.

Eldon bowed to Grandma as deeply as he was able. It

would seem that he, too, felt the need to greet her with the utmost respect. I rather liked him for it. "M'lady."

What I didn't like, and most certainly didn't expect, was for Grandma to wave her hand and fling Eldon against the basement wall, keeping him awkwardly pressed into the concrete halfway between the ceiling and the ground. She conjured three darts out of thin air and threw them, which all landed on Eldon's leg—the impaired one. The darts grew bright, burrowing themselves into his body.

"What the—" I stopped talking in order to grab Serafina by her middle as she tried to push past me to come to Eldon's rescue. Whatever Grandma was up to, I didn't want Serafina to get hurt by being in the middle of it.

"You called her for help." Serafina's tone was accusing. "And this is how she's *helping*?"

"Just…wait and see, okay?" I'd doubted Grandma once too often in the past, this time I wanted to give her the benefit of the doubt, no matter how bad this looked. She told me she agreed we should help Eldon, and I wanted to take her word for it.

"*M'lady*," Grandma repeated his earlier words as she smiled mildly at Eldon. "How do you know to call me that?"

Eldon's voice didn't waver, despite the fear he must be experiencing over being held high against the wall and weird wiggly things making a home inside his body. I could've told him not to be afraid, except I had no idea what the hell was going on. "From the power that I sense from you, I would say that you're very much deserving of that title."

"I'm the head of the Aequitas clan, a charter member of the Vengeance Council. Tell me, Prince Eldon"—Grandma watched Eldon with unblinking eyes—"is Trust the Wise still advisor for the royal court of Dualsing?"

Eldon's face registered his shock. "You know the true name of the changeling plane? And you know Trust?"

"We were friends. A long time ago."

Why would Grandma have contact with anyone from the changeling world? I thought back on my surprise upon discovering that Grandma knew Gregory the mercenary, and couldn't help but wonder just how connected Grandma was to the shadier characters throughout the planes.

"More than you think." Grandma turned toward me, reading the questions from my mind. "Being in my position, I interact with creatures from all walks of life. In every facet of the Cosmic Balance. No matter what the official party line *du jur* the Council happens to maintain. Maybe one day it will be you doing the same thing."

Did Grandma just say that in the future I might become the matriarch of the family? Yeah, over the disapproving dead bodies of 97 percent of all the other family members, with the other 3 percent too busy to protest because they were neck deep with their vengeance assignments.

"M'lady, to answer your question." Eldon cleared his throat. "Trust is no longer the royal advisor of the court, though he has secretly been my private counsel for as long as I can remember."

"Where is he now?" Grandma asked.

"I don't know," Eldon replied softly, the anguish clear in his voice. "Upon my sister Deirdre's return, she killed our mother so she could start her reign right away. Then she took away the brownies' pay, doubled the pixies' workload, and imprisoned Trust. She also ramped up efforts to send out triple the number of changelings to the world by the end of this year."

"No," Serafina breathed. "That's terrible. And I'm so sorry about your mother, Eldon. I didn't know her very well, but to be murdered by her own child—"

"I know. I don't know how to feel about it." Eldon sighed wearily. "My mother had spent eighteen years pining after the child she lost rather than caring about the one right in front of her, yet I can't say I got a lot of satisfaction seeing how things backfired on her."

"I hate to say it, but I'm not shocked about Deirdre. The first time I met her was when she killed my cousin Gabriella." Serafina shook her head. "I was horrified by the complete lack of hesitation in her decision to do so."

"My twin has gotten the worst of both worlds—cruel selfishness from her changeling blood and an arrogant disapproval for other supernaturals from the vengeance demons. I was in the middle of planning Trust's rescue and overthrowing Deirdre when she surprised me. And now I'm here. And I can't return home." Anger and frustration filled Eldon's voice.

"Ah, and here we are, getting to the heart of the problem." Grandma seemed to pay no attention to the darts, which had turned into some kind of neon-colored vapor seeping out of Eldon's leg. They dissipated as soon as they left his body and he appeared no worse by having endured it. What the heck was *that* all about? "You want to return home, don't you? You still want the throne, no?"

"I did. I still do. I can do right by the minorities like Trust, the brownies, and the pixies. Hell, I'll even be better for the rest of the world. My sister already has plans in motion to ramp up the switching practice. That would not happen under my reign."

From the corner of my eye, I could see Serafina looked disappointed.

"No." Grandma shook her head. "You want the throne because you want power. First and foremost. Helping all those unfortunate creatures comes a close second, but still a second."

Wow, she was really good at calling him on his shit.

"Since when do people want the throne for the right reasons?" Eldon shot back. Huh, the guy was being just a bit too proud about doing the wrong thing. I could see where he and Serafina could clash. Though raised by changelings, her sense of right and wrong had always been bang on. The difference in their values had to be the reason why she returned to the vengeance plane alone. "And who are you to interfere with what should've been Dualsingian's internal affairs anyway?"

"Just some food for thought, Prince Eldon. From a friend." Grandma released the holding spell she had on Eldon. He slid down the wall and hit the ground, then got up on his two feet, perfectly balanced. The movement was so fluid and painless that it took me a few seconds to realize that something was definitely different from before. "A friend who's just given the full function of your leg back."

Serafina ran to Eldon. I let go of the breath that I didn't even realize I had been holding. Now I was glad I didn't doubt Grandma. Okay, I did for a little while there. But at least I didn't act on it.

Serafina stopped in front of Eldon as he shifted his weight from one side to another, testing the co-ordination of his legs, marveling at his newfound agility. She looked like she didn't know what to say to him.

"Prince Eldon, I took the liberty of restoring your physical strength, though I can't do anything about the magic that was stolen from you," Grandma said.

"Why?" Eldon asked with a mix of wonder and suspicion.

"First of all, to thank you for looking out for Miss Advocatus all those years when she was at Dualsing."

"I would've done it anyway," Eldon said.

"That's not the point. She was a vengeance demon on foreign soil and the kindness you showed her is appreciated. Secondly, I would like to balance out your disadvantage in this current world, considering the loss of your magic. As a daughter of vengeance, I do truly believe in fairness. And then of course"—Grandma paused for dramatic effect—"I want to make sure that you have the ability to run and not drag my Megan down."

I beamed at her calling me "her Megan." Despite the trouble I might be getting myself into very, very soon, a part of me felt this amazing joy, basking in my gran's love.

And I loved her cut-to-the-chase practicality. I saw a reflection of her in me.

So now Eldon had the strength of an able-bodied mortal. Kinda useless in a supernatural fight, but at least not a burden to carry around when things got rough.

I just didn't know how rough it was going to get.

❧ 6 ❧

FIRST RIGHT OF VENGEANCE

IT WAS WELL after midnight when Grandma left for the Council. Before she went, she added her own brand of magic to the house's protection, in case Sui-Ling decided to grab Eldon and make a run for it.

Grandma knew right from the start that I was going to help Eldon. That was why she healed him. And she was right. I couldn't *not* help.

I packed as much as I could realistically carry for the upcoming escape. The plan was to get Eldon out of the house and then "accidentally" lose him once we shook Sui-Ling. Still, it would be good to have a backup plan. Hey, I was the girl whose life was threatened during a routine, low-risk co-op assignment, and I almost got tricked into releasing the ultimate Big Bad. I believe I could stand to have a little bit of paranoia.

I packed fairy dust, which I had stashed in my old bedroom inside empty tampon tubes—it was quite a feat hiding them from my trickster half-brothers. I took two cans of Blue Unicorn, magical energy drinks that would allow me to display illusions of power, and I enchanted half a dozen magical manuals to be penny-sized for the road. One never knew when she might need to look up valuable information from resources such as *1001 Wild Herbs and How They Can Kick Start Your Vengeance Career*.

I divided what I had into two portions. One for me; and one for Serafina. Without the vengeance background or the magic to wield any spells, there was no point creating a separate pile for Eldon—not that I would trust a changeling with them anyway, even one I was trying to rescue.

I barely got everything into two duffel bags when I heard a raucous noise from the front lawn, a mix of hoarse shouting and metal clanging.

I ran.

When I hit the living room, I saw Serafina and Eldon on the staircase, making their way out of the basement to check on the commotion. I shook my head and waved them back. It would be best if they stayed completely out of sight. I waited until they returned to their sanctuary, then I squared my shoulders and opened the front door—

To the sight of a circus.

My parents' vibrant green lawn was now littered with tiny tents that looked to be made from rags, the birdbath and pink plastic flamingo barely visible. The tents must have gone up through magical means; otherwise, I would have heard their construction.

There were over a dozen goblins, males and females alike, gathered in the clearing at the center of the tents and producing a great deal of noise as they trash-talked, cursed, and brandished their swords at each other. In the context of goblin culture, that meant they must be among friends.

They showed off their prized daggers, flails, and axes, weapons that were made with the superior craftsmanship that their race was famous for, and polished to gleam like mirrors.

If only they'd taken the same care in washing their grimy-looking tents.

The goblins' stocky bodies, which only came to my waist, bumped into each other in a mock show of dominance, their spirits high with every bone-crashing impact.

Just how the heck were they able to bypass the house's protection? And why were they here now, when hardly anyone had visited my parents' place in the last two decades? Were they here for Eldon, too, like Sui-Ling?

With a sinking feeling, I stepped onto the porch and closed the front door behind me.

"A-hem," I coughed.

They ignored me.

Calling upon my magic, I sent sparks to catch the tips of a few tents on fire. The sight of the fire soon sent the group screaming as they frantically raced to find water to douse the flame. One resourceful fellow started kicking at the birdbath, hoping to get access to its water.

For Hades's sake, my mama would kill me if harm came to that silly birdbath. It was a battle keeping that thing on the lawn considering Dad's constant objection to it. Hastily, I put the flame out with the snap of my fingers.

"A-hem," I coughed again.

This time, the goblins stopped and listened.

One, a clan chief from the look of the hammered silver helmet on his head, stepped to the front. His body was covered from head to toe in a wide assortment of chain mail and armor plates that were surely as heavy as he was, if not more so. In a low, gruff voice with a menacingly plodding pace, he said, "We ya from da Reavaz clan of da goblins. I um Greexet Pickbolt. We ya here for da changeling."

Oh no, not another one.

Did Fir blurt out the knowledge of Eldon to somebody at

the bar? That rat bastard! He promised not to tell. He swore in the name of Fleur, for Hades's sake.

The goblin chief's next words banished that idea. "Miz Neringah posted it onah Twitter. So don'tah even t'ry to deny it. She even provided ze general permishion for us to be on zis lawn."

Looked like my nosy neighbor did more than spy this time. All the home protection spells had a built-in exclusion for the household's immediate neighbors—otherwise they would be attacked every time they accidentally crossed the boundary while mowing the lawn. It was the same idea if kids came over for birthday parties and sleepovers, a blanket exclusion that allowed the neighbors' guests to bypass the protection. What we didn't expect was for Miss Neringa to provide an open-ended consent for anyone who stepped onto our lawn. *Our* lawn. All they had to do was read the tweet, and the invitation stood.

So much for top-notch security.

Foiled by technology and someone who had no life.

And if the news of Eldon was on social media, soon there would be a riot happening right on my parents' front lawn. How was I supposed to make a quiet escape? How was I supposed to protect Eldon if everybody wanted a piece of him?

Suddenly Sui-Ling appeared in front of Greexet, her post at the parkette across the street abandoned. She seemed to have arrived at the same horrifying conclusion I did regarding the magnitude of the problem we were about to face.

"Mr. Pickbolt," Sui-Ling began diplomatically. "The house of Aequitas had already promised to present my organization's case in front of the Council. I can assure you that all the formal procedures will be followed in determining the proper order of vengeance. If you can be so kind and take your leave, I'll make sure to file your concern under the proper classification and forward you the appropriate paper-work to fill out."

Looked like the girl wasn't just the muscle. She was also the politician.

Greexet dismissed Sui-Ling's words with a wave of his dinner-plate-sized hand. "Papah-work? Zhat's bullroar! Lookzie here, Mizzie. Ze changelings had done us goblins wrong, and he *iz* going to pay. We have every right to get 'im. Even ze Council can'tah deny us zis vengeance."

His words were greeted with loud cheers from his kins-men, along with blade clanging that went on and on like a kissing request at a brutish version of a wedding reception.

If my original plan to quietly get past Sui-Ling was blown to hell, maybe I could shift gears and keep her distracted with the goblins. Hoping to draw the chief into a conversation, I asked him, "Just how did the changeling wrong you?"

"Zhose tricky bastards switched zheir babe with one of my ancestor's babes." Greexet leaned closer, his hoarse voice filled with anger. "And zhey stole ze secret for forging ze Unforgeable Sword."

"Sorry, the Unforgeable Sword? I thought that was just an old legend. A myth." I frowned.

"No it iz not! Ze Unforgeable Sword *was* real. Ze changeling learned its secret before it was lost to time for me people." Greexet sighed.

"Well, it's not like the market has ever been flooded with this invincible weapon." I shook my head.

"If the changelings weren't able to master the making of the sword," Sui-Ling added, her eyes gleaming with triumph, "then no harm was done. No grievance means no vengeance needed."

"No harm done?" Greexet's eyes narrowed to dangerous slits. "While it iz true zhat ze traitor was only able to take half-learned skills back wis him, zhat was enough to kick start an explosion of knock-offs. For ze first time in history, our customers were introduced to ze alternative of cheap goods. Ze day ze world moved away from ze genuine craftsmanship to embrace mass production was ze start of me people's decline. Wis less demand for our goods, many of us could no longer stay togezher as a clan. Children started moving on to ozher more modern profeshions, like ze mechanics or, worse, ze awful *telemarketers*. Tell me, miz, iz zhat what you call 'no harm done'?!"

Alright, harm was definitely done when he put it that way.

"If, upon careful examination it is determined that your people had suffered, it would no doubt be classified as vengeance well-deserved," Sui-Ling conceded.

Greexet snared. "'Upon ze careful examination'? You mustah be kidding me."

"Think of it this way." Sui-Ling dropped her diplomatic tone. "What makes your clan, the Reavaz, the representative of your race to claim this vengeance? And more importantly, out of all the races the changelings have wronged through the ages, what makes you believe that the goblins truly have the first right of vengeance? We have to perform a thorough investigation with due diligence."

"Due diligence, me goblin ass! Everybody else, zhey ain't here. *We* are. And we are going to get ze changeling!"

Another wave of weapon banging exploded from the goblins and I used the noise as cover to slowly retreat. I was still on the porch, and all I had to do was inch backward until my back hit the front door.

The first right of vengeance was often a note of contention even amongst the most cut-and-dried cases. The idea was that whomever was the first victim of an injustice got to have the first right to benefit from the relief and comfort brought on by the act of vengeance. The goblins and

Sui-Ling could go at it for a while. In the meantime, I could make off with Eldon and Serafina.

And it wouldn't be a moment too soon. The big fish, like the Council and Sui-Ling's group, would try to use Eldon to wreak havoc on his entire race. The likes of the goblins, though, would be happy with just tearing Eldon apart.

"We have ze first right!" Greexet roared.

"No, *I* have the first right," a female voice rang through the lawn, stopping me in my tracks. Damn, I hadn't moved backward enough to touch the front door yet.

A tall, blonde woman with a willowy figure stepped from the large hole that appeared on the lawn. Despite her entrance, her long dress was unsoiled by dirt or mud. There were ivy and wildflowers adorning the woman's outfit, making her look more at home in a magical forest than a suburban lawn with streetlamps and fire hydrants.

She had the face of an angel. Her skin was flawless and milk white, her movements graceful, and there was an ageless quality to her. She could be sixteen or thirty-six, or a lot older than that.

As she stepped fully from the hole, the ground closed behind her feet. The grass, smooth and even, as if it had never been disturbed. Damn, another user of Miss Neringa's all access pass.

She approached the group. "I am Eldratha, the elf queen of Orlagroth. I have the first right of vengeance. My ancestor, Livana, the Head Queen in all elvendom, was tricked into sharing her beauty formula of Eternal Youth."

"If stealing zhat secret was any more successful zhan what zhey did with ze Unforgeable Sword's," Greexet sneered, "zhen how come I've seen me fair share of ugly women in me life?"

His clansman laughed. One of them shouted, "Zhey're not as ugly as you, chief!"

Considering the goblin males considered scars and deformity to be a point of pride, that was actually a suck-up-to-the-boss compliment, not an insult.

Eldratha huffed. "Regardless, the beauty formula was stolen from us and sold to the human plane. Since the beginning of time, mortals have been clamoring for the ultimate anti-aging secret. What the silly fools don't realize is that all those so-called new and improved anti-aging products on the market are really just the same old thing derived from my ancestor's original recipe. Incomplete formula or not, it was theft by the changelings and retribution shall be ours."

"Well, zhat still does not mean you got ze *first* right. Beauty is only skin-deep. Ze sword is mightier." Greexet snorted.

The elf queen looked down her nose on the soot-smudged clothes of the goblins and swept her elegant fingers over her long shiny hair. "The quest for beauty has always come before the desire for warfare, and warfare was what made the skills of your kind necessary. Without the beautiful Helen, there would have been no need to launch a thousand ships."

Okay, she kinda had a point there.

And it looked like she might have possessed some brawn to go with that beauty. From where I stood, I could see half a dozen animated shrubs inching closer to the goblins on the fringe of the lawn, while thick tree roots slowly crept their way out of the underground, waiting to ambush the goblins.

The engine of a bus hissed as the vehicle pulled up at the stop across the street, but I was too distracted to care. My inner trickster smelled the potential for chaos and wanted to grab a front row seat with some popcorn. My inner vengeance demon prompted me to start retreating toward the house again, satisfied that the different players on the lawn would now have even more to fight about and would forget all about me.

I did a miscalculation, backed into a large flowerpot beside the front door and almost stumbled. Luckily, all the goblins were surrounding Eldratha and Sui-Ling, not bothering to pay me any attention. I turned away from the crowd and smiled at the sight of the front door. I would be out of sight soon, then I would lock the door, wrap the house in a thick layer of anti-neighbor protection, and figure out a way to get Eldon out of here without going out the front.

Hunkering down was my best course of action right now.

But as I reached for the doorknob, three new voices chimed in the ongoing argument between Eldratha, Sui-Ling, and the goblins. "Stop it, all of you. *We* have the first right! Where's Little Meg, we want to talk to her right away."

The voices sounded old and young at the same time, like the hoarseness of old ladies had overlapped the ringing laughter of teenage girls.

Without turning, I knew exactly who had just arrived. The Three Fates.

I bounced away from the front door quickly, hoping that in the few seconds of the newcomers gawking at the surrounding, and everybody else gawking at them, no one caught sight of me trying to escape into the house. If the legend about elf royalties' power to command anything organic was true, then Eldratha could get to me before I closed the door and figured out how to override Miss Neringa's all access pass. The porch and the door were both, after all, made of wood. Heck, she could bend the wood and trap me in a makeshift prison while getting Eldon, if her plan of shrubs and tree roots involving the goblins was anything to go by.

Stealth was of the essence.

I waved in acknowledgement to the Three Fates, who used to call me something a lot nastier than *Little Meg* when I attended my grandma's ball as a child. I guessed they were trying to be nice in order to get me to hand over Eldon. Fat chance.

The Three Fates were retired auditors of regulated destinies. Nobody ever used the word "disgraced" in association with them, but let's just say that their retirement wasn't entirely voluntary. The trio tried to look as powerful and intimidating as little old ladies carefully folding their return bus passes into their handbags could. No magically constructed tents or ground-opening portal for these three girls—they were pensioners on a budget.

I must be getting jaded, for I found myself being less surprised about even more people showing up than the fact that these three old ladies had enough technical know-how to read Miss Neringa's tweets to come here.

To my relief, Sui-Ling blocked the Three Fates' way as they tried to reach me, effectively focusing their attention on her and away from me. "Greetings, Clotho, Lachesis, and Atropos. It's an honor."

Anyone who'd ever picked up a history book in the supernatural world would know the Three Fates' names, but I got a feeling that Sui-Ling's education at the ancient order would've covered a detailed account of their careers.

"Don't you *greetings* us, young lady." Clotho wagged her finger at Sui-Ling. "We meant what we said. We own the ultimate first right of vengeance."

"Get in line, you mizerable hags!" Greexet hissed.

Hades help me. Soon there would be as many claims to the first right as there would be different versions of *Spiderman*.

I had to go. Like, ten minutes ago. But I was good and well stuck with these supernaturals, armed with either ancient blood, advanced magical skills, or sheer blunt force.

"What makes you think you have the first right?" Eldratha rearranged the full skirts of her beautiful dress as she gave the

Three Fates' worn white robes and mall-bought shoes a once over. She didn't seem very impressed.

"Why, we're the changelings' most wounded victims, and the first," Lachesis explained. "Whenever they switch a baby, they don't just steal his or her childhood. They change that child's destiny. Every thread that we planned to weave on the tapestry that is the child's life, everything that is going to make that child the person they are meant to be, is completely destroyed. From political allies that should have been made in prep school, to the proper breeding that could only come from being raised in a world of privilege, down to their lifelong attitude toward power, money, and relationships, everything is rewritten."

"It was a huge blow to our credibility." Atropos's chin quivered, her gaze lost in memory. "People began to question the value of having regulated destinies. Eventually everyone started buying into that 'you could be whatever you want to be' nonsense. The changelings robbed us of our career, our reputation, and our rightful place in the Cosmic Balance. What do you have that could compare to *that*?"

Eldratha and Greexet simply glared at the Three Fates.

I could see where they were coming from, though. The changelings had robbed them of their self-identity just like they did with that of the children they switched.

Self-identity. That was it—my ticket outta here.

The tricksters and vengeance demons both had their versions of the illusion spells, though one camouflaged for the sake of performing trickery, the other for the purpose of administrating vengeance.

What if I, the hybrid of trickster and vengeance demon, created an illusion channeling both kinds of magic?

Usually, I either do a vengeance spell, or a trickster spell. The only time I ever tapped into both sides at the same time was a few months ago, when I had to fix a little damage called the-end-of-life-as-we-knew-it.

Despite all the progress I'd made in getting my two natures to meld with one another, to say that I was a little nervous about doing an experimental hybrid spell under pressure was an understatement.

I began building up my magic—both sides of it—and my pearl pendant grew bright in response. Concentrating, I created an extremely area-specific illusion, blocking just that light, a dead giveaway that I was gearing up my power.

"Thank you for sharing your story, Clotho, Lachesis, and Atropos. As I've already told Eldratha and Greexet, your claim is noted and proper assessment will be performed," Sui-Ling droned on, carefully explaining the claim process as she understood it. She might not be from the Council, but with the absence of Grandma she had taken over the role of the bureaucrat—with the goal of advocating for her own group's interest, of course.

Any impression of this being a fair and straightforward process was bullshit. It was going to be one big drawn-out mess, with many levels of appeal and counter-appeal.

With my rising anger over the changelings' wrongdoings, my inner vengeance demon struggled for dominance. To counter it, I envisioned the tricksters playing a joke on the changelings, having them accidently do a switch back, and didn't find out the children they thought they kidnapped were really their own kids until eighteen years later.

It worked, and my power continued to grow, sourced equally by my two natures in a perilous balance.

Meanwhile, the Three Fates took a long, appraising look around them, Sui-Ling's words deaf on their ears. They didn't have a single weapon in hand, yet they looked as confident as if they were carrying an Unforgeable Sword of their own.

Clotho's hands kneaded and pulled at something invisible.

"Oh, sisters, suppose I have a closer look at their threads of life?"

"Yes." Lachesis narrowed her eyes. "I could do a proper measurement and see if any of their lives are unnecessarily long."

"Then I can cut the threads." Atropos made a scissoring motion with her fingers. "Or tie them into endless loops, making their lives a pointless pit of disappointments."

Greexet made a signal to his clansmen, and they crowded around. "Shut up, you crusty old bitches! I got ze most men here. Zhat changeling's mine. So stepah aside. And zhat same goes wis you two."

He pointed at Sui-Ling and Eldratha. Sui-Ling responded by having her wings burst out of her back, and the elf queen drew a spike-lined whip from her belt. When the whip hit the ground, the air filled with the sizzling smell of burnt grass.

This was my moment.

I cast an illusion spell across the entire lawn, inclusive of every supernatural within the three house radius. The image of a fake Megan remained on my spot as I moved toward the door for like, the millionth time, but this time unseen.

I had my hand on the front door knob, congratulating myself over the success of the spell,

when yet another new voice rang out across the lawn. Well, new for this occasion anyway. I recognized that voice, and he damn well didn't come here because he was tipped off by Miss Neringa. "Sorry to inform you, ladies and gentlemen, but collectively my clients have the first right that trumps all rights."

The voice was Gregory's.

❧ 7 ❧

CLASS ACTION VENGEANCE

THERE COMES a time in every girl's life when she kicks herself for *not* kicking a certain guy in the nuts when she had the chance.

This was that moment for me.

For the occasion, Gregory had dressed in a formal suit, hidden his vengeance wings, and carried a briefcase. He even put on a pair of reading glasses. He looked perfectly civilized, but I knew the bastard for the thug-for-hire that he was.

I understood from the start that his reasons for finding Eldon had to be darker than what he claimed, but *this*? He used me. He used me to drag my friend and grandma into this mess. And for what? So he could play lawyer and make a big fat profit?

My rage over seeing him dissolved my illusion, which wasn't very stable to begin with, being the experimental spell that it was. I barely made it back to where Fake Megan was before the illusion officially bit the dust.

I stalked toward Gregory. The group of goblins, who were psyching each other up for a fight just moments ago, jumped out of my way. Smart of them. I was in a murderous mood and it wouldn't be a good idea to stand in my way right now.

"Interesting seeing you here, *mercenary*." Sui-Ling tossed her last word at Gregory like it was an insult, giving me the satisfaction to see that she was no fan of his, either. It was no surprise that someone from an old-school ancient order would look down on mercenaries, as it was considered extremely shameful for vengeance demons to use the gift they were born with for profit.

"Sui-Ling." Gregory nodded. "Long time."

"Not long enough," she muttered. I couldn't help but wonder how they came to cross paths before.

With a flourish, Gregory pulled out multiple copies of a legal-looking document from his briefcase; he then passed them around as if my parents' lawn was some damn boardroom.

"What the hell is going on? What are you doing here?" I demanded as he pushed a stack of papers toward me. Not expecting that movement, my arm reached out automatically to block his, my reflexes a gift from my combat training at Demon U.

Upon impact, Gregory drew back his arm right away. The papers fell but didn't scatter on the ground, due to the staple holding them together.

Though my skin had only made contact with his for less than a second, a tingling sensation traveled from my arm to the rest of my body, and I trembled involuntarily. It was as if my body remembered that time when Gregory gave me a piggy-back ride in order to gain safe passage to the boot-legged plane. The hardness of his muscles, the heat radiating from his torso...

Dammit. My emotions, jumbled by my failed hybrid spell, must've somehow magnified the effect of that acci-dental touch, which only got me madder. I needed to focus on my murderous rage *toward* him, not my attraction *to* him.

To buy myself a moment to compose myself, I scooped up the fallen paper. I even made a great show of shaking the dirt off it.

"Everyone, please turn to Exhibit A at the back." Gregory acted all business-like, though his gaze skirted around me. Was it because of our touch, or my questioning about his purpose here?

It has to be the latter, I told myself.

Seeing that everyone else, including Sui-Ling, seemed to be taking him seriously, however begrudgingly, I flipped the offending document to the back, not caring how I practically ripped its staple off.

By the yellowed street lamplight, I read.

Exhibit A turned out to be a three-page list of supernatural species big and small: trolls, dwarf giants, lesser faes, brownies, pixies, leprechauns, and even boogeymen, and the signatures of their leaders. These middle and lower class creatures weren't exactly on the top of the totem pole in the Cosmic Balance. In fact, if there was a common theme on the list, it was that every single name on it was considered too weak, too odd, or too intellectually challenged for polite vengeance society.

"My consulting firm, Clear Vengeance, is representing these clients." Gregory's voice rang clear across the lawn as everyone stared at the document, dumbfounded. "I can prove to you that each of my clients has ancestors who were wronged by the changelings. Some of them even have children held at the changeling plane as we speak."

If or when the changelings got punished, there was no guarantee that the little guys would get their fair share of healing relief. These fringe creatures that Gregory represented would totally get overlooked in the sea of bureaucracy and prejudice. I had to admit, it was smart of them to join forces together. Too bad in the process they had allowed themselves to be manipulated by Gregory. He stood to gain quite a bit of profit in this endeavor.

"So you have the strength in numbers"—Eldratha waved her hand dismissively—"but by definition, the first right of vengeance is a test based on chronological order. A combination of many wrongs done on later dates cannot trump one single wrong from an earlier date."

"And you assume that would be yours." Gregory looked like the Cheshire cat. I could tell that he was glad that the elf queen brought up the issue of timing priority, because he already had an answer for it. If I weren't so mad at him I would be just a little impressed by his display of utter cunningness. "My clients have both the strength in numbers *and* the earlier dates. What you have to understand is how a criminal evolves."

"Yeah, I'm sure you know a lot about that," I muttered.

Gregory ignored me. "Every criminal mastermind started out with minor crimes, and many serial killers practiced on small animals before they moved on to bigger targets. The changelings were the same. At the beginning of time, they began their questionable tradition by switching much weaker supernaturals with their own. Those with less valuable skills to impart. Those with less magic to guard their babies. And yes, those too insignificant to wield weapons, to enjoy beauty treatments, or to have regulated destinies. It was only *after* they became successful with these weaker supernaturals that they moved onto more and more powerful targets. Therefore, without a doubt, the first right of vengeance belongs to my clients. Our claim is indisputable."

Even I had to admit he had a point. There was a good reason why Santa Claus's annual naughty list fetched such a high price in the vengeance world—not every kid on that list ended up being big-time criminals, but almost all big-time criminals began their career by being on that list.

I knew that Gregory would always be gunning for his own profit, and it wasn't like we had any sort of relationship that would give me any right to his loyalty whatsoever. Sure, I found him hot, but it wasn't like we even went on a single date. Not that he'd asked, and not that I'd say yes. I was pretty sure I wouldn't. Maybe.

But at the end of the day, our entire interaction could be summed up to him coming to my aid once, wherein I promised him a boon in return that he came back months later to cash in. That was pretty much it. So I totally didn't understand this sense of betrayal cutting through me. Like I was deeply disappointed in him or something. I told myself it was simply because I was ashamed I didn't do more home-work on the guy before getting Serafina and the rest of my family involved in this mess. Ashamed and horrified. Yeah, I was going to stick with that.

Sui-Ling launched into her trademark response de jour, "As I already told those in presence before your arrival, Gregory, all these claims would have to be fully investigated—"

"Do my clients' claims not have the Ring of Vengeance to them?" Gregory cut straight to the point.

The Ring of Vengeance was like the ring of truth humans talked about—this certainty of rightness of someone's claim that a vengeance demon could sense. It was an instinct we were born with, but had to learn to trust over time.

Something in Sui-Ling's hard eyes shifted. She felt the Ring. And damn him to hell, I felt it, too. His clients owned this vengeance fair and square.

From the disgusted looks on the faces of Eldratha, Greexet, and the Three Fates, they knew defeat when they saw it as well.

"Look," Sui-Ling sounded both irritated and impressed, "I get it. Even I have to admit your claim is solid. But there's still a procedure that has to be followed. It's best if we wait for the Council's verdict—"

Gregory snorted. "Would your plan be to wait, if you'd managed to sneak off with the changeling without the Council's knowledge?"

Sui-Ling glared at him, then she thought of something and narrowed her eyes shrewdly. "Oh, Gregory, what will your dear old dad say about all this?"

Gregory's lips thinned. "He has no say in this."

"You're going to embarrass him in front of his peers."

"This is business." Gregory tried to pretend that the mention of his father didn't bother him, but one muscle kept jumping on the right side of his jaw.

"Bastard," Sui-Ling hissed. I got the feeling she meant it more than the common curse word. She knew he was illegitimately born. In this aspect, the respectable vengeance society was forever stuck in the fifties—the only thing more cringeworthy than being born out of wedlock would be to go rogue, which Gregory had also done.

Despite my anger at him, a part of my heart softened a little wondering about the circumstance that had forced the younger Gregory to choose the path of mercenary.

I indulged that soft fuzzy feeling for half a second, before squishing it like a bug.

The goblin chief exchanged glances with his underlings. Suddenly he gave out a battle cry. Weapons raised, they all charged toward Gregory, clearly hoping to use their sheer strength of numbers to bag the changeling while they still had a chance.

Without thinking, I reacted. I flanked Gregory while Sui-Ling did the same on the other side. In such close quarters, using magic had too great a risk of backfiring, so hand-to-hand combat was employed instead. Together, Gregory, Sui-Ling, and I blocked weapon after weapon. Just how many knives did one single goblin carry anyway? Sui-Ling and I glanced at each other, both unbelieving that we were defending Gregory. But dammit, it was the right thing to do. Even the Three Fates tried to help. They had no chance to examine the life thread of the individual goblin within the herd that was rushing toward us, but they helped by trying to trip them or hit them with their handbags.

Eldratha, the elf queen, covered her delicate nose and said in disgust, "What *is* that smell?"

She must have had a super-sensitive nose, for even after she said it, it took another few seconds before the odor hit me. It was the stink of ten thousand unwashed socks all in one punch.

The ground shook at my feet as the groans of ill-tempered beasts filled the entire neighborhood block.

"Mee wand san veng ginze, too!"

"Veng ginze gooood!"

Oh crap, ogres. Looked like they got wind of the all-access pass, too. Who had ever heard of *them* checking tweets?

❦ 8 ❦

THE ESSENCE OF CHAOS

FROM WHAT I understood from animated movies, humans paint ogres in a rather romanticized light. Sure, they were supposed to be violent and destroyed everything in their paths, but turned out they were simply misunderstood.

In reality, the stereotype regarding ogres was pretty much correct. There wasn't much heroic or off-beat charming about them. They were dumb as soup and attracted to conflicts like a trickster to chaos. For all they knew, *veng ginze* was a type of pizza. They heard about it, and now they wanted it because everybody else did.

As a pair of ogres tore around the corner of the street, uprooting a cedar tree the width of a garden shed in their path, I stole a glance at the others around me. Eldratha and the Three Fates looked ready to flee; the Three Fates had taken out their return bus passes, as if clutching onto them tightly would make their means of escape appear out of thin air. The elf queen was already waving her hands at the earth, presumably trying to re-open her passage in the lawn. The pair of ogres—no, wait, make that two pairs—roared and headed straight for us like monstrously oversized quarterbacks.

Only Greexet and his goblins seemed excited by the prospect of the impending fight. If I thought they'd already taken out most of their weapons during our brief scuffle earlier, I was dead wrong. They had barely gotten started. The goblins now pulled out swords, knives, and daggers from every part of their bodies, many of which made me wonder how they could have survived as a race given the need to sit down or bend down at *some* point in their lives.

The ogres, towering monsters over ten feet tall, smashed through the white picket fence, taking out ours and the neighbor's, and proceeded to trample across the lawn. Didn't they learn from HGTV how expensive sodding was? Didn't they know how hard it was to get neighbors to agree to chip in for the fencing? It was unforgivable.

I felt a tug at my sleeve just as I started calling on my vengeance power, like Gregory and Sui-Ling already had.

"Try reaching for your trickster power, sister," Fir whispered in my ear.

Where the heck had he come from? I didn't remember seeing him around me. My entire focus was on the ogres, mind you, but I would like to think I'd notice if someone got close enough to me to be whispering in my ear.

"Come on, Megan, for the sake of Fleur," my half-brother hissed.

I took his advice and tapped into the naughty, fun-loving side of me, though I had no idea how that was supposed to help me in a fight with the—

In a fight with the what, exactly? Once I allowed my trickster side to take over I could see that there was no damage to the lawn except where the goblins set up camp.

No gigantic ogre feet. No mighty ogre roars. No awful ogre odor.

No ogres at all.

Everything was an illusion, created by a spell I could now recognize as one of Fir's latest creations called the Blind Panic.

The aim of the spell was to create and feed chaos, and *that*, it did. With my trickster side allowing me to actually look, I could see now that everyone was running around, fighting or fleeing the fake monsters, while ignoring the perfectly visible Eldon and Serafina heading our way. They carried the duffle bags that I had packed earlier and were smiling. Fir must have made sure that she and Eldon were immune to the influence of the Blind Panic spell.

"Alright"—I turned to Fir—"this probably seems like the wrong time to ask, but *why*? What are you *really* up to?"

I needed to know why my half-brother suddenly wanted to help us, because it wasn't the first time I fell victim to his trickster nature. He loved me to pieces, but he was prone to throw me over for a really good round of trickery. Memories from the Aequitas ball he crashed were still fresh in my mind.

"Always so suspicious." Fir put his hand over his chest as if he was heartbroken, but I wasn't moved. For all I knew it could all be an act. "I assure you, my intentions are completely noble."

I narrowed my eyes.

"Alright, they are noble because I get something out of it, too," Fir corrected. "Eldon is family."

"What the heck are you talking about? What family?" I asked incredulously. "His plane has been closed since almost the beginning of time. You'd never seen him in your life until now."

"Yes, but according to our oral history all the great deceivers of the Cosmic Balance such as tricksters, cuckoos, and changelings are distant cousins. And family helps out each other. Besides"—he shrugged—"if word got out that I allowed Eldon to be captured, it'd be bad for my rep. We can't afford for him to be punished. What if the rest of the world sees this and gets the idea to start going after the rest of us? We have to stick together."

As he spoke, the scene before us became even more chaotic. Clotho and Lachesis were fighting with Eldratha in a desperate bid to get into the earth passage the latter had opened up. Taking advantage of the elf queen's reluctance to cast spells given the tight space, the elderly Fates were downright dirty in their fighting. There was a lot of name-calling and face scratching. Then, with a mighty yell, Clotho grabbed a lock of Eldratha's pale blond hair and pulled.

And ended up with the elf queen's wig in her hands.

The look on Eldratha's face as she touched the short, spiky, jet black hair poking out of her head was so hilarious, I couldn't stop myself from laughing. It was like that actress who played the platinum blonde heroine in the *Game of Thrones*; she was a natural brunette.

Atropos, unlike her other two sisters, chose the fight option rather than flight. She aimed a very unladylike kick to Greexet's groin, and promptly took a couple of his swords for her own protection against the ogres she thought were still coming for her. I wondered what the little old lady thought she could manage with them, until I remembered that this was a woman who had spent eons doing nothing but cutting threads. She ought to know her way around sharp objects.

Then, as if my parents' poor lawn wasn't crowded enough, one hunched figure appeared, teleporting to land just at the edge.

Once the dust settled, I could see that the new arrival was a troll carrying a leprechaun, who carried a brownie with an array of pixies and fairies clinging to his hat and hair.

Wait. Troll, leprechaun, brownie, pixies, and fairies?

When did I see that combination of supernaturals just recently?

Gregory's Exhibit A.

The group of supernaturals hovered around the edge of the lawn. Maybe they didn't have Miss Neringa's access pass. Maybe they got used to keeping their distance from the mighty vengeance demons. Either way, rather than coming any closer, they called out to Gregory.

Gregory was doing this strange dance where he was dodging imaginary ogres and collecting all the legal documents scattered by everyone at the same time. I almost laughed at the sight of his beautiful leather briefcase getting dented by the trampling goblins, and his precious documents smudged with dirty footprints of all sizes.

"Where is he?" The young brownie jumped at his spot, trying to see past the goblins, which were at least five inches taller than him. He looked so hopeful and earnest. If I didn't know better I'd say he was asking after a pony, not a changeling he contracted someone to capture and get revenge on.

The troll beat his chest. "Me. Want. Change-chee-lane."

"Is he ready for vengeance now?" The high-pitched voice of a purple-winged fairy carried over all the other sounds.

Gregory dived around the feet of an imaginary ogre and reached his clients, the briefcase clutched to his chest. "You guys shouldn't be here."

"We want to be here." One of the pixies said in a sad voice, "Our great-great-aunt was captured by a changeling just before he returned home. We never knew what became of her."

The leprechaun frowned at the chaos surrounding them. "I didn't expect to see ogres. Ogres! What are they doing here?"

"I'd like to know, too," Gregory muttered.

I didn't bother listening to the rest of the clients questioning and pleading with Gregory. Those were his clients, after all, not mine. Gruff or emotional, they were his to handle.

Take that, traitorous jerk!

While the chaos continued in the yard, I let Fir tug me away. He led our little group toward the swan-shaped birdbath.

I stared in disbelief as Fir stopped in front of the birdbath and twisted the stone swan's neck to the right with an audible click, making it angled in such an unnatural manner that it looked like someone had offed the poor creature, which would have been ghastly if its tongue wasn't rolling out in a totally goofy way.

The water of the basin drained away, revealing a cross-dimensional threshold.

"I found a loophole in the fine print of that spell Dad used to ward the house. I made this passage a long time ago to sneak beer in," Fir explained, then he winced. "Such a tough spell to crack, and our friendly neighborhood giantess bypassed it all with a twitter mention. There's something to be learned here."

"Maybe another day. Let's just get out of here for now," I urged.

Eldon stumbled back from the cross-dimensional threshold and looked at Fir with genuine regret and a hint of embarrassment. "I appreciate the help, but I won't be able to go through that."

"I know all about your restrictions, cousin." Fir leaned closer and winked. "This one doesn't cross to other planes, only crossing distances within this one. I fixed it to a pedicure spa across town."

Eldon breathed out with relief. "Thank you."

"Thank me after you get through. It's going to be a tight

squeeze. I did the best I could, but I'm afraid the passage is only as wide as the actual size of the water basin. I have to sneak the beer in, drink them, and lose some weight with the treadmill before I can go get more again."

I eyed the water basin, which was barely wide enough to fit a brownie through. Fir was right. It was going to be tough to get through it. Damn my child-bearing hips.

❦ 9 ❧

THE PERFECT IMAGE

FOR A FINAL DISTRACTION TO cover our departure, Fir created an illusion of a much-better-groomed version of Eldon—glossy hair, fancy royal outfit, rosy cheeks—and projected him smack into the middle of the lawn. It was the perfect image of what one might expect of a fae prince, had he not been found half-dead in a dark alley and hunted by creatures both light and dark.

Everyone caught by the Blind Panic spell paused, then turned away from each other and started going after Fake Eldon.

"Wait—" Gregory nearly got trampled as the troll bull-dozed past him, followed by the leprechaun and the brownie. I was suddenly reminded of the first time I met Gregory, when his client—an overweight woman in a shapeless, yellow polka dot dress—charged toward him, almost going over the balcony and taking him with her.

Man, the guy didn't have a lot of luck with his clients.

One of the pixies caught her wings in a thread dangling from Gregory's button and, impatient to rush off, yanked herself free by burning a clear section of Gregory's shirt off. I ought to be focusing on Fir, who was having a heck of a time squeezing through the basin passage with his pot belly, or at the very least take a moment to admire the impressive display of hard coiled muscles on Gregory's partly bare torso, but the tattoos on his chest caught my undivided attention.

In the vengeance demon world, females centered their power using the pearls in their earrings. The male equivalent of this practice was a little more different. At the Becoming —the vengeance version of the bar mitzvah—the guys receive an elaborate tattoo over their chests. Spells are woven right into the patterns, which encourages mental clarity and the focusing of power. With Gregory's chest exposed, I realized that we had another thing in common—a seemingly half-ass Becoming gift. Back when Grandma was pretending not to love me, she gave me a necklace made of a single pearl that was supposed to be a diss on my Becoming. Of course, I'd since then found out that the single pearl held more power than the standard issue earrings, but there was no doubt that the half-finished design on Gregory's chest was meant as anything but an insult.

I took a moment to examine it further. While the protective spells in the center of the pattern were intact and probably fully functional, the designs on either side were anything but. On the left side of the tattoo was a dragon, symbolizing loyalty. The outline of the dragon was complete, but only a random scale or two on its body was inked, and it was done so with dull-looking dye. The whole thing was a far cry from the norm, which involved a riot of vibrant colors filling every space of the design. As for the right side, well, it was supposed to be a proud declaration of the vengeance house that the person belonged to. On Gregory's chest it was deliberately vague. I could make out an oval shape that could either be a shield or a cauldron with twin stars on it, and something on top of it that could either be an upright sword or a dagger. Or a Popsicle stick. Though I doubted it.

It was as if the tattoo artist had to leave to use the bathroom and never came back to finish the job.

This was a direct homage to Gregory's bastard status. Saying loud and clear: "We have no choice but to give you vengeance power, but don't you dare think for a second you could ever be one of us."

I could identify with that.

With Fir finally through the passage and pulling Serafina from the other end, Eldon was next. Still getting used to his newly functional body, he looked at the three foot high basin as if he wasn't quite sure how to climb to the top of it. I kneeled in front of him and patted my thigh, gesturing him to use it as a step stool. He looked at me gratefully.

"Don't get used to it," I warned. "This is the first and last time I'm going to kneel to your royal-pain-in-the-ass highness."

That brought a smile to his face as he placed one foot on my thigh and braced his hands on the edge of the basin. "Have no worry. I would not expect you to—"

Then he was yanked off me by Sui-Ling. From the furious look she sent my way as she held Eldon by his throat, she had somehow managed to see through Fir's illusion.

"Enough games. We're at the close, dear."

Chaos still reigned all around us, meaning the spell held for everybody else. With Fir and Serafina already gone from the lawn, by the time I jumped onto my feet it was too late. Sui-Ling had conjured up a portal and disappeared into it with Eldon.

Damn.

❧ II ❧
THE CHANGELING INHERITANCE

❧ 10 ❧

BEYOND OMISSION

"Megan, how come you two didn't follow us?" Serafina pushed herself out of the basin, returning to this side of the portal. Fir followed shortly after. She looked around in alarm. "Where's Eldon?"

I opened my mouth to answer her. I needed to tell her what happened, but at the same time assure her that all was not lost. Sui-Ling wouldn't dare do anything to Eldon until her superiors had finished negotiating with the Council. We had time to fix this.

Before I could get the words out, a second passage opened up right behind Serafina, and out stepped Grandma Aequitas and Sui-Ling.

Yet something was wrong.

Rather than her mesmerizing dragonhide cat suit, Sui-Ling was now wearing a sweatshirt and yoga pants that were two sizes too big for her.

And Eldon was nowhere in sight.

"Gran, what's going on?" I rushed to her.

"Where's Eldon?" She looked around the lawn at the chaos surrounding us.

"Gone." I jabbed a finger Sui-Ling's way. "She took him."

"No, I didn't." Sui-Ling shook her head, her disheveled hair a mess. Wasn't it smooth and sleek just moments ago?

"Why the heck are you denying it? I *saw* you!" I accused.

"No. What you saw was someone who *looked* like me. An imposter."

"What?" Serafina, Fir, and I shouted at the same time.

"I ran into Sui-Ling, this real one in front of me, on my way to see the Council," Grandma explained. "She had just been attacked and was trying to seek our assistance."

"I got wind of the changeling and was on my way here when an assailant sneaked up on me. She knocked me out and took my outfit." Sui-Ling crossed her arms and dug her nails in her animal-printed sweatshirt in disgust, tapping her kitten-heel boots. Some Good Samaritan with questionable fashion sense must have lent her that top and the baggy yoga pants. It was a long way to fall from the skintight, magically-enhancing dragonhide. It would be kinda funny, if it was under any other circumstance.

I couldn't believe that the girl who took Eldon wasn't the same as this one who was currently in my presence. Physically they were identical, down to the dark hair which fell to her waist like a curtain, disheveled or otherwise. Whoever the imposter was, she'd perfected the trickster charm called the Lookalike, or something similar to it.

"Were you able to see what the assailant looked like?" Grandma asked.

"No, I didn't get a good look. She jumped me from behind."

"So it could even be a guy," I suggested.

"The essence felt female, but then that could be false as well."

"So we got nothing." Fir whistled.

"No, but when I find the bitch, or the bastard, I'm going

to make them pay," Sui-Ling vowed. "Whoever jumped me has been walking around pretending to be an agent of the Condor League, wearing my clothes and mimicking me like a cheap Chinese knock-off."

We all just looked at her.

"What?" She shrugged. "I'm Asian and therefore, the only one who can make that analogy without being politically incorrect."

I suddenly remembered what the fake Sui-Ling said about her age and being an Asian woman. Then I realized that the imposter was no cheap knock-off at all—she'd managed to copy both Sui-Ling's appearance and personality to the tee, and knowledge, too, if her cryptic conversation with Gregory about his daddy was anything to go by. Sui-Ling had been expertly duplicated. Like an evil clone or something.

That suggested an enemy way more sophisticated than the type who picked up their supplies and spell books from a trickster's joke shop.

Grandma and I exchanged a look; she had arrived at the same conclusion.

Fir proceeded to de-activate the Blind Panic. The lawn was like a warzone, littered with shoes, trampled tents, dropped weapons, and scattered legal documents. Eldratha's blond wig laid over a leprechaun's green hat, with a troll's enormous and dirty toenail poking out of it like some weird version of an English fascinator.

During the panic, someone had thrown fairy dust toward the imaginary ogres in a futile attempt to halt their movement. As the breaking dawn began to light the street, the tiny fairy dust clouds settled, making the yard a minefield of random and spontaneous magical transformation. I couldn't believe I'd been up all night over this whole craziness.

Now that Eldon was gone, there was no reason to linger

anymore. Greexet, Eldratha, and the Three Fates all went home; so did Gregory's clients.

Sui-Ling was silent as she watched Grandma lead me, Serafina, and Fir inside for a private conversation. She would be waiting.

I pointed a finger at Gregory. "You. Stay."

"Is he going to listen?" Fir sounded doubtful.

"He will." Sometime earlier, while I watched Gregory reassuring his clients about his commitment to their contract, I had an epiphany.

He owed me. A lot. He just didn't know it yet. He would stay because he wanted to learn from me who had Eldon, but I just realized that I had something on him that would make him mine to use rather than the other way around.

Grandma's face was grave when she turned to face us in the living room. "I just received word on who has Prince Eldon."

"Who?" Serafina hadn't said a word since she discovered that Eldon was taken. Her silence was more alarming than her, well, alarm.

Grandma wove another privacy spell over the gazillion other ones we already had over the house before answering, "The Greys."

"What?" I shouted.

The Greys. The secret society the Council was supposedly going after. The bane of my existence, the organization that almost succeeded in using me to bring the end of life as we knew it. They had Eldon? This was bad news.

"They made contact with the Council soon after they snatched Eldon." Grandma held up her phone. "They want to negotiate."

"The Council wouldn't consider talking to them, would they?" I watched Grandma's face anxiously. "I mean, come on, those bastards tried to end the world."

Grandma sighed and gestured for us all to sit down. She waited until everyone was seated before speaking again. "You have to understand, Megan, the Grey's actions were only fully witnessed by you. There are those in our world who don't put a lot of weight in the words of a, er, a..."

"Half-breed," I finished the sentence for her. I could feel her relief in not having to say the vile word herself.

"The changeling prince on the other hand," Grandma continued, "is a very seductive prize. From the Council's point of view, he could be the key to tackling one of the oldest and continuing cases of unresolved vengeance. He could be instrumental in the greatest rallying call in history."

"Talk about a golden PR opportunity," Fir muttered.

"What do you know about PR?" I asked my half-brother. "You're a full-blooded trickster. I thought you hated all that corporate and polite society stuff."

"Hey, tricksters gotta make a name for themselves, too. That's PR in a way, you know. Megan, you have no idea how many doors opened to me after the Aequitas' ball."

Grandma glared at Fir over the mention of the ball fiasco, then sighed again. "He's not wrong. This situation is both a crisis and an opportunity for the Council. Inaction at this point could only hurt them. The cat is, as the humans would say, already out of the bag, and there's simply too much anger stored up for the changelings throughout the Cosmic Balance for it to go away on its own."

"Yeah, I saw that firsthand last night," I said darkly.

"The Council is going to be under a lot of pressure to invade Dualsing, isn't it?" Serafina asked, her voice catching.

The pitying look Grandma sent her way told me what I needed to know. Serafina's eyes filled.

"I'm so sorry, dear. I know a part of you still considered it home, and I'm sure not everyone there is necessarily bad. I'll do what I can to shift the focus away from Eldon, bringing attention to the fact that the Greys have blatantly taken what should've been left to the Council's judgment."

"Appealing to the pride of the Council is good under normal circumstances, but in this case, it's pretty weak compared to the juicy reward of bagging a changeling. You don't hold out much hope it'll work, do ya?" Fir asked Grandma point blank.

"Fir!" I didn't bother to keep the warning out of my voice. The last thing I wanted was for him to offend Grandma. We had to stick together.

Grandma said in an even voice, "No, I expect it's going to be an uphill battle, or even a lost cause."

Serafina gasped in horror. Grandma reached over, patted her hand, and continued. "The marching drum of war is in the air. Everyone is too busy sharpening their weapons to listen to reason. The prince's kidnapping made this matter more politicized than ever. He's the perfect bargaining chip for the Greys."

"Then how about we take that bargaining chip away from them?" I heard myself say.

"Megan," Serafina began. "I appreciate all the help you've given me, but I don't want to get you into any more trouble. This is my fight."

"*Our* fight," I corrected. "It stopped being just your fight once the Greys came into the picture."

"Our fight!" Fir winked as he pumped his fist in the air. "This is going to be so much fun."

"Maybe for a full trickster, but not for Megan." Grandma looked me in the eyes. "Know this, my granddaughter. The Council is already not happy with you for not going straight to them when you first realized who Prince Eldon was. They fully plan to deal with you after this is all over. You have to understand that you'll be in an even worse position if you continue with this course."

Did I really want to incur the wrath of the Council? Of course not. Up until now, technically, I hadn't been working against the governing body of my profession outright. So okay, I had played dumb; but there was a big difference between "accidental" omission and open defiance. If I went off and stole Eldon right out from under the Council, there would be hell to pay.

But this matter was no longer about the need to help a friend or the desire to prevent someone from being punished unjustly.

It went much beyond that.

The Greys were now involved, and the world couldn't afford to have them hold such a power over the Council's head. No good could come out of that alliance.

And I'd seen how the bitter fight over Eldon was creating divides among the supernaturals rather than unity. If it was bad now, it'd only be so much worse in the aftermath of a direct attack on the changeling plane. The changelings had pissed off a lot of people over countless generations. The calculations of who got what vengeance relief would be stuff of accounting nightmares. Even if the division was done as fairly as possible, nobody was going to believe it to be so. It would lead to conflicts and ill-feelings between all parties, even accusations of corruption, real or imagined, directed at the Council.

A vengeance of that size was the last thing the world needed. If my history class—whichever part I hadn't slept through—had taught me anything, it was that winning the war was often a very small part of the story. The aftermath was the real struggle.

The Greys would be right there, waiting to take advantage of the resulting discord like the vultures that they were.

The entire Cosmic Balance might not want to believe that the Greys had a twisted agenda, but I know what I saw.

I nodded at Grandma solemnly, letting her know I knew exactly what I was getting myself into. What I stood to lose. What I stood to gain.

Potential school suspension or further alienation from vengeance society was a small price to pay to thwart the Greys. I had no idea how to do it, but I couldn't live with myself if I didn't at least try.

Whatever Grandma was able to read from my mind, it made her a believer. She looked at me with pride in her eyes. "If you're going to do this, Megan, you have to hurry. Take Eldon away before formal negotiation starts between the Council and the Greys."

Alright, time for more information.

I turned to Fir and Serafina. "You both mentioned something about Eldon having restrictions when it comes to cross-dimensional travels. Can you explain more?"

I had to know what we were up against not just in regard to our enemy, but our own inherent limitations.

Fir scratched his head. "Oh, that. Well, physically a changeling's body just isn't built for constant traveling across the planes. They can try, but each crossing weakens them until they can do it no more. Like when a fuse is blown and that's it."

"Each changeling could endure about two round trips in a lifetime," Serafina added.

"That's the reason we tricksters eventually lost touch with them. Hard to bond with someone when you only get to see them and get into trouble with them twice in your life." Fir appeared deep in thought; it was strange to see, since he was rarely the serious type. "Come to think of it, maybe that's why they started switching in the first place. It was before the age of the Internet and e-commerce, meaning an ordinary trade industry wouldn't have worked with them. So they send their kids out to swindle their host families, making the most out of their lifetime travel limits right off the bat."

"As for Eldon," Serafina said, "there's a once-in-a-lifetime trip that every changeling who was never switched out into another plane takes when they come of age. That counts as one of his round trips."

"And being dumped onto the human plane gets it up to one and a half trips," I concluded. Then it occurred to me. "We took him to this plane. That's used it up already!"

"No." Serafina shook her head. "The earth and vengeance planes are parallel to each other and therefore don't count as two. He still has a one-way trip left. But with his magic gone, his body won't have enough tolerance for it."

"So even if we could rescue him from the Greys, and that's a big freaking *if*, we could only stash him in either the human or the vengeance plane. He couldn't go home."

"Exactly," Fir confirmed.

"We have to find a way. Somehow. And we'll have to do it quick once we rescue him," I decided.

Serafina frowned. "But, Megan, I already explained it. He can't. Besides, it may already be too late. As of now, False Sui-Ling might have taken Eldon somewhere that used up his one-way trip."

"He *has* to go back home," I said firmly, "otherwise he'll end up dead. Think about it. They'll never stop hunting him. Heck, he's probably being tortured as we speak."

From the way Serafina's face paled and her body swayed, I could tell that she'd already known that was a possibility and had likely been trying hard not to think about it. But I was enough of a jerk to say it out loud to drive home my point. I needed her to understand that Eldon couldn't possibly stick around. But seeing how she was affected by my words, I cursed myself inwardly. Causing her further stress was the last thing I wanted.

"Look," I gentled my voice, "as long as he remains in our world he is a catalyst for conflicts. I'm so sorry. I wish things were different, but they're not."

"Serafina, dear," Grandma's tone was filled with sympathy, "let him go. Give him the chance to try to win back his crown. Allow nature to take its course as it's meant to."

A tear rolled down Serafina's cheek. She nodded her agreement. "As it's meant to."

"Great." Fir cracked his knuckles. "Now that we've decided what to do, the question is, how?"

"Let's start off with Serafina's locator spell." I didn't have a full plan. Not yet. But finding out where they were keeping Eldon, even if we weren't ready to go there yet, seemed like a pretty good first step.

———

"Enough is enough!" I hollered at Fir. "Turn the lights back on."

With the return of the lights, I managed to catch an exhausted Serafina before she pitched over onto the living room carpet. Twenty minutes of non-stop locator spell had been too much for her. The bright overlapping maps had been twisting into one another rather than logically sorting themselves out like the last time. As Serafina fell, they winked out of existence.

Serafina opened her eyes, her voice barely above a whisper; beads of sweat soaked the hair surrounding her forehead. "I can't find Eldon. Something's blocking our connection."

Looked like I would need to use another resource at my disposal. And part of me was looking forward to that.

❦ 11 ❦

INNER LEGAL BITCH

WHEN THE GOING GETS TOUGH, the tough go ass-kicking.

With the last of the early morning gloom chased away by what was promising to be a bright and sunny day, I closed the door to the house and walked up to Gregory. Grandma headed for Sui-Ling, most likely to sort out the political end of things, but my focus was all on Gregory. I took in his good-looking, traitorous face, and his shirt, magically mended, covering his firm and broad chest. I told myself I was disappointed that it was all covered up because I wanted another look at the symbol of his house. Some additional tool of blackmailing could come in handy one of these days.

"You owe me," I told him flat out.

"Excuse me?" He frowned.

"You owe me. A boon, a favor, a debt...whatever you want to call it—you owe me. You broke your promise to me." I had come to realize that I needed to beat this guy at his own game. He wanted to get mighty offended when I suggested that there was no honor among thieves? He wanted to play dress up and pretend to care about formality? He dared to suggest that mercenaries have their own code of conduct?

Well, then he better be prepared to meet my inner legal bitch.

My daddy's job as an arch vengeance demon wasn't all about descending on serial killers all menacing-like and swooping them off to vengeance. Most of the world's true psychopaths hid behind a façade of civility; from those causally dismissing massive chemical spills to those raging wars in the name of fantastic-sounding principles and values. Growing up I'd spent many hours at the dinner table listening, fascinated, as Dad discussed his work days of "cutting through the bullshit" and "getting the bastards where it hurt the most." And sometimes that was done not through fists, but through paperwork and contracts.

The little daddy's girl in me who was weaned on such tales smelled an opportunity.

"You promised me that what I had to do for you was legal and didn't involve trickery," I accused.

"And it didn't."

"It's true, the little trip to retrieve Eldon from the human alley technically didn't," I conceded. "But what I was forced to do *after*, did."

The discovery of Eldon had a domino effect of forcing me to open my trickster mind to sense the Blind Panic, and I sure as hell was getting myself into trouble with the Council. How did that not involve trickery? How was going against my own governing body not an illegal act? And it wasn't like Grandma was entirely thrilled by the risky business I found myself in, even if she supported my decision given the circumstances.

Her stamp of approval, my butt.

I saw the moment Gregory reached the same conclusion on his own. He cursed softly.

"The conditions by which my co-operation was initially obtained have not been met." I sent a prayer to the universe that the Mercenary Rules of Conduct, which I'd never read and I doubted was even publicly available, agreed with me on this. "And by extension, the contracts you have drawn up with your clients, the fulfillment of which is dependent on my help, are also on shaky ground. Your only hope is to make things right with me before the Council comes up with a way to out-claim your clients. Otherwise you'll have to redo all existing contracts and their attached claim to vengeance with the new, later date."

Anyone worth their legal salt knew the importance of contract dates. In this game of who-got-to-get-what-vengeance-relief, claims made with earlier dates trump those with later dates. If Gregory was able to pull off this class action vengeance, it would be one of the greatest of its kind in vengeance history, and Gregory stood to gain a *lot*. He would not want a legal technicality with me to derail his plan.

I had the bastard and he knew it.

I was never the type of girl who liked to trap a guy, but with Gregory, I was willing to make an exception.

"What do you want?" he asked softly.

Well, what do you know? It worked. It just occurred to me how weird it was, that a people who were considered outlaws by vengeance society had rules in place that took more care about doing things the right way than the ones in power often did. Well, since it worked to my advantage, I wasn't complaining.

"Help me find Eldon. You started all this by enlisting my help to figure out where he was. An eye for an eye, a location for a location."

"Why can't Serafina help you?"

"She's been blocked. She can't do it. But somehow you knew to find him in the first place. How did you do it? You must know something."

Or knew someone who did. At the very least, he might

have contacts that knew how to find the Greys, and by extension, Eldon. Considering I didn't have a lot to go by, it was something.

Gregory took a deep breath and I could practically see him mentally sifting through his options, his expression turning from annoyance, analytical, and finally to resignation, with even a dash of grudging admiration. Then his eyes flashed with renewed determination. "I'll help you. But once the changeling prince is located, all bets are off."

"Alright." I would cross that bridge when I got there. I understood where Gregory was coming from. Right now, with Eldon missing, nobody was getting any vengeance done anyway. He might as well help me. Besides, I was pretty much the only person in the world who had an intimate knowledge of what it meant to deal with the Greys.

We were useful to each other. For now.

"Should we shake on it?" Gregory asked, offering his hand, a hint of challenge in his eyes.

A little giddy from my success at getting his co-operation, I didn't stop to wonder what that look was all about. It was too late by the time my arm swung up and his hand clasped mine.

Unlike the long, bony fingers typical of tall men, Gregory's hands were large, his palm padded with warm flesh. My own hand felt freakishly small in his, and the tingling sensation I felt earlier again enveloped my body in one breathless moment.

Then the moment passed, and I pulled my hand back with as much dignity as I could manage.

I wasn't happy with myself. But from the frown on Gregory's face, neither was he.

❧ 12 ❧

THE ORACLE

GRANDMA RETURNED to the Council while Gregory took the rest of us to meet his contact. By "us" I meant me, Fir, and Serafina. I couldn't leave Serafina behind because she had every right to be there. I couldn't shake Fir because, well, he was Fir.

I was expecting to go to a bar, a nightclub, or a gambling hall. Someplace clandestine I assumed mercenaries would operate from. Gregory ended up taking us to the most non-supernatural and non-menacing place that had ever existed on the human plane.

A supermarket. The discounted, price-matching type, with bright fluorescent light bulbs and infinite boxes of mac and cheese on sale.

"Seriously?" I shook my head at the carts of perfectly wholesome apples and oranges, so different from the seedy lairs I had pictured.

"This way." Gregory gestured as he led us to the deli section of the store. The unmanned counter displayed various sausages and hams. Next to the counter was an entrance draped with vertical plastic strips. A sign taped to one of the strips said "Employees only."

Gregory pushed aside the plastic and headed in. We followed closely.

"Let me go in there on my own first." Gregory stopped walking, holding back the plastic strip curtain.

"No," Fir, Serafina, and I answered as one voice. We were so coming in there with him. I didn't trust him as far as I could throw him.

He sighed. "Alright. But be warned, the mercenary world is...different than what you might think."

What did he mean by *different*? Like, meeting in the meat freezer with butchered pigs all around us? Dumpster-diving at the back with hobo-looking informants? I had no idea what mercenaries actually looked and acted like save for Gregory, and I had a feeling he might not be the norm.

After the barrier of the plastic curtain, we crossed a small tiled room to another door.

This door opened onto a dark hallway, hypnotic siren music echoing in the background. The air was filled with the smoky clouds of overpowering incense, making my eyes water and my throat dry. At the end of the hallway, a scantily clad female fire demon with a whip in her hand waited. In contrast to the supermarket plastic, a jeweled and beaded curtain hung from the doorframe. She leaned casually against the doorframe, but there was nothing casual about her. She was dressed like a belly dancer, with an exposed navel, a glittered bra top, and a skirt embroidered with gold metal coins. Grey clusters of asbestos ash lined her shoulder bones, elbows, and kneecaps; those clusters could instantly expand to cover her entire body in a fire.

So, this was a nightclub of sorts, after all? Couldn't say I was expecting anything different, as per Gregory's warning.

"Pete. Long time no see," the she-demon greeted Gregory,

her voice sultry like the music in the background. She referred to him by his mercenary street name, the I'm-oh-so-harmless moniker "Pete."

Then the she-demon turned her eyes to the rest of us and asked, "Who are these people?"

"Clients," Gregory replied.

"Partners," I declared at the same time.

The she-demon looked from Gregory to me, Serafina, and Fir, then back. She crossed her arms. "Partners, really? I thought you said you'd gone solo and that's why you've been too busy to spend time with me. And two of these people are vengeance demons. They don't even need your service. So what's really going on?"

"It's complicated," Gregory said.

The she-demon pouted. The wounded look would have looked cute on a young girl, but on her it just seemed childish and manipulative. "It's been months since you played with me. You promised."

Ewww. I didn't even want to know how exactly Gregory had been *playing* with Miss Ample Bosom. Not that it was any of my business. But, let me say it again. Ewww.

And no, I wasn't jealous. Just grossed out. Really. I thought his taste would be a little less crass, and his sexual partners a little more discreet. Geez, I had learned all sorts of unattractive qualities about Gregory in the last twenty-four hours. He would have stayed a lot sexier in my mind if he'd never come around and collected his damn boon.

"Just go get Mel, Candy. I'll come back to see you soon. Right now I have business to attend to." Gregory reached out and tugged a strand of hair behind the vixen's ear, his voice affectionate.

I couldn't help but roll my eyes. The girl who dressed like a stripper was named Candy. How cliché was that?

Gregory noticed my eye roll and seemed to realize he was

forgetting something. He turned back to the she-demon. "Don't bother keeping up with the illusion for these three, Candy. These aren't paying customers for Mel."

"Why didn't you say so sooner?" Candy's voice shifted higher on the register. No longer deep and sultry, but like a little girl's. The image of the tall, sexy girl shimmered, leaving behind a witch no older than six or seven in her jammies. The whip in her hand turned into a *My Little Pony* figure with a long, pink polyester tail. The incense cleared from the air, the siren music stopped and the room was now lit up with regular standing lamps.

I looked at Gregory questioningly.

He coughed. "Mel. He, er, he believes in a professional environment for the line of work that he does."

All the details of the nightclub scene were nothing but an illusion, conjured by a little girl who was probably just starting elementary school. All those words that she said to Gregory, being put into the context of who she really was, fit perfectly now. She wasn't a clingy flirt. She was just a child who wanted her friend to come play with her.

A part of me wondered why Gregory felt the need to clarify the situation. Then I wondered why I would want him to care enough to do that.

"You're really good, you know?" Fir said admiringly to Candy. "I totally bought the whole thing. I didn't even pick up a single stray vibe of witchcraft. You're going to be spectacular when you grow up, young lady."

Candy gave Fir a brilliant smile, pleased by his compliment.

Sure, she would be extraordinary when she grew up. But at this age, being this talented made her vulnerable. There were many magic-sucking creatures who would love to make a meal of her raw talent. What the heck was she doing in the shadowy world of mercenaries? Shouldn't she be in one of those schools run by the witches' unions, where she would be protected?

Gregory leaned toward me and whispered, his eyes never leaving Candy, "Candy did go through the regular witchcraft education system for a while."

It unnerved me that he seemed to understand the questions whirling in my head. So I forged ahead. "What happened?"

Candy, like any child, was ignoring the grown-ups and chattering to Fir about the various tricks she used to make her illusion so realistic. Fir, in turn, told her about the magical tracking app he was working on. Gregory leaned closer to me.

"The system failed her. Monsters came to her home. Her mom grabbed her and her baby brother and ran. Mel took them in, and ever since then her mother does odd jobs around the office for him."

Candy stopped talking and winked at Gregory. "You don't have to whisper. I know the story. I was there. I'll go find Mel now. I'm filling in for a few hours. Ma's off taking Teddy to the doctor. She thinks he's got pixie flu. *Pixie flu*, what a baby!"

And off Candy went, disappeared through the bead curtain.

Gregory laughed. "That little brat!"

When he turned toward me, the first genuine smile I'd possibly ever seen was on his face. It took years off him and made it feasible that he and I were approximate in age.

Then, of course, I had to ruin it by asking him more questions.

"You mentioned Mel wanted to present a professional image to the outside world. Just what kind of work does he do that would require the whole shebang of incense, siren music, and gypsy hip scarf?"

Gregory's face immediately became guarded. "Look, I want you to keep an open mind."

"Uh-oh, that's what people say when they're going to tell me stuff that would make me want to close it."

"Mel is an oracle."

An oracle? We were here to visit a two-bit fortune-teller? Like, we're going to try finding Eldon with crystal balls and tarot cards and stuff? The last time Mom followed a seer's advice, she ended up playing a role in bringing forth the *Trick of the Century* rather than preventing it. The paradox of prophecy? Yeah right. More like the seer was talking out of her ass.

This was how Gregory planned to help me? Was this guy pulling my leg?

"Megan," Gregory warned, "I can't have you disrespecting Mel."

"How could I? He's the fortune telling dude called *Mel*. Can't he at least make his name a bit more exotic, like Melchior or something?"

"No. He never had to. They just called him The Oracle here."

I was about to laugh in his face when Fir gasped. "The Oracle. *The* Oracle? Megan, the guy is the stuff of legend. Very selective clientele. Super secretive."

I bit back a snotty comeback. Beggars couldn't be choosers.

"You consider Candy part of your family," Serafina stated. She was staring after the still swaying bead curtain, the only original decoration in the room that turned out not to be an illusion. She had been quiet through this mission thus far, so I paid attention when she did speak.

Gregory nodded in confirmation. "We outcasts stick together. The family I choose is the only family I have."

I wasn't sure what it would be like to create a family with

members of your own choosing. I could bitch about the high-strung vengeance society all I liked, but when it came down to it I had a pretty nuclear immediate family, made up of a pair of loving parents and half-siblings that, while different from me in nature, were there for me in their own ways. What was it like to not have that support system at all?

"And yet you're using a fake name with them," I pointed out. I was being a jerk, but I couldn't afford to feel bad for Gregory, not after all the vengeance class action business he had dragged me into.

"Pete *is* my real name. To me," Gregory emphasized. "The only people using 'Gregory' are Lady Aequitas, you, my mother, and—"

He stopped himself, but I already knew what he was going to say. The only other people who used the name he was born with were those who knew about his bastard origins, who would never accept him as Candy and his self-made family would.

I couldn't help but think that in our own ways, Gregory, Serafina, and I were all outcasts. I was a hybrid, Gregory was a bastard, and Serafina was a constant reminder of her family's shame. Gregory might have become a friend, like Serafina, had we met under different circumstances and he wasn't such a treacherous ass.

"So how does it work?" I asked Gregory, eager to move away from my own train of thought. "Mel uses whatever voodoo he's got to see stuff you can use, and then you give him a kickback?"

"Something like that." He, too, looked relieved that we were moving on to another topic.

Candy came through the bead curtain before I could ask more questions about the business arrangement. She announced, "Mel's ready for you now."

I snorted. "If he's the Oracle with the capital 'O', he

would've known that we were coming without someone having to run in to tell him."

Fir kicked at me.

"Be nice." He pulled me closer and whispered, "I think this guy is the real deal."

"Sure he is."

Fir gave an exasperating sigh. "Megan, you are a supernatural. You're born of magic—two types of magic, actually. How could you be so closed-minded about fortune telling?"

"I'm not. I have no problem with the supernatural stuff. I just don't like scammers." I couldn't exactly tell him about what happened with the terrorist video that had gone viral a few months ago, now could I? Mom had set events in motion that brought forth the *Trick of the Century*, when she went about preventing it from happening as per an oracle's instructions. So much for all that mumbo jumbo.

"It worked well enough to get you to find Eldon in the alleyway that first time, didn't it? Give this guy the benefit of the doubt."

I had nothing to say to that. Maybe Fir was right. Maybe there was something to future prediction. Maybe my wariness toward Gregory was coloring my perception of those associated with him.

I followed Candy along with the others, pushing the bead curtains out of my way just a little too hard; the colored glass beads collided against each other in an annoying chorus like tiny mocking bells.

Suddenly, it was as though we stepped into the make-believe land of television—straight onto the set of *Doctor Who*. Behind the bead curtain was the control room of the TARDIS—from the Matt Smith years, not Capaldi, thank you very much. Countless bright buttons and levers surrounded us, and there was even the severed head of a Cyberman lying on the ground.

The TARDIS shook, the familiar sound of the TARDIS taking off through time and space echoed around us. The smell of burnt metal and old books filled the air, which to me was always the scent I mentally associated with the Doctor. I had no idea what other people thought the TARDIS smelled like, but right now, it was as if my imagination had become reality.

"What the hell?" I looked around me. I would go out on a limb and say that my surrounding was an elaborate illusion. One that was disturbingly custom-made to speak to my inner geek. Yet no amount of rationalization could get my five senses, which were screaming at me that everything was real, to shut up.

Fir took it all in, awestruck. And who could blame him? Illusions this detailed surely took hours to perfect. If Candy's little handiwork was flawless, then this Mel guy was a god amongst magicians.

And for a trickster, illusion was the bread and butter of the trade.

"Like it?" A man in the image of Peter Capaldi materialized in front of us. Sigh. I would have preferred a Matt Smith illusion. I was obviously being toyed with.

"I'm Mel. I had foreseen that you would doubt my gift, Miss Megan, and I understand that you're quite into human pop culture. I hope you're pleased with what I have put together on your behalf."

I gritted my teeth. "You're good. I'll give you that."

He was either a really good wizard or a really good visionary. Either way, he might be able to help with my present dilemma.

"Are you a mind reader as well?" I narrowed my eyes on the image Mel projected of himself. "Did you pull my dislike of Capaldi from my head?"

"That one is too easy, dear. I don't have to be a mind

reader or a seer to bet Capaldi wouldn't be a lot of people's favorite."

He had a point there.

Mel must enjoy tormenting me, because he kept his Capaldi appearance as he took Serafina's hands into his. "Lady Serafina."

Serafina shook her head. "No one has called me that since I left Dualsing."

"That is true, and the title didn't help you get an ounce of respect even when it was used, did it?" Mel chuckled. "But regardless, once a lady, always a lady."

I coughed, drawing Mel's attention back on me. Though his touch on Serafina seemed more respectful than leering, I still felt better when he let go of her hand. She'd gone through enough as it was.

"Now, about Eldon—" I began.

"Prince Eldon," Mel corrected.

"Fine. About that. You *knew*." I stated that as a fact, with no room for denial. "You must have known from the moment he landed on the human plane."

"Actually, I knew a little earlier than that, dear. The poor prince would have been laying in that alleyway for quite a long time if he had to wait for me to tell Pete, Pete to tell you, you to tell your friend, and you girls to get to him, don't you think?"

"How did you do it?" I asked curiously.

"I have a gift predicting disturbances in the Cosmic Balance. Not the big waves, mind you, just minor ones. When this knowledge is used in an intelligent manner, it leads to satisfactory results."

"You mean when partnered with someone like Gregory, it leads to satisfactory profits." I remembered what Gregory stood to gain with the class action vengeance and wondered what Mel's cut was.

"Indeed. But you're not here just to criticize my way of life, are you?"

Gregory bowed to Mel with a respect I'd never seen him display, even toward his own clients. He pointed at me. "Mel, I'm honor-bound to help this vengeance demon because I have misled her in the initial process of the class action. We're at a standstill until I repay my debt to her."

Mel's gaze didn't waver. If I expected to see annoyance at being asked to do extra work for free, it wasn't there.

"If there was a debt incurred, then the debt is ours to share, son," Mel replied with the same affection Gregory seemed to feel toward him.

"Thank you, Mel," Gregory said with deep humility.

"The truth is, I already knew you were coming." Mel turned to the rest of us. "I suppose you're here to figure a way to send Prince Eldon back, so I did a reading on the Cosmic Balance."

"And?" I prompted.

Mel looked me up and down, his eyes settling on my bosom for longer than was decent. I was about to call him on it when he answered, pointing at the same boobs he couldn't tear his eyes from, "Your magic is the answer in this dilemma, Megan. Part of the answer, anyway."

"What?" I looked down at my pearl necklace. Oh, he was looking at *that*.

"You need a way to boost the prince's tolerance for cross-dimensional travel because he's bound by the limitation of his race. Can you think of anyone who could open tough-to-open passages, and in fact, almost accidentally helped the Absolute Good and Evil escape their prison?"

Me.

Wait a minute. "How did you know about this? My grandma made sure none of that's public."

Even Gregory, who'd aided me in that fight, didn't have all

the information, because he wasn't in the room when I confronted the Absolute Good and Evil.

Mel smirked. "We mercenaries live on the fringe of society, remember? We have our ways."

"Just how am I supposed to boost Eldon's tolerance?" I asked. A part of me was glad I could be of help in the matter, the other part was a bit nervous about playing such a key role in it.

"You'll know when the time comes."

"How?" I persisted, feeling a little ill about going in completely blind.

"I assure you, you can do it," Mel said, declining to explain further. "The greater challenge will be opening the portal to begin with. It's not an easy task, and it's different than when you did it for the Absolutes. They *wanted* to leave their prison. They *wanted* to be found. The changelings don't. And they have done their damnedest since the beginning of time to avoid just that."

"Then how do we do it? You mentioned I was part of the answer. What's the rest of it?"

Mel pointed at Serafina. "Her. My glimpse of the future shows that Lady Serafina holds the other key to this dilemma."

Serafina frowned. "But I'm incapable of going back. I haven't the means to do so. When I was in Dualsing before they returned me home, they had me wear a pendant called the Eye of Sebille. It encouraged the symbiotic bond between me and Eldon's sister."

"We heard whispers of such jewels. So they are indeed real." Mel smiled.

"There's one made for every kidnapped child trapped in Dualsing," Serafina confirmed. "Though I suspect the one I wore was extra fancy, given the status of Eldon's sister."

"And it served as a bridge for your exchange, yes?"

Serafina nodded. "The bond between us grew stronger until the day we traded places. But once I returned to the vengeance plane, the Eye detached itself from my neck and latched onto my counterpart's body. It disappeared with her when she went back to Dualsing. Since then, my connection with her and Dualsing is gone. I can't go back."

A gleam of triumph flared in Mel's eyes. "Ah, but can you not think of anyone else who might still have that kind of a connection?"

"The only people tethered to Dualsing would be the changeling children living in our world right this moment." Serafina's eyes widened. "Alpha and Beta!"

"What are you talking about?" I asked.

Serafina turned to me excitedly. "When I was at Dualsing, it was my job to keep track of the whereabouts of the changeling children. Of course, I didn't know what the job was really about at the time, or who they were. But there were two changelings on the same plane as Eldon's sister. They were given the code name Alpha and Beta."

"You're telling me that there are two changelings running around the vengeance plane right now, masquerading as one of us?" I asked.

"At least as of a little over a year and a half ago, yes," Serafina replied. "And if the authorities ever find out, these changelings will never be free again."

Or worse. I didn't voice my thought out loud. If the Council knew about the changeling kids, the loss of freedom might be the least of their worries. The Sui-Ling type would want to see what made them so hard to detect, and that knowledge could only come from torture and experimentation. I would like to think that our society was civilized enough for that *not* to happen, but this was the first time in vengeance history that they had a chance to see what made a changeling tick, so anything was possible.

"Maybe I never thought about them until now because deep down I didn't want to," she murmured. "A part of me hates myself for not connecting the dots sooner, and the other part wishes I never did."

"Don't be so hard on yourself." I put my hand on her arm. "Who knows how the whole bonding and exchange ritual works? Maybe if the kids are discovered, the Dualsingians are just going to abandon them or something. You know how they say you're not supposed to touch baby birds, or else their mothers won't care for them anymore? Maybe it's like that."

"I thought that bird thing was just an old wives' tale?" Gregory began.

"You never know, there is always some truth in myths." I glared at Gregory. Didn't he realize I was trying to cheer Serafina up? "Anyway, if you knew and told the Council, everything would be screwed up and the vengeance kids would've been stranded on Dualsing for good."

"I suppose you're right, Megan." Serafina straightened her shoulders. "Mel, how can Alpha and Beta help get Eldon home?"

"If you can locate these kids, Eldon can piggyback ride on their bonds with Dualsing. One kid's bond might be strong enough, but two in combination is even better," Mel replied.

"Do you remember where they are?" I asked Serafina excitedly.

"I-I think so." Serafina took a deep breath. She waved her hands, conjuring a map against the ceiling of the TARDIS. This one was as clear as the one she had created when we had first tried to find Eldon, with no entanglement like the last one. It was a world map depicting the vengeance plane.

Serafina magnified North America, and further enlarged the southwest side of Lake Michigan.

"That city." Serafina pointed at Chicago. "This is where

the changeling kids were placed on the vengeance plane. Hopefully they're still there."

Fir slapped his thigh. "Of course!"

We all looked at him. He explained, "Vengeance Chicago has one of the highest population of tricksters on the entire vengeance plane. There's something there that makes us thrive. Maybe the wind or something. I assume whatever enhances our magic there is probably doing the same for our changeling brothers and sisters, helping to mask them from the vengeance authorities."

Serafina highlighted a point at downtown Chicago. "That was where Eldon's sister was. She was on the rooftop of a skyscraper at the time."

"These"—she made another two dots—"are the spots where Alpha and Beta were relative to her position."

She transposed onto the existing map something that looked like Google Streetview. "If I remember correctly, Alpha was walking downtown, between these two buildings, and Beta was in a two-story house in the suburb."

Even having witnessed a previous demonstration of her skills, I was still impressed by what Serafina could do. For the first time in what felt like forever, I was optimistic. We had two—count it, two—leads, with firm locations we could chase down and send Eldon on his way using the abilities that Mel was confident I had. I grinned at Serafina, then quickly dropped it when I saw how miserable she looked. Damn, I kept forgetting that while for me, the departure of Eldon would mean getting rid of all the things that could go wrong in my world: the Council leading the planes into war, the Greys gaining the upper hand, and the chaos in the meting out of vengeance; but to Serafina, it meant saying goodbye for the second time to someone she obviously cared about.

I didn't miss how Gregory used his cell phone to snap pictures of the map on the ceiling before Serafina shut it down. That would be Gregory, making sure he wasn't left out of the next phase of the plan, looking out for angles he could exploit later.

I glared at him only to find him with a deep frown on his face as he looked at the screenshots on his cell. Weird.

Fir was practically dancing on his feet. "I can't wait to meet these long-lost trickster cousins. Wait until I tell everyone!"

Under my frosty look, he added, "After. *Way* after. Maybe never."

"It better *be* never," I grunted.

"So which one should we go after first?" Fir asked.

"Alpha," Serafina and Gregory said at the same time. As if regretting his words, Gregory's mouth thinned and he said no more.

"Visiting Alpha first makes sense," Serafina explained. "From the record, it looks like he might be the younger of the two."

"The older and the closer they are to being exchanged, the more of their changeling personalities emerge," Fir reasoned.

"And the more...difficult it might be to convince them to help us," Gregory added.

"Alright, Alpha it is." I clapped my hands together, then I asked Serafina as something just occurred to me, "You referred to Alpha as a 'he,' is that so?"

"I'm not entirely sure." Serafina frowned. "That word just comes to mind when I think of Alpha."

"Maybe your instinct knows something you don't. Let's go find out." I turned toward the door, then stopped and glanced back at Mel. I couldn't bring myself to thank him, not when he was in this with Gregory to turn a profit, and was only helpful because they wanted to move forward in obtaining it.

So I opted for a convoluted form of compliment instead. "So, you got any last words, advice, or wisdom to impart?"

Mel gestured toward Serafina. "Yes. Catch her."

"Huh?"

I had barely started moving when Serafina collapsed onto the floor.

❦ 13 ❦

IN SERAFINA'S SHOES: LOSS

So IT WAS DECIDED. We would first try to find Alpha based on the information I'd given the group.

I should feel excited at the prospect of making progress, but all I could feel was dread. Dread of being too late in reaching Eldon. Dread at sending him back to Dualsing in what would likely be a suicide mission.

Or maybe I was focusing on what might happen in the future, because I couldn't bear to imagine what might be happening to him right at this moment.

I wanted to scream in frustration, but all I could do was follow the group out of the sci-fi-inspired room in a brisk and orderly fashion.

Until Mel pointed at me and told Megan to catch me.

Before I could ask him to clarify his instruction, my eyes rolled to the back of my head and I plunged into a world of ice and darkness.

Cold, so cold.

I was lying on a metal surface, with straps cutting into my arms, legs, and torso, tying me down. I knew the surface was metal because there weren't any clothes to insulate my back from it. I was naked save for a sheet covering my middle.

With these blasted binds, I might as well still be impaired. My legs are just as useless now as before.

I hope Finny is alright.

Those weren't my thoughts. They were Eldon's, as evidenced by the mention of that leg, and the fact that he was the only one who had ever called me Finny.

It wasn't me who was thinking those thoughts, and it wasn't me who was half-naked on a cold metal slab somewhere dark and unknown. Amazed and terrified at the same time, I realized I was somehow experiencing what Eldon was feeling, and hearing what he was thinking.

The bond of love that we'd once shared, which had allowed me to hone onto his location in that wretched human alley but was somehow severed upon his kidnapping, had resurfaced. It allowed me to leave my body behind and seek out Eldon through some kind of involuntary astral projection, much like how I once did with his sister.

Someone turned on a single fluorescent tube, the harsh light lit up the strange room that resembled a cross between a morgue and a ritualistic shrine.

Now that I was aware I wasn't actually on a metal slab, my perception shifted. I could no longer feel the coldness of metal behind my back. Instead, I took on the perspective of the body-less spirit that I was, floating a couple feet above Eldon's body.

I looked at him. If I had had a body to gasp in horror with, I would have.

Though Eldon's body lacked any physical wounds, there was no doubt in my mind that he'd been tortured. It was there in the grayness of his skin, the dark circles around his bloodshot eyes.

I forced my gaze to leave him and examine the room in

greater detail, hoping for some clues that could help identify his location. There were the things one might expect from a human hospital, such as the metal slab and the high-tech instruments, but the floor was painted with ancient symbols, and in the corner there was a table with two-dozen spent candles.

I looked back at Eldon. There was a mix of fear and defiance on his face as he looked up at the person who'd just turned on the light and entered the room.

The false Sui-Ling.

For reasons unknown, the Greys' agent had decided to maintain that disguise. The smooth dragonhide she stole hugged every inch of her body.

False Sui-Ling grinned at Eldon as she leaned over him. "So, is your highness ready to talk?"

Eldon remained silent.

"So far the only thing we've established is that you're royalty, and I didn't get that using *this*." False Sui-Ling pulled out a wand and looked at it with a bemused expression. The wand was made of oak, and hand carved with an asymmetric yet utterly sharp end. It was well polished; one would expect no less refinement from a society of the Greys' caliber. "Your mannerism betrays your breeding, and breeding is the one thing I recognize and could relate to. You sure you won't tell me anything useful before we begin again? I hate hurting someone of a respectable bloodline, changeling or not. We'll send you home right away if you're willing to tell us where to find it, I promise."

"No," Eldon spat, his lips pulled back from his teeth in a snarl.

"Very well." False Sui-Ling shrugged and traced the wand over Eldon's formerly impaired right leg. Then she moved it toward his upper body.

The wand touched his chest and nothing happened. I was

just about to breathe a sigh of relief when Eldon screamed in pain, his right leg shaking in spasms, almost yanking free of the restraint. False Sui-Ling then moved the wand onto his abdomen; just like before at first nothing happened, then Eldon's right leg seemed to be assaulted by invisible forces. The pain I saw on his face, compared to his usual stoic bearing, was absolute.

I couldn't run to him. I couldn't help him because I didn't have the physical form to do so. All I could do was stand there and see him suffer. The sense of helplessness was driving me insane.

Since my return home, many had been skeptical about my capability to become a true vengeance demon. I was too gentle, they criticized. But now, in the face of Eldon's agony, I longed for the body I'd left behind at Mel's place. I had no doubt my wings would have no problem bursting out of my back, my pearl earrings charged to a glowing brilliance, ready to aid me in wreaking destruction on Eldon's tormentor.

But all I could do was resist the urge to panic, and focus on something I could be useful for.

Like figuring out how the mysterious torturing worked.

Why was it that his right leg seemed to be in such great pain, when the wand only touched it at the very beginning, and was nowhere near it as the agony hit? Why was it that touching every other part of his body brought on pain for his recently healed leg?

By the time False Sui-Ling traced the wand over Eldon's right leg again, I understood.

Megan once showed me a human toy called the Wooly Willy. It was a cardboard depicting a cartoon face. Sealed in hard plastic with iron filings, you used a magnetic pen to direct the filings to where you wanted them to deposit on the cartoon face, adding "hair," "beard," and "eyebrows" onto it. False Sui-Ling was using the same principle, drawing out the vengeance magic that was used to heal Eldon's leg, and depositing it onto other parts of his changeling body.

The rest of his body raised arms against the foreign magic they perceived as a threat, and started attacking his own leg much like a host body rejecting a transplanted organ. In essence, False Sui-Ling was torturing Eldon using his own body.

It would be clever if it weren't hurting the boy I'd cared about most of my life.

"Finny, what are you doing here? Leave now! I don't want you to see this." Eldon's voice brushed over me. I blinked and looked around, realizing that there were now two Eldons—one lying on the metal slab, covered in sweat and seemingly dead from torture, the other standing right next to me in an immaculate royal outfit, as substance-less as I was.

False Sui-Ling frantically tried to find a pulse on the Eldon on the metal slab, angry that her prisoner might have eluded her through death.

I swallowed and asked Eldon, "Are you...dead?"

"No, I'm not. I'm just getting a reprieve using a spell called Playing Dead, something we learned from our trickster cousins a long time ago. Once I was out of my body, I found you here. I don't have a lot of time before I get pulled back down there, Finny. You have to leave, now."

Even in pure spirit form, I could tell that Eldon had been through a lot of pain. "Not until I can find some clue as to where you are."

I looked around. It was just a room with white walls and no windows. It wasn't revealing a lot of details to his whereabouts. He could be anywhere. On any plane.

"Just go, Finny," Eldon begged. "There's nothing here you can learn. Just go so I know you're far away from this. I can bear anything if I know you don't have to watch it."

Seeing the anguish and concern in his eyes, I realized something.

"You cut off our connection after your capture, didn't you?" It was the only explanation that made sense.

His expression was unapologetic. "Yes. And now you broke through my block. Don't do it again. Now *go*."

I squeezed my eyes shut and bit back a sob.

How many times was I supposed to lose him? I lost him to strategies and planning when he learned of my inevitable departure from Dualsing, though unbeknown to me at the time, he was secretly plotting to keep me there. I lost him to greed and ambition when I refused to take part in the conspiracy, knowing I was only one of the two reasons he wanted the crown. Now, right this moment, I was losing him to pain and torture. And I would lose him yet again, for good this time, when my friends and I managed to send him home.

I opened my eyes to a sea of faces above me. Megan, Fir, Mel, Gregory, and even Candy. They stood over me, talking among themselves.

"My ma is the one good with the healing spells. I tried everything I could think of," Candy was saying to everyone. "She's not waking."

Megan's eyes jumped to mine and widened. "She's awake!" She crouched on the floor next to me. "You okay?" she asked with concern.

I lifted a hand to my cheek. It was wet with tears. "I'm not sure I'll ever be."

✣ 14 ✣

ONCE WAS AT HOGWARTS

"So Fake Sui-Ling never showed her true face." I paced back and forth after Serafina told us about her experience.

"Or *his* true face," Fir pointed out. "It could be anyone under that disguise."

"Maybe it's someone we know." Gregory really knew how to brighten my day. "Maybe there's a way to ferret him or her out."

"Nah. Too many candidates." I shook my head. "The Greys are a group of arrogant, bigoted vengeance demons who hate anyone they consider not pure enough to walk the planes, right? I can list at least twenty families who didn't want to invite me to their children's birthday parties because I had trickster blood in me, and that's just the first grade. If I had received a penny for every vengeance demon who'd ever given me a dirty look or a cold shoulder, I would have been super rich by the time I had finished elementary school."

A look of understanding came over Gregory's face. We might not have a lot in common, but I bet my experience growing up as a hybrid was similar to his as a bastard.

"If we can't even be sure if there's a traitor already planted in our lives, what are we going to do?" Fir asked.

"We continue on," Serafina said quietly. Now that her tears were dried her eyes shone with determination.

"She's right," I said. "We move forward."

———

With Serafina's map, we knew the exact intersection of the windy city where Alpha's presence had last been recorded.

Fir pulled some strings with a few relatives in the city I had never even met before, and off we went to Chicago, our teleporting completely off the books. We couldn't afford the Council finding out about these changeling kids. Thank Hades they were always underestimating the resourcefulness of tricksters. Arrogance was definitely their weakness.

Our destination was the Loop, Chicago's central business district. It was home to City Hall, and an abundance of theatre houses and high-end hotels. Fir, having been to the city a few times before to visit our relatives and attend the annual Tricksters Unite Convention, became our de facto guide. We teleported to an empty private parking area behind a sushi place, and from there he took us to the intersection of North Canal Street and West Madison Street.

There was nothing here except row after row of office buildings. Plenty of banks, venture capital firms, and insurance companies, but none of those were places someone under eighteen would hang out. There wasn't even a single school in the next five blocks.

Even vengeance society had need of a financial district. The difference from the human one was, of course, the vengeance aspect: the banks had special safety deposit boxes for highly dangerous, licensed-by-the-ounce fairy dust, the venture capital firms invested in vengeance-tracking apps, and the insurance companies offered policies for risk of legal dispute over the first right of vengeance.

The fur would be flying at the latter if this war on changelings actually happened.

I squinted at the setting sun, just peeking between the clouds and the tall buildings. I couldn't believe that nightfall would soon be upon us. Was it really less than forty-eight hours ago that I was happily punishing some mean old lady at a hospice? Those were the simple days.

"Now what are we going to do?" Gregory asked the question that was probably on everyone's mind.

Before coming here, having the exact location that Alpha had been seemed like a solid, and even easy, lead. But now, looking at this busy intersection lined with soaring skyscrapers and more people in suits than the national average, doubts started to creep in. Sure, Fir and Serafina claimed that they'd know when they saw Alpha, but there was a sea of people here, and we didn't have a physical description of the teen. And just because he passed by here over a year ago, there was no guarantee he would again any time soon.

I squared my shoulders. Time wasn't our friend here; we had to keep going. "We know two things about him: his most-likely gender, and the fact that he's probably in his late teens, being this close to returning to the changelings. I suggest that we divide into teams, and do some scouting. I can go with Fir and take the left side of the street, Gregory and Serafina can take the right. Shouldn't be hard to spot a teenager in Suits Central."

If he's here to begin with, a cynical voice in me whispered. I ignored it.

All along the street level were chic delis catering to the business crowd. As Fir and I walked down the block, we passed at least three or four of them, filled with local office workers.

Suddenly I saw a group of teens with backpacks coming out of one in the next block, frozen yogurt cones in hand. They looked so out of place in the land of the suits, which was just what I had hoped to find.

I ran straight to them, dragging Fir with me. With his potbelly, my half-brother wasn't exactly fond of the excursion, but I didn't want to lose sight of the teens.

I startled them with my approach, making one teen almost drop his treat. They were dressed in torn jeans and stained sports jackets, different from the neat and conservatively dressed miniature adults I went to high school with, but there was no doubt that the teens were vengeance demons.

I turned to Fir and raised my eyebrow, but he shook his head, indicating that none of the teens in our presence was Alpha.

But who was to say they didn't know where Alpha might be?

"Hey, guys, where are you from?" I asked. "I didn't know there was a school around here."

Urgency might have made my voice harsher than I'd intended. And the teens, who were probably still in their rebellious phase, didn't react well to it.

"Why should we tell you anything? Who the heck are you?" one of them, the ringleader by the look of him, demanded. Despite the bravado, his eyes darted nervously. In fact, the entire group looked uncomfortable but defiant, as if they were caught doing something they shouldn't.

Judging from the backpacks, the yogurt treats in hand, and the day of the week it was—Tuesday, a traditional extended school day for vengeance high school, I was willing to bet that these guys were in the middle of skipping classes.

Great. Young, defensive, and pack mentality, not a good combination.

"Hey, man, it's not *who* they are, it's *what* they are." The ringleader's Number Two sniffed the air and everyone else did the same. I saw the moment they smelled the trickster in me and Fir. Their demeanor changed from worried to disdainful.

"Oh, I know where these two are from." The ringleader smirked. "The welfare office."

They all laughed. Shabbily dressed or not, the teens had the same arrogance as any other vengeance demons.

"Ahem." Fir coughed, muttered for my ears only, "See how it's done, girl."

Fir wrapped himself in a new trickster spell he had recently invented called Your Worst Nightmare. It caused its victim to see whatever they least wanted to see. The group of teens paled, then all talked at the same time, fighting to be heard.

"Good afternoon, Mr. Doctus," the ringleader said in an overly-bright tone to Fir.

"We have a spare class. We're not skipping, I swear." Number Two was quick to cave.

"Please don't tell my mom," another teen begged.

"I'm going to overlook this," Fir said sternly, "if you get the hell out of my face and head straight back to school."

The teens didn't need any more encouragement. To their hastily retreating backs, Fir added, "And go to the nurse station and tell them to vaccinate you for the pixie flu with the fattest needle they got."

Gregory and Serafina had caught up with us just then. Fir gestured. "Come on, let's follow them. These kids might be going to the same school as Alpha. Maybe he was here because he was skipping class as well."

"We found no teen in our search." Gregory shrugged. "So we might as well."

We tailed the teens as they ventured back to class. Their path took us through alleyways, parking lots, and side streets all the way to the metro. Three stops later, free for them on Tuesday, not for us, and a few more local twists and turns, they arrived back at their school. It had been a complicated route, but all in all, the trip had taken no more than fifteen minutes.

Now I knew why this intercity school didn't show up on our radar when we looked at the intersection's surrounding area—it was outside of the five-block radius we set. But if the teens know where they're going, there was definitely enough time to go out, grab a yogurt, and get back, all within one skipped period.

Besides, at that age, doing these things wasn't about being logistically worthy. It was about being part of a social group and bonding over the danger of being caught.

I should know, since they usually bonded over not inviting me to such outings.

I stopped in front of the high school and pointed at the name of the school, which was carved on a flat block of stone over the arc of the front entrance: Sir Advocatus Public High.

I elbowed Serafina, "Now is that irony, or a sign?"

"Did you just say a sign? I thought you don't believe in fortune telling." Merriment danced in the depths of Gregory's eyes. "Feeling the effect of having met Mel?"

I shrugged. "I decided to keep an open mind."

After all, Mel did give me adequate warning about catching Serafina.

"So," Fir asked Serafina, "which one of your relatives is this Sir Advocatus referring to?"

Serafina shook her head. "I've lost track of who got what high school named after them."

"Fair enough. Whoever it is, they got the equivalent of having their portrait hung in the bar's bathroom anyway," Fir commented.

"Why do you say that?" I asked curiously.

"Look around you," Fir replied.

The high school consisted of one tiny main building and more than a dozen portable-converted classrooms, which, judging from rust leaking from their frames were originally intended as a temporary solution. There was graffiti spray-painted all over the brick of the main building and the vinyl exterior of the portables, and weeds ran rampant in the school ground.

"This is worse than any vengeance school I've ever attended," I breathed. There was an air of neglect about the place, and my heart went out to the kids who had to spend their formative years in this environment. I thought no child was supposed to be left behind in our civilized society. What the hell was this place?

"Come on," Fir said as he led us into the main building, "we need to find the administrative office."

If the outside looked bad, the inside was no better. There was paint peeling from the yellowed walls, and the floor tiles were chipped in places. Walking on them posed a dangerous risk for those of us wearing kitten heels.

As we passed by the lockers, I saw a few of their doors were dented from repeated kicking. Just like everything else, the lockers were vandalized.

Then there was the smell of cigarette smoke coming out of a half-open door of a girl's bathroom. Why in Hades were these vengeance demons' kids getting into the human habit of smoking? Our metabolism processed that chemical crap right out of our systems before the associated high of addiction could be fully enjoyed, leaving one with nothing but stinky clothes.

This was truly and fully, a slum school.

Being born into a suburban neighborhood and going to school in the same area, I had no idea such appalling conditions existed in the public education system. I mean, I watched enough human teen movies to know such places existed, but the poor state of things were generally settings to show off either an exceptionally devoted math teacher or some sort of hip hop prodigy from the hood.

Reality was stark and sucky.

The administrative assistant, who was busy filing her nails, was no more charming. Her disinterest in helping us with the student records came less from her concern about privacy and more from her inability to do her job. Nothing had been filed since, like, never.

"That was...unproductive," Gregory said dryly.

"Well, you're the mercenary." I glared at him. "Shouldn't you be like, threatening her with bodily harm or bribing her with the latest nail color or something?"

"I would if she actually had any information of use." He chuckled.

I sighed. I was hoping that if Fir or Serafina were able to physically touch the record of attending students, they would be able to identify Alpha. We would have to find another way.

"Fear not, there's hope still. There are faint traces of changeling signature all around us. Alpha has been in this school. Maybe still is. I can feel it. We're on the right track." Fir gestured for us to follow him back to the locker area and held out his hand to Serafina. She took it without hesitation. With their hands joined, they started walking by the lockers one by one.

"We're going to do this the old-fashioned way. Hopefully we can sense Alpha, or sense his stuff when it's close by, or even better, if he bumps into us in the hallway," Fir explained as he and Serafina walked farther ahead.

The school bell rang.

In an instant the hallway was filled with students heading to their next class, most of them with their winter jackets on, either hurrying out to the portables or returning from them.

Most of them did more chattering and lingering than rushing to class, but then given the extended school day, who could blame them?

The crowd surge separated Gregory and I farther from Fir and Serafina, but there was nothing to do but ride it out.

Another surge—this time triggered by a group of jocks horsing around and the people trying to avoid them—almost knocked me over. Gregory reached out and steadied me, my back brushed against the hard muscles on his chest.

When he let go of me, I felt a wave of disappointment.

"So." I coughed, mentally searching for something to talk about, feeling suddenly like Gregory and I were alone with each other rather than being surrounded by students. "I assume you've gone through the vengeance education system before?"

"Some of it," he said noncommittally. "More so than Candy had been to witchcraft school."

Great. Just because I was rattled by getting into the guy's personal space, didn't mean I wanted to give him the impression that I was trying to fish for his personal information. I couldn't care less if he'd been in school long enough to read *Vice and Vigilance*, a classic novel about five vengeance demon sisters that was a staple for literature classes.

"You probably didn't miss much." I shrugged. "They got meaner by the grade."

"I have no doubt. I did miss out on *Of Vice and Men*, though." Gregory appeared thoughtful. "Ironically, I read it *after* I left school. Just picked it up from a bargain bin one day and started reading."

It was weird how I happened to be thinking about assigned course material just now. "Wait, you read the required reading when you don't have to? What's wrong with you?"

"I have to. How else am I going to keep up my language

skills so I won't get tripped over by a technicality in a contract?" he said, deadpan.

I couldn't help but laugh, and he joined in, self-mockery danced in the depth of his eyes.

Then we both stopped laughing abruptly, as if disturbed by how unguarded we were for a second there.

We kept walking.

Weird. There was an area ahead that everyone avoided. Initially I thought it must be a bad patch of the floor, or something gross to be avoided, until the kids went on their way and I managed to get a closer look.

On the floor was a large patch of green goo. The mass was constantly reshaping itself, one moment it looked like a body of water, and then it transformed to look like a mold of hard jelly. No matter how the goo changed though, it remained within a certain parameter on the floor.

As we watched, the goo rippled back to liquid form only to have parts of it firm up and form letters on the surface. The letters, solidified in a darker color of green, read:

NEVERMORE,
P.

Then under the words, a date from seven years ago.

Even the most negligent of school janitors would have gotten around to cleaning the mess up in seven years. The fact that it was still there, after all this time, could only mean that whoever put the vengeance magic there had made sure it was good and permanent. It reminded me of the Weasley twins' final act before they left Hogwarts.

The words and the date dissipated, and in their place was something like a cartoon, a series of images forming in slow motion. It featured a symbol that, had this been the first time I was seeing it, would have made no sense.

The symbol comprised of a dragon on one side and a shield on the other. The shield was encrusted with two diamonds, and there was a sword positioned upright on top of the shield. The cartoon was a continuous loop of the dragon taking flight. As it flew off, it clutched the sword between its teeth and pulled it out of the shield, crapping a disgusting load of green gooey crap onto the shield.

Huh.

The sign off of *P*.

Gregory's half-done tattoo.

I turned to him. "You haven't just been to vengeance schools before. You've been to *this* school. That pool of goo was your way of saying 'screw you,' wasn't it?"

Gregory's upper lip pulled back in the start of a sneer, as if his instinct was to deny my claim. Then he smoothed out his facial features and he squared his shoulders.

"Yes, I was a student here," he confirmed softly. "People didn't take my bastard status kindly. I dropped out at thirteen, soon after the Becoming. The goo was my last act before leaving."

It was his way of taking what was given to him by birth and owning it, shame and all. That was the day he became Pete, the fiercely proud mercenary with the capital *P* sign off.

I glanced at the green goo again, trying to memorize the symbol of Gregory's house without looking like I was doing it. I was never very good at recognizing the different houses' coat of arms. To me they all looked the same. Each slight variation in the angle of the sword tilt, the number of stars on the shield, the size and position of them, made them different. Hopefully, with all the Vengeance 101 tutoring that Serafina received, she would be able to tell me what house Gregory's scumbag father had come from. I'd ask her later. Much later. After we had dealt with the current crisis.

The green goo had once again returned to its liquid form with the word *Nevermore* in its center. Gregory pointed at the letters, his tone matter-of-fact. "You got the nod to Edgar Allan Poe, right?"

"Of course." The vengeance English class threw in a human poem here and there. "But I admit I always liked the *Simpsons* version better."

An awkward silence fell on us as the true meaning of his initial lack of disclosure to me sank in.

I thought of how he didn't say anything about being a student here, even when we walked straight into the administrative office, and even when we were talking about being in school just now. Maybe he figured the staff might have changed guard in seven years. Maybe he was hoping we wouldn't come upon the gooey section of the school.

His gamble had almost paid off, as the administrative assistant showed no sign of recognizing him.

That was, if I hadn't made the connection with him and the goo.

I knew how tough high school could be. Yet even with my challenges, I had a warm immediate family to go home to at night. I had no idea what Gregory's mom was like, but his dad obviously hadn't cared enough to offer the mother and child financial support nor the protection of his name.

Despite Gregory's clinical description of his former bullied life, that kind of childhood had to leave a scar. Just what did it take to drive someone out of school and make him turn his back on any chance of ever becoming a respectable member of his race? Just how desperate did the situation have to be, that joining the shady profession of mercenary seemed like a better alternative?

Gregory looked at me, his eyes full of silent challenge. He

must hate being forced to open up about that vulnerable period of his life. His jaw hardened, as if he was waiting for me to mock him, or worse, insult him with my pity.

And no matter how ticked off I was at him for dragging me into the whole changeling mess, I couldn't do it.

Instead, I gave him what both of us needed at this moment, which was so not holding hands and bonding over having shitty high school years. I gave him something he could work with—my anger. "You asshole. You didn't bother to tell us about this place when we first mapped the intersection. Are you trying to get Eldon killed? You realize that if he dies, nobody is getting anything, right?"

Gregory blinked, looking surprised yet grateful for the direction I was taking our conversation. "Well, I didn't think of it at first. It was a long time ago and the frozen yogurt trips never even crossed my mind. Only losers went out for frozen yogurts."

"What did *you* do then, while they were gone?" I asked.

Gregory grinned. "I went up to the roof and drank Blue Unicorns with their girlfriends, of course."

There it was. That flirtatious side he used as a shield; when we both knew full well that just like me, he had never made the type of friends that he could skip class with.

I smirked. "You needed to get high on Blue Unicorns to impress a bunch of losers' girlfriends?"

"No, I was impressive enough so that they were the ones who offered to go up to the roof with me. And they were the ones who *supplied* the Blue Unicorns."

I tried to imagine all the cool kids' girlfriends going after Gregory behind their backs. I wondered what the teenage version of Mr. Dark-and-Handsome would've looked like. He would still be a boy like the rest of them, his shoulders and chest not as well-developed as now, but I imagined that his handsome face, his defiant spirit, and the lure of the forbidden would have been enough to make the average teenage girl swoon.

Hey, Megan, my inner voice said, *just because we decided to be nice out of decency, can we not get carried away here? He's still the enemy, albeit a co-operating one for now. Can you, like, stop drooling over him for five seconds and get on with the mission? You know, that one where you're trying to prevent an all-out war?*

What do you think I'm trying to do here? I asked my inner voice.

I dunno. First you met his "family," now you're at his old high school. If I didn't know better I'd say you're going steady.

Shut. Up.

"Hey, I think we found something," Fir called out from the locker area. With one last look at the puddle of green goo, I walked over to where Fir and Serafina were. Gregory followed.

The students had mostly settled into their next class by now, and whoever was still loitering in the hallway couldn't see us. Fir had put up a protection shield around us, making this section of the hallway appear deserted. It was a good thing, too, because he was pawing over stuff from a locker, one which I had no doubt he'd forced open.

"What is it?" I asked. "Is that Alpha's locker?"

Fir held out a chemistry textbook. "Put your hand on this."

I did as he requested. Nothing.

Then after a while, *something*. It wasn't anything based on logic, just an impression of fresh-baked bread and clean laundry, all the comforts of home.

And family.

Yes, that was it. Something about the textbook reminded me of the rightness of a loving family, a sense of conviction that the owner of the book was kin, yet the energy signature wasn't of anyone from my immediate family.

Fir took the textbook from my hand, put it back into the locker, then held up a magnetic photo frame with a picture of three teens in football gear. He pointed at the middle one. "That's our changeling."

Serafina nodded. "I agree. He's Alpha."

"His last name is Agricola. Thomas Jadrien Agricola." Fir flipped through what looked like a binder for math.

Agricola in old Latin meant *farmer*. It was a typical working class vengeance family name. Just like humans, vengeance demons had developed their surnames by using their professions as identifiers. It was another instance when the planes mirrored each other. Mr. Doctus, the teacher whom Fir was pretending to be in order to rein in the teens on the street, for instance, had a last name that meant *to teach*.

Given the type of school Alpha, or Thomas, was going to, it was no big shock that he wasn't with an influential family. The question was, why? I thought the whole point of the switch was to steal secrets from the rich and powerful.

Armed with an actual full name, we went back to the administrative office. Fortunately, the administrative assistant was nowhere to be seen, and we were free to snoop around. Unfortunately, trying to locate one single student record in a sea of unfiled ones was like finding a needle in a haystack.

Until I saw a note lying on the ancient fax machine among the spams, indicating that Alpha had called in sick this morning. Just who the heck used a fax machine to report absences anymore? Didn't anybody at this school hear about emails, texts, or online forms? I made a mental note to have a chat with Grandma about pouring resources into this school. It needed a much better staff and better equipment.

Fir snapped a picture of the note while I ran a simple Internet search of the home address from the fax number. We were now ready to visit Alpha.

❧ 15 ❧

PENCIL PUSHERS

ALPHA'S HOST family lived in one of those condos that people who couldn't afford to buy multi-million dollar houses, but still wanted to be in the city, crammed into. The tiny units themselves weren't that badly maintained, though the rent dollars definitely could've gone further in more suburban areas. Apparently the rich families who lived in houses in the same area sent their kids to private schools, so updating and maintaining the public school was never a priority.

All this, we learned from Fir as we made our way to Alpha's home.

"I don't get it," I said as the elevator closed with a *ding*. "Why isn't Alpha placed with a richer and more prestigious family, if the changelings want the best bang for their buck?"

"My guess is that hosts aren't always chosen based on money or power, but whether or not they're strategically important in the long game that the changelings play." Serafina thought for a moment. "My own case is actually the exception, not the norm. It's not every day that a changeling princess gets switched, and it's not every day someone with my family background happened to be born around the same time. Mine was what was considered a switch of equals, between matching, er..."

"Royalties?" I offered.

Serafina flushed. She was never a big fan of her so-called privileged life. I didn't blame her. Since birth, her social status had brought her nothing but pain. "We no longer have royalties, Megan."

"Yeah, but your family practically is. Mine, too, if they actually considered me one of them." I laughed self-deprecatingly. There was a time when it would have really bothered me; now it was just a fact of life. I had enough love in my life to not let it get to me much.

"Anyway," Serafina continued, "from my understanding a switch like mine and Eldon's sister is quite rare. In Dualsing, most of those sent out are children from the middle-class, and they don't always get matched with the wealthiest families. It's all a matter of luck and timing."

"They're earning their way up the changeling society by switching," Gregory commented. Count on him to be able to see the upward mobility angle.

Serafina nodded. "It would seem so."

The elevator door opened and we filed out. I threw up a privacy shield around us at the waiting area to finish the conversation, keeping my eyes in the direction of the hallway where Alpha's unit was.

"So what do we know about Alpha's host parents? Why were they targeted?" I looked at Gregory, who had made a few calls on our way here. I assumed he was hitting his contacts to find out all he could about the environment in which Alpha grew up. If we were to turn the teen to our side, we had to know who he was, and what knowledge he was supposed to unknowingly steal from his host family.

"Pamela Dorothy Agricola and Harold Zachariah Agricola," Gregory recited. "Both working as entry level clerks for the Department of Service Administration; their main job responsibilities seem to be the filling out and filing of various federal forms."

"Bureaucratic pencil pushers." I knew I liked to talk about the vengeance demons in the field as if they were the only kind in existence. But the truth was, the field agents were whom I *aspired* to be, what my co-op hours would hopefully train me for. Not everyone got to be James Bond. Somebody always ended up doing the paperwork nobody else wanted to do. "What's the point of placing a kid with *them*? What value could they possibly be to the changelings?"

"Don't underestimate those working behind the scenes, Megan. They're the ones with the *real* magic," Gregory cautioned. I wondered if he wasn't just talking about the government worker ants. "The little guys are the ones who see everything from tax returns, expense reports, to the logbook of the Council members' bodyguards. They know who eats at what restaurants, who has money for extra pension contributions, and who placed their kids into gymnastics class and where. Some of my most valuable intel comes from these 'pencil pushers,' as you'd call them."

He had a point.

It wasn't until now that I realized my ambitions of being certified as a front line worker had always colored my perception of those on the supporting side. Not on a conscious level, but by pursuing the licensed career with an utter single-mindedness, as if it was the end all and be all, I was in a way belittling every other job there was out there.

A sobering thought.

"Okay. Let's pay them a visit. Hopefully Alpha is up for a talk, being sick from school and all." I headed toward unit number 806 to the left of the hallway. "Fir and Gregory, why don't you two wait outside? All four of us showing up at the door may be a bit much. People tend to open their doors to girls more often than boys."

Fir and Gregory looked at each other. They both weaved a quick invisible spell around themselves, practically in sync.

I rolled my eyes. Looked like nobody wanted to miss the fun.

I fished a tampon tube out of my bag. Long ago I'd learned to take the cotton out of unused tampons and use the tubes to hide stuff from my nosy half-brothers. A safe bet they wouldn't be too curious about *that*. Yes, female vengeance demons got PMS, too, but the pain was better controlled with magic, and the bitchiness was channeled into good old productive vengeance.

I shook the tube, sprinkling de-aging fairy dust all over my face and body. I bought it on sale and I had just enough of it for Serafina and me. I passed the tube to Serafina and she put the rest on herself. From the mirrors in the hallway, I could see that we looked just like the eleventh-grade versions of ourselves.

Alpha was in that grade, according to his chemistry textbook. I conjured two backpacks and gave one for Serafina to carry.

I knocked on the door of 806.

Nothing.

Suddenly, I was aware of noise coming from the apartment.

I knocked again. Someone was running in the apartment; a man yelling and then what sounded like a woman, begging him to calm down.

Then I could see the light from the peephole disappeared, suggesting that someone was looking at me and Serafina on the other side. I tried to look as innocent as possible.

The door opened.

A woman in her forties with swollen eyes and untamed hair looked at us tentatively. "May I help you girls?"

"Hi, ma'am. We are Thomas Jadrien Agricola's classmates," I said in a squeaky, teenage voice. "We heard that he's sick so we wanted to come and see how he is. We brought him some class notes." I gave her my most I'm-so-harmless smile.

The woman's fingers tightened around the doorframe. Her lower chin was shaking. She looked at a spot behind her, possibly at the man who was yelling earlier. Then she seemed to steel herself. "I-I'm afraid Thomas isn't available right now. Maybe, um, you can come back tomorrow?"

"Don't tell them to come back tomorrow, Pam." I could hear the man as he hissed. "Just tell them to go away. This is a family matter. We'll handle it."

He kicked something in the foyer in apparent frustration, and a shoe tumbled behind Pamela. He must have kicked the front hall shoe rack.

"I'm sorry, girls. This just isn't a good time." Pamela sighed, starting to close the door.

I planted my foot between the door and the doorframe. "Oh, I don't think so. We're coming in."

I pushed the door open and walked through the threshold as I shook off the de-aging fairy dust. Serafina did the same while Fir and Gregory made themselves visible again. Pamela backed against the shoe rack, her face pale as a sheet of paper. Then she tripped over a shoe and fell onto the floor.

I helped her up. "Ma'am, you alright? I apologize for the entrance, but we really must speak with Thomas."

She started crying.

"Go away! Leave my wife alone." The man whose voice I'd heard earlier came into full view, his face twisted with fear and anger. He was wearing his pajamas, and he had a full day

LOUISA LO

of beard growth. Looked like he might've called in sick for the day himself. "We don't want you here!"

"Harold, let the authorities help. They're going to find out sooner or later," Pamela pleaded with her husband. Then she turned to us. "I'm so sorry. My husband is never like this. He's under terrible shock. We all are."

"The authorities?" Fir and I echoed. My half-brother had the most amused expression on his face. I doubt he'd ever been mistaken for the law before.

"Help? How are they supposed to *help*? There's no fixing this," Harold spat, then to us, "Just go away!"

The civil servant must have been drinking, I realized as he staggered toward us with bloodshot eyes, his movement menacing had he not had a potbelly and a pair of weakly erected vengeance wings.

Fearing our combined effort would hurt him, we all held back thinking that someone else would prevent the wobbly, disheveled vengeance demon from crashing into us. Then when it was apparent nobody was doing anything about it, and the collision seemed imminent, we ended up each sending out a blast of energy at the same time.

Harold flung from the foyer and crashed into a loveseat in the living room. Pamela screamed and ran to her husband, checking him over for injuries. He seemed knocked out but otherwise fine. The woman looked up to us with fear in her eyes. She took in the multiple pairs of vengeance wings now filling up the foyer, and swallowed.

"Are you here to arrest us?" she asked.

"What?" Gregory, Fir, Serafina, and I looked at each other in confusion.

"You're from the Council, right? I can sense your strong magic."

"Ma'am"—Fir stepped forward—"do I look like someone the Council would send?"

Pamela's nostrils flared and immediately her shoulders dropped. The realization that we were not the authorities seemed to have calmed her down. "No. Maybe not you. You're not even a vengeance demon. Again, my apology to all of you. My husband is not his usual self. He's never been like this in all these years we've been married, I swear. We've just been about scared out of our minds, that's all. They're not going to understand at work, and...and..."

Pamela sniffled and struggled to catch her breath.

"Slow down." I tried to project tranquility into my voice. "Tell us what happened."

Despite my words Pamela was getting herself worked up all over again. Her breathing became so shallow, I was afraid it was the start of an asthma attack.

Serafina, who came from a long line of healers, put her hands over Pamela's and started to synchronize her own breath with the older woman's. Then she slowed it down and somehow got Pamela to follow her lead. Eventually the latter was calm enough to speak again.

"They're going to wonder how we didn't see it." Pamela's voice was full of sorrow. "And if we're this unobservant, then maybe we don't deserve to work with sensitive information anymore. We're going to get fired from our jobs, aren't we? And forget about work, how am I going to face my own parents ever again? How could I tell them about Thomas? I ought to have known. What kind of mother am I?"

"You found out Thomas is a changeling, didn't you?" Gregory asked quietly.

Pamela started shaking. "Who are you? All of you? How do you know these things? We've told nobody."

"We're here to help. My friend here"—Gregory pointed at Serafina—"is a leading changeling expert."

I raised my eyebrows but didn't contradict Gregory. I supposed being held captive at Dualsing most of her life would make Serafina somewhat of an expert on changelings. She sure knew a heck of a lot more than this pair of hapless host parents.

Pamela straightened up from the loveseat and with one last glance at her unconscious husband, led us to a bedroom at the end of the hallway wordlessly.

She opened the door.

It was one of those dream bedrooms that one would expect to find in a home decor magazine. A picture perfect boy's bedroom, with a bed in the shape of a pirate ship, and a wide collection of football gear and video games littered all over the place.

The Agricolas might not have had enough money to send their child—or whom they thought was their child—to private school, but they sure spoiled him with what income they had at their disposal.

A boy sat on the bed crossed-legged, facing the wall. His tiny frame seemed too small for the wide shoulder pads carelessly dangling on one of the ship mast bedposts. He swayed himself back and forth repeatedly, as if obsessing over that single motion was all that mattered in the world. I put my senses out and found no weird energy vibes, despite how obviously upset he was.

No weird energy vibes, not even a stray bit of strange magic, and that was exactly what was wrong.

I detected vengeance magic in the air and Fir's own brand of trickster power, but nothing else. Nothing that would suggest the presence of a changeling.

The kid in front of me was no changeling—he was a vengeance demon. The exchange had already taken place.

"It happened last night." Pamela hugged herself by the doorframe. "We woke up to Thomas screaming, but by the time we got to his room, he was gone. And *he* was here." She pointed an accusing finger at her real child.

"You must've heard the stories about how changelings work. You might even have caught wind of the recent rumors about them." Gregory asked softly, "Why didn't you contact the authorities right away?"

"I never thought this could happen to us. We're just a regular family." Pamela's eyes filled. "My baby. I'll never see him again."

I was just about to point out that her baby was right there in the room with us, but Serafina shook her head. She leaned closer to me, and murmured, "Don't bother. She believed all her life that the changeling was her child. Right now, even the idea of thinking of the kid on the bed as hers is going to feel like such a betrayal."

Pamela sighed. "Harold is up for a promotion. If his boss knew we'd been fooled in such a humiliating manner... And my mother. She babysat Thomas for two years straight so I could go back to work after maternity leave. She loves him. How am I going to tell her she'll never see him again?"

Pamela seemed very obsessed about what people around her would think, but I didn't hold that against her. Sometimes focusing on others' reactions was a way to not deal with your own.

"Wait." I held up a hand. "I thought Alpha, I mean, Thomas, is in the eleventh grade. He's not of age. How come he went back?"

"Actually, he just turned eighteen last night. He was always more of an athlete and he got a little behind in school, that's all. He loves playing football. Oh, the way he throws a spiral..." Pamela started counting all of Thomas's supposed talents in the sport, but I glanced at Serafina and realized that she was no longer listening. Her eyes were riveted to the boy still rocking himself on the bed, the one that his real birth mother treated as if he wasn't in the room.

I should have known that Serafina would be drawn to

him. The kid had suffered the trauma of being ripped from everything he'd known, all to go from one household that didn't want him to another.

Serafina gently approached him. "Do you mind if I sit next to you?"

The rocking continued.

Serafina sat at the edge of the bed. "What name do they call you by in Dualsing?"

The kid didn't look at her. I realized I still kept calling him a kid despite the fact that he was technically an adult. I guess it was because of his small frame and how utterly lost he looked. "Dain."

"Hello, Dain." Serafina smiled at him though he wasn't looking at her. "I was raised in Dualsing, too. When I was there, I was called Lady Serafina, from the House of—"

"Sebille." He stopped rocking abruptly and looked at her, his gaze burning into hers. "I know who you are. You were celebrated before the queen's return. They handed out candies to us in your honor."

Serafina blushed. "It wasn't much of an honor, was it?" Then she seemed surprised by something. "You knew about the exchange process then?"

"Yes." Dain nodded. "After the queen's return they no longer kept the secret from the underage. So we're all aware of the practice. I just never thought I was going to be one of *them*."

"You are one of *us* now." Serafina put her hand on his. "It's going to be okay."

"These people hate me." Dain glanced at his mother.

"They're in shock. Give them time."

"We couldn't have come at a worst time," Fir muttered to me. "This sucks."

"Not as sucky as it's going to be in a few minutes." Gregory pressed a finger to the device attached to his ear.

"We have to go. Now. I've been listening to the police scanner. A neighbor just called the authorities about all the disturbances. They're on their way. We can't be here when they arrive."

I tugged on Serafina's elbow. "Let's go, hon."

Serafina opened her mouth as if she was going to say something to Dain, then closed it, seemingly lost for words.

Dain turned back to the wall and started rocking again.

We beat feet out of the apartment just in time. Two vengeance demons teleported outside the Agricolas' door as we stepped into the elevator. There would be no hiding the freshly returned child now.

"Poor Dain," Serafina said in a voice that was sad beyond her years. "I wish there was more I could do for him."

"Later. When this is all over. I have every faith you will think of something." I put my arms around her. I couldn't even imagine how it felt to have no roots whatsoever. It was truly humbling how there was always somebody who had it harder. I was again reminded of my good fortune of having a close-knitted immediate family. "Just survive this current crisis first, alright?"

She nodded.

We were all silent as we exited the elevator and walked away from the condo structure as nonchalant and innocent looking as possible.

"Even if we had found Thomas before the switch, it might not have done us any good," Gregory said suddenly, looking up from his phone.

"Why do you say that?" I asked curiously.

"He most likely wouldn't have helped us anyway."

"How would you know?"

"I saw enough to know. The video games in his room weren't all human ones like *Call of Duty* and *Assassin's Creed*. Quite a few of them are patented by the Geekomages."

The Geekomages was a small group of human geeks who achieved supernatural power through an overdose of fandom, and they were like radioactive spiders with programming skills. They were an emerging race that many of the older species were wary of, but there was no doubt they'd help shape the high-tech world we all lived in now. Bill Gates, Mark Zuckerberg were among their leaders, with Steve Jobs faking his death so he could continue his work on the vengeance plane. He was starting to attract too much attention.

The video games put out by the Geekomages were designed to be technically challenging, involving complex math and problem solving skills. If Thomas the changeling was playing them then he couldn't be that dumb.

"I also saw a bunch of framed winning pro-line tickets," Gregory added. "In consecutive weeks. These games are magic-proof. The kid had to be betting and winning not using luck, but probability calculations."

"Then why the heck did he fall behind in school two years in a row?" Fir asked, puzzled.

"He was a jock, a popular kid—judging from all those pictures with the cheerleaders—and I'm guessing someone who failed his grades not because he wasn't smart enough, but because he was lazy and bored. I just went through his Facebook page. The kid sounded arrogant and entitled. He probably wouldn't help us with our cause even if we'd found him on time. Discovering his changeling heritage would just make him pat himself on the back affirming what a special little snowflake he was."

"So one chance down, one to go." Fir opened the portal to our next destination. "Let's hope the next one will be both willing and available, and that just one kid will be enough for what needs to be done."

Here was to hoping.

❧ 16 ❧

SOUP KITCHEN

I HAD NEVER BEEN aware of Chicago's status as a trickster mecca of sorts, though I should've known based on how many trick-athons were hosted in that city that Fir had tried to drag me to through the years. Ashamed as I was of my trickster gene growing up, I avoided those invitations like a dude avoided Celine Dion concerts.

The point was, I knew very little about the different Chicago suburbs. So it was a surprise to me that the place Beta resided turned out to be at a rather affluent community called Hinsdale. The "two-story house" Beta lived in was more like a seven-bedroom Queen Anne mansion, with two acres of accompanying green space. There was something very old world and charming about a Queen Anne, and the blue and white structure in front of me, with wrap-around porch, was a classic beauty. I wish I'd seen it in broad daylight, but evening had fallen by the time we got there.

"Pretty fancy gig for a commoner from Dualsing." Fir whistled.

"As I said before, it's all a matter of luck and timing," Serafina said.

"What do we know about the parents?" I asked Fir and Gregory. Between the two of them somebody would have dug up the intel we needed.

Gregory gave me a blank stare. He'd been inexplicably mute since our teleportation to the edge of the property. Weird.

"Caroline Isabelle Sumpsi and Louis Maximilian Sumpsi," Fir said.

"Wait a minute. Sumpsi, as in from the House of Sumpsi?" There was a Sumpsi on the Council since the inception of the governing body.

"Caroline and Louis are the black sheep of the family," Fir explained. "This house is more like a place of exile."

No wonder. The Sumpsis usually lived in residences similar to the Advocatus family estate. The Queen Anne, while splendid, wasn't exactly in the same caliber.

"What did they do?" Serafina asked.

"Louis is the second son of the current generation of Sumpsis. He was groomed to take over the business side of the family while his older brother, Macallister Sebastian Sumpsi would take over the political mantle. But Louis decided to follow his life-long dream to become a scientist. A *supernatural* scientist. Flash forward ten years, and he's actually doing okay. He's a research fellow at Northwestern University, Chicago, on the human side. The pay sucks, though."

"Lucky he and his family got a place to stay on this plane then," I said. "Hold on. He reached that turning point in his life only ten years ago, that means by then, the switch would have happened already."

"Exactly, Beta would've already been here." Fir's smile was rueful. "I guess my changeling cousins didn't see that one coming, huh? Here they are thinking their kid is going to bring back all sorts of corporate secrets, and they ended up with the latest string theory or something."

"Don't underestimate the Dualsingians' ability to make use of the most obscure or unexpected information," Serafina cautioned. "When Beta goes back they would make sure to take him for everything he knows."

"Stop calling him Beta. His name on this plane is Pedro Amos Sumpsi. Get used to calling him that before you go in," Fir cautioned.

When Serafina tracked the whereabouts of Alpha and Beta back at Dualsing, she captured their location at a single point in time. Luckily, in Beta's case, she got him when he was at a permanent residence.

"What about the mother?" I asked.

"She supported her husband's decision. They stayed together. By all accounts they're a happy little family. They're active members on this Facebook group called Geek Supernatural Parents. Anyway"—Fir slapped me on the back—"I'm going to sit this one out like the way you wanted me to do the last time, Megan. Black sheep or no, barging into the middle of one vengeance demon household is my limit for the day. I'll wait for you at the back."

"I'll join you," Gregory said immediately, which was rather suspicious. I gave Fir a look and he winked in return, silently promising to keep an eye on Gregory. I could be paranoid, but what if Gregory was taking the opportunity to cook up something that would free him from his obligation to me? Who knew if he had any loop-hole-finding lawyers in his back pocket? I thought maybe we had a moment there at Advocatus High, but who knows, and who was to say that meant he wouldn't screw me over if he could?

As for Fir, though, I was strangely confident that he wouldn't be tempted to leak anything on Eldon to his trickster friends, even though rumors must be spreading like wildfire in those circles and the chaos was like a drug. Fir knew what was at stake. Tricksters might be mischievous and devious in general, but they were loyal as hell when it came to protecting their loved ones. With the entire Cosmic Balance at risk, that pretty much covered everyone Fir had ever loved.

Before we rang the doorbell, Serafina and I had decided on no disguises this time. Our initial plan was to go for the images of fellow country club members. But after Fir told us about the father being the black sheep science nerd of his family, the society girl look could seem a bit out of place.

Besides, Pedro was only two months shy of his eighteenth birthday—we made sure of his age this time—Serafina and I weren't that much older than him. It wouldn't be that suspicious for us to call on him.

I rang the doorbell. My senses told me that only two people were home. Let's hope that one of them was who we were looking for. Both power signatures *felt* vengeance, but then the changeling's would be masked to give off that false reading anyway. It would've been like that even when he was a child, without his knowledge or consent. But Serafina could identify Beta once she got close enough.

A middle-age woman of generous girth, rosy cheeks, and wearing a white apron came to the door. She smiled at us. "May I help you girls?"

"We're here to see Pedro Amos Sumpsi," I replied.

"You must be his ride to the soup kitchen. Hold on a sec. He's just getting ready. The dear boy made scalloped potatoes using my recipe and it turned out amazing. But it still needs to cool down and be packed up. Now where did I put those oven mitts?"

The chattering of the woman, who seemed to be the cook, was rapid fire, and I couldn't get a word in edgewise. We followed her into the foyer, then the kitchen to the left of that, as she hunted for her oven mitts. "Ma'am, we're not with the soup—"

"Oh, Pedrrrro," the woman called out in a singsong voice toward the direction of the stairs. "Your ride is here!"

I exchanged a look with Serafina. Either the kid was at the soup kitchen because he was a real sweetheart, or that he had no choice because he was there for required community service. Given the purpose of this visit, I found myself hoping for the latter. Remembering how haunted Serafina looked when it came to Dain, I almost wished this Beta kid was a jerk who had to be strong-armed into helping us. Forcing compliance was at least something tangible I could work with. Ruined lives and profound sadness? Not so much.

In a minute a lanky, almost sickly looking kid in thick-rimmed glasses came down the stairs clutching a book in his hand. He had eyes only for the cook and the casserole dish on top of the oven. "Sorry, Minnie, I got caught up in something. It's not burnt, is it?"

"No, but your friends are here."

Pedro looked at us for the first time, and shyly looked away. Great. We thought not going for the society girl appearance was enough to look less suspicious, but it would seem that the guy wasn't used to talking to any girl at all.

Minnie shooed him away. "Go on to the living room and wait with your new friends, I'll finish the rest."

She winked at Serafina and me, pushing us out of the kitchen as well. I could feel her inner pleasure, an almost physical thing. She was so glad Pedro was interacting with girls.

Great, first we got the jock, and now, a bookish Harry Potter.

We all got into the living room. It was as big as the entire apartment I shared with Rosemary, my human roommate, but nowhere near as grand as Serafina's family estate house. I wondered about Pedro's host father. Not exactly roughing it here, but I did admire the guy for standing up to his family. I knew firsthand how it felt to be a black sheep.

"I already called them and said I don't need a ride." Pedro frowned. "I was just going to wrap up the dish and pack it into my bike's basket and go."

I looked at Serafina, who nodded slightly, confirming that Pedro was indeed a changeling.

"Actually, we're not from the soup kitchen. We're here." I began, "because there's something we have to talk to you about."

Pedro swallowed. "Are you here about the raccoon-bat at Uncle Macallister's? I swear he wasn't trying to hurt anybody. He just didn't like being hit by golf balls, that's all."

"Huh?" The confused look on Serafina's face and mine said it all. Raccoon-bats were feral giant bats with a penchant for dropping balls on golfers. Why did Pedro think it had anything to do with our visit?

He blushed. "My uncle was teaching me golf at his place. Trying to get me interested in more respectable stuff, you know? I...er, I released the raccoon-bat that he trapped. I thought maybe you girls work for him."

Aha! Sneaking around letting raccoon-bats off the hook. So the shy boy wasn't so meek, after all.

"No. We work for no stuck-up Council members." I laughed. Then I sobered up when I realized that I was about to break some pretty bad news to a person who appeared to have a kind heart and didn't have the slightest inkling to his true origin. Damn. Why did I always end up with the hard stuff to do? Where the heck were Fir and Gregory when the real going got rough? It didn't matter that Pedro would've known in a few months anyway, if things had been allowed to run their course. Instead of the changelings, I was the asshole who was going to put an end to his innocence. I hated myself for that.

"Hey, why don't you sit down?" I gestured to the sofa nearest Pedro.

"What is this about?" Pedro stayed exactly where he was, suspicion shone in his eyes. Ah, he wasn't dumb, either.

I sighed. "There's no easy way to do this, so here goes."

Pedro listened intently as I talked about the Dualsing tradition of baby switching. Most of the basic stuff he would've already heard, but not in detail and not in the presence of someone who had lived through it. I explained how Eldon got kicked out by the changelings and became the most wanted on almost all the supernaturals' lists. Every now and then Serafina interjected with details, some I never even knew about.

We went through the whole backstory and the big picture stuff, covering everything except how all of that would affect Pedro on a personal level. I really, really hated getting to that part.

So I did the extra cruel thing, however unintentional, which was to keep beating around the bush. I ignored the many pointed looks Serafina sent my way.

"Look, I don't think I need another detailed rundown on the cross-dimensional limitations that the changelings face." Pedro's hands were now clutching and unclutching the fabric of his pants. "Can you please just tell me why you're here, and what any of this has to do with me?"

"It's alright, Megan." Serafina's hand found mine. "I think deep down he already figured it out."

"Figured out what?" Pedro whispered.

I took a deep breath. "You're a changeling. You're currently the only one assigned to this plane." Unless more were sent here after Serafina left Dualsing.

Pedro sat down heavily on the sofa that I had previously offered.

"Look, I really hate to lay all this on you." Now that he knew the truth, I couldn't keep the rest of it in. "We need your help to prevent the Council from going to war with the changelings. There are other forces at work here. I can go into the details later, but basically a group of people are trying really hard to destroy the world, and we're asking you to help us save it. I know it sounds so corny, but it's the truth. And I'm so, so sorry about all this."

We sat together in silence for a long time.

I knew what I said was a lot for the kid to process. I was essentially telling him that his entire life was a lie. And we were asking him for help before he even had time to process it all.

"How do I know you're telling me the truth?" he demanded after a long while.

Ah, after the shock, here came the denial.

As I opened my mouth to answer him, there was a loud screeching noise in my ear, as though concert-grade speakers were sending out feedback directly into my brain.

"May I have your attention please," a female voice spoke inside my head with the tone of a seasoned television announcer. "This is an emergency cross-dimensional broadcast on the vengeance public psychic channel."

I exchanged a look with Serafina, confirming that she, too, was listening. I'd heard of the existence of such a channel, but it was never used before in my lifetime. I supposed it was a little like the police scanner Gregory had been listening to, but rather than actively seeking to tap into it, the broadcast forced its way into our heads, whether we liked it or not.

Pedro frowned, puzzled by how both Serafina and I had suddenly gone utterly silent.

The psych link worked entirely by the virtue of vengeance

blood—even diluted, in my case—and Pedro's inability to hear the broadcast was proof beyond doubt that he was no vengeance demon.

Serafina offered him a hand and he took it. His eyes widened as he, too, was able to hear the broadcast through his physical connection with her. His eyes filled with tears as he came to the same conclusion as I did with regard to his heritage.

I would have taken the time to comfort him if I wasn't so focused on what the announcer was saying, a sense of unease settling deep into my bones.

"...be able to reach most regions on the vengeance plane and beyond. If you're listening to this, it means you are a vengeance demon by birth. If you're not a vengeance demon and are listening in by other means, we ask that you tune out this broadcast immediately. Failure to do so will result in vengeance unprecedented."

I rolled my eyes. Anyone who took the time and effort to listen in to what they shouldn't be listening to wouldn't be dissuaded by a simple, hard-to-enforce warning. It was typical Council-talk. It was worse than the anti-privacy warning before human movies that never deters anyone from pirating.

"An hour ago the Council reached an agreement with the Greys and have gained their full co-operation in opening the passage to the changeling plane. As of this moment, we are at war with the changelings. With the support of other super-naturals including the reapers, the banshees, the tax fairies, and all of the four major witches' unions, the attack will be a long-anticipated action that will benefit all of us in the Cosmic Balance..."

My stomached rolled and threatened to eject the jumbo hotdog I'd grabbed on the street while still in downtown Chicago. The announcer droned on, but my mind already zoomed in on the most important facts.

They were going to war.

They'd agreed to jump into bed with the Greys.

And contrary to what they claimed, not everybody in the Cosmic Balance was going to benefit. The reapers, the tax fairies, and the unionized witches...all of them were the type the Council favored due to their "respectability." Not a single one of Gregory's clients were even mentioned. Didn't the Council realize what a mess this could become? A lot of supernaturals already didn't like them, and being denied vengeance would focus that resentment and unite them all.

Serafina and I looked at each other with our mouths open. I was sure the horror in her eyes reflected the same in my own.

"Crap!" The single curse word exploded from Serafina, which was so unladylike and so out of character for her that I didn't know whether to laugh or to be horrified.

Well, war was pretty horrifying, so there was a lot of that going around.

The Council was playing directly into the Greys' hands by allowing itself to get dragged into such a polarizing war. At best, the Greys would no longer be hunted. At worst, the ensuing conflict *after* the war would weaken the Council, making it ripe for picking for the Greys. After the Greys finished with the Council, they could then do away with the Cosmic Balance and bring back the Absolute Good without contest. It wasn't the first time, in vengeance history or otherwise, that a superpower was brought down by the very ally they chose.

"You've been telling the truth. About me. About the changelings," Pedro whispered, pulling his hand from Serafina's and hugging himself. The scared and anguished look on his face was a stark reminder for me to put the big picture stuff aside for now and concentrate on the misery of the young person in front of me. "I'm one of those changelings they're going to war with."

"Their quarrel is not with you." Serafina shook her head. "It's with *them*. You haven't done anything wrong."

"Haven't done anything wrong?" Pedro gave a mirthless laugh. "I got switched. My sole purpose here is to steal what knowledge I can from the people I care about. I was sent here to rob them blind!"

"Pedro, I might've had the exact opposite experience from yours, but I know this"—she leaned closer to him —"I've never met a Dualsingian who felt half as bad about the switch as you do now. It shows that where it matters, you *are* your vengeance parents' kid. They raised you well and you know what's right and wrong. Hold on to that."

"I don't want to hurt them," Pedro stated. "And I don't want to go to that changeling plane and live among those people and have them learn all about my dad's research because of me."

He looked at Serafina, and then at me. His face fierce. Now *that* was a kid I could see freeing raccoon-bats at the risk of his stern uncle's wrath. "If I help you, will you promise to help me stay on this plane? Maybe arrange for me to take a short trip to some nearby planes and max out my lifetime tolerance? Please, I'll do anything to avoid returning to those thieves. I couldn't stand the idea of it."

After the shock and denial, here came the bargaining. And who could blame him? I would do the exact same thing if I was in his shoes. I had to admire the kid for thinking on his feet, even coming up with that idea of purposefully blowing his own travel limits using knowledge we'd just given him.

"Sounds like a good plan," I acknowledged. Then something occurred to me. "But what about your counterpart?"

"My counterpart?" Pedro echoed.

"You know, the vengeance demon who had been kidnapped by the changelings so you could take his place? He's trapped on Dualsing as we speak." I turned to Serafina. "Can he come home if Pedro stays?"

"I don't think so." Serafina shook her head.

Pedro paled. "You're saying that if I don't go back, I'll be condemning someone to a life of second-class citizenship, never getting to know his real parents? And my parents, they'll never know their real child?"

"Wait." Serafina chewed on her lower lip. "Maybe there *is* a way for both the switcher and the switchee to stay on this plane."

Hope flared in Pedro's eyes.

"When my switch happened," Serafina explained, "there was about a ten-second overlap when I got onto the vengeance plane already, but Eldon's sister hadn't gone back to Dualsing yet." She shuddered. "It was a long ten seconds. She was trying very hard to kill me."

"What?" Pedro and I both barked.

"Long story. I'll go into it later. The point is, they had me put on a necklace called the Eye of Sebille at the time, and once I got on the vengeance plane, it detached itself from my body and went onto my counterpart's. The Eye helped guide me here, and then it took Eldon's sister home. I assume there's a similar procedure in place for your return, Pedro."

"If we can make sure the jewel couldn't attach itself to you, or go back to your counterpart"—my mind was going a million miles an hour, thinking of all the spells I knew to contain magical artifacts—"we can come through the switch with both of you remaining on this plane."

For the first time since he found out about his heritage, a genuine smile touched Pedro's lips. But of course, there was a price to our help—he had to play the role we needed him to play in the grand scheme of things. "So do we have a deal, you help us prevent a war and we help you avoid returning to the changelings?"

"Deal," Pedro said without hesitation.

I turned to Serafina. "Do you think just one kid is going to be enough for the ritual?"

"Yes." Serafina looked at Pedro with pride. "His heart is true. That's potent magic. Even at his most miserable, he cared about his counterpart, someone he never met and is going to be competition for his parents' affection. It makes the connection between them steady and strong. It'll help open the passage to Dualsing."

———

At Pedro's insistence, Serafina and I distracted Minnie while he packed up the dish of scalloped potatoes and covertly sent it to the soup kitchen using an express delivery fairy. No point having it go to waste, he said. Besides, the cook might get worried if he took off with the dish still in the house.

"I'll get going now, Minnie." Pedro hugged the woman whom he obviously cared about as more than a mere servant, his thin frame dwarfed by her girth. "Please tell my parents I'll be late tonight."

I sincerely hoped that the matter would be resolved by then.

Fir and Gregory waited for us at the far end of the two-acre lot, but I didn't mind the walk. It gave me some time to think without the social obligation to make small talk.

Now that we had secured Pedro's help, I found my mind turning back to that vengeance public broadcast.

I wished I could speak to Grandma. The very public announcement of the Council to join forces with the Greys, despite her opposition, was driving home how strong their will to go to war was. That in turn suggested that they would not look kindly upon anyone who stood in their way.

If I continued forward with my plan to stop this war, I would not only be standing against the Council, the governing body I was honor-bound to serve, but also the Greys, whose extensive network—legitimate and otherwise—I'd only scratched the surface of. Both fights, win or lose, would ensure I would not have a place left in the vengeance world.

Talk about a point of no return.

I'd worked hard to win a place in the vengeance society, and I was so close. I got into the right university. I got into the right co-op program. I got into my second year with a good academic standing. But I couldn't back down now, not when the fate of the world hung in the balance.

The edge of the property came too soon. Stone half walls accompanied an open wrought iron gate that was as strong as it was beautiful. Gargoyles stood on the top of the stone walls, and a gilded coat of arms adorned the gates, displaying the heraldry of the household. The back entrance was built to convey a sense of awe and majesty, while the fact that it was wide open and there was an amateur-crafted wooden wind chime tied to the gate spike said something quite to the contrary.

I liked Pedro's parents, and I'd never even met them. I hoped he got to stay with them, and I hoped they wouldn't give a damn about his origin.

I looked absently past the coat of arms, which was built into the intricate pattern of the gate. I was too busy searching for Fir and Gregory to pay it much attention. Then my mind processed what I was looking at and I stopped short.

I looked closer at the heraldry on display. In the center of the golden coat of arms was a silver shield, bejeweled by two sparkling red diamonds. A sword, with a guard that curved toward the blade, sat upright on top of the shield.

Gregory.

Gregory was an illegitimate member of the House of Sumpsi. Since I seriously couldn't see Pedro's father being the love 'em and leave 'em type, judging from the noble son he managed to raise, that left his uncle, Macallister Sebastian Sumpsi.

Member of the Council, Minister of the Vengeance Ethics Commission.

Suddenly, what Fake Sui-Ling, who possessed the same knowledge as her real counterpart, had said to Gregory made perfect sense.

"Oh, Gregory, what will your dear old dad say about all this?"

Gregory's lips thinned. "He has no say in this."

"You're going to embarrass him in front of his peers."

"This is business, and I won fair and square."

So Pedro had, in fact, been switched with Gregory's younger cousin. Was that the real reason why Gregory chose to stay outside the house? Why Gregory had initially suggested visiting Alpha first? To delay coming here?

Speaking of the devil, Gregory headed for us with Fir. Gregory caught me staring at the coat of arms, and his lips thinned.

"Hey, Mr. Mercenary, I assume you heard the broadcast and filled in Fir. Being a man of the shady trade didn't like, cut you off from that psych link or anything like that, right?" I said brightly, even injected a touch of sarcasm, purposefully steering clear of any reference to my newly acquired knowledge.

Gregory studied me briefly, no doubt assessing if I was going to spill the beans in front of everyone. So I forged ahead. "You heard the list of the Council's allies. Well, sucks to be your clients right now."

I might needle the guy every chance I got, but I wasn't about to divulge his origin secret to the group.

The House of Sumpsi was just as powerful as the Advocatus, and when the situation with Pedro was made public the embarrassment would not be any less. Gregory could have used all this to his advantage, to rub it into his birth father's face publicly, or even tried some good old-fashioned blackmailing. As far as I could tell, he wasn't about to do that. If he did, his father would've come swooping in, and we wouldn't have been able to leave with Pedro undetected. I suspect that Gregory chose to not press his advantage for precisely that reason.

No, I wouldn't expose his heritage. A jerky thing to do aside, it would also be stupid. After the public broadcast, the chance of his clients getting justice had just gotten way slimmer. His lessened reward for fulfilling his contract with them meant there was less incentive to play ball with me. It wouldn't do to encroach on the remaining goodwill between us.

Better to keep it light and comfortable with our normal jabs and insults.

Gregory's shoulders relaxed and he snorted. "Sucks to be my clients? Sucks to be those who keep me from serving them."

"You just try anything, mercenary," I warned, "and I'll see to it that every fringe character from here to the siren plane thinks you're helping me because you've gone soft. Good luck getting any clients after *that*."

With my taunt, the last of the wariness dissipated from his eyes. I found myself feeling a sense of satisfaction at having managed to spare him some pain and embarrassment, beyond what business motivations would call for.

And wondered, for the first time, if I was the one who'd gotten soft.

❦ 17 ❧

IN SERAFINA'S SHOES: AMBITION

My mind wandered as Megan and Gregory bantered back and forth. Being at odds with one another seemed like a strange kind of courtship, and if I had been the kind of friend that I'd vowed to be for Megan, I should've been paying more attention to it, but I couldn't. The public broadcast had left me badly shaken.

Regardless of what the Dualsingians had done to countless supernaturals through the years, regardless of what they'd done to me, that plane was home to me for over seventeen years. I'd made friends there. I'd loved and lost there.

I couldn't stand the thought of it burning up in flames.

And Eldon...every second we couldn't get to him was another second of pain for him. I put up a relatively calm appearance in front of my friends, but inside I wanted to kick and scream in frustration. Blinding panic threatened to overwhelm me during every waking moment. It helped when we were trying to convince Pedro to join us—at least I had something else to focus on. Now I had nothing but my own thoughts in my head as we walked away from the Sumpsi estate.

Megan said something about having to call in the cavalry, and we were heading to an animal shelter on the human plane to regroup.

We teleported to the shelter. Megan had taken me here to volunteer on a few occasions. Having only been introduced to the art and science of teleporting upon my return to the vengeance plane, I was adequate at it at best. It usually took me a moment to reorient myself after the experience, and upon my arrival on the human plane, the spinning in my head didn't ease.

Massaging my solar plexus, I opened my eyes.

And found myself not having arrived at the shelter at all.

I was back to the dark hospital room where Eldon was. Fake Sui-Ling was nowhere to be seen. Once again there were two Eldons. One, healthy and whole, was "floating" in midair next to me. The other one, with eyes shut tight and scorch marks all over his body, was on the slab.

"You're back." There was unguarded joy on his face when he first saw me, then it turned into a scowl.

"Yeah, I guess I am."

"How? I blocked you."

"I don't know." Maybe the act of teleporting, which was really a thrust through the veil between planes, fueled by my worry for him, had managed to reopen my connection with Eldon without my conscious effort.

"She's going to be back soon. Please go," he pleaded.

I didn't have a lot of time. I had no idea how long I could remain here. "Eldon, listen. These people who are hurting you—they just made an alliance with the vengeance Council."

"I know." He curved his lips, but there was no humor there. "They were very eager to get the information out of me in hopes of honoring that deal. Hence the burn marks. They're starting to get a little more creative with their torture."

"We're coming for you," I vowed.

"I know you are. And then I'll return home."

There was something in his tone that resembled eager anticipation, which he couldn't hide from me in our current form. It made me sad and angry at the same time.

"You do want power, don't you?" I stated softly. "Not just because of what's best for the Cosmic Balance, or what's best for me. You really want power for itself."

"Lady Aequitas was right about that." His eyes held no apology. "I want it. I've suffered for it. I'm going to suffer more still before this is over. I deserve a chance to sit on that throne."

"Even if it kills you?"

"Yes, even if I end up crushed under it."

Even if it broke both our hearts.

The words, unspoken, lay between us as we stared at each other, bound by our own version of right.

"Finny." His hand moved as if trying to reach toward me, then lowered. "Please leave me to my pain, and allow me the delusion that the more I suffer now, the more deserving I will be of the crown when I take it from my sister."

"I'll go." My voice was strangely emotionless, given how I was feeling inside.

"Finny..."

"Call me Serafina. I'm not Finny anymore."

❧ 18 ❧

NEW DEAL

WE TELEPORTED into a storage room of the shelter Rosemary, my human roommate, volunteered at. Was it really just two days ago that I was living among non-magical folks and stealing chocolate chip cookies from the kitchen?

It was already well into the evening, but the shelter was still open. Most of the volunteers had day jobs and could only help out at night anyway. And cats were nocturnal, so they were actually a lot less grumpy when taken out of the cage for a brush and groom in the dead of night.

The storage room, being right next to the grooming area, was where they kept the blankets, kibbles, and cat litter. A good thing, too, because the first thing I saw out of teleporting was Serafina diving face down, unconscious, onto a pile of large dog towels. Thankfully, she landed in the basket for fresh laundry.

I rushed to her and flipped her over so she could breathe. "Oh no, not again."

"Is she alright?" Pedro demanded anxiously. Then, "What do you mean, *again*?"

"Another long story. She's fine, I think." Her breathing

was even, just knocked out cold. These fainting spells of hers were happening far too often for my own comfort.

She came to after five minutes or so, and I helped her up.

"You okay?" I asked.

"Yeah," she said in a quiet yet determined voice. "But we have a job to do. A war to prevent."

"That, we do." I took a careful look at her. Unlike the tears from her last venture into astral projection, she was dry-eyed and exceptionally calm, which wasn't necessarily an improvement. But if I wasn't going to push Gregory about his heritage, then I sure as hell wasn't going to push Serafina about her out-of-body experiences.

To everyone in the room, I said, "Alright, listen up, people. We're staying here with Rosemary while we sort a few things out. We want to be nice and help her out while we're here. So when we go out of this room, we all grab a groom kit and an animal and start brushing, okay?"

"But I'm allergic to fur," Fir whined.

"Grab the short hair ones and start clipping some toe nails." I snapped, "No excuses. Being on the human plane is our best chance to stay off the radar. It's either the shelter or the hospice of my current target. Believe me, this is far less depressing."

Current target. In my head, I was still thinking of Sandra Hogan, the power tripping ex-ER nurse as my current target. Would she really still be mine to torment when this was all over? If the world ended up going to hell, did it even matter?

I opened the door and there was Rosemary working on a German shepherd. I enchanted it so that in the perspective of the two humans in the room—Rosemary and her boyfriend, Jordan—our group were entering through the proper entrance to the grooming area, not piling out of the storage room like thieves in the night.

"Hey, Rosemary," I greeted her.

"Megan!" Rosemary's sweet round face split into a wide smile. "I was so happy to get your message. So, you mentioned this is like a group volunteer day for work?"

Fir snorted. I ignored him.

"Yeah. This is kinda like an impromptu volunteer blitz. For a few hours after work." I nodded at her boyfriend. "Hey, Jordan."

"Hey, Megan. If you and your friends can come over here, I'll get you set up."

We got our animals and tools, and I settled us at a corner table. I put a muting and illusion spell over the entire room, making sure Rosemary and Jordan couldn't hear us or see anything their human eyes shouldn't.

Gregory had a Maltese on his lap. He said with wonder in his voice, "This dog is so well-behaved he's practically a rag doll."

"Only with us vengeance demons. They have the instinct to know who their handlers are," I explained.

"Mine isn't that well-behaved," Fir complained. His Labrador retriever puppy was all over the place, yelping and licking his face, and just wouldn't sit still.

"Like I said, she knows who and what you are," I said pointedly. "Guess which part of her you're bringing out?"

"Ha." Fir stuck out his tongue. I would've told him to be more mature but then I reminded myself he was already way more mature than most in his race. More mature than Fir on a regular day, even. "And where's *your* animal?"

That was right, I didn't get myself one.

"I have to call in the cavalry." I replied.

"And who might that be?"

"Esme." My half-sister was smart and powerful, and had started to build a network of contacts in the upper crust of vengeance society that the likes of me or Gregory wouldn't be able to access. I needed her in the tasks ahead.

"I thought Esme is on holiday off plane with her mom somewhere and you aren't able to contact her." Serafina frowned.

"Not through the normal channels, we can't. But there's another way."

I took a deep breath and closed my eyes. I gathered my energy as if I was getting ready to teleport, but instead of sending my body to a specific destination across the planes, I projected my thoughts like a heat-seeking missile toward wherever Esme was.

I need you, sis.

As kin and two supernaturals who had passed life force to each other before, there was a strong bond between me and Esme. Tapping into that connection across an unknown number of planes wasn't impossible. However, it wasn't going to be pretty.

The pressure in my head built like it was trapped in a metal crown that was two sizes too small.

I repeated the message. It was like shouting into the howling wind and having no idea if I was heard.

Everything was a blur and the room was swimming. Voices came to me like they were underwater. I thought I could make out the alarming tones of Fir, Serafina, and Pedro. Then a pair of strong arms surrounded me. Instinctively I knew it was Gregory's.

Then to my horror and utter humiliation, before I could even process the idea of being in his arms, I started puking. As if I was having the worst case of food poisoning, with bad shell fish and spoiled milk.

"Megan, stop it." Gregory shook my shoulders urgently. "You're hurting yourself."

I used everything I had left to blast out the message one last time, then I let go of the bond and slumped into Gregory's arms.

Then everything turned black.

———

When I came to, all evidence of my vomiting was erased. I was still in Gregory's arms, facing away from him. Good. I was so embarrassed I couldn't look him in the eyes.

"What the hell was that, Megan?" Fir demanded. All of my friends were looking a little green. Rosemary and Jordan, thankfully, remained oblivious.

"I got the message sent. I think." I straightened and taking my cue, Gregory released me.

"You scared us," Serafina reproached.

"It has a few side effects," I admitted weakly. I would've gone for false bravado, but my queasy stomach was still settling down. "At least I didn't have temporary loss of certain motor functions, like in some extreme cases."

"You're not making us feel better." Fir rolled his eyes.

What I did should only be used in case of extreme emergencies. But I figured this mess is as extreme and urgent as they come.

Though not knowing exactly where Esme had to come back from, I got a sense that it was really remote, probably without immediate teleporting access. It might be a few hours before she got here, so we settled back into the clip and brush motion.

We worked in silence for a while, and I worked on interacting with Gregory without thinking about how I puked my guts out in his arms. Very sexy. Er...not that I wanted to be sexy in front of him, but it was just not a side of me I would want anybody to see.

Detangling a very matted long hair Himalayan cat—how did this pure breed end up in the shelter, I wondered—was a two-person job, and Gregory helped hold the kitty down when he was done with his Maltese so I could work on its sensitive belly. As the fur began to fly, I couldn't help but remember that the first time Gregory and I met was to fight over the vengeance claim for a mother dog and her puppies.

We'd come full circle.

After we were done with the Himalayan, I turned to Gregory. "There's something you and I need to discuss. Alone. But do you mind if I have a chat with everybody else first?"

Gregory nodded. "I'll explore this place a bit."

He left the room.

Serafina, Fir, and Pedro looked at me curiously.

I asked Serafina, "Once the passage to Dualsing is opened, what's the longest you can keep it that way?"

Serafina bit her lower lip. "With the help of Pedro, and if we're really lucky, I could hold it for maybe an hour. But why would we want to do that? I thought we were just going to send Eldon back?"

"Because there's one factor we haven't considered yet—all the other supernatural children currently trapped in Dualsing, including Pedro's counterpart. If the Greys and the Council manage to crack Eldon before we get to him, then they would gain access to Dualsing. It's going to be an all-out war on that plane, and these kids will be smack in the middle of it. For all we know, the changelings are going to use them as bargaining chips."

Serafina and Pedro looked at me, dawning horror on their faces. Never mind Pedro trying to avoid being returned home —his counterpart might be held back from the switch anyway.

"We have to get them out of there before all hell breaks loose, and we should do it at the same time we get Eldon home." It was time to think strategically. I was an Aequitas. I was from a family that, in the medieval days, had been known for its military genius. Time to live up to the family name, whether the rest of the family considered me one of them or not. "Serafina, do you know anyone in Dualsing who would help us?"

"There were only two who have ever been nice to me other than Eldon. Alina the pixie and Trust the dragon. Alina is too young and fragile, and Trust is captured from what Eldon told me."

"Well, somebody recently told me not to underestimate the little guys." I glanced at the door where Gregory disappeared through, remembering his defense of the "pencil pushers." "Can Alina help us find those children fast?"

"I think so. She used to assist me in keeping track of the changeling children. Maybe she could use the same skill to locate their counterparts on Dualsing."

"Alright. Sounds like a plan then," I said, getting up from the table.

"So what is it that you want to speak to Gregory about?" Fir's eyes gleamed with speculation. "Or is that code for making out? I saw you and him looking funny back there by the iron gate."

I mentally winced, feeling like a bug under a telescope. Whatever this *thing* I might be experiencing with Gregory— root cause ranging from undiagnosed brain damage to overactive imagination induced by stress—I did not need to have it happening with my nosy brother poking around. He would make something out of nothing and run with it.

I rolled my eyes. "If you must know, I'm about to give him a new deal, an offer he can't refuse."

Once the words were out of my mouth I kicked myself for how corny it sounded. The *Godfather* reference sounded totally cool in my head.

Just goes to show how rattled I was by Fir's shrewd observation.

———

Gregory was at the infirmary of the shelter, where the more injured new arrivals recuperated after receiving medical attention.

I had a feeling he would be drawn to the wounded and damaged. That was one thing we had in common—beside both being outcasts.

He was standing by a small incubator hosting a ferret with a bandaged paw. The animal kept trying to bite his bandage, but then Gregory leaned closer and suddenly it relaxed and stopped fidgeting.

"Hey," I greeted.

He tensed and turned away from the ferret, as if he hated being caught at a moment of tenderness. I thought about not pushing it, then I decided I'd done that once too often recently.

"Getting soft?" I teased.

"Done with being Pukie Miss Puke?" He shot back.

And with that, we were back. Time to get to the point of getting him out here.

"Gregory, so far I've been getting your help by threatening to hurt your clients' claim to vengeance. But you heard the broadcast. There's not much hope for small fishes like your clients now. The Council is going to put their allies over anyone else. You have less reason to help me now than you did a few hours ago. But we still need your help. We're heading into unknown territories at Dualsing and we need your improvisation skills. And we need you to not screw us over. So how about I offer you something else to keep you around?"

Gregory raised his eyebrows, then a smile teased at the corner of his mouth. "You're sweetening the deal without any prompting. I keep forgetting how practical you are."

I shrugged. "I'm a realist."

I told myself it was simply a good strategic decision, not because the little things I'd observed in the last day had slowly warmed me up to him. But that damn ferret wasn't helping as it crooked its head toward Gregory, let out a contented sigh, and drifted to sleep.

"So what is it you would like to offer me?" There was respect in his voice now. No mockery, but genuine respect from one pro to another.

"The full financial benefit of getting the supernatural kids back to their rightful parents." I briefly explained the rescue plan. "Fir will be a hero among the tricksters just for returning Eldon, and anything more would be considered a sell-out from their bohemian worldview. Serafina doesn't care for the glory, and it would attract unwanted attention for Pedro. That leaves just you and me, and I'm willing to give you my half in exchange for your help. You mentioned once that some of your clients have children held by the changelings even right now. Getting those kids will give you something to take back to them. It's not the vengeance claim they hoped for, but it might be even better. At the very least you can earn out your retainer—I assume you took it—while not burning bridges. As for the rest of the kids, those that don't belong to your clients, well, that's where the real pay dirt is. You can collect rewards for their safe return. Getting their own flesh and blood back aside, the rich families would pay extra to keep the switch as quiet as possible. You might even make new clients out of them at the end of the day."

I listed out all the benefits of the new arrangement for Gregory in one breath—thank Hades for my supernatural lungs, then I waited for his reaction. It wasn't every day that I proposed something to a mercenary and a part of me was nervous. Threats of legal technicality was one thing, a business deal between two equal partners was quite another. It wasn't something we covered in Demon U, where at the end of the day, vengeance demons were an order-taking bunch.

Gregory's face split into a big smile and he offered me his hand. "You got yourself a deal."

High on my jubilance at the successful negotiation, I totally forgot about what happened the last few times we touched—not counting the puke-in-his-arms incident because I was too out of it to note any physical reaction. I went for the handshake, then pulled my body back when the tingling sensation once again started at the point of contact. I jerked back just a little too, well, jerkily, lost balance, and ended up on my ass on the floor of the infirmary.

Gregory grabbed hold of my wrist and pulled me up. "You're okay?"

Gregory smelled of sandalwood and pine nuts, offset by the crispness of oak bark. And his large and callused hands, in such sharp contrast with his aristocratic blood, held me firmly against his toned body.

Alright, maybe I felt *something* while I was in his arms earlier, puke or no puke.

"I'm...okay." Was that breathless voice really mine?

He paused, then tightened his hold and breathed in my scent. Then his head lowered toward mine.

I closed my eyes.

It felt strangely right to do that, my logic already thrown out the window when my butt kissed the floor.

Talk about kissing...

In a moment of flaring desire, my wings burst out of my back. It was a common indicator of unchecked passion, except Gregory was holding onto me when it happened. The blast of energy ejected me from his arms as if we were doing a throw jump in figure skating, and remarkably, both of us managed to land on our feet.

I hastily pulled back my wings, but not before noticing he had to do the same with his.

Breathing heavily, I backed away, the full impact of what just almost happened hitting me like a freight train. I almost kissed Gregory.

Let me repeat. I. Almost. Kissed. Gregory.

What felt right just seconds ago now felt like a trick of the mind, and my cheeks grew hot at the thought of my wings coming out in such an embarrassing manner.

Vengeance courtship was still stuck in the Victorian era, and the wings didn't make an appearance until, like, the thirtieth date. Not that this was a courtship, but still.

Maybe mercenaries did things differently...

Not. Going. There.

There was a war to prevent, and it took no pity on my frayed nerves.

"Let's get back," I managed, and walked toward the groom room, not bothering to check if Gregory was following me.

It wasn't every day that a girl was glad of having an Extinction Level Event to distract her.

————

"What happened to your face?" Fir demanded upon my return to the groom room, with Gregory a few steps behind me.

"What are you talking about?" I asked.

"It looks like you're in a 'before' picture of a hemorrhoid cream commercial."

Ouch. In hopes of heading off Fir's inquisitive observation, I weaved a spell over myself that should suck out all the stray lustful vibes and leave no hint of whatever the hell it was that had just happened. Sounded like I might've gone overboard and looked like a sour prune or something.

The downside was, both Serafina and Pedro now looked stressed, probably thinking I had a falling out with Gregory that might derail everything.

"Of course she does," Gregory interjected. "Megan has just agreed to give me her entire share of the profits for my trouble."

I looked at Gregory. He was smirking with infinite arrogance, the mask of his mercenary jerkiness fully back on. None of our shared intimacy was on his face.

Schooling a scowl on my own face, I pretended to go off in a huff, grabbing myself another long-haired cat to groom along the way.

It was Gregory's turn to cover for me, and I liked it.

———

An hour or so later, a pale Esme staggered into the grooming area. She looked even worse than I feared and was rubbing her forehead. I weaved a quick spell to keep Rosemary and Jordan engrossed in their task as I rushed forward and put my arms around her. She squeezed me tightly then collapsed onto a nearby chair.

"Let me help her." Serafina knelt down and took Esme's hand. As Esme's pearl earrings went from near transparent to a healthy luster, and color returned to her cheeks, I knew that Serafina was sharing her life force with my half-sister, recharging her.

I tugged at Serafina's sleeve. "Alright, my turn. You have to conserve your strength for the fight ahead."

Serafina stubbornly held onto Esme's hand. "I'm fine. I've been having a lot of excessive adrenaline and energy. I have plenty to share. This way we both get something out of it."

I kicked myself for being so focused on the big picture that I failed to truly see what a bag of nerves Serafina must have been. She was so quiet that sometimes I forgot she had a full reserve of raw vengeance power, a ticking time bomb that was not above being triggered by volatile emotions.

After a long while, Serafina finally released her hand. I noted that there was no change to her own coloring after the energy transfer, suggesting that she was telling the truth about having more than enough to give.

Esme sat up, her eyes full of concern for me. "Megan, what happened? I was in the middle of climbing up Mount Olympus when suddenly the headache began, and I lost the ability to move my right leg. I almost fell to my death at forty thousand feet above sea level. I would have if my mother hadn't been there."

A wealth of emotions rose within me, I couldn't decide which one to process first.

Horror, that I'd almost cost Esme her life.

Love, that despite what I'd just put her through, her first concern was for me.

More horror, as I realized how hard she would've had to push through her pain to get here from where she was. Mount Olympus was a plane that was abandoned at the same time their gods were abandoned by humans. Every year the plane drifted farther and farther away from both the vengeance and the human planes, and in a few more generations accessing it would be a distant memory. You don't get any more remote than that. It took a while for the negative side effects of our contact to wear off, and Esme would've had to travel for miles in pain before getting to the exit point of the plane.

I winced. No wonder she looked like hell when she got here. That was why the method of communication that I employed was reserved for extenuating circumstances only. "I'm so, so sorry that I almost got you killed. I have a good reason for calling you on your vacation, I swear."

"What is it? Your message sounded like it was coming through water. I couldn't pick up your exact words."

"Then how come you knew to come running?"

"I could sense the urgency of it. And I figured you wanted me to come alone. You know how hard it was to shake my mother after what almost happened?"

As it turned out, the plane which Mount Olympus was on was so remote, Esme and her mom didn't even hear the Council's broadcast, so her shock was complete when I told her the whole story.

"You should've called me the moment you came in contact with the changeling," she hissed.

"I didn't even know what I was facing until I was neck deep in it." I tried to downplay the whole thing.

She gave an exasperated sigh. "I would rather you call me and give me a splitting headache then find out later that you'd come face to face with a member of the Greys again. You don't know who's masquerading as this Sui-Ling. She sounds dangerous."

And there it was again, her protectiveness of me. Just a few months ago, Esme was trapped next to me while the Greys attempted to push me over the edge using my own anger and fear. I doubted she was going to forget that anytime soon.

"To be fair, I didn't know she was the bad guy when she first showed up. If I'd known I would've set all four of my brothers on her."

"Megan, don't try to make light of this." Esme's jaw hardened. "All the way here I was worried for you, wondering how bad this is."

I lowered my head and dropped the cockiness in my voice. Esme was right; this was no laughing matter. I thought I was easing her mind by downplaying it, but I wasn't. "I'm sorry."

"It's okay." Esme's hand, which was fisting and un-fisting the fabric on her pants, relaxed. "Tell me your plan."

I introduced Gregory and Pedro to Esme. She already knew Fir and Serafina.

"Gregory." Esme gave him a once-over, then realization dawned on her face. "This is the mercenary you mentioned before, right?"

Gregory's eyes lighted up in amusement, as if he was wondering what exactly I had told Esme about him. Esme glanced back at Gregory, clearly not done with her speculation.

Not ready for yet another person analyzing what even I didn't understand, I said just a little too brightly, "Yep, we got a team full of interesting people. There's Gregory for the muscle, Serafina and Pedro for the passage opening, you for the respectable cover, and Fir for...well, simply being an evil genius. Now all we need is a good base of operations with some heavy security, and I know just the place to go."

✺ III ✺
NATURE VS. NURTURE VS. CHOICE

❧ 19 ❧

THE ENEMY OF MY ENEMY

You know what they say, the enemy of my enemy is my friend. I certainly hoped that was true, even if those friends turned out to be obnoxious evil-villain-wannabes who had been the bane of my existence since the first time I laid eyes on them.

I took our little group to the Bureaucracy. It was a downtown night club on the human plane catering to supernaturals on shore leave. They came here looking for a place to let their hair down, may that said hair be a troll's coarse wisp, or Medusa's live snakes.

The club was owned and run by the Off-Blacks. Yes, you heard the name right. It wasn't some sort of politically incorrect racial reference, but a group of elves who were into worshiping the Absolute Evil. In deference to the fact that they weren't quite as evil as their master yet and needed a reminder to be bad, they called themselves the Off-Blacks.

Similarly, the choice of name for the Greys, who followed the teachings of the Absolute Good, stemmed from their desire to be a lighter and lighter shade of grey until one day they would be as pristine white as their idol. To be frank, the two names sounded like some sort of botched marketing campaign for a new laundry detergent, or in the Greys' case, an erotica book title. I would snigger if the Greys hadn't been such an effective pain in my ass, or the Off-Blacks not so pathetic in their attempt to be *eeeeevilllll*.

But the main takeaway was that the Off-Blacks and the Greys hated each other, and I was going to use that to serve my purpose.

The first time I was at the Bureaucracy, I came to get some information out of the Off-Blacks. Instead, I was magically ejected out of their office and dumped in the alleyway next to their building. Once I got out, I couldn't get back in no matter how hard I tried. I'd since figured out how to visit the Off-Blacks using other means, but that first experience taught me just how good their security system was.

Since these guys were making a living by posing as clair-voyants, it was inevitable that they would have a lot of unhappy customers wanting their money back. Hence the need for the world's best supernatural security system, which in turn made the club an ideal place to hide. Esme was off connecting with Grandma—being considered respectable, she was the perfect person to fly under the Council's radar at this point. We would take a rest here until she came back with the latest intel. I'd like to say we were going to set up the ritual that would take us into Dualsing right away, but the truth was, I'd gone almost forty-eight hours without sleep and it was taking a toll. There was only so far a Blue Unicorn could take you, and I was on my last can.

When Esme had been kidnapped, I'd interrogated the Off-Blacks for information to find her. After the dust settled and one of the Greys' agents, Dan Pillar, was captured, I had a decision to make—did I turn the Off-Blacks over to the Council or release them?

It was Fir who convinced me to let them go, arguing that

the Council would've laughed and done the same anyway, as they never considered anyone not of vengeance blood to have anything worthwhile to say. Besides, he claimed, you never knew when you'd need someone like that on your side.

Like now.

I suspected Fir's original suggestion to live and let live didn't have much to do with the current scenario, though. In the course of helping me torment the three silly Evil-Lites, my half-brother had formed a weird rapport with them. Somehow, the catch-me-if-you-can attitude of the Off-Blacks was a perfect foil for my half-brother's flamboyant personality, and much to my annoyance, they had become fast friends.

So yes, I had figured out a way around the club's security system. But no, that wasn't how we were going to roll tonight. Instead of sneaking around, we were *welcomed* in by the bouncers, through the front door, thanks to Fir's VIP status.

The Bureaucracy was a three-story complex. The bottom two floors of the building had the usual club fanfare: loud music, dim lighting, and patrons dressed in party clothes at least one size too small. There was also plenty of Blue Unicorn and regular human beer flowing around. The top floor, however, held a labyrinth of rooms, each of them an underground market of a different sort, trading in all things legal and not entirely legal, from spell ingredients, love potions, to magically enhanced "super-pets."

Talk about spell ingredients, this place was like a football-field-sized pantry for all our prepping needs. That textbook I took with me, *1001 Wild Herbs and How They Can Kick Start Your Vengeance Career*, actually had an old recipe for herbs that might help with the ritual. Why not, right?

The bouncers ushered us directly up to the top floor, much to the audible complaints of the people in the long line for the stairs. I guessed that was what they called VIP access. Once we got onto the landing, the loud music of the lower floors faded to an ambient level thanks to a built-in privacy spell. There was a small balcony right off the landing that overlooked the party below, with a wrap-around lounge sofa. Seated on the sofa were the three members of the Off-Blacks —Bonaventure the Third, Wistari, and Naracion. Surrounding them were half a dozen buxom brunettes in mini-skirts and fuck-me boots.

The three detangled themselves from their entourage of admiring females and pulled Fir into a group hug. All four of them squealed and giggled like little girls.

"Fir, how have you been, man?" Bonaventure the Third slapped my half-brother on the back none so gently.

"Bo, Wis, Na! So great to see you." Fir laughed.

I rolled my eyes. As I mentioned before, I did that a lot with this bunch, especially when the Off-Blacks were over at my parents' house for the Trickster Cup Playoffs or *Halo*. It was truly amazing that the three guys were totally able to get over the fact that the first time they set foot in that basement was when they were being tortured for information. Maybe the humans were onto something with that tidbit about goldfish memories.

"I read about what happened with that bank robber and the Nerf gun. Was that you who pulled the switcheroo?" Wistari asked.

"You know I never trick and tell." Fir was grinning from ear to ear, scratching his potbelly.

"Bullshit. You posted that Nerf gun on Instagram." Naracion grabbed his phone and proceeded to find the virtual proof.

Bonaventure the Third leaned closer to Fir and winked. "Next time, bro, give me a heads up so I can use it to prop up my Prediction of the Week, will ya?"

The men roared with laughter, but then Bonaventure the Third's eyes landed on me and the merriment on his face cooled by quite a few degrees. He cocked his head, taking in the rest of our little group and his frown deepened as his gaze lingered on one person, then another. "What the hell is this, man? You've brought enough vengeance demons here to form a siren's girl band. Friends don't take killjoys to friends' place of business."

Picking up on his disapproval, his fan girls—mostly succubi who dined on the excitement and sexual energies of this place—sneered at us with soft hisses.

"Don't worry. I might be a vengeance demon, but I'm a mercenary," Gregory explained.

"And I'm on hiatus," Serafina offered.

I jumped onto the I'm-a-different-kind-of-vengeance-demon wagon. "And I'm a—"

"Hybrid. We know *that*, Megan." Bonaventure the Third's lips thinned. "Are you here to arrest us again?"

"I would hardly call that first time an arrest," I argued. "It was just a little capture and torture. Come on, Fir was tormenting you, too, and you forgave him fast enough."

"Fir and I, we're the same kind of people." Bonaventure the Third folded his arms in front of him, a gesture immediately mirrored by his two sidekicks. "Whereas you bring us nothing but grief."

"Not true. This time I'm here to offer you something really fun and mutually beneficial. I swear."

The Off-Blacks didn't seem to be listening; they were too busy sniffing the air around them. Then three pairs of shrewd eyes homed in on the bookish Pedro, who looked so out of place in this house of loud music and dirty trading.

"Speaking of the same kind of people." Bonaventure the Third gave Pedro a wolfish grin. Pedro took an involuntary step back, and Gregory inserted himself in front of the kid, partially blocking him. "Why, hello there. Don't be shy. Aren't you just all kinds of interesting? You got a similar signature as

Fir, yet you're no trickster. You're a, well, I don't believe it! You're a changeling!"

"We need to talk. Privately. *Now*." I threw a look at the Off-Black's succubus girlfriends, who had now also started testing the air around Pedro. From the secret smiles tugging at their lips, it would seem that they, too, had come to the same conclusion as the three stooges.

Great. First Fir, then these guys and their girls. Looked like Sui-Ling's organization went about it the wrong way when they spent millennia trying to figure a way to detect the changelings—all they had to do was ask the darker creatures. Typical vengeance demon arrogance.

Every moment out in the open at this club, a place that catered to the aforementioned darker creatures, was an additional risk that more people would discover who Pedro was. An image of supernaturals fighting over Eldon on my parents' lawn came to mind. We needed to be in one of the back rooms, and it needed to happen yesterday.

"And why should we do that? What's so tempting about your offer?" Despite the dismissiveness he was trying to convey in his voice, the calculating look on Bonaventure the Third's face told me he was beginning to grasp the seriousness of the situation. Guys like him really kept up with the news, and by now he would've heard all about the public broadcast, whether or not it was supposed to be exclusive to vengeance demons or not. He would've known all about the alliance between the Council and their sworn enemy—the Greys. When your enemy gained a friend, that was bad news indeed.

"I'm giving you a chance to stick it to the man."

———

We were in a private back room, and the boys had gotten rid

of their female companions. It was a tight fit, but at least it was just as hard for the Off-Blacks to try anything funny as it was for us to defend against it.

"So let me get this straight." Bonaventure the Third did his best to pace along with his sidekicks, but kept knocking into one or both of them in the tight space. "You want us to hide you, help you rescue the current public enemy number one, then take him back home. And you want us to do all that at great personal risk to ourselves, with no profit whatsoever?"

"It's a steep bargain when you put it this way," I admitted. "But look on the bright side, you get a chance to say 'screw you' to the Greys. And you know what their endgame is. You know what bringing back the Absolute Good would mean."

A new world order with an unforgiving take on justice, and a drive for honesty at all cost. No more watered-down Blue Unicorns, fairy wand knock-offs, and women with magically enhanced bosoms. No more impure creatures, either.

"Yeah, but our own master will also have a shot at getting out, too," Wistari countered.

"Maybe we should take the chance, no?" Naracion puffed out his chest.

I narrowed my eyes at the Off-Blacks. I'd long suspected that despite all the big talk about striving to be as evil as they could possibly be, if the Absolute Evil ever knocked on their door, these boys might just pee in their pants. It was like the difference between saying you wanted a certain radical politician to win the election and having him actually come into power and start giving you a real dose of what his ideals truly meant.

"Alright, let's say for a moment that the Absolute Evil managed to escape as well. Hooray. Then your mighty master is going to go after the equally mighty Absolute Good. Two powers, evenly matched. Geez, it's going to be a war that'll get dragged out for centuries. They're probably going to have to take over this little club for their war effort. The first floor would make a nice field hospital. Second and third floors could be used for interrogation. How's that sound? What else have you got? Gold? Goblin-made silverware? Well, not anymore. It belongs to your master."

The Off-Blacks looked at each other and swallowed. It was clear that they preferred their little slice of capitalist paradise to remain a place of excitement, not pain. And to stay theirs. Who could blame them?

"What? No takers? Come on, guys. It's going to be so much fun it'll be criminal. You can either be annihilated by the Absolute Good, or be dragged into the ultimate fight between Good and Evil."

A long pause.

Bonaventure the Third said with as much dignity as he could muster, without actually admitting that I had a point, "We'll assist you in this venture of, as you called it, sticking it to the man."

✥ 20 ✥

GOODNIGHT OR GOOD MORNING

WE SETTLED in for the night, though it was actually already early morning, in the large attic of the Bureaucracy. We needed to rest before Esme got here. The Off-Blacks left and headed off to who-knew-where, hopefully not to betray us. I doubted it, but you never knew.

The last song before the club closing had finished playing, the mean drunk who had been cursing like a sailor in the alleyway below quieted, either from passing out or getting sober enough to move on. Everyone waved the standard sleepover charm and conjured a pillow and a blanket, making themselves comfortable on the floor.

Fir was surrounded by a good selection of flasks. Some borrowed from the Off-Blacks, filled with herbs and various ingredients for the ritual, and some straight from his own backpack for personal enjoyment. He took a swallow from a flask of Hell Fire Whisky, and was dead asleep before his head hit the pillow.

I noticed the forlorn look on Pedro's face as he hugged the blanket to himself, and wondered what was on his mind. Was it his first time away from home? Or was he upset that his parents might be worried sick? Out of fear of placing them in danger, we'd agreed not to contact them except to send them a short text saying he was staying at a friend's for a few days. Not very plausible given his less than active social life, but we really couldn't afford to tell them what was happening until it was over.

Gregory was more prepared than the rest of us. He opened a compartment attached to his belt that contained a magically miniaturized futon, a night table, a rug, and even a book. He found a corner, turning everything back to their regular size. He adjusted the futon into a half-sitting position, sat on it, and promptly opened the book to a marked chapter. I wasn't sure if I should be impressed by his preparedness, or wonder about a lifestyle that made it necessary. Mostly I just wanted to find a discreet way to peep at the title of his book. Was it *Of Vice and Men*, or something similar?

I figured after the almost-kiss we shared, I was justified to have a little curiosity.

Except ever since the aforementioned incident, I'd been avoiding looking directly at him. How could I possibly get the title of the book without looking straight at the person who was holding it?

I took a deep breath and decided to get on with it. I turned, cranked my neck, and looked.

It was *Baking with the Cake Boss*.

Seriously?

Gregory noticed my stare, lowered the book, and said defensively, "I try to stick to light reading right before bed. My mother's fortieth birthday is coming up. I want to surprise her."

So his mother had him when she was very young, a lot younger than his wealthy and powerful father. And Gregory loved her.

With a sweet tooth and being a regular viewer of cake-making TV shows, I found myself excited over the fact that Gregory could bake. I wondered if his cake would be theme-based, and if so, would it feature any motorized parts, and for fondant would he be using chocolate, my favorite...

Stop fantasizing about his baking, that would only lead to fantasizing about him feeding you cake pieces by hand, or being naked under an apron...

Hey, who's letting her imagination get ahead of her here? I thought you are supposed to be my rational side.

I forgot. Anyway, back to the script: we hate him, we hate him, repeat after me—

—oh, come on, you gotta admit, the guy's got a hell of a back story. Born in shame. Embarked on a shady career at an age when many were still children. Resourceful and smart. Even loves his mom and that group of mercenaries he considers family...

Now you're gushing. I'm so embarrassed for the both of us.

"Okay, everybody. I'm sleeping now," I called out in a voice that was just a little too loud and squeaky, and abruptly casted a spell of instant darkness around myself, not caring if Gregory wondered about my lack of response to his explanation. I just didn't trust myself to continue that conversation without drooling, and not just over the cakes.

My words were greeted with varying degrees of grunts, sighs or in Fir's case, a snore.

How I envied my half-brother.

I thought it would be hard to fall sleep, given the event-filled days, the state of the world, the act of roughing it on the floor, and thoughts about Gregory that my conscious mind refused to process. Yet sleep came easier than I thought. Well, maybe not deep sleep right away, but I was soon drifting in and out of that state halfway between dreamland and wakefulness.

Then the ground shook.

"What the heck!" Fir cursed, his collection of flasks

shaking and crashing into each other in a chorus of musical jingles, their contents spilling onto the floor and soaking his blanket. I wasn't sure if he was more outraged over being roused out of his sleep, getting his bedding wet, or the lost alcohol.

I was caught in that paralysis between awake and asleep, my body already relaxed but my mind still sharp. As I laid there while the world shook around me, I willed more adrenaline to pump into my bloodstream and get me going again, for my body to catch up to my brain. I really, really hated the feeling of helplessness while trapped inside my body. Seemed to have enough of that happening in the last year.

By the time I got up from the floor, the tremor had ceased.

Only to restart half a minute later.

By the time the Off-Blacks came into the room with Esme in tow, a third tremor had come and passed.

I kept trying to tell myself that the tremors had nothing to do with Eldon or the changelings or anything that was going on in our lives right now, but deep in my guts I knew they were somehow connected.

"Look what we've got here. Another vengeance demon," Bonaventure the Third announced, rolling his eyes.

"Hey, Esme," I greeted her.

"Megan." Esme glanced at the Off-Blacks and looked at me questioningly, her eyebrows raised. She must be puzzled by the company I'd chosen to keep. I would be, too, if I wasn't so desperate. Strange times made strange bedfellows, and nothing united people like a common threat. Besides, the Off-Blacks really weren't bad guys, despite their fascination with evil.

"Meet Bonaventure the Third, Wistari, and Naracion." I pointed at them. "They own this club and have agreed to hide us. So, what have you got for us?"

Esme bit her lip, her gaze strayed to the Off-Blacks again.

"It's okay," I assured her. "They're our friends. Kinda. So were you able to find Grandma?"

"Yes, but it's very bad news. In the Council meeting Grandma was basically outvoted in the matter regarding Eldon. Then a group of Council members called a vote on the alliance with the Greys out of the blue, and that got passed by majority, too. The public announcement is a result of that meeting." Esme shuddered. "I'd never seen Grandma so angry before."

I would imagine she must be. Gran had been in politics for decades, had built her own network of contacts and spies from the ground up. It took work to blindside someone like that, especially when as of yesterday the Greys were officially the enemy.

And now we were on the verge of war as a result.

"Where is she now?" I asked Esme.

"She's scrambling to rally her supporters. Quietly."

I'd never thought the words *scrambling* and *Grandma* would go together. It further drove home that we were on our own.

"What about these quakes? Do you know what caused them?" Gregory asked.

"I do. From what I can learn from Grandma, they are the side-effects," Esme sighed and continued, "of the Council trying to breach the inter-dimensional barrier into Dualsing with a very, very dull knife."

Serafina paled. "They broke Eldon?"

"No, and that's the problem." Esme reached over and laced her fingers with Serafina's in a show of support. "He refused to tell them anything, so the Council and the Greys gathered the best hags they had, and tried pushing through to the changeling plane using Eldon's body as a locating anchor. Without his consent."

"Well, good luck with that." Fir snorted. "Without a

changeling's active involvement or jewels like the Eye of Sebille, the passage wouldn't be fully formed even if a partial address could be pulled. It would be like trying to cut through a rubber tire with a plastic knife—lots of bouncy resistance that gets you nowhere."

"Is that what the tremors are all about?" Pedro asked.

"Half-formed passages are unstable, and they build up tension at the very core of the planes involved," Fir explained.

Horror dawned on Serafina's face. "These aren't just seismic activities we're experiencing. The Council is literally tearing the planes apart in the quest for vengeance."

"No, not for vengeance," I said softly. "For pride and power."

I turned to Fir. "So you're sure that they're not going anywhere with this plastic knife experiment?"

"I'm positive," Fir confirmed. "But the problem is not whether or not they could get through the barrier. If they keep up these small tremors for over a day or so, there'll be irrevocable damage to the vengeance plane on a structural level."

"Urgent as that is, we need to get a few hours of rest." I looked around me. Though everyone seemed genuinely eager to get on with our rescue plan, and every minute was painful for Eldon, there was no doubt that we were on our last leg. The mind might be willing, but our bodies had reached the limit. The jarring to wakefulness from that very first tremor simply put us on yet another roller-coaster ride. We had to rest if we were to bring our A game.

When the next tremor hit, I snapped my fingers, throwing a shield called the Bubble Boy around the attic. I'd occasionally use this spell to block out the sound of the alarm clock, and often it worked just a little too well. So hopefully it would help us get some real sleep.

Bonaventure the Third's eyes fell to the mess of broken

flasks around Fir. "We'll go get the ingredients replaced while you rest."

Luckily while the club might be closed, most of the black markets in this building never did.

The Off-Blacks left. Everyone settled back down into their makeshift beds.

Except Serafina.

That was my last thought as I closed my eyes, the last image I saw was of her standing by the window, staring into the breaking dawn.

————

I woke up about two hours later. I could've slept for much longer, dead to the world that I was, but instinct alerted me to danger. I forced my breathing to remain slow and even, my eyes shut but not too tightly, and sent out my senses.

Fir, Esme, Gregory, and Pedro were all deep asleep. Serafina was still by the window. There was a stillness in her spirit that felt unnatural, awake or not. I would make a bet that she was in some kind of trance. Two foreign energy signatures were present in the room, hovering just below the ceiling of the attic.

I slowly opened my eyes a little. I expected to see a pair of banshees, or fairies. Anything that could fly or float in midair.

There was no one.

Even with the heavy black-out curtains and the Bubble Boy shield blocking the early morning sunlight, the room wasn't so dark that I couldn't see anything if it was there.

I closed my eyes and put my faith in my senses again. There they were, unmistakable, two distinct cores of power looming over me and my friends.

Well, that explained why I never heard anyone barging in, or the blaring of the Off-Blacks' many alarms. Our uninvited guests were substance-less. Or at least they could take on that form.

"You can open your eyes again, dearie," a voice, cold as the last blast of winter, said. "We knew the moment you were awake."

I sat up slowly and looked at the spot where my mind's eye told me two supernaturals were. I made out the forms of two women as they descended to the floor. They appeared to be dressed in white. I think. I couldn't be sure. Their images flickered, they kept appearing and disappearing from view until I realized the best way to look at them was through my peripheral vision.

I knew that the boogeyman and certain vengeful spirits could materialize and de-materialize at will, but I never heard of any supernaturals that seemed to exist slightly out of phase with the plane.

I glanced at my friends and kin. They were still sleeping. Enchanted to sleep, most likely. None of them were too shabby in the magical department, and I doubted I was the only one who had the alertness to *not* sleep through this.

"Who are you?" I asked the strangers. They were beautiful in an otherworldly way, all light blue skin and willowy. There was fluidity to their movement as they drifted toward me.

"We're drawn to plagues and sufferings, but we're no healers," the first one whispered against my ear, her voice sly and musical.

"We frequent trenches and battlefields, but we're no Valkyries." The second one circled behind me, blowing the hair at the back of my neck.

"Is this supposed to be a riddle? I hate to spoil your fun, but I got nada." I forced my galloping heart to calm down. I couldn't afford to show fear in front of these unknown entities. "You'll just have to spell it out for me."

The first one snarled as her formerly gracious manner

vanished. "You insolent child. How dare you speak to us this way. We are succubi."

"You don't look like any succubi I've ever seen." I crossed my arms. These women were statuesque, not curvy. Though the Off-Blacks' girlfriends were as haughty as they were fashionable, they were nevertheless affectionate to their targets. These two women had an infinite coldness in their core beings, as if they would not give a damn even if the world got blown to shit. Giggling, lively, earthy temptresses, they were not. "No succubus ever requires me to look indirectly at them in order to see them."

"Those so-called succubi you have encountered in the past are not a true representation of our race. They're just our handmaidens. We are their queens. I'm Pandora. And my sister is Hilda." Pandora gave me a regal tilt of her head.

Oh great, one was named after a mythical character who released all the evils out into the world, and the other, stemmed from the Norse word for *battle*. I was getting a good feeling about this already.

"Those girls work for you, huh? Oh, is that why you know to be here?" Probably the same reason they knew how to get around the Off-Blacks' sophisticated security system. Even my own Bubble Boy shield had now been neutralized. There was nothing like an inside job. Damn, I didn't count on this when I picked this place to hide.

"We're true succubi. We feed off the tragedies and miseries of the world. All the worlds." Hilda glided to the motionless Serafina and gently brushed a strand of hair away from her face. Then she turned Serafina around like a statue so I could get a good look at her. My friend's face was frozen in an eternal stare, her body as rigid as a rock.

"What have you done to her?" I grit my teeth.

"Poor little dear. So trapped inside her own body." Pandora smiled mirthlessly at me. "Now that you know what we are, you must understand why we cannot allow you to prevent this war that the Concord Council is so hell-bent on. The conflict would provide us delicious energies for years to come. Pain and suffering speaks to us, sorrows call to us like a sexy dessert."

It was one thing to have a race of creature that fed on a few lustful vibes here and there—one might even call it healthy, like the grazing of an overgrown pasture or something—but to exist entirely to make a meal of other peoples' unhappiness? To use their grief and sorrow like a food bank? Wow. Just. Wow.

And here I was, thinking we needed to keep an eye out for supernaturals who might be after Eldon for vengeance. This was infinitely worse.

And if I wasn't even taught about the existence of these succubus queens in school, then how was I supposed to fight them?

❧ 21 ❧

IN SERAFINA'S SHOES: LOVE

I COULD HEAR the confrontation between the succubus queens and Megan, but try as I might, I couldn't move my body to take a stand by my friend's side.

I couldn't even make use of my own vocal cords, let alone a limb.

When I'd first experienced the numbness, I'd thought it was due to extreme exhaustion. By then everyone around me had dozed off. I was the only one who couldn't allow herself proper rest. Proper rest I needed for the upcoming fight.

But then I realized that I wasn't just exhausted, I was immobilized. I was fully conscious but trapped. Megan once talked about how her childhood sleep paralysis turned out to be a real attack by the Greys. I had never experienced sleep paralysis, real or presumed, but my predicament fit Megan's description.

I felt Hilda's icy fingers on my cheek, and through the sisters' conversation with Megan, learned the true purpose of their visit.

I tried to sort through all the knowledge that my tutors had given me about the various supernaturals, but came up blank regarding the royal succubi our intruders claimed to be. It didn't sound like Megan knew a lot about them, either.

Pandora was boasting about sexy desserts of pain and sorrow when Megan chimed in. My friend could speak, though I had a feeling it was only because the succubi had allowed it. In fact, I think Megan and I were conscious, unlike the rest of our friends, due to the same reason. Perhaps the royals enjoyed toying with us.

"What are you going to do to us?" Megan asked softly. Her voice was calm, but I knew inside she must be angry and afraid.

"We won't kill you, if that's what you're asking. We'll keep all of you in stasis like your friends here. You'll be able to see and hear everything as the world descends into chaos around you. But you won't be able to do anything about it." Hilda grinned. "This way we get to feed on your increasing angst and helplessness, while keeping you out of the game entirely. It's quite ingenious, if I must say so."

"By the time you're released from our spell, it's going to be a brave new world," Pandora said.

"And then you'll be killed," Hilda said.

"But not by us," Pandora clarified. "The Absolute Good will do the job nicely."

"Wait, you know about the Absolute Good?" Megan's eyes widened.

"We're in the business of pulling energy from supernaturals, dear. And along with their essence we get their secrets as well. Call it an occupational hazard," Hilda said smugly.

"You're aware of the Absolute Good and their agenda, yet you're still helping to usher them in? Don't you realize you're going to be persecuted as well? I don't see them looking kindly upon some sucker of lust and life energy." Megan must be running out of options if she was trying to reason with ones who would not be reasoned with.

"We'll go into hiding. By then we would've saved up enough energy to last a few lifetimes over, for both consumption and to ensure our disappearances. We'll die of old age before the Absolute Good can find us. So what do we care if the world goes to hell?" Pandora shrugged.

"So said the major polluters about climate change," Megan spat.

My heart sank. Megan, for all her disdain for politics, was always smart about not closing any door for the sake of survival. She wouldn't be so openly defiant to the queens if there was still something to be gained with keeping good manners. Her choice of words could only mean that all hope was lost.

I couldn't be kept in suspension. I couldn't. Eldon needed me. My friends needed me.

Pandora and Hilda waved a spell over Megan as she tried a desperate charge toward them, immobilizing her. Then they started working on an enchantment for our entire group.

To my surprise, magically enslaving everyone seemed to be taking a lot longer than I thought it would. Then I realized that was because the succubus queens were trying to accomplish a second goal at the same time—synching and knitting everyone's varied power signatures together in a manner similar to plating a meal at a buffet restaurant.

A little meat and vegetables here. A little carb there.

A little trickster and changeling magic here. A little vengeance demon power there.

True to the succubus queens' claim, we were to become their energy popcorn as they stood and watched the world burn.

As the people that I cared about across all the planes—Eldon, Alina, Trust—suffered and died.

Only to have my friends in this room eventually meeting the same fate.

Not on my life.

A massive tremor shook the building. The queens didn't react to it, though it was at least three times as strong as the others before it. And it was continuous, not sporadic. It was as if they were wrapped in another Bubble Boy spell and I wasn't.

Maybe it wasn't the ground, but me who was trembling. My teeth rattled and I was shaken to my very bone, yet the pictures hanging on the wall remained still. The vase on the side table was not in danger of shattering.

"It isn't you who's shaking, nor is it the ground of the vengeance plane. What you're experiencing, Lady Serafina, is the ripple effect of the quakes originating from Dualsing," a grave voice I recognized all too well said. A miniature dragon the size of a large hound came into my view. He was Trust, Eldon's pet dragon and secret royal advisor.

I'd seen two radically different versions of Trust when I was at Dualsing. There was the disguise he'd shown to the rest of the plane, with cataract-clouded eyes and scales discolored from old age and lack of polishing. Then there was the real self that he'd only allowed Eldon to see all those years— eyes clear and full of intelligence, gleaming scales, surrounded by a light shimmer of gold.

The Trust I saw now was somewhere in between, with his pearly scales losing quite a bit of their luster. Nowhere near beaten, but not in his full glory, either.

The last I heard of his fate was that he was captured by Queen Deirdre, Eldon's sister.

"Trust, how did you get here?" I found that I could not only speak, but move my body freely now. "And where *is* here?"

I assumed I was still physically at the club's attic, though I wasn't entirely sure. I could see the succubus queens and my friends in front of me, but ever since Trust appeared the scene had a grayed, foggy quality to it, much like how Megan described her experience in the Shadow World.

"Nowhere. And everywhere. The partially-formed passage into Dualsing is changing the rules of magic and thinning the veil between planes. Our spirits are together at a place that is of neither plane."

No wonder Megan and the succubus queens didn't notice Trust, just as they didn't notice the tremors. We were not technically there with them.

"So you're saying that the tremors I'm feeling right now are an echo of the quakes from Dualsing, and not from the vengeance plane itself?"

Trust nodded. "The partially-formed passage is unnatural, and the vengeance plane is not the only one paying for it. The quakes are much, much worse in Dualsing. After all, we're the one being invaded. A lot of structures have collapsed. A section of the Mirage Palace is in ruin. That's how I was able to escape from my prison."

I bit down a sob. Dualsing had been my home for most of my life. The Mirage Palace might be magnificent, but most royal subjects on the plane lived in mud huts, and such dwellings were no match for the quakes. And Alina...was she alright? I had a horrifying image of the young pixie getting her wings crushed by flying debris, injured and trapped in a small crack in the ruins somewhere.

My race, my *real* race, was responsible for this.

"It's not your fault." Trust seemed to have read my mind and his voice was a sea of comfort I didn't deserve. "Things are happening as it was foretold. Just as Queen Deirdre was foretold. The true ruler of the changelings must be allowed to rise to the challenge and lead us out of the rubble of the past."

"Trust," I gasped. "My friends and I are trying to get Eldon back to Dualsing. But if his sister is destined to lead the people out of this crisis and beyond, then we would be sentencing him to certain death."

"The crown is not meant to be his." Trust bowed his head. "I deeply regret misleading him all those years, encouraging him to believe he *could* win the crown. I did it because Queen Deirdre was foretold to be one of the most terrifying queens in Dualsingian history, and I was desperate to find a way out for my people. I can see now that you cannot fight destiny. Prince Eldon knows that now. I already went to him. I'll hold the connection so you can talk to him. There's something he must say to you. I'll ensure your privacy, even from me."

Trust faded to near-transparency while Eldon materialized. Like before, he projected an image of himself in an immaculate outfit fit for the royal court. I could only imagine how he looked in reality.

"Finny," he said.

I didn't have the heart to correct his use of my old name, not right now, so I simply nodded.

We stared at each other for a long while. I opened my mouth, then closed it again. What could I say to him that didn't sound hollow and superficial? To ask him if he was fine, when he was clearly not? To assure him that my friends and I were coming to rescue him, when we'd been hitting one road-block after another?

"I know." With the two words Eldon reminded me that we did, after all, grow up together, and words weren't necessary.

I swallowed. "Trust said you have something to say to me? What is it?"

Eldon took a deep breath to steel himself, his eyes intense and determined. "Listen to me. Find a way into Dualsing. Block the half-formed passage from that side. Fight energy with energy and neutralize the tremors. Find Trust and Alina when you get there. The Molten Amber will help, too, because they can sense my will in you. Make a deal with Deirdre if you have to. She can't be trusted, but she'll want to survive this so she'll cooperate."

"Wait. What?" My head was spinning, and it had nothing to do with the tremors. The Eldon I knew craved power at all costs. Why would he suggest I make an alliance with his sister?

Something on my face must've betrayed my disbelief. Eldon's face twisted into a sad smile. "Is it really that hard for you to believe that I want to do the right thing this time around?"

"I...I..." I wished I was a better liar. Truth was, I didn't know what to make of his plan. "What about you? How can I go to Dualsing and save you at the same time?"

"You can't. You have to leave me to my fate." Eldon took both my hands in his. His palms radiated heat despite the fact that he was formless. "Would you believe me if I tell you that when I found out about the attack on Dualsing, I realized that I love my people more than I love the crown? They're suffering, Finny. I could feel their fear and panic. Trust just told me the real prophecy, and I'm going to respect it. If being led by Deirdre is what it takes for the Dualsingians to survive and thrive, then I won't stand in the way. I'm going to be the best king I could be by not trying to rule at all."

Just when I thought I had Eldon all figured out, he surprised me. Pride swelled within me. "You're doing right by your people. You *are* a great king, Eldon."

"Thank you." He smiled ruefully. "I've wanted you to say those words to me for years, but I never dreamt it would be under these circumstances."

Tears ran down my cheeks. I tasted salt on my lips and bit into them. I'd given up on what was supposed to be real and what wasn't in this spiritual realm. There were tears and pride in my soul, and therefore I could taste them on my lips.

"Don't cry, love," Eldon said softly. Then he cocked his head, as if listening to something. "Another tremor is coming to the vengeance plane. Ride it. Break out of your stasis. Go to Dualsing."

Eldon stepped away from me and with a nod to the near-transparent Trust, both winked out of sight.

For a long moment, all was quiet.

I looked around the attic. The succubus queens were almost done "packaging" me and my friends into a perfect combo of harmonized, ready-made energy meal, adding layers of shields over us as humans would put plastic wrap over leftovers.

The tremors Eldon predicted hadn't come to the vengeance plane yet, but the strength of the continuous ones from Dualsing was strong within me, reminding me of the duties he had entrusted me with, and the enemies in the attic who threatened my ability to fulfill them.

When the tremor finally hit the vengeance plane, I reached for it. Then I combined it with its more powerful counterpart on the Dualsingian side. I sent the amplified burst of vibration toward the succubus queens, breaking the trance they had cast and knocking them off their feet.

❧ 22 ❧

A PLACE MOST SAFE

I COULD DO nothing except remain on my spot as the two damn parasites waved one layer of ensnarement after another over us.

Suddenly, strong magic burst from Serafina's direction, lifting the succubi up and then crashing them onto the floor as if they were rag dolls. Before they even landed on the ground I felt their hold on me loosen. My body, which was in the middle of charging toward my enemies when it had been frozen, tried to finish the last command my brain had programmed it to do.

So that was how my arms and legs drove me into a dead run, smacking my face right onto the ground with my wings poking out from the back.

And I wasn't the only one experiencing an awkward thawing. All around me, my friends were struggling to regain their footing while gearing up for a fight.

The vengeance power of Esme and Gregory, and the trickster power of Fir filled the charged air, weaving in with the changeling power of Pedro. Thanks to the succubi's expert braiding of the different types of magic, my friends could now turn the power combo against them.

The succubi liked to feed on energy, huh? It was time for a little binge eating.

The combined power hit them like a sledge hammer, and the succubus queens cried out and withered on the floor.

Abruptly, all their movement halted, and they collapsed entirely, like puppets with their strings pulled out.

For a moment none of us moved, afraid that it was just a ruse to get our guards down. But after a few minutes, we approached the queens tentatively.

Wisps of cobweb began to cover their bodies. Their eyes were closed, faces peaceful as if in a slumber.

Like sleeping beauties, if sleeping beauties were blue-skinned parasites.

Before our eyes the cobwebs formed two hard-shell cocoons and we couldn't see their faces anymore.

"Are they dead?" Fir asked.

Gregory touched one of the cocoons with the toe of his shoe lightly, and it wobbled like a tipped-over, supersized Russian doll.

"No." There was regret in his voice. "Looks like the energy overdose pushed them into some kind of hibernation."

"Fitting, given the snakes they are." I watched a nature documentary once. There was this ginormous snake that swallowed an entire calf and then just lay there and couldn't move for weeks. Talk about the ultimate post-food coma.

Hopefully the succubus queens stayed short-circuited for a long time.

With a bang to the door, the Off-Blacks rushed in.

"What the heck is going on?" they exclaimed. "There was a barrier around the attic and we couldn't break through."

Fir proceeded to tell them what happened, concluding with, "Dudes, you gotta find less treacherous girlfriends."

"You saw how hot they were," Bonaventure the Third protested. "How would I know they were reporting the going-ons to a bunch of murderous hags?"

A debate sparked about what to do with the pair of dormant succubi. Fir and the Off-Blacks gleefully argued for merciless torment. Pedro and Esme chimed in, calling for civilized treatment to our prisoners. Gregory supported Fir and the Off-Blacks, but believed the goal of torture should be to obtain sellable information. Given the *occupational hazard*, as Hilda had called it, of their feeding habit, Gregory might be onto something there.

Ever the businessman.

As a group we decided to leave the decision until after we dealt with more pressing issues. The cocoons were miniaturized and placed into Gregory's secret compartment along with his mobile living room.

In a way I was glad of the debate because it gave Serafina the time she needed to compose herself. When she was ready, she told us what she'd experienced. What Trust and Eldon had told her.

Despite Eldon's instructions, there was no way we would just let him rot with the Greys. There might just be enough of us to handle the new complications.

The good guys gotta try, right?

———

"So, let me get this straight. Again." Bonaventure the Third paced back and forth across the attic floor. "Your original plan was to open the passage to Dualsing and return the changeling prince. Then the mission was extended to rescuing the kidnapped kids as well—which we, the Off-Blacks, will see no profits for. And now, we're *not* returning the prince, but we're still rescuing the kids, and on top of that we're going to sucker-block the Council's half-formed passage from the other side. And oh, we'll try to save the prince anyway, even though he ain't returning home ever again. Did I get that right?"

I winced. "Yeah, it sounds a little finicky when you put it that way."

"Thought so."

I remembered the conversation I had with Mel the Oracle not so long ago.

"And just how am I supposed to boost Eldon's tolerance?"

"You'll know when the time comes. I can assure you, you can do it."

When what time came? Turned out Eldon wouldn't be needing any boosting, because he wasn't going back to Duals-ing, after all.

Was it because Mel wasn't that all knowing, or that what he saw was only choices and possibilities, but not absolutes?

Who knew?

As to what Serafina said of Trust's prophecy? Well, that was a whole lot of nothing. So it sounded like Eldon's sister and her people would survive at the end of the day, but that didn't mean the Council's campaign wouldn't end badly for the very people who launched it. In fact, in manga, there were always tons of fists flying madly as the target of a conflict clawed his or her way out of the battle dust. I wouldn't be surprised if that would be what happened with Eldon's sister, the flying fists being the Council beating itself.

––––––

With the Bureaucracy compromised, we needed a new base

of operations. Somewhere unexpected, safe, and able to hide Pedro's increasingly strong changeling signature.

Before changeling children were placed with their hosts, their bodies were programmed to emit energy signatures that mimicked whichever race they were assigned to. The magic was set on an unconscious level, but now that Pedro was aware of who he really was, that safeguard was deteriorating. It was as if his body figured out there was no need to exert the effort to hide anymore. Since we met him, his energy signature had become more fragmented—with the top note of vengeance demon and the undercurrent of changeling. Anyone who took the time to examine it would discover that the upper layer was merely an illusion.

So our new digs had to be able to conceal that secret, on top of being so off the radar that we could perform the passage-opening ritual in peace. I ran out of ideas, but Fir said he had the perfect place. So we packed up everything, including the new herbs that the Off-Blacks prepared, and followed him.

"You've got to be kidding me, right?" My jaw sagged as we squeezed ourselves out of my parents' birdbath. We stepped into the late morning sun, the neighborhood waking up around us. With all that had happened, we were behind schedule.

"Don't worry, Miss Neringa is asleep. She's still recovering from the excitement of all the happenings, according to her tweets. Also, I have a pre-built concealment from the birdbath right into the house. How do you think I've been able to go to so many drinking parties and never get caught?"

I waited until we all filed down to the basement, adding extra precautions to the house until it felt like we were wrapped under a zillion layers of protection, before rounding on my half-brother. "Why are we coming back here? This is the dumbest idea ever. Have you forgotten there was a freaking mob at our doorstep less than forty-eight hours ago? Lynch. Mob. At. Our. Doorstep."

Fir shrugged. "Precisely. They've already been here. It's the last place they'll look now."

"But once they start looking, *really* looking, even the strongest protection won't prevent them from smelling Pedro."

"Yeah, they'll smell him and assume that it's the lingering changeling scent from Eldon. *Think*, Meg, it's so dumb, it's perfect."

"Okay, I'll give you that." I thought there must be something depressingly symbolic about going back to mommy and daddy's basement. Again. But desperate times and all.

———

Everyone got settled into one seat or another in the messy basement. It was kinda like musical chairs with an assortment of mismatched furniture—love seats, futons, and even video game chairs that looked like driver seats ripped out of a car. Gregory stole a sofa seat from Fir, earning him a dirty glare, and gestured to Pedro to sit on it. He patted Pedro on the back before hunting for a seat of his own. Pedro gave Gregory a grateful smile.

They had developed quite a rapport, just like two people who were new-found cousins would, despite the fact that Gregory was illegitimate and Pedro was a fake vengeance demon.

I headed toward Pedro with Serafina mirroring my action from the other side of the room. We both noticed how deeply troubled the kid looked when he thought no one was looking, and had the same notion to comfort him.

"You're doing okay?" I asked him.

"Yeah, I guess." He avoided my eyes.

"Don't worry. Your part is easy breezy. Just help us open the passage to Dualsing and wait around until we come back. Then afterward we intend to keep our promise about helping you stay on the vengeance plane."

"No, it's not that." Pedro hesitated. Then he seemed to decide on something. "Listen, can I come along?"

"What?" I nearly shouted. Gregory gave me a questioning look and I pulled Pedro closer.

"What the heck are you talking about?" I hissed. "You know what's waiting for us there? *I* don't even know what's waiting for us there."

"I can help," Pedro insisted. "I'm sure of it. My body is designed to mask my own energy signature. I think I could extend that to help make everyone else's untraceable."

"But, *why?* Why would you want to go there?" I puzzled. "You told me you want no part of that plane."

"Look"—Pedro's eyes were pleading—"a part of me really, really wants to see Dualsing. Just once. It's where I was born, and I'll never get another chance ever again. Please."

Now that he put it that way...

Serafina and I glanced at each other. Hades knew we understood the need to learn about one's origin. The poor kid was neck deep in a conflict that just days ago he wouldn't even have known he had to choose a side for. How could I blame him for being curious?

"Alright, but you have to promise you'll stick close to the group." I forced him to meet my eyes, and this time, he did.

"I will."

———

"Alright." I got everyone's attention. "We're going to divide ourselves into two groups. Esme, Fir, the Off-Blacks and me, is one. Our mission is to infiltrate the Council headquarters and rescue Eldon."

"We call the place The Tree. It's on the vengeance plane. I can get us in." Esme sat up straighter. "They're holding the prince somewhere in there. Wherever he is, that's where they'll be trying to get the passage fully opened."

With a name like The Tree, an image of some kind of sky-reaching elven dwelling came to mind. But it was actually underground, so the proper name should really have been the Root. It was just sheer dumb luck that the part-time job Esme took to pay for her masters and recent vacation was located at the Tree. It wasn't entirely surprising, given her excellent vengeance track record, high grade point average, and respectable family name. The job was administrative rather than fieldwork, but it was a stepping stone to take on a more political role in vengeance society.

Speaking of which.

"You sure you want to get us in?" I asked Esme softly, trying to convey the risk I knew she was taking.

"Yes," she said just as softly, meeting my eyes.

I nodded. It was her choice.

"The second group," I coughed and continued, "is made up of Gregory, Serafina, and Pedro. Their job is to go into Dualsing, gather the kidnapped children, and get them out of there. Then Serafina will neutralize the half-formed passage on that end."

"Sounds like a lot of work with too few people involved," Fir muttered, doing the math. "You have what, six people on team one and three people on team two? Why aren't there more people on the second team?"

"Two reasons. One, team one must be in position to take Eldon by the time Serafina is ready to close out the passage. The minute she starts they're going to swarm around Eldon to find out what's happening. But if we take Eldon too soon then they'll know something's wrong anyway. So timing is crucial. Hence more man-power to make sure it happens according to plan. Besides, it's not just about the rescue, we're also taking away the Council and the Greys' only means to form another new passage."

"What's the second reason?" Bonaventure the Third demanded. He and his two sidekicks seemed none too happy that they weren't assigned to the Dualsing trip, and in a way I could understand. Like the tricksters, the Off-Blacks had something in common with the changelings—deceit and the art of illusion. It was natural they would want to check out Dualsing, which was exactly the reason why it wasn't a good idea.

"It's a *stealth* mission," I emphasized. "It works better in smaller numbers. Serafina has lived there most of her life. Pedro is a changeling and can give off the right magical vibe while masking the wrong ones. And thanks to his occupation, Gregory has more sneakiness than even a trickster. I don't need more people drawing unnecessary attention to the group."

"How do we know when Serafina begins reversing the passage on that side, without us being able to communicate?" Esme asked.

"You'll feel it," Serafina said quietly. "The vibration being imposed on Dualsing is going to start bouncing right back to the vengeance plane."

I glanced at Serafina's face. I expected to see worry and nervousness there, but instead, there was a calm determination radiating from her. It must be killing her that her skills were required at the Dualsing leg of the mission, and she couldn't be on the team that was coming for Eldon. But there was also an unmistakable glow about her that even the present situation couldn't dim. It was the glow of someone in love.

And the glow of someone who had finally allowed herself the luxury of truly loving back.

————

"Sneakiness." Gregory came to me after the meeting and repeated my earlier words. "I'm chosen for Dualsing because I have more *sneakiness*."

Everyone was busy doing their own preparation and didn't pay us any heed. We were more or less alone.

"Sneakiness. Resourcefulness. Whatever. Just fill in the blank to whichever description you like more." I shrugged. I wasn't about to admit that there were more attractive qualities I found in him, like his dogged determination to make a life on his own terms, or his willingness to abide by the mercenary code even if it went against his bottom line.

"You're aware you're sending me on a mission with no one to keep me in check except a gentle girl and a young kid. Are you sure I can be trusted?" he murmured.

"Are you sure Serafina is a gentle girl?" I raised my eyebrow at him. "She seems to be on a tear."

"Nevertheless, she's new to this game. She's no match for me in, um, sneakiness. Neither is Pedro."

It was true. By allowing him to retrieve those children and return them to their families as I'd promised him, I was trusting him with a lot. He could screw us over twelve ways to Sunday, such as making a more profitable arrangement with the changelings and even throwing in Pedro to sweeten the deal.

But it was on the latter point that I was confident Gregory would come through.

I tilted my head. "You think I didn't notice you quietly boosting the kid's energy every time you gave him an encouraging pat on the back? The kid has never been trained to be on the field. He never learned how to conserve or focus his energy. He should have been dead on his feet by now, given the succubus attack and sheer exhaustion, but he isn't thanks to you. You like the kid. You wouldn't try anything funny with him at risk."

Or with the other children's lives at risk, actually. Just like with Candy, he had a soft spot for lost kids because he'd been one himself. Gregory might be many things, but my gut was telling me he wouldn't jeopardize this mission.

He smiled ruefully, then stepped closer, his eyes full of challenge of another kind. "What about in general? Do you also believe I wouldn't try anything, er, *funny*?"

With him right in my personal space and our faces inches from each other, memory of our near-kiss flared in my mind. I knew exactly what he meant by *funny*.

"We'll figure it out after all this is over." I took a step back. "There's always a chance we won't survive."

He chuckled. "Such an optimist."

23

THE TREE

THE TREE WAS an underground facility that used an ancient tree's trunk as an access point on the ground level. It was a ten thousand year old great basin bristlecone pine located in the White Mountains of California. Members of one of the witches' unions called the Anorites Coven had stood guard since the very beginning days of the Council. It was a tradition very much like the human Swiss Guards handling security for the Vatican.

Esme, Fir, the Off-Blacks, and I teleported to the valley where the Tree was located; we landed about a mile out and prepared to walk to the entrance. The Tree was equipped with the expected high-security perimeters for headquarters and teleporting within them was impossible.

Before crossing the magical boundary, Fir took out a cream lace parasol and gestured for me to take it. It was a beautiful piece of embroidery with intricate patterns, and the early afternoon sun filtered through its various loops and openings.

The parasol was strangely fitting to the woodland we were passing through, but not really appropriate for carrying into a vengeance headquarters. But I'd learned to trust Fir's methods, so I took the parasol. Then he gestured for me to pass it to Esme, which I did.

Esme held the parasol and frowned. "What is this for?"

"I mean, it's very steampunk and everything," I said. "But we need to get through the safeguard, not go to ComicCon."

"This baby is perception altering," Fir explained. "As long as we physically touch the parasol once then stay within a few feet of it, we're covered. When the witch who monitors the entry looks through her synch mirror, all she'll see is Esme."

"She'll see me holding *this*?" Esme sent the parasol spinning slightly. "Wouldn't it look suspicious?"

"They'll just see you alone. No parasol. No me. No Megan." Fir reassured her, "I've been getting my inspiration from human myths and legends all over the world. Figured there might be some truth behind them. In the grand scheme of things, humans dismissing magic is a pretty recent occurrence. There's an old Asian myth involving ghosts being stuck in certain locations, but able to travel to other places if a consenting mortal is willing to carry the umbrella it's hiding under. I tweaked the concept a bit to make it more demon friendly."

"But what if they don't use the synch mirror? What if they're into camera surveillance?" I asked.

"These are traditional die-hards." Fir winked. "Do you really think the Council would've allowed them to use anything from the last century?"

He had a point.

I looked around for the Off-Blacks, but they were already invisible, with not a stray vibe of elf, giant, or anything else in the surrounding area. If I didn't know they were around, I wouldn't think anything was out of place at all. I made a mental note to look into their camouflage techniques.

It felt like forever before we arrived at the clearing where the great basin bristlecone pine stood. Esme tapped three times on the trunk, and a door opened, revealing an elevator made entirely of wood. Following Esme's lead, we stepped into the chamber. The door closed and down we went.

The interior of the elevator was smooth and free of railings, leaving me with nothing to grab onto as we reached near free fall. A scream stuck in my throat. I held it tight, fearing that the chamber was being monitored. I should've asked Fir if the parasol altered audio perception as well.

I tried to think of something to distract myself. There were now six people in the tiny room, yet I didn't feel any of the Off-Blacks bumping into me. If they were here—and I assumed they were—how the heck did they manage to mask not only their visual presence but also their physical? Some sort of shrinking spell? Or space manipulation?

The descent decelerated as suddenly as it had started. The door opened, and Esme stepped out into a marbled lobby with a lone witch at the reception desk. Esme flashed the girl her employee identification card. "Hello, Sapphira."

"Hello, Esmeralda." Sapphira smiled, addressing my half-sister by the long form of her name in a show of vengeance formality. "Coming in early to prepare for Undersecretary Regnum's town hall this evening?"

"Yeah. Just a few things."

"Have a good day."

"You, too."

We passed through the lobby and into a passage to the left. We took another to the right, walking until we arrived at a central hub that was connected to a large network of tunnels. Esme chose one and walked in, then turned left, then another two rights, her sense of direction like a homing pigeon. It felt almost like we were in some kind of ant colony, with twists and turns every few feet, and doors appearing at random, likely leading to ever more tunnels. I was so glad to have activated this new trickster app that Fir just designed, the last bugs shook out thanks to him talking it through with Candy when we were at Mel's. It automatically tracked the places we'd passed through and would create a map for the return trip. I supposed such an app would be invaluable if a trickery ever went wrong and a trickster had to make a hasty getaway.

We passed vengeance demons here and there. Sometimes on their own and sometimes traveling in groups. Esme politely greeted all of them, and not once did anyone sense something was off with her.

"We can talk freely here," Esme said, stopping in a deserted tunnel and touching the smooth wall next to her. "Now that we're in the actual network itself, these walls are embedded with Molten Amber. They absorb sound so that the words spoken in one section of the tunnel can't be heard in the one before or after it. It's an effective way to keep the areas insulated from each other."

"I remember Serafina mentioned the Dualsing palace having the same stones within its walls, but it sounded like those on that side did nothing but light the way." I squinted at the wall, which looked like any other boring, cement wall.

"That's because those Molten Amber were probably forced to work there, rather than being invited to work like they do here. Illuminating is just the most basic thing these hidden gems can do. They could absorb sounds, cleanse the spirit, wipe out negative vibes, and they never, ever reveal your secret, not even to the Council. We are completely safe talking here."

"Well, it's a cool idea not to have any off-the-book political chats monitored and recorded, but the Council are control freaks. Why would they choose to trust something they can't fully control?"

"It's tradition. What can't be controlled by them also couldn't be controlled by others."

"No, it's arrogance."

"It's creepy, that's what it is. I can feel all my evilness being drained away," Bonaventure the Third complained as the Off-Blacks materialized before us. The materialization was in two stages, visual and then a return to true form. They were briefly visible in their morph shapes. I caught a glimpse of them before the morph and saw that the self-proclaimed evil villains were disguising themselves as cute little cartoony purple bats. No wonder they didn't bump me in the elevator.

I wasn't about to tell the Off-Blacks that they were probably more irritating than evil. After all, we were on the same mission together, cute purple bats and all. So I turned my attention to Esme. "So, Undersecretary Regnum, huh? You didn't tell me you're working for her."

"It's supposed to be confidential." Esme blushed. Realization dawned on me why she chose to keep that a secret. As an Aequitas who *didn't* have a trickster side, Esme had vengeance opportunities thrown at her that I never would. She was trying to spare my feelings. And up to a few days ago, I would have actually cared enough about my place in that society to be hurt.

"How far are we to the Pond?" I changed the subject.

The Pond was the entry to the restricted area where they were holding Eldon. That was also as far as Esme's clearance could take her. We didn't know the specifics of how to get past that because we didn't know what to expect. Even Grandma didn't know because the safeguards rotated randomly. Hopefully between the trickster and black marketeers among us, someone had the skill set, come what may.

"Not far at all. Just a couple more turns. That's why I stopped here."

"Tell us where to go, and you get out of here before the shit hits the fan."

Hurt and confusion crowded Esme's eyes. "We agreed I'd come along."

"Two words, sister: Undersecretary Regnum."

"What about her? I don't get it." Esme frowned.

"It's not her. It's what working for her represents. You have a bright future in the vengeance society. I'm not going to ruin that for you. Besides"—I winked at her—"I might need a friend in high places one of these days."

"I'm not a friend. I'm your sister." Leave it to Esme to take everything so literally.

"I know. Please, I promise to call for you if something goes bad, okay?"

Esme looked at me for a long time. Finally she sighed. "I'll be on standby. Call me at the first sign of trouble."

Or the second. Or the third. Let's face it, I would try to not call her at all.

I transformed myself to look like one of the girls Esme had greeted on our way here. Then Esme handed me the parasol before heading back in the direction we came.

Esme's direction was accurate to a tee, and the Pond was actually, well, a real pond. Well, at least until it randomly switched to some other safeguard later. The tunnel widened then sloped downward to accommodate a body of water about the size of two full-length swimming pools. The water was murky and green and it was impossible to see to the bottom. On the far side of the Pond was a clearing, which led to two tunnels on each side of it.

A boat was moored on our side of the Pond, next to a small wooden dock. A lone figure waited for us there.

Sui-Ling.

The real one or the Grey's substitute, I had no idea.

She walked toward us, the nasty-looking sword swinging

from her hip as always. At least it wasn't unsheathed. But I was familiar enough with her skill to not let my guard down.

"Hello, Megan." Sui-Ling nodded at me, seeing through my glamor with no trouble at all. Then she gestured at the spot where Fir was, though he was supposed to be invisible due to the parasol in my hand. "And this is your trickster brother, I believe."

I warily lowered the parasol and allowed Fir to be visible again. There was no use pretending if Sui-Ling had already figured it out.

"How did you know?" Fir asked Sui-Ling ruefully. "I just invented this spell."

"No, you just *reinvented* it from an old Chinese legend recorded by a Victorian scholar. My grandmother told me the story when I was a child. So naturally I recognized all the signs."

"*Your* grandmother or *Sui-Ling*'s grandmother?" I asked, remembering how Sui-Ling's pretender was able to pick up both the original's personality and knowledge.

"Oh, I assure you, I *am* the real Sui-Ling." She took out the sword and unsheathed it. Fir and I jumped back in alarm, pulling our magic around us. But Sui-Ling simply grasped the sword's long handle and twisted, revealing a hidden compartment inside the handle, and picking a small tube out of many that were hidden there. I was reminded of those human screwdrivers that contained multiple removable tips for the everyday handyman.

The selected tube was some kind of mini aerosol can. She squeezed down on its button and moved the can around as if she was spraying Lysol into the air, and the Off-Blacks materialized and fell to the ground. The aerosol can must have contained fairy dust that neutralized concealment charms.

While Bonaventure the Third, Wistari, and Naracion scrambled off the floor, Sui-Ling neatly put the aerosol can back inside her sword handle. The can jingled as it slid back into its own slot. But that couldn't be right. I'd learned enough from *Weapons & Self-Defense 201* to know that the worth of a sword wasn't just based on the quality of the blade. The weight and density of the handle helped balance the swordsman's grip and increase maneuverability. I'd never heard of a handle that wasn't solid, unless—

"That sword is just for show, isn't it?" I asked her.

She grinned. "Of course."

"Why?" Fir asked as he helped the Off-Blacks off the ground.

"For distraction. When everyone is busy looking at the sword in the Asian chick's hand, that's when they're not looking at the gun in her *other* hand." Sui-Ling sheathed the sword and handed it to me, handle first. "Here. A message from Lady Aequitas to prove I'm the real Sui-Ling. She said she's looking into something and cannot come join you right away. Just open your senses while touching the sword. She said you'll understand once you do."

I gripped the handle. Immediately, in my mind's eye a short, three-second scene replayed over and over of a fat bird's poop landing on ten-year-old Cousin Fred's head.

That was the shared, re-synched memory between Grandma and myself. It had a special meaning because it demonstrated that even back when she was pretending not to love me, she was watching out for me and punishing my bullies behind my back.

The memory was sweet but not politically significant. Not likely something that would have come out during an interrogation, in the very unlikely event that the Greys had managed to get the drop on Grandma. It was indeed a message from her.

That meant the girl in front of me was the real Sui-Ling.

"You're on our side?" I asked incredulously.

Sui-Ling held up a hand. "I wouldn't go as far as that. But the alliance with the Greys is causing great discord throughout the planes. It has to be stopped."

"And how does the Condor League feel about the whole thing?" Fir asked.

"My superiors are very...politically minded."

"In other words, they want to cover their asses. So how are you going to help us, you-who-are-technically-not-on-our-side?"

"I'm honor-bound to not assist you in the rescue." There was a silent message in Sui-Ling's eyes I couldn't quite decipher. "But I would turn a blind eye to your presence here."

And with that, she left the dock.

Fir and I looked at each other. He shrugged. "It went better than I thought."

"That's because you aren't the one who was un-transformed against your will and made to kiss the ground with your forehead. Crazy witch," Bonaventure the Third muttered.

Fir and I got into the small boat. With limited seating, it made more sense for the Off-Blacks to resume their invisible bat forms. Considering the Pond was the entry point to the restricted area, I was expecting the alarm to start blaring once my bum hit the seat, or a demand for passwords. Nope. Na-da.

It turned out, getting into the boat was easy, getting the boat to move was a different story.

I tried lifting the oars, but they wouldn't budge. The oars were just lying there, settled loosely into the oversized oarlocks on each side of the boat, but like magnets they simply refused to detach from their positions.

With the oars being so stubborn and our goal so close, I was tempted to jump into the water and swim across. A look over the side and I had changed my mind. Even up close, I still couldn't see all the way to the bottom. The surface rippled as if there were eel-like creatures swimming underneath it.

The waves had a hypnotic effect on me, making me focus my entire being on its ebbs and flows. I barely registered Fir's frantic poking at my arm.

Until High Judge Edbert Llewellyn Advocatus, Serafina's uncle, dropped himself on the seat opposite of me in the boat, causing it to wobble and me to stop thinking about what creatures might lie in the pond.

I winced, remembering that while both the Off-Blacks and Fir were currently invisible, I wasn't. I was too shocked to even leap up and fight.

Yet High Judge Advocatus looked right through me, staring straight ahead, his eyes blank. He settled into the seat, picked up the oars, and began to row us across the Pond. He didn't seem to have the same problem as I did with them.

As we came to the far edge of the Pond, the judge reset the oars and stood. Without a word, he stepped from the boat and onto the shore. He made his way down the tunnel on the left, and that was that.

After a few seconds, I dropped the parasol on the belly of the boat, my muscles felt like I'd run a marathon.

"That was...happily anti-climactic," Fir commented dryly, visible again.

"What happened?" I whispered, nerves still jangling.

Fir pursed his lips, then a smile slowly spread over his face. "When Sui-Ling said she'd turn a blind eye to our presence, she meant she'd help us by turning on the Blind Eye spell."

"The what?" Bonaventure the Third dropped down to the boat with his sidekicks. Naracion cried as he tripped over the parasol and almost felt into the water.

"The Blind Eye spell. It's an old trickster classic not a lot of people know how to do anymore. Her secret society must've retained the knowledge for it." There was awe in Fir's voice. "Long-lost tricksters spells. Creative weapons. General unpredictability. I like this girl."

I didn't like that gleam of interest in his eyes.

"Seriously, like, *don't*," I warned him. "She's a vengeance demon who knows her way around a human gun. No. Crushing. On. The. Secret. Society. Vengeance. Chick. No. Matter. How. Helpful. She's. Been."

"Killjoy."

❧ 24 ❧

IN SERAFINA'S SHOES: HEIR

AFTER MEGAN, Esme, Fir, and the Off-Blacks left for the Council headquarters, I sat cross-legged on Megan's parents' basement floor and gestured for Pedro to do the same. I scattered the herbs provided by the Off-Blacks in a spiral pattern and said, "We'll begin."

"I don't know what to do, Serafina," Pedro said with a tremor in his voice, his hands fidgeting.

"It'll come to you naturally," I promised.

I took a deep breath, remembering how my connection with Deirdre had brought my spirit to the vengeance world when I was still physically at Dualsing, making me an unwilling witness to Cousin Gabriella's murder. "Being this close to your return date you might have started sharing a bond with your counterpart already."

"I haven't been feeling any bonds," Pedro insisted. But his eyes shifted away just a bit too quickly.

"How about now?" Gregory had been standing at the back, but now he walked close to Pedro and offered his hand. Pedro took it, then his eyes widened.

"What's happening?" I looked from Gregory to Pedro.

Gregory had an unreadable expression on his face, while Pedro looked like he'd seen a ghost.

"My birth father and Pedro's host parent are brothers," Gregory explained. "My blood relation to his counter-part amplifies and magnifies Pedro's connection with him."

Hope rose in me. Gregory had just made my job so much easier. I would like to say that I'd made a mental note to share the new information of his origin with Megan, but truth be told, I was so focused on the tasks ahead I might not remember to. The faster I could do my job, the faster Eldon would be away from his tormentors.

"I can feel my counterpart now," Pedro whispered in wonder. "He's like someone who exists in my blind spot. Always been there. A white noise I've been dismissing without realizing I was doing it."

"Good," I said excitedly. "What else can you feel? Focus on something on your physical body."

"My neck," Pedro breathed. "It's hurting. Something heavy is—"

"Weighing it down?" I guessed.

"Yes! It's so heavy I can feel a migraine coming."

"What you're feeling is the weight of a very large pendent. Turn your head left and right. Can you feel it?"

Pedro did as I asked. "Yes. Big pendent. And sharp. The chain is cutting into my flesh."

The Eye of Sebille. Or a version of it similar to the one I wore on Dualsing, currently assigned to Pedro's counterpart. The jewel was probably enchanted to have a more humble appearance in order to not raise too many questions, unless Pedro's counterpart resided in the royal court like I did.

"Close your eyes. Keep the feel of the pendent with you," I instructed. "Now open your mind's eye. What do you see?"

Pedro's eyebrows knitted together. "A marketplace. With a lot of fruit and vegetable stalls. I come here to deliver melons for my dad every week, but really I was always hoping to see her."

"Who?" Gregory asked.

"The girl that I love," Pedro replied, his voice took on a dreamy quality.

No, not the girl that Pedro loved, but the girl that his counterpart loved. Pedro was picking up not just visual images, but thoughts and feelings from him as well. That was important. It meant that with the help of Gregory, their connection was strong.

I tried not to think about the fact that this innocent crush would come to nothing, as his counterpart wasn't destined to stay in Dualsing any more than I was. Even if we never interfered, all too soon this stranger would have the only life he knew ripped from him.

"Wait, all the stalls are overturned. There are apples and oranges rolling on the ground. Oh Hades, the ground itself is shaking. The market is deserted. I knew coming here it probably would be. But still I'm hoping to find her. Hoping she's okay. I don't know what to do if something happened to her." Panic began to seep into Pedro's voice.

These must be the strong earthquakes that Trust said Dualsing was experiencing.

"Pedro, can you give me some more descriptions? Something specific?" I would need that if I wanted to create a proper anchor to the plane.

"It's early afternoon just like here on the vengeance plane. There's a maypole in the center of the market. It's lying on the ground now. Some of the ribbons are no longer attached to the maypole."

"What color are the ribbons?"

"Purple and white."

Maypole. Purple and white ribbons. That must be for the Malarinshu, a festival commonly celebrated in the Yogubo province. It was a far-fringe farming province southeast of the Mirage Palace. If Pedro's counterpart was delivering produce to the market there, then his social standing in Dualsing was far lower than what Pedro enjoyed on the vengeance plane.

Fortunately, it would be a lot easier to enter Dualsing through a less guarded rural region than trying to barge right into the palace. I waved my hand over Gregory, Pedro, and I, clothing us in local attire that would help us blend in with the Dualsingians.

"Is there a storage area in the market? An enclosed structure of some kind?"

Pedro turned his head to the left and pointed. "There."

"Describe it." I pulled my magic around me. Gregory's hand remained in contact with Pedro's, while I shot out a hand and gripped Pedro's shoulder. Through our connection, I felt Gregory lending Pedro not only the strength of his magic, but something else. Something he was trying to hide from us, but nevertheless palpable and powerful.

His compassion.

Megan was right in trusting Gregory. I had to remember to tell her that when I saw her again, even if I forgot the other things.

"It's a small hut made of yellow brick and a red door," Pedro continued with his description. "The door is half-closed. I can see buckets of cherries inside. Some buckets are on their sides. There is a thin layer of straw on the ground. That's as much as I can see."

That was enough. We were ready.

"Keep in your head the image of that hut. Imagine the fresh smell of the cherries as they rolled on the straw and bumped into each other," I instructed Pedro. Then I closed my eyes, waving my free hand around to mentally "paint" the hut's interior as Pedro had described it. "Gregory, close your eyes, too."

When I was transported back to the vengeance world, I didn't step through a portal to do so. I soldiered through the grand ball and fireworks that were supposedly being held in my honor. I was then escorted into a private chamber in the queen's wing, which was fully decorated in anticipation for Deirdre's return. At the stroke of midnight, with the Eye of Sebille around my neck, my surroundings simply dissolved and reshaped themselves from that of the Mirage Palace to the front of the Advocatus family estate.

My instinct told me that this would be the same manner in which I would go back to Dualsing now. The bond between the two switched children would be the anchor for transport, with Gregory and me tagging along for the ride.

When I got the details right, down to the color of the hut door and the slightly bruised surfaces of the cherries, I took a deep breath and opened my eyes.

We were sitting on the floor of a small hut exactly as Pedro described, with straw underneath us but thankfully no crushed cherries. Gregory immediately waved a spell of invisibility around us. Not that we needed it, nor did we require Pedro's ability to mask our energy signatures, after all. The hut, and the entire market, were practically deserted. There was only the ceaseless sound of wooden boxes and stalls as they rattled against each other while the never-ending quake continued. I could see several cracks on the wall—it was a miracle that the hut was still standing. Things were definitely worse here than on the vengeance plane.

"My counterpart is near. He's searching the market for a sign of the girl he likes. He wants to make sure she's alright. Should we go talk to him, Serafina?" Pedro lowered his eyes, sounding as if it was the last thing he wanted to do. He, too, knew what our arrival meant for his counterpart's pursuit. If we intercepted him now, he might never find out what happened to his love.

"Let him go for now," I said softly.

Gregory raised his eyebrow.

"There's no use chasing after the kids one by one," I added. "The spell I'm going to use to retrieve them encompasses all of them in one fell swoop. Our first step should be to get inside the palace."

Here was to hoping that Pedro's counterpart would be able to find his sweetheart and spend some time with her before they were pulled apart forever.

Gregory took a deep breath, testing the air. "The magic on this plane is older and very potent, but still follows the same pattern and style as any other magic I have encountered. I think we should be able to teleport on this plane like we normally could. At least to the boundary of the palace grounds."

"I think I can do better." I closed my eyes again, remembering what Eldon told me.

Find Trust and Alina when you get there. The Molten Amber will help, too, because they could sense my will in you...

I had no idea how to find Trust, all I knew was that he'd broken out of his prison. And there was no way for me to be sure if Alina was even in the palace when the quake started, given the new queen's brutal rule. She could've been exiled along with her kind for all I knew. But the Molten Amber would most likely still be in the Mirage Palace, since it would be a monumental task to remove them from the very walls they were embedded in, and things that stayed out of sight and didn't talk back had a way of flying under the radar.

Since arriving at Dualsing, I could hear the Molten Amber's humming in my mind. It was faint at first, but growing stronger now. It was a sad song speaking of forced servitude and homesickness, amplified by the vibrations shaking the ground.

Eldon was right. They could feel his will through me, and they wanted to help.

An image of an alcove appeared in my mind. I recognized it as part of the Mirage Palace right away, as its floor and walls had a design using quartz and smooth white marble that was quite distinctive.

The alcove was screened off from the main hallway, offering a measure of privacy. I was grateful the Molten Amber had chosen it as I watched the tunnel open up in the palace.

I heard gasps from both Gregory and Pedro and opened my eyes.

There was now a tunnel opening in the hut. I knew that it would lead to the alcove I'd pictured in my mind. By invitation of the Molten Amber.

"Come on." I grabbed Pedro by the hand and gestured for Gregory to follow us.

We took a single step in through the tunnel opening and walked out of the other end into the alcove. I was amazed the Molten Amber was able to get us past the palace's heavy protection entirely. The Dualsingian, a race of thieves, were always so proud of their complex security system.

The Molten Amber, impregnated with countless palace secrets and political intrigues, were more powerful than anyone had anticipated, far beyond their intended purpose of being nothing but pretty lights illuminating the halls. The powerful magic reminded me of Eldon's original ambition in his befriending of these beings.

And what it took for him to give all that up.

"Thank you, Molten Amber." I touched the wall lightly, respectfully.

I peeled back the screen covering the alcove and looked down the palace hall. The long corridor was deserted. Just as I remembered, instead of having natural light coming through windows, the walls gave off a soft dim glow as hundreds of thousands of Molten Amber lighted the way in the royal residence.

The very magic of the place seemed diminished somehow, and the tremors were stronger here than at the marketplace. There was a silent scream in the air, as if the palace itself was a sentient being in pain.

There was debris in the hall and damage to sections of the wall, those areas darkened, their glow snuffed out. I looked down the corridor and saw that were a good number of dark patches along the way.

It felt strange being back in the palace, a place I never thought I'd see again in my lifetime. It felt even stranger because it wasn't at all how I'd remembered it.

"Should we even be here, Serafina?" As we moved out of the alcove, Pedro's eyes kept darting around as if he expected a monster to lurk behind every column and drape. I couldn't blame him. This was the first time he'd ever been on the soil of his own people, and he wasn't exactly seeing the best of what it had to offer. Not to mention, if he was discovered on this trip he might be stuck here for the rest of his life. I admired his courage for wanting to be part of this despite his fear.

"We have to," I stated. "But we should keep a low profile. I don't think there are a lot of people around, but you never know."

Make a deal with Deirdre if you have to. She can't be trusted, but she'll want to survive this so she'll cooperate...

The operative words here being "if I had to." It would be wise to avoid Eldon's sister if we could. She was the foretold ruler of Dualsing. She was prophesied to rise to the challenge and make her people thrive. But it was never said how she was going to do it, or how many deaths she would cause.

Or who she would betray.

My eyes were drawn to a marble column that had fallen to the floor and cracked into several sections, exposing pieces of Molten Amber to the air. The Molten Amber had hardened, losing their natural fluidity. Their edges were turning a grayish, non-transparent color. My instinct told me they were dying, though I didn't understand how. Maybe they couldn't be in direct contact with air.

I needed to do something to help.

I picked up a smaller piece of the marble column and put the Molten Amber next to the still intact wall. The dying fragments immediately liquefied and joined their healthy brethren. I did the same with the other debris, with help from Pedro and Gregory for the heavier ones, until all the damaged Molten Amber on the column had rejoined the protective fold of their family. The wall grew bright with hundreds of Molten Amber as they lit up as one for a few seconds, then dimmed back, as if to express their collective gratitude.

"You're welcome. I wish I could do more, but I'm in a hurry," I murmured. "Eldon sent me here to do something very important. Do you know where Alina the Pixie might be?"

The Molten Amber lit up again and rearranged themselves into a straight line with an arrow, pointing toward one end of the corridor.

"Thank you again."

We followed the light. At the end of the passage, the Molten Amber in that wall did the same and pointed us to the right direction again. They were acting like runway lighting, until we were practically sprinting just to keep up. But they winked out whenever we were near the presence of a passing Dualsingian, allowing us to conceal ourselves in time. It happened twice. We crossed paths with a young servant I had never seen before and a disenfranchised minor noble who handled security when I was living here. Both looked disheveled and hurried, and they didn't notice us. From our hiding place, Pedro stared after them in a mix of fear, longing, and curiosity; they were the first of his kind he'd ever seen in his life.

We passed through a breezeway. Today, there were no unicorns grazing there, all of them having likely fled the palace. No wonder. The very magic of the palace felt vanquished. Unicorns were infamous for being avid chasers of good tidings. They went wherever fortune favored and had no loyalty toward any specific race or kingdom. They could bring additional prosperity to an already blessed place, but could also further weaken it upon their abandonment of it when times were bad.

We approached the east wing, an area that was not embedded with the Molten Amber at all. By then I already knew where Alina was. I had intended to go there after finding her anyway.

I gently touched the last wall that was still glowing. "We'll go on from here. You have my gratitude."

The Molten Amber grew bright and then winked out.

"Where are we going?" Gregory asked.

"The Observatory." It felt like I'd worked there a millennium ago. Had it really been only a little more than a year? The dread of visiting it mixed with the anticipation of seeing my sweet pixie friend again.

"Is this where you used to track the changeling children?" Pedro asked.

I nodded, adding, "Yes. Though I didn't understand at the time what I was looking at."

The Observatory had a massive library with records on every changeling ever switched. Hopefully, it would shed some light on their counterparts who were currently still at Dualsing.

We passed a long row of unmarked wooden doors until we reached the last one. It would lead us up to a tower I knew only too well. At the top of the stairs was the door that opened to the Observatory. The thick walls and heavy drapes had been designed to block out as much light and sound as possible, so once we stepped into the Observatory an eerie quietness enveloped us. Slipping into my old habits, I walked as lightly and quietly as possible. I could hear Gregory and Pedro doing the same, their footfalls becoming almost imperceptible.

The dome-shaped ceiling, usually bright with mesmerizing lights outlining the maps where changelings had been placed, was dark and dormant, leaving us fumbling in the dark.

Here in the hushed silence, the chaos of the earthquake was but a distant memory, the floors here were still. Ironically, after finally getting used to the constant vibration, my body felt off balance.

The Observatory must have been built to withstand a lot of stress and damage. This made sense since it hosted the means of tracking one of Dualsing's most valuable assets—the children that it sent out to the world to steal for them.

"Alina," I whispered, desperately hoping that the Molten Amber was right, and my longtime friend and companion was close by.

It didn't take long for that wish to be granted. A streak of light made a beeline toward me like a cannonball on fire; its speed was only surpassed by the mad string of chatter that accompanied it.

"OhSerafinaisitreallyyouImissedyousomuchhowhaveyoubeenIthoughtIwouldneverseeyouagain!"

"Slow down." I laughed, having said those exact same two words to her as I'd done every time I came in here in the past. Tears ran down my face as the little pixie dropped the lantern in her hands on the closest surface and smacked face-first onto my upper arm, recovered, did a somersault and went back for another hug. With my wet cheek this time. Then she did a happy dance with a series of gravity-defying pirouettes, then dive bombed me with a kiss on the other cheek.

"Serafina. I'm. So. Glad. To. See. You." Alina struggled to slow down her words despite her excited emotions. "I've been hiding here for a long time waiting for you."

"I missed you, too, my friend." I sniffled. Then her words sank in. "Did you say you've been hiding here?"

She nodded. "From the queen. Things haven't been well for my kind since her return. Then the earthquakes hit and the queen tried to capture all the minor magical creatures and suck out their power to fight the shakes. My ma and her sisters left while they still could. Even Mr. Lichen left. I stayed behind because Trust told me I'd be of use to you. He said to wait for you here."

"Alina." I was touched by the little pixie's loyalty. She could have escaped, but she risked staying for my sake.

I didn't know what to say, but she seemed to understand and said, "Don't worry about it. Trust said I could help, and I want to help."

"Speaking of Trust, do you know where he is now?" I asked.

She shook her head. "No idea. The dragon was being all secretive."

Alina's eyes widened when she took in Gregory and Pedro behind me. She sniffed at the air, flew close to my left ear and whispered, her voice fearful, "What are they? One smells like a Dualsingian, but different. The other one has such a stern note to his magic, and yet so...so..."

"Familiar in a way?" I guessed. "Did he remind you of me?"

She tugged at my earlobe twice. I took that as a double yes.

"Alina"—I pointed at Gregory—"this is Gregory. He's a vengeance demon, just like me. Our race is the guardian of the Cosmic Balance."

I bit my lip, preparing myself for Alina's reaction. What would she think of my true identity?

Alina merely nodded. "You and I had always suspected that there was something different about you, didn't we? After you left I learned that you're not a Dualsingian, but frankly I don't care what you really are. You'll always be my friend."

I beamed at her. Deep down that was always my fear—that my long-time companion would turn away from me in horror or disgust if she ever found out who I really was. I couldn't tell her how much her acceptance meant to me.

Alina greeted Gregory. "Nice to meet you, Gregory."

"Nice to meet you, too," Gregory replied in kind.

"And do you remember the book of Eglantina-Six?" I asked Alina.

"How could I not? It was our last assignment together." As small as her eyes were compared to mine, I swear I could see tears sparkle in hers. "And Trust explained to me the true function of the Observatory."

"Gamma turned out to be the queen. Alpha just got back to Dualsing. And this"—I pointed at Pedro—"is Beta."

Alina's mouth turned into a perfect *O*; she drew close to me again and whispered, "Is he as evil as the queen?"

"No. He's nice," I assured her. "He goes by the name of Pedro on the vengeance plane."

Alina flew to Pedro tentatively, and once she decided that he seemed alright, circled him three times in quick succession. Then her face split into a grin. "Hi, Pedro."

"Hello." Pedro smiled back at the pixie.

"Now that I know what to expect from vengeance demons"—Alina sniffed the air again—"I'll say you smell like a Dualsingian with a sharp hint of vengeance."

Pixies were known for their keen sense of magical detection, far more advanced than both changelings and vengeance demons, so I was surprised that Alina seemed fooled by Pedro's automatic masking of his true nature.

Pedro shook his head. "No. That's just my cover. I was *designed* to smell like a vengeance demon. That's not what I really am, unfortunately."

"Are you sure? Because I could swear it!"

"You guys, I think we have to get a move on." Gregory coughed. "Megan and her group are probably in place by now."

"What is he talking about, Serafina?" Alina asked.

I briefly outlined my plan to her. "Can you help us?"

"Of course. Wait." Alina zoomed down and retrieved her lantern. "Okay, let's get the raw material for the Reveal."

The Reveal was a spell that I was taught to locate a changeling who was sent out into the world. I'd never done it with their counterpart at Dualsing, not to mention at a much higher volume. I had no idea if it would work, but I had to try.

With the lantern in hand, Alina led us to the back of the Observatory, where a long row of bookshelves was built right into the wall. These shelves held the heavy volumes of Observatory records. I was never permitted to get near the shelves —Mr. Lichen, my mentor, would always pull the volumes I needed for my shift.

The volumes were filed chronologically, with the ones on the left frayed almost to the point of deteriorating, and the newer ones on the right I worked on before, such as Eglantina-Six, Marigold-Twelve, and Oda-Four.

We picked out the volumes with the most recent cases

recorded; Gregory and Pedro carried the lot of them to the desk in the center of the room.

I waved at the dome-shaped ceiling overhead. A mass juxtaposition of maps materialized on a backdrop of royal blue, each a bright line of a different color. I did another wave, and most of the maps disappeared from view, leaving only those connected to the volumes on the desk.

There were a total of twenty-three overlapping maps, meaning there were twenty-three planes out there that currently had children kidnapped by the Dualsingians.

"I recognize some of these maps," Gregory breathed. "Some of them are home planes of my clients. The dwarf giants, leprechauns, and trolls."

"Didn't the dwarf giants discover a ruby mother lode a decade ago?" Pedro's eyes were calculating.

"A few years back the trolls accidentally came across a way to make sparkling fart wines. It's the choice drink of Freshmen Week initiation since it is gross but harmless." Gregory seemed to be getting where Pedro was going with this.

"And according to *Popular Vengeance Science*," Pedro added, "the leprechauns have just come up with a way to use their rainbows as a source of alternative clean energy. They're just waiting for the patent to be approved."

"All of these races have trade secrets that are worth stealing." Gregory smiled. "All the more reason my clients would be pleased to have their real children back."

Time to see just how many children in total were kidnapped from the twenty-three planes.

I pulled the thought of Eldon around me. If the task in front of me was more complex than any I had ever done, then the anchor I was using—and the love that it represented— was also stronger than it had ever been.

Alina blew out the candle inside her lantern, the maps

now the only light in the room. They shone brilliantly above us. I waved my hands over the patterns like a paintbrush, revealing dots that represented the changeling children on each plane.

There were about a hundred dots.

I breathed a small sigh of relief. The number was within the normal range that I'd suspected, considering switching was more about strategic placement than bulk dumping. Looked like Deirdre hadn't fully implemented her plan to ramp up the switching yet.

Show me your twins on Dualsing, I commanded.

The overlapping maps disappeared along with the dots. I experienced a moment of panic until another map appeared. A single large map.

The map of Dualsing.

And on it, the hundred dots showing the locations of the kidnapped children.

"Gregory, you have a contract with your clients." I offered him my hand and he took it. "You have a legal obligation to these kids. That gives you the right to defend them."

I turned to Pedro. "Pedro, your people have robbed these kids of a proper childhood. You have a moral obligation to them. That gives you the right to recover them."

Pedro took my other hand.

Through Gregory I could feel his clients' love for their missing children. I added that love to the guilt and shame Pedro was feeling, for he was a good person and was genuinely horrified at what his people had done to others. I poured all that emotion into the map of Dualsing overhead until the dots grew in brightness.

"Call to them," I told Pedro. "All of those kidnapped kids should be psychically linked to you now."

A look of wonder crossed over him. "Yes, they can hear

me. Some are confused. Some are afraid. My counterpart simply...recognized me."

"Hold the connection." I let go of both Gregory and Pedro's hands. "Tell them what you can about the situation but keep it brief. They already know about the switching practice so that should make it more believable. I'll call the Molten Amber and arrange to have them teleported here immediately."

When they had all arrived, Pedro and I would open the passage and send them to the vengeance plane, and from there, to their real families. The mass exodus of the kidnapped children from Dualsing should trigger a reverse effect on the changeling children out in the world, as nature balanced itself again.

That was my theory anyways. Soon to be tested.

I needed it to work; once it did I could neutralize the Council's passage, and in doing so, give Megan the signal to rescue Eldon.

"Wait," Pedro said softly.

"What's wrong?" I asked nervously. "Are the links destabilizing?"

"No, nothing like that." Pedro took a deep breath. "When it's time to leave, go on without me."

"What?" Gregory and I shouted simultaneously.

"What are you talking about?" I grabbed Pedro's arm. "I promised you this is not going to be a one-way trip, and I won't let it come to that. It *doesn't* have to come to that."

"Yes, it does," Pedro said.

"I don't understand," I said.

"Serafina, I'm a changeling." Pedro looked resigned and incredibly sad. "I tried to deny it. I tried to hold onto my old life. But now I know I'm meant to stay here. To balance out my counterpart's return home. It's the only way. Otherwise nobody can be where they're supposed to be. I know it in my bones, and I think deep down you do, too."

"Pedro—" I pleaded.

"And it's not just that." Pedro's gaze became faraway. "Now that I'm linked I could hear the kidnapped kids. And the changelings they're bound to. I'm one of them—not one of the victims, but the wrongdoers. I'm a Dualsingian. It's in my blood, and this plane pulls at me in ways I never even knew possible. That's the real reason why I needed to come here, though I couldn't admit it to myself at the time. It had nothing to do with bravery. This plane has been calling to me ever since I found out the truth. I hate everything my race stands for, but I cannot leave. This is my home."

Tears rolled down my cheeks. Maybe it was I who was in denial. I knew exactly what he was talking about. The first time I stepped foot on the vengeance plane, I was terrified, but I knew I was home. I knew I was where I belonged, at long last. How could I object to how Pedro felt just because he was a changeling, not a vengeance demon, and there was much less to be proud of?

I hugged him. "You've got a stronger sense of right and wrong in you than most vengeance demons I know. Don't ever forget that. Don't ever lose it. And you *are* brave. So brave."

"You'll go to my parents and explain everything?" Pedro choked.

"Of course," I promised.

"I wish I had been honest enough with myself to see what was coming and say a proper goodbye to them in person myself. To me they'll never be my host parents. They're my *parents*. Simple as that." Pedro's eyes filled. "And tell Minnie I'll miss her. She's more than a cook to me. She's family."

"We'll make sure they know that. All of them." Gregory's voice was filled with emotion. "I'll go with Serafina to visit them after this is all over. I hope you adjust well here, cousin. We don't share a drop of blood, but it doesn't matter. I'm proud of you."

"Me, too." I swallowed. Time was running out, no matter how much I hated what came next. Holding onto the psychic threads with all those kidnapped children was a huge strain on Pedro, though he refused to let it show.

"And I'll help you adjust to life here." Alina circled Pedro once, settling on his shoulder. "I'll be your friend."

"Thanks." Pedro smiled at the pixie. It gave me great comfort knowing that two of the people I loved the most in Dualsing would have each other to lean on.

"I'll tell the Molten Amber we're ready now," I said.

Before I could do that, the sound of clapping came from the entrance to the Observatory.

"What a touching moment, right before the act of treason." The familiar voice of a girl echoed into the room, chilling me to the bones.

The sound of snapped fingers, then the chamber filled with blinding light. The extreme brightness effectively rendered the map overhead unreadable. Pedro swayed, trying in vain to hold onto his fading connections with the kidnapped children. Gregory shot out a hand to steady him.

Half the lights blinked out, but the damage was done. I could no longer see anything on the ceiling, my eyes trying in vain to adjust to the sudden change in brightness.

A flame-haired girl wearing an elegant wine-red silk gown walked toward us. She was about my age. Large almond eyes, full lips, and glowing skin...her face could only be described as glorious. Floating above her hand was a bubble, and in the bubble was something so out of place with the fairy tale surrounding that it took my brain a while to process it for what it was.

A pair of miniature floodlights. Designed by humans and powered by magic.

"One of the many offerings from the traders." The girl grinned and raised the partially switched off floodlights.

"Deirdre." The last two times I had seen Eldon's sister had resulted in attempted murder by her. It wasn't exactly a fond memory. And now there was so much more than just my life at stake. I glanced in Pedro's direction, and Deirdre caught it. She dismissed him, seeing nothing. Truth was, she was eyeing Gregory, viewing the mercenary as a much greater threat.

Upon the entrance of the queen, Alina hid behind Pedro. Pedro started to ask Gregory a question, but was silenced by a look from Gregory. Gregory, his eyes never leaving the queen, stepped in front of Pedro.

"We meet again, Lady Serafina." Deirdre chuckled. "We share a bond, dear, and that kind of thing doesn't truly go away, even if your ability to read my mind is gone, I knew you were here the minute you stepped onto my plane."

"I'm not here to help Eldon win back the crown, if that's what you think. In fact, he doesn't want it anymore. I'm here to help stop the tremors."

"Liar! My brother no longer wants the crown? Can't you at least make up a lie that's a little more believable?" Deirdre spit out. For a small moment her glamor slipped and I saw the dark circles under her eyes and her left cheek scratched and slightly bruised. The attempted invasion of her world was more damaging than she let on.

A glance at my face told Deirdre that I had seen what I wasn't supposed to see, and it only made her angrier. She started toward me.

"She's telling the truth." Pedro tried to come to my defense, but was held fast by Gregory.

Deirdre hissed in Pedro's direction. "Hold your tongue, my *subject*. We'll deal with your treachery later."

While Gregory tried to calm Pedro down, Deirdre took the mercenary's momentary distraction to blast him with an attack spell. Seeing what was coming, Pedro tackled Gregory to the ground, but not before the spell hit Pedro and left a deep gash from the tip of his shoulder to his elbow.

Then the two rolled to the side, putting their combined weight on Pedro's wound. The teenager cried out in pain.

The second blast of the spell knocked them both out. In Pedro's case, it was an unintended mercy.

But that left just Deirdre and me.

And Alina.

The young pixie started screaming Trust's name, as a talisman or a call for help, I wasn't sure. Deirdre snarled and Alina flew into hiding, too afraid to make any more noise.

Deirdre turned her attention back to me.

"Well, third time's the charm. Don't you think?" She smiled and started circling me.

Deirdre started hurling waves of spells at me. It was difficult to block them because they had the form and appearance of existing vengeance spells, but their underlying cores were infused with the cunningness and slyness typical of changeling magic.

"Not bad, am I?" Deirdre laughed, moving in a deadly dance of aggression. "Considering growing up they thought I was a Powerless."

I was too busy surviving to make a witty response. Evasive maneuvers were all I could manage.

My familiarity with the Observatory's geography was my only saving grace. I dove behind century-old antique armchairs and hid behind massive bookshelves. After so many close calls, my natural instinct was to escape. But my training kicked in.

Upon my return to the vengeance plane, I'd learned quickly from my physical combat tutor that I didn't have it in me to be an aggressive fighter. So he taught me how to patiently wear down my opponent through the art of careful observation and energy conservation.

So though it might appear I was losing the fight with Deirdre, I was actually learning and assessing.

The dark circles told me Deirdre was exhausted. The scratches and bruising on her face told me she'd slipped up, and could again.

But not right this moment. One of her spells snaked around my ankle, cutting through me like a barbwire. Knowing the importance to keep moving, I yanked at my ankle, tearing my tendon in the process.

I cried out, intense agony shooting through my body as blood gushed out.

Then I spotted it.

A built-in nook at the foot of the wall, obscured by a solid oak table.

I forced my injured body to move, to roll into the space that was barely large enough for me. Then I sent one illusion to cover the spot and another to create a fake version of myself, continuing to duck Deirdre's attack.

I blocked out the pain and forced myself to listen to her burst of spells.

It had a certain staccato ebb and flow to it. A pattern I could discern because as she said, we were still somewhat connected. The punishing frequency of the bursts themselves, which didn't give room for a proper power reload, told me that she was fueled by anger, and with anger came blind spots.

I saw my opportunity after a particularly brutal round of assaults on my fake self. Deirdre was getting closer to hitting her, and took a few seconds to recover.

The best time to attack is when it looks like they've managed to get you too busy to do so, my tutor's voice whispered in my ears.

I sent everything I could muster into a spell called Blow A Fuse, which was similar to what our group had done to the succubus queens.

As Deirdre pulled power from her core, getting ready for another round of assault, I sent mine along with it. It made her magic just a bit off balance, so that the next spell she tried to hit the fake me with, it backfired on her. The energy contracted inward, right back to her core, knocking her to the floor.

The fake me dissolved.

Limping over to where Deirdre's feebly withering body was, her moans filling the Observatory, I thought I would feel fear, regret, or even a hint of remorse.

No. All I could think about were the minor supernaturals who'd suffered under her reign, and all the more who would suffer if she carried on.

I always thought I didn't have it in me to cause harm, but in that moment I really wanted to.

The sound of a door being ripped from its hinges rang through the room.

"Stop," Trust said by the entrance. "The heir of Dualsing must be allowed to carry out her destiny as it was foretold."

❧ 25 ❧

THE FURIES

WE FOLLOWED the same route that High Judge Advocatus took after he had left our boat. It was safe to assume that as a member of the Council he would be going to the most secret areas of the headquarters and would lead us to where Eldon was being held.

"Megan." Fir elbowed me, gesturing to the guards at the end of the upcoming passage, the first people we'd encountered since leaving the boat.

They were a pair of tall grunt reapers. Dressed in full black suits, the signature outfit of their kind, they looked like they hadn't smiled in decades. Geez, the Council really took no chances when it came to surrounding this area with their most trusted loyalists. The dignified reapers weren't the type to play rent-a-cop for just any occasion, which told me that we were at the right place.

While so far the Blind Eye spell was doing an adequate job of preventing us from being heard and seen, getting *past* the reapers was another matter. How were we going to cruise by people who walked the line between life and death, and from whose eyes nothing escaped?

"Well. I figured we'd come across reapers at some point, so I came prepared." Bonaventure the Third, reverted to his true form, took out a tube of gooey black paste from his coat. "Here, slather this on your face."

I took a slab of the black paste and sniffed at it. It smelled like paint and rotten bananas, and it had a slow burning sensation. "What is this?"

"Ground maggots from the Grimmian Forest." Seeing the appalled look on my face, Wistari explained, "The only thing that could confuse a creature of both life and death is its familiar. Maggots feast on dead things, but in doing so they create new building blocks of life."

"Isn't the Grimmian variety poisonous?" I asked.

"Yes, if you have it on for too long it'll stop your heart," Bonaventure the Third confirmed. "Which is why Wistari, Naracion, and I are staying here. Our body mass is less than yours, and the poison is faster acting for us."

Fir and I smeared the maggot paste on our foreheads and cheeks like it was war paint. With that much of the paste on our bodies, the slow burning sensation had intensified to a sharp, searing pain. It was as if the maggots were still alive and attempting to bite their way into the blood vessels under my skin.

"Take this. For later." Bonaventure the Third offered me and Fir each a handkerchief. "We'll try to confuse the reapers' senses further from this end."

Knowing we didn't have much time, Fir and I took the offering and walked up to the reapers. My eyes began to water, and I fought to keep the tears in my eyes. Mixing the paste with my tears was a sure way to spread the poison over a larger area of my skin. It felt like there was a ton of rocks crushing my chest, and worse than the physical pain was the onslaught of grim despair, a voice urging me to lay down and die.

I kept walking.

Just before my vision was lost I got close enough to see the reapers looking right through us and knew we were successful in our invisibility.

Fir took my hand and guided me past the reapers and onward.

"We're in the tunnels now," Fir whispered. "The reapers can't see us anymore."

I let go of his hand, took out the handkerchief, and wiped off every trace of the maggot paste off my body. My vision returned, the pressure on my chest eased, and gone were the negative emotions of ultimate doom.

I glanced at Fir and gasped. There was blood oozing out of his ears.

"It looks worse than it really is," he assured me while wiping the blood off. "You had it bad with the eyes, I had it bad with the ears. We all got our weak spots."

Fir and I continued walking, knowing our allies would be waiting for our return. I felt feeble and unsettled, as my body processed through the poison that managed to get into it. There was a sluggishness to my heartbeat I didn't like. I felt utterly exhausted, like I'd just run a marathon.

I hoped Gregory, Serafina, and Pedro were faring better on their end. Thinking about Gregory got my heart beating a little faster, or more normal in this case. Who knew he would be good physiotherapy?

"How's your heart?" I asked Fir.

"Better than yours, probably." Fir rubbed his chest ruefully. "Must be all the laughter keeping it strong."

I was a little afraid of encountering another labyrinth of tunnels, but thankfully we now seemed able to go on a straight path. Good. I would hate to do rounds of *eeny, meeny, miny, moe* and get lost as a result.

After another few minutes of walking, a sense of pure

dread threatened to overwhelm me. Judging from Fir's pale face, he was feeling it, too. There was a pungent energy signature in the air that smelled like antiseptic, as if we were at a human hospital and the place was rubbed down with bleach. Too unnaturally clean. Too sterile. Too clinical.

The powerful energy signature was coming from around the next corner. Someone was probing the air in the surrounding area with unrelenting tenaciousness. The scan swept through us, actively seeking out any stray energy vibes or abnormal happenings. It was different from the good old standard detection method any respectable vengeance demon would employ. There was something ultra-no-nonsense and overzealous about it. No mercy and no hesitation.

I had no idea why the Blind Spot was able to withstand such an unforgiving scrutiny, but the probe couldn't lock on to us, but simply maintained a constant, nerve wrecking broad sweep.

Well, time to bite the bullet.

I took a deep breath and turned the corner, expecting to see a group of the most advanced arch vengeance demons waiting for us.

What the heck?

There was no group of arch vengeance demons around the corner working together to probe the passageway.

Three cribs formed a triangle in the tight tunnel, leaving would-be passersby no room but to squeeze around them. In each crib was a newborn vengeance demon, a month old at most, fast asleep on their sides, their wings miniature and undisguised. The art of disguising one's wing was a skill learned later in life.

There were repeated patterns drawn on the ground comprised of a dog's head with snakes for hair like Medusa. And three carved words: Alecto, Megaera, and Tisiphone. These were the names of the three Furies, ancient avengers of broken promises and violent crimes, keepers of justice and order. According to legend, they were the founders of the vengeance demons race, like Mitochondrial Eve was to modern-day humans, or Fleur to the tricksters.

There was an ancient belief that vengeance newborns were the most connected with the Cosmic Balance, and they would cry out if they sensed injustices.

Three cribs, three newborns, the patterns and words on the floor. The whole set up was meant to invoke the spirit of the Furies to enhance the natural senses of the babies, to use them as a security alarm system.

Let me say it again. The Council had sunk so low as to using babies to work security. All just to guard Eldon? Really?

Was this why Grandma couldn't come to us earlier and why she sent Sui-Ling instead? Was this the *something* she said she was looking into, why she couldn't join us? I totally couldn't see Grandma being on board with this, no matter how ruthless she was. There were certain lines you just don't cross.

Grandma must be in the heart of the Council now, dealing with the lot of them. I had to go to her.

But how did we pass the kids if it meant hurting them? How could I do that if that was the price?

"We're not going to hurt them." Fir elbowed me, as if reading my mind. "These vengeance kids are already either drugged or enchanted."

"What?" I jumped.

"Take a more careful look. That deep sleep isn't natural."

"How do you know? You're a trickster."

"Who do you think got stuck babysitting you when Mom and Dad went on date nights? You think I wouldn't know real vengeance baby sleep if I saw it? The wings have this twitching and spreading movement, as if the babies dream of taking flight and wreaking vengeance havoc before they can even walk or talk. Your dad assured me that all newborns from his race sleep like that."

Now that Fir mentioned it, the miniature wings were tamely settled on the babies' backs. Damn, those kids must be really out.

"That means somebody who's also following the high judge had already disabled the alarm and passed through here." Horror forced its way through my weakened heart. "We've kept a fair bit of distance between us and the high judge after getting off the boat. Someone else must've been in front of us. Or maybe he or she was even flying above us on the boat, just like the Off-Blacks."

I ran forward, squeezing past the tight space between the cribs. Then I came to a halt and looked back at the babies. Fir waved me away. "Go, Megan. I'll take care of them. Maybe a tickle from my trickster beard is enough to scare these babies awake. It sure worked for you. Once I'm outta here I'll send them to safety. Anyway, *run*."

I did.

I jogged through the tunnel, abandoning discretion now. I had to assume whoever was in front of me had already either triggered or disabled the other alarms. Either way, the time for stealth had passed.

I came to a stop in front of a bunker-like metal door. I listened. No sound came from the other side. I steeled myself, turned the handle, and pushed in.

I was wrong. The baby alarm disabler wasn't following High Judge Advocatus.

He *was* High Judge Advocatus.

❧ 26 ❧

THE COUNCIL AND THE GREYS

I WALKED into a room that looked like a cross between a medieval torture chamber and a mad scientist's lab.

Eldon was lying unconscious on a metal slab, with instruments all around him like he was in a sizable operation theatre of some human medical drama. In stark contrast, ancient symbols, created with the same paint and brush strokes as the ones by the three cribs were scrawled on the floor surrounding him. A single fluorescent lightbulb was installed on the ceiling, but it wasn't turned on. Instead, the room was lit by a few dozen candles, placed in tarnished silver candlesticks that the Phantom of the Opera would be proud to have in his lair.

Unlike those by the cribs, the symbols surrounding Eldon were glowing, casting the entire slab in a cylinder of blinding light. On the ceiling, where the light beam hit, was the Council's half-formed passage that was giving the Dualsingian plane all those lovely earthquakes. It looked like what any cross-dimensional passage should look like at the beginning of its formation—a piece of normal space warped like a vortex of a whirlpool, except that it couldn't move past this stage. It was trapped at half open, with the space involved set in a constant pattern of twisting and untwisting itself.

"Hello, Megan." High Judge Advocatus revealed himself with a dry smile on his face. Now I wished I hadn't sent Esme away. I could use the back up. On the other hand, being discovered like this was the exact reason why I didn't want her further involved.

"High Judge Edbert Llewellyn Advocatus." I took my time addressing the guy by his full name. Slowly enunciating each syllable. Anything to drag things out. I had no way of alerting Serafina's group that I'd run into problems. I could only hope to distract the high judge long enough so that they could complete their work without interference. "How are you? How's the Council rocking? That changeling there is looking good. How's the interrogation coming along?"

High Judge Advocatus frowned. "Sarcasm doesn't become you."

"Of course it does. Trickster blood, remember?" I knew I was being totally ridiculous, but what else could I do? I couldn't beat the guy. All my allies were busy elsewhere. It was obvious I didn't come to the Tree and get lost trying to find the ladies' bathroom. I had tried to hide Eldon before, for Hades's sake.

"Do you know the trouble you're in, young lady?"

"I got this far, didn't I?"

"Only because I *allowed* you to pass through the Furies."

Realization dawned. "You mean it was *you* who disabled the kids they were channeling through?"

"Of course. And in case you're wondering, my action has the full support of the Council."

I cast my eyes around for something, anything, I could use to gain an advantage. Instead, I saw more and more Council members as they appeared in the room, until almost all fourteen members were there. Including Macallister Sebastian Sumpsi, Minister of the Vengeance Ethics Commission, Gregory's father.

Everyone was there, except Grandma, longtime honorary member of the Council.

A chill pierced deep into my heart. "Where's my grandmother?"

High Judge Advocatus chuckled. "Now the little trickster has finally decided to become serious."

I clenched my fists at my sides, barely containing my rage. "Where is she?"

"She left. She abandoned you, Megan. She knew you were coming, but she left you for us to deal with."

No, that couldn't be right. She loved me. I'd doubted Gran's love time and again, the last time being when I was tricked by the Greys. But she had never failed me, even when I didn't know I could rely on her. I wasn't about to trust the words of an arrogant ass like High Judge Advocatus over a lifetime of love.

"What did you do to her?" I narrowed my eyes on him. If Grandma didn't abandon me, and she wasn't here, then what happened? What could possibly explain her absence from the very Council of which its modern version she'd helped shape?

High Judge Advocatus smiled. "Alright, enough games. We're at the close anyway, dear."

Who in the last two days had more or less said the exact same words to me?

The Fake Sui-Ling, by my parents' birdbath, before taking Eldon with her.

I stared at High Judge Advocatus. "You were the one who masqueraded as Sui-Ling!"

"As I said, enough games. I have to thank you, Megan." High Judge Advocatus bowed formally to me. "Without you we would never have come this far."

"What the heck are you talking about?"

"We ran into each other when you visited my niece, remember?"

When I went to enlist Serafina's help in finding Eldon, upon Gregory's request.

"You listened in on our conversation," I breathed. That was how the fake Sui-Ling was able to replace the real one and get to my parents' house so fast. In trying to help Eldon, I was the one who set the Greys on his trail, which inadvertently got him captured and tortured. Irony was a bitchy fairy I intended to slap.

When I survived this.

High Judge Advocatus had to be a member of the Greys then. But he was also a Council member. Just how did that work? Especially since he didn't seem to be acting against the Council's wishes.

I'd doubted Gran's love time and again, the last time being when I was tricked by the Greys.

Like how the high judge was trying to get me to believe the worst of her just now.

"There has never been an alliance between the Council and the Greys, has there?" I looked around the room; at each of the Council members Grandma had called friends and allies for decades. "You're not working with them. You *are* them. You were one of theirs all along. That's why you weren't all that hot on pursuing all those leads that Dan Pillar provided on the Greys."

The extremists who wanted vengeance demons to stand by the Absolute Good and rule the world with an iron fist, and the governing body of the said vengeance demons, were one and the same. Great.

All humor faded from High Judge Advocatus's face. "You're sharper than I've given you credit for. Your grandmother came to the same conclusion. Too bad I wasn't able to finish her off before she escaped."

Finish her off? My heart squeezed painfully. Just how badly was Gran hurt? She must be in horrible shape if she couldn't even warn me about this trap.

And a trap this was. I had no doubt of it now.

"What the hell do you want from me?" I spit out. I directed my question to High Judge Advocatus, aka Fake Sui-Ling, who seemed to be the leader of the group of traitors.

And what traitors they were, to the very Concord they'd sworn to protect. I mean, I knew they were strict about following rules, and that they were assholes in general. But to bring about the destruction of existence as we knew it? I thought deep down there was decency in them. I thought working for the Council meant I was fighting for something. That was why I worked so hard to get into Demon U, to be licensed by their system, to play their game and measure my own success in accordance to their standards.

Suddenly, my previous worry about not being able to go back to vengeance co-op seemed laughably trivial.

"Not just from you, but also from my niece. We need you both. Where is she, anyway?" The high judge looked around as if Serafina would magically show up. "The Eldon that Serafina last talked to was actually controlled by us. The poor lovesick fool never knew the difference."

My jaw dropped. "How could that be? Listening to Serafina, there had been no doubt in her mind that the Eldon she saw was his true self."

"Oh that." High Judge Advocatus waved his hand. "We'd managed to gain some access to his memory. Enough to mimic him. The principle is the same as when I assumed Sui-Ling's identity. All the talk about being willing to forsake the claim to the throne and asking her to leave him to his fate? That was all us. It took an idealist to believe something that naïve. Believe me, dear, once you taste power, it's not something you give up on."

"So your plan was to get Serafina all mushed up with a self-sacrificing Eldon, so she'd come straight here to save him?"

Well, they thought wrong. Serafina chose to follow the plan the Council thought she would reject. She had gone to Dualsing on Eldon's advice and left me to rescue him.

Damn, what kind of mess had Serafina, Gregory, and Pedro walked into with that kind of misinformation? What kind of mess was *I* in the middle of?

❧ 27 ❧

IN SERAFINA'S SHOES: ADVISOR

"LADY SERAFINA." Trust the Dragon placed himself between me and Deirdre, forcing me back a couple of steps with his sheer size. The dragon was miniature no more, in his full glory of shiny scales and golden aura. It outshone even the flood lights.

I nearly stumbled due to my injured ankle. Trust caught me by my sleeve using his teeth. "My apologies, but I cannot allow you to kill the queen."

He lifted the semi-unconscious Deirdre and gently adjusted her into a more dignified position. "As I said before, we must allow the heir of Dualsing to carry out her destiny as it was foretold."

"Her destiny? You mean her reign of terror?" I looked at Trust disbelievingly. "To what end? So she can continue to hurt and kill? So she can make her people thrive by kidnapping more children? That would only ensure support for the Council's war effort and drag out this conflict. To what end are you willing to see your own predictions through?"

I put a hand on both Gregory and Pedro, waking them up from the attack spell they were caught in. Alina zoomed out of hiding, conjuring a roll of bandages, and quickly patched me up before moving on to Pedro.

Gregory helped Pedro to his feet.

"M'lady. Queen Deirdre is foretold. There's no disputing that." Trust seemed unfazed by my outburst. "Her reign is meant to be violent. Fortunately, it's also supposed to be short-lived. Her destiny was to be in captivity for the rest of her days."

"What?" Gregory, Pedro, Alina, and I all said at the same time.

Trust blew mist from his nose, and when it reached Deirdre's wrist, it twisted into rope and bound her.

"I was the advisor for fourteen Dualsingian monarchs." Trust stood tall and proud, stretching to his full size. "I have lived for a very long time and there is still life left in me to serve this kingdom yet. I intend to—"

"You're going to rule Dualsing yourself, aren't you?" Gregory guessed.

"Will anyone allow me to finish my sentences?" Trust sighed. "No, boy, I'm not going to rule this kingdom. *He* will."

Trust pointed at Pedro.

"Me...me?" Pedro stuttered.

Trust turned to Alina. "How's the wound on his arm?"

"It healed itself. It went shallower before my very eye, then it was gone," Alina whispered, a strip of bandage still clutched in her fingers. "How did you know?"

"He's the true heir to the Dualsingian throne," Trust said simply. "He's almost unkillable now that he's stepped onto our soil again."

I tried to remember Trust's exact words to me earlier, realizing he must have misled me on purpose.

"Things are happening as it was foretold. Just as Queen Deirdre was foretold. The true ruler of the changelings must be allowed to rise to the challenge and lead us out of the rubble of the past."

Trust never actually said Queen Deirdre was the true ruler of the changelings, now had he?

"I'm the true ruler of Dualsing." The words from Pedro came out as a half-question.

"Yes, you are." Trust nodded at Pedro. "And your reign is going to be a long and prosperous one. I have waited many years for your arrival, your majesty. You'll guide our people on to a new and different path, one that moves away from the nasty business of switching out children. Times have changed. As a people we must develop a new identity. We need a self-sustaining modern economy and something distinctively ours that we can offer the world. And we need allies that are not only friendly because of our stolen information. You're the key to this renaissance."

"Why me? I'm not even royalty." Pedro frowned.

"Precisely. You were born a commoner, without the conniving nature bred into the changeling nobilities. You were nurtured in love and raised with the vengeance demon's sense of right and wrong. You are well versed in modern day science and technologies. You'll be a fair and wise ruler, and I would be honored to be by your side." Trust bowed to Pedro.

Maybe that was what Alina meant when she said that Pedro smelled like a Dualsingian with a hint of vengeance. Maybe being raised in such a manner had made him a vengeance demon in all the things that mattered.

Pedro paused, a look of wonder crossing over his face. He smiled tentatively, the first real smile he had since arriving at Dualsing. He might have resigned to stay on this plane out of obligation, but now he had something to look forward to, a way to change the very things he dreaded in his own race. He said to Trust formally, ruler to advisor, "The honor would be all mine."

He then turned to me and took my hand in his. A warm sensation spread through my body, all the way down to the tips of my toes, repairing the tendon in my ankle in the process. My bandage fell away from me. Pedro stared at it and whispered, "I knew how to heal you. Somehow, I just knew."

I flexed my ankle in wonder. "Thank you."

"Serafina"—he dropped my hand gently—"would you think it strange if I tell you that a small part of me isn't surprised at all? About everything?"

"It's meant to be." I felt it deep in my heart.

"No switching practices from now on," Pedro vowed, clutching his fist to his heart.

"Countless families will thank you," I said.

"It's the least I can do given the sins of the past. It'll take time for my people to find that new identity Trust mentioned." Pedro thought for a moment. "You probably won't hear from the changelings for a very long time. As a people we have a long way to go before finding our new place in the Cosmic Balance."

"I'll help." Alina drew close, though she seemed a little in awe to be in the presence of the new ruler, the heated towel she used to wipe his face just moments ago dangling awkwardly in her hand.

Pedro grinned at her. "I'm counting on it. I'm going to need to hear from representatives of the other races in Dualsing. We have to work together to survive, and that means listening to voices both big and small."

Alina beamed at her new monarch.

Trust coughed. "Lady Serafina, please apologize to Prince Eldon on my behalf again for misleading him. I didn't have the vision about King Pedro until you left Dualsing. Working on only partial information, I spent years grooming and encouraging Prince Eldon to be the ruler he'll never be. By the time I found out about King Pedro, Prince Eldon had become far too ambitious, and I was afraid of telling him the truth."

What Trust didn't say out loud was that he was afraid Eldon would've tried to kill Pedro in order to secure his throne. Remembering the old Eldon, the one who was willing to trap his own twin sister on the vengeance plane and never allow her to know her true heritage, I knew Trust wasn't entirely wrong in his reservation. I might've done the same if I was in his position.

"Don't worry about it. Eldon has come to see the damage of that ambition in himself. He'll understand," I reassured the dragon.

"I would sincerely hope so," Trust said.

"Goodbye, your majesty." Gregory offered Pedro a bow.

"Goodbye, cousin." Pedro pulled Gregory into a hug instead.

"We're not really related," Gregory reminded Pedro.

"And you're not really my subject," Pedro retorted.

Both guys smiled at each other.

Alina gave my shoulder a fierce hug. "I'm going to miss you, Serafina." She sniffled.

"Me, too, I hope we'll see each other again." I, too, would miss one of the only friends I'd ever had on this plane. But knowing she would no longer be under the reign of Deirdre did give me hope that I'd left her in a good place.

"So, are we ready to go?" Gregory asked me.

"Yes, we are," I said. I retraced my steps to where we were before Deirdre's interruption, with the hundred dots representing the kidnapped children overhead and Pedro psychically connected with them again. I sent out my request to the Molten Amber; and all the kidnapped children teleported to the Observatory.

Kids from a wide range of ages filled the room, each of them an untapped well of supernatural power. They were all understandably frightened by their new surroundings, and it took a bit of time to calm them down. Once they did, Pedro and I sent them to a day care center on the vengeance plane that Gregory had made arrangements with. They would be safe and cared for there until we could deliver them to their real families.

Once the kidnapped children exited Dualsing, another set of kids immediately teleported into the Observatory. There was a little guy in a full green hat and suit, clearly a leprechaun, and a troll in brown rags that reached almost to the ceiling of the dome.

The changeling children had come home.

Some of them bore similar physical appearance to supernaturals that could be found on the vengeance plane, others were enchanted to blend in with whatever races they were assigned to. Their bodies were covered in illusions such as wings, horns, hunchbacks, crocodile-like skin, and in one case, even gills and fins.

These children were more badly shaken by the transition than their counterparts. Not only because their connections with Pedro were across greater distances and thus less clear on what to expect, they also weren't aware of the switching practice as their counterparts who resided on Dualsing were. On top of that, the persistent tremors on Dualsing didn't provide a very warm welcome.

The child with the gills and fins, a changeling assigned to the underwater-witch tribe, started hyperventilating like a fish out of water. She had gone into shock over being in a non-aqueous environment even though physically her changeling body was perfectly capable of it. There was no reasoning with a lifetime of conditioning, though, and in the end Trust had no choice but to look her in the eye and place her in a suggestive trance, convincing her brain that she was still under water.

Part of my heart went out to the young girl, and all the other children; but another part was terrified of what might be happening to Eldon as more precious time had come and gone.

When Pedro and I finally tried to close the Council's portal, it didn't go smoothly. The opening on the vengeance side might be at a defined point of space, but that wasn't the case on the changeling side.

Because it had been formed without Eldon's consent or the use of jewels such as the Eye of Sebille, the portal was not stabilized. It sought to lock a location at Dualsing to establish a two-way network, but couldn't, and the entire changeling plane suffered for it. It was like a tornado that was constantly on the move, coming close to touchdown many times but never quite landing, leaving damage in its wake. How could one close a passage that wasn't technically opened on this end?

One cannot neutralize something that wasn't there for one to neutralize.

Pedro offered his hands and I clasped them in mine. Using the subtle patterns of the tremor, we tried to pinpoint the ever-shifting "twister" that was pressing itself into the very fabric of this plane. It proved to be evasive, until suddenly there was a push from the other end of the twister itself, compelling it to face us head on.

It was likely an attack from the Council, but also an opportunity.

Despite being hurled onto the ground by the force of that energy blast, Pedro and I threw everything we had at it, finally sealing the portal.

When the seismic activity on Dualsing ceased, we knew we had been successful.

We said our final goodbyes to Trust, Pedro, and Alina. It was time to leave Dualsing. While it took work to get *into*

Dualsing, returning to the vengeance plane was just like any other regular teleporting. Gregory and I arrived at the outer boundary of The Tree. Fir, the Off-Blacks, Esme, and Sui-Ling were waiting for us at the pre-designated spot.

"Where's Megan?" Gregory and I asked at the same time.

"She's still in there," Esme replied. "We think something's wrong and we're going back in."

My surprise at seeing Sui-Ling must have been obvious, because Fir shrugged and said, "She's the real deal, and she decided to help. Common enemies make strange bedfellows. Right, Sui-Sui baby?"

Sui-Ling gave Fir the death stare, which was totally lost on him as he was too busy leering at her bosom. "*Bed* has nothing to do with it."

❧ 28 ❧

THE DOUBLE DARE

"WHY?" I asked. "Why did you want Serafina to come rescue Eldon?"

"Megan." The high judge *tsked*. "If we tell you everything, then what's the challenge?"

Before we could continue our good-guy-versus-bad-guy confrontation like in any self-respecting B-rated human movie, the portal overhead winked out of existence.

Just like that. For something that twisted and untwisted six ways from Sunday, it was anti-climactic. One moment there was a vortex of warped space, the next everything was back to normal, as if the passage had never been.

So much for the Council's attempt at reverse psychology; Serafina followed their advice and eliminated their handiwork.

I barely had time to appreciate the irony before a strong shockwave lifted me off my feet, knocking me to the floor like a bowling pin.

"How do we know when Serafina begins reversing the passage on that side, without us being able to communicate?"

"You'll feel it. The vibration being imposed on Dualsing is going to start bouncing right back to the vengeance plane."

The expression on the high judge's face as he picked himself back up was thunderous. The rest of the Council looked just as dour and bitter.

Despite the trap I found myself in—and the return of the heaviness in my chest as I got up—my face split into a triumphant smile.

"What have you done?" High Judge Advocatus bellowed.

"What do you mean?" I asked innocently. "I've been here with you the whole time. That wasn't me."

"Serafina." Realization dawned on the high judge's face.

Time for some more distraction. Help might just come in time if I dragged this out long enough. For the first time since stepping into the room, I felt a glimmer of hope.

"Okay, let's just say for argument's sake that it *is* Serafina. That would be rather disappointing, wouldn't it?" I grinned, my eyes sweeping across the other Council members, hoping to engage more people to talk to me. "If she'd come here as you had hoped, what is it that you'd intended to accomplish with her?"

No one answered. These guys obviously hadn't watched enough human movies, where the bad guy always reveals his plan to the trapped heroes in a grand show of miscalculated arrogance.

I addressed Gregory's father directly. "Minister Sumpsi, what about it? What's the end game here? You can tell me. It's not like I'll be able to repeat it to Gregory. You know, your son? The one who happens to be a mercenary?"

That did it. Macallister Sebastian Sumpsi's eyes flashed, the mention of his illegitimate son a sore point. Good. "He's *not* my son. No child of mine would behave so shamefully."

"The half-ass tattoo on his chest says otherwise," I countered. "So kill me. Or not. But just tell me what the heck you were hoping to achieve. Let me know why I've been running around like a dog chasing its own tail for the last few days."

Minister Lawrence Harrison Lex—father of Madeleine Abrianna Lex, my nemesis from Demon U—stepped from the back of the crowd and considered me for a minute. Unlike the others, he was deadly calm, showing none of the anguish of having their grand plan derailed. I knew without a doubt that Minister Lex had already considered me dead. A chill came up my spine, and I forced myself to straighten it. "If Miss Advocatus had come here, we would have liked her to revive the changeling, for one. He seems to be in some kind of coma. Also we had hoped that she could help strengthen our passage."

"You mean your *former* passage? How did that work out for you?" I gestured to the ceiling, which was now normal. I knew I shouldn't push my luck, but I couldn't help it.

A muscle jumped on Minister Lex's face. "Don't be coy. We graciously answered your question. Now it's time for you to fulfill a request of our own."

"Is that what the high judge meant when he said earlier that he needed both Serafina and me? Alright, so what is it that you want me for?" I asked.

"Our request of you has always been the same, young lady," Minister Lex explained.

"Are you still on the whole *getting-your-boss-out-of-eternal-prison* business? Haven't you learned anything from Enid and Damarion's failure? You remember Enid, right? My mentor from Demon Co-op who tried to get me angry enough that I would open the portal to ultimate annihilation? I'm not about to fall for the same trick twice, so where do you go from here?"

High Judge Advocatus tilted his head as if he was receiving some news that pleased him immensely. He then smiled. Like a pack of wolves, all the other Council members did the same. An icy feeling hit my guts.

One collective snap of fingers from the Council members and Serafina, Gregory, Fir, the Off-Blacks, Esme, and Sui-Ling stood before me. Pedro wasn't there, but I assumed he was kept somewhere safe until we could fulfill our promise to him.

"Look who we've found wandering above our headquarters." Minister Lex chuckled.

Serafina cried out when she spotted Eldon, unconscious on the slab. She tried to run to him, but Esme and Sui-Ling grabbed hold of her. Those two, with their combined professional vengeance training and familiarity with our governing body, were the quickest to act as they read the situation in front of them with troubled eyes.

High Judge Advocatus was ever helpful in clarifying the Council's intention. "Well, Megan, let's see if we can get you to change your mind about releasing our master after seeing all your friends being tortured to death."

"Releasing your master?" Esme frowned. "The only masters that would need Megan's releasing are the Absolute Good and Evil. But that would mean you're the...the...no, it can't be!"

Comprehension dawned on her face, and she wasn't the only one.

"Wait." Bonaventure the Third laughed, gesturing at High Judge Advocatus. "He's one of *them*?"

"I'm afraid so. The entire Council is," I muttered.

Serafina gasped at High Judge Advocatus.

"Uncle Edbert." Serafina shook her head in disbelief. "How could you be involved with the Greys? I-I just can't imagine."

"*I* can," Gregory hissed, glaring at his own father.

The older man glared back. "I wish I'd never allowed your mother to keep you. Stupid girl."

"Don't you dare call my mother names." Gregory started toward Minister Sumpsi, then the mercenary was clawing at his own throat, his face turning blue. He fell to a kneeling position. I ran to him and cradled his head in my middle.

I chanted the counter spell to Minister Sumpsi's magic, and Gregory coughed, breathing heavily. I helped him to his feet. I might've won this battle, but I was so screwed in the war.

All my friends were here. There was no one else who could come riding to our rescue. Pedro was too young. Grandma was off injured somewhere. I knew she'd come to my aid if she could, and the fact that she wasn't here meant she *couldn't* be here. Whether I made it or not, I could at least try to get some people off the hook so they might regroup later.

I pointed at Sui-Ling. "This girl is not even *on* our team. She was probably fighting our lot when you grabbed them."

"And *this* one?" I poked Gregory in the shoulder. "I freakin' hate his guts."

Gregory just rubbed his throat, as if telling the world he understood that I liked him far more than I let on.

Not. Helping.

And in the end it didn't matter. The Council members conjured gold metal rings between their palms and sent them toward us. In my case, the metal ring expanded and looped over me, caging me in its circumference. For my friends, the rings contracted and settled right over their hearts. For a moment, there were no ill-effects from the rings; then everyone's faces started contorting with pain.

"The Menlonyn Rings are impregnated with over a thousand kinds of pain to be experienced by the heart. How long do you think your friends will last, Megan?" High Judge Advocatus mocked.

"Don't listen to him," Esme gasped.

"Ah, Esme. I'd almost forgotten to deal with you in all the excitement." High Judge Advocatus shook his head at the star student of Demon U. "I can't say I'm truly surprised by your actions, dear, but I'm still very disappointed."

"Screw you," she spat.

He *tsked*. "Such language."

Despite the pain they must all be feeling, my friends shouted out encouragement, all warning me not to give into the Greys' demand, not to give in to my anger, that they would rather be tortured than to lose the world.

One by one my friends, family, and yes, my would-be lover fell to the floor in agony, and there wasn't a damn thing I could do about it. Serafina held onto her arm as if it was broken, crying out in pain. Gregory shivered and curled up as if he was abandoned in an arctic wasteland; Fir raked his hands all over his body, yelling, "Fire ants! Fire ants! Get them off me!"

The rest of my friends exhibited reactions from pains such as severe migraine, fire, stomach ache, and in the case of Bonaventure the Third, a kick to the groin.

The experience of a thousand pains, indeed.

Panic and despair threatened to overtake me, only to be drown out by my fury. How dare they hurt my friends that way? Who did they think they were? I would make them pay, I swear.

Oh come on, Megan. We've been through this before. They're just trying to get you so angry so that this brain of yours will produce the resonance that would release the Absolute Good and Evil. Don't fall for it, my inner voice, which sounded like Fleur, my ancestor, warned.

My angry mind didn't care about the logic of it. My chest,

already tight due to my earlier ordeal, threatened to explode, and my ears rang as my blood pressure rose. All the adrenaline pumping through my body seemed to open up a new avenue in my brain.

Or one that had been opened only once before.

I felt almost giddy as the floodgate separating the two sides of my opposing nature—vengeance and trickster—showed a sliver of an opening. I could do this. I could trick the Council members with illusions they had never seen before, making them run around this room thinking their friends were their foes, and vice versa. I could fool them into hurting each other, even killing each other. How's that for a perfectly executed vengeance?

No! You've only just begun to fully tap into your inner trickster, and that's in a controlled setting, Fleur's voice rang in my head.

Yeah and who was teaching me how to do that? Grandma. Who's hurting now? Grandma. I want to make these bastards pay!

With my growing anger, heat radiated from my pearl necklace as my power geared up. A humming started in my head, and in the center of the room, a new passage was forming in response.

It was the sight of that passage that finally knocked some sense into me. I'd been tricked. Again. And I couldn't even afford the shame that went along with it as it would only lead to more anger and a wider passage to the Absolute Good and Evil's prison.

Well, if there was one comfort, it was that this time around the formation of the passage wasn't nearly as far along as last time. Yet with my white-hot emotions, I was still feeding the widening of the passage whether I liked it or not. My eyes strayed to my friends. Trapped as I was, I couldn't do anything for their suffering, but I could still close the passage. The only thing I could control now was me, and my torrent of emotions.

So I took myself out of the game.

I threw my body into an emergency shut down, like that time when Dan Pillar tried to kill me and I pretended to be a corpse. The Council might think that I had fainted out of stress and panic, but I was really weaving the Playing Dead spell all over myself. It was the first spell learned and last spell forgotten, and as natural to a trickster as making honey was to a bee.

And therefore the hardest to detect, even by the oh-so-sophisticated vengeance demons.

With luck, my Playing Dead would halt the emotional turmoil that was feeding the passage formation, putting a stop to it as effectively as removing all the firewood from a chimney. I wouldn't know beforehand whether it would work, as my unconsciousness was what would cause the cutting of the power.

It was only a stop-gap measure, as my friends and I were still trapped by the Council. Not to mention, I felt like a Judas for abandoning them, though they would be the first to point out that the fate of the world took precedence over individuals.

Hopefully the Council would stop torturing my friends once they realized I was out.

I set myself an internal timer to wake up in an hour, and sank into nothingness.

Or at least what I expected to be nothingness.

There was always nothingness whenever I used Playing Dead, including the time with Dan Pillar. In that case, one moment I was closing myself against the scorching heat that he was blasting my way, the next I was half buried in a dumpster with rotten banana peels on my face.

Not this time.

I didn't black out. I was...floating. Floating in a transparent, aqueous world full of moss-green water. I didn't want to move. I didn't have to. A gentle wave carried me back and forth, rocking me like ocean current would to a forest of kelps. There were no worries here. No thinking. No gravity. Just swaying.

Then I felt another mind, a consciousness if you will, getting close to me. The waves were drawing us together, as if we were two Cheerios in a bowl of milk in those human commercials. Like recognized like. As the other mind got closer, I could tell that he—yes, it was a he—didn't seem to be enjoying this kingdom of thoughtlessness as much as I was.

"Megan," the mind shouted at me, reverberating through the water, stretching my name in an almost incomprehensible echo. But there was a sense of urgency in the echo, nevertheless.

I moaned, not wanting to let go of this numbness that had enveloped me. There was something terrible lurking at the edge of true wakefulness. I could feel it. And I wanted nothing but to stay in this tranquil land of lost thoughts forever.

"Megan!" The mind was right next to me now. "Snap out of it. Your friends need you."

I sighed and spoke, the sound of my voice muffled even to my own ears. "Go away. I don't have to wake up for another hour."

I didn't even know that I knew that until I said it out loud. With the return of knowledge came a flicker of self-awareness. It had the burnt taste of anxiety to it.

"In another hour you might not have a body to wake up to. If they can't get you to wake up and co-operate soon, they'll just kill us all."

That got my attention. I sat up and found myself floating on the moss-green ocean rather than being in it, a wooden board under my body supporting me.

Eldon sat on a wooden board of his own; we floated next to each other, bumping gently against each other in the waves. His royal highness was in a pristine royal uniform of some sort, all shiny brass buttons and braided ropes, and not a splash of water on his person.

"Where are we?" I asked.

Eldon shrugged. "Wherever we go when we Play Dead."

"You know about the spell?" Of course he knew. Tricksters and changelings were distant cousins; they must've shared this ancient magic way back when. Eldon didn't simply pass out cold on that slab table—he did it intentionally, like me.

And now we were in this world outside of the world together.

"I'd never used Playing Dead before," Eldon explained. "But it just came to me when I thought I couldn't bear the torture anymore. I was never told you can be conscious during it, though."

"Me, either," I admitted.

"Is the Council's passage gone?"

"Yeah."

He breathed a sigh of relief. "Thank Fleur. I've been trying to help Finny close it from this end, pushing the passage to take a more corporal form on Dualsing so she could pinpoint it and neutralize it. But being in this world I couldn't tell if it worked."

"Hold on. You're okay with the passage going kaput? That might be your only chance to go back home." And to win the crown, which was what he'd intended on doing before the Council had us believe otherwise.

Eldon gave me a glare. "Just because the Council used me to convey certain information to Serafina for their own end, doesn't mean I wasn't on board with the message. They thought they were using me, but in fact I was using *them*. I was in full control of that last conversation with Finny, and with Trust's help I managed to block out certain parts of it without the Council ever knowing the wiser. They thought I was telling Serafina to go to Dualsing as a vague suggestion, an impossibility that would herd her toward coming for me. Instead, I was passing her specific information to make sure she could follow through with it."

"Like which allies to contact and such," I realized.

"And what to do about the Council's passage. I made sure the Council didn't know what Finny would be up to." Eldon's lips curled in satisfaction.

"You must have needed energy to help close the passage. How? We're in the land of thoughts and dreams," I asked, feeling like there was something I wasn't seeing, a missing piece of the puzzle that was staring me right in the face. Then I got it.

The tunnels throughout the Tree were lined with Molten Amber.

"The Molten Amber will help too because they could sense my will in you." That was what Serafina said Eldon told her.

"...but the Council are control freaks. Why would it choose to trust something they can't fully control?"

"It's tradition. What can't be controlled by them also couldn't be controlled by others."

Well, maybe that wasn't true, after all.

Eldon smiled. "You figured it out, huh?"

"You used the Molten Amber."

But there was more. It was in the hint of sadness in his smile. The Molten Amber was a conduit, but a conduit was different from an energy source. So where did the energy come from?

"You paid a heavy price for closing that passage, didn't you?" I guessed.

"A necessary one," Eldon said softly. "I poured the core essence of what made me a changeling into that push. It was the only thing I had at my disposal that was strong enough. As a result, I not only have the physical strength of a mortal, I *am* a mortal now. It's for the best anyway. I could never be used to open a passage to my people ever again."

It was then that I truly believed Eldon's claim that he had given up on the changeling crown. He was really going to be the best king he could ever be, by not trying to rule at all.

I admired that. And I was so happy for Serafina. Well, once they stopped torturing her.

Speaking of which...

"I have to go back," I told Eldon.

"I expected nothing less, Megan." Eldon nodded. "I don't think there's a rule saying you can't be awake before the hour is up. I'll be right behind you."

I blinked and got up from my wooden board, except it had now become the floor. I was at the lab with the Council again. Fortunately, the Menlonyn Ring that was my prison dissipated as I stood up. I had a feeling Eldon had something to do with it. My heart beat steadily, my earlier weakness gone.

The Council members were too busy debating among themselves about what to do with my friends to immediately notice my emergence from Playing Dead. It would seem that while they had no problem torturing the likes of Sui-Ling, Esme, and Serafina, there was some hesitation about how it would look if they were actually killed, especially in regard to the backlash from the Condor League.

The passage I had formed was gone, as I'd gambled it would be.

My friends, semi-alert, lay where they had fallen. Though their torture seemed to have stopped since I Played Dead, they were severely weakened and in no shape to fight. Eldon still made a very good show of being out, though I knew he must be awake as well.

I brushed imaginary lint off my shirt, then coughed.

The Council members turned toward me and their jaws dropped.

"Megan, dear, you came to." The high judge attempted to hide his shock. I would bet that he had tried many ways to wake me up and had been unsuccessful. The fact that they were discussing the disposal of my friends probably meant they'd given up.

"No, I *chose* to come to," I corrected him. "During my time away I had an epiphany. Eureka. Inspired. Whatever you call it."

"What do you mean? Inspired, as in by my master?" High Judge Advocatus actually looked strangely hopeful. Well, I was supposed to be able to bring the Absolute Good back, so maybe it wasn't that big of a stretch that I could be touched by it on a more personal level, right?

"No." I didn't bother to elaborate, to tell him that what really inspired me was Eldon's idea of being the best ruler by not ruling at all.

Using the same principle, I realized that in order to be the best vengeance demon I could ever be, I had to not care about being a part of this plane at all.

"Then what are you talking about?" Minister Sumpsi demanded, throwing his hands up in the air.

"You guys really do hold all the cards here, you know. You're way more powerful. You've got my friends. You're well-connected and could make our lives miserable." I counted the Council's advantages on my fingers. They weren't anything my enemies weren't aware of. Then I grinned. "But you have one weakness."

"And what is that?" Minister Lex's tone was full of dismissiveness.

"You need me alive. You need me alive and well on this plane." After all, I was a living, talking get-out-of-jail card for their master, with *living* being the operative word. They could torture my friends and family all day, but they dared not cause me any real physical harm. Even when Enid was pretending to hurt me, she was careful never to deliver any fatal wounds.

The Council members said nothing. I took that as a good sign and plunged on.

"But, you see, I have no problem leaving this plane, if it means my loved ones would be spared from the judgment day that the return of Absolute Good will bring forth." I wasn't saying I was dying to be a martyr or anything like that, but in order to embrace my true competitive edge, I had to take a long hard look at the score and know exactly how far I was willing to go if it came to that. And I needed my enemies to see that, too.

Still not a single word from them. I kept on talking, working it out in my head as I spoke.

"What we have here is what the humans call mutual assured destruction. Let us go and leave us be, or I'll open the portal to your master's prison and jump right in before anything could escape out. That's gotta seal the passage up good, don't you think? From the legends, I know the prison can't be opened from their end, not by anyone. That means not even me."

"You...you would not dare." High Judge Advocatus's voice was full of fury—and a hint of un-disguisable fear.

"You're talking to a girl who's backed into a corner and got nothing to lose. I'm the only vengeance demon and trickster hybrid born in like, forever. I'm your hope, your best chance to keep your fanaticism going. Do it for the new recruits if nothing else. Think about it, as long as I stay in this world," I coaxed, my tone changed from confrontational to drenched in honey, "I could slip up. I could get pissed off and open the portal. Different life stages...new crisis...accumulated heartbreaks through the years...all that could add up to a moment of weakness for you to swoop right in, and voilà, *Hello, Absolute Good*. You never know. As long as I stay on this plane, that is."

"You're talking about a cease fire," Minister Sumpsi said slowly.

"I'm talking about taking a bet on my weakness."

To secure the safety of me and my friends and to earn a reprieve for the world, I was counting on the Greys' confidence in their ability to get me in the end. I was banking on their need for hope, and my own determination to resist them day after day. It was a contest of wills I'd have to engage in from now on, my only possible advantage was to be less arrogant than the bad guys.

And that meant acknowledging that I wasn't infallible and beyond temptation, and that this could really come back and bite me in the end.

It wasn't perfect and it certainly wasn't a final resolution for the whole mess, but I was learning that absolutes were bullshit anyways.

"What do you say?" My eyes traveled from one Council member to another. They all looked disgusted and angry. "Hey, if you don't want to take the deal, you can always try to get another vengeance demon to hook up with a trickster, but that might be harder than bringing forth the end of the world."

As if to demonstrate what I was saying, a moaning Fir reached up and scratched his butt cheek and accidently brushed against Sui-Ling's thigh. Well, maybe not so accidently. Sui-Ling gave a swift kick to knock Fir's hand away.

"There's one more thing you should know." Serafina picked herself up from the floor and addressed the Council. "I got into Dualsing before coming here."

The Council members took a collective intake of breath and exchanged greedy looks with each other. Though they already figured Serafina must have closed their portal to Dualsing somehow, to hear that she was actually able to get onto the changeling plane was something else. I could practically hear the Council members plotting how they could take advantage of Serafina's access to Dualsing. If they couldn't have their master returned, then at least they could wage a great war in the name of justice. I wondered why Serafina would want to share the information about Dualsing, but she gave me a look that told me there was a good reason for her reveal.

"While it is true that I was able to get in," she continued, "I had a great deal of help. A changeling who was living on the vengeance plane helped me open the passage. But he's gone now. He'd decided to stay with his own people."

"You hear that?" I asked the Council, hiding my own shock at her words. I was rather fond of Pedro. He was a good kid. "Just in case you're thinking about capturing Serafina to open another passage into the changeling plane. It won't work because she can't do it alone."

"And I won't be able to help you, either," Eldon said. I had no idea when he got up from the slab, but there he stood beside it. "I've shed the last of my changeling essence. You will no longer be able to use me as an anchor. If you don't believe me, use your senses."

It was comical how in a few moments the Council members' faces went from hopeful to suspicious then to bitter. Their senses must have confirmed that Eldon wasn't lying.

"So no war for you." I helped my remaining friends off the floor. They looked like hell, but there didn't appear to be any long-term effects from their ordeal.

High Judge Advocatus said, "Even if we are to reach an agreement about releasing you and your friends, Megan, there's still the matter of the war and public opinion. The Council must be seen as keeping its word."

Ah, so we were down to negotiating the specifics now. That was practically a yes to my proposal.

"What, you want my help in getting you out of this hole you dug yourself into, with all those promises made of ultimate retribution? Fear not. I might just have something to soothe the beast of popular opinion." I turned to Serafina, "Did the children all make it back okay?"

"Yes. They're at a secret location as we speak. There are about a hundred of them," Serafina replied.

"You see? A hundred kidnapped supernatural children just got rescued. They're from a cross section of the Cosmic Balance," I told the Council. "Gregory already has the right to the financial benefit of this operation, Fir got the street cred for helping our changeling cousins, but the Council can take the official recognition. Spin it whichever way you want. Make yourselves legendary heroes in the face of the evil changelings, or whatever. How's that for appeasing the populace?"

I stole a glance at Gregory, hoping he wasn't too pissed off by the idea of his old man getting undeserved credit due to his own actions, especially considering the choking incident earlier. But to my surprise he seemed strangely smug about it. It was his father who looked as if he'd been asked to swallow a lump of rotten cabbage.

"You're willing to let us claim this victory as ours?" Minister Lex said incredulously.

"Yes. Take all the glory you can stomach, as long as you leave my friends and family the hell alone. And no 'accidents' befalling them, either." I'd finally come to understand that the things that were valued in the world I was trying to be a part of—the co-op credits, vengeance markers, and social recognition—were all but an illusion, a distraction from doing the actual right thing, and I had as little use for glory as a mercenary ever did.

"That...that could do. That could do very well. The press will love us, and our reputation will grow," a Council member who was responsible for public relations and inter-species liaisons breathed. I could practically hear the wheels turning in his head and see white smoke coming from his ears.

High Judge Advocatus huffed. "But even with tangible results, the public would still need to feel that the changelings did not get away with their crimes. They need someone concrete to blame and to be brought to real justice. The wrongdoers couldn't get away with their bad deeds. That's the essence of a good vengeance."

Oh, the irony of the words. There would be no good vengeance if the intention wasn't pure, and if the purpose of the fight wasn't just. I could see that now.

"You want someone to bring to justice. How about her?" Serafina carefully took out a small casing from her dress pocket. A Barbie doll suspended in the center of it. At close examination, it wasn't a plastic toy, but a real, pixie-sized girl all dressed up in silk fineries. She appeared to be asleep.

"Deirdre," Eldon exclaimed.

"May I present to you, Deirdre, queen of the changelings," Serafina introduced the miniature figure on her palm. "We had captured and miniaturized her."

I now understood why Serafina had been so open about having been to Dualsing. There was no point hiding it because she had been planning to reveal the ace in her, well, pocket.

"Her changeling essence is gone, just like mine." Eldon's eyes were wide.

Serafina nodded. "We made sure that the Council would not be able to use her to get into Dualsing."

There were many burning questions I was dying to ask

Serafina. Like how did they manage to capture such a prize, and who the heck was ruling Dualsing now? Again, later.

High Judge Advocatus looked at Serafina as if he was seeing her for the first time. "It would appear that I underestimated you, niece."

"Thank you, uncle," Serafina said, deadpan.

"The changeling queen is wanted for the murder of Serafina's cousin, plus all the kidnappings committed during her reign." I grinned. "You guys can have a very open trial. Make a TV circus out of it. The public digs that kind of drama. Especially with her exotic beauty and the royal title. How's that for a distraction?"

The Council member responsible for media relations looked like he was about to pass out from excitement.

I didn't feel too bad about the indignity and likely life imprisonment that awaited Deirdre. That was the problem with being a bloodthirsty psychopath—not a lot of people would be too outraged by your punishment, even when it was dished out by people who were just as horrible.

"And the new ruler of the changelings has vowed that there will be no more switching," Serafina added.

"A return of the kidnapped kids, a gain of a prisoner, and obtaining the promise of no more kidnapping," I counted the three points on my fingers. "You don't even need a lot of spinning to make this look good."

Now High Judge Advocatus smiled. They all did.

So it was decided. The Council went back to looking righteous, and my friends and I went back to our lives and pretended we didn't know they were not only assholes, but the very enemy they claimed to fight against. All was peaceful.

At least for now.

EPILOGUE #1

RE-SURFACING from the Tree was a bit of a shock. After spending what felt like an eternity underground, the waning twilight seemed incredibly bright and such a miracle because a part of me had wondered if our group would be able to make it out at all.

"A lot of downed trees here," Megan observed as we made our way out of the boundary of the vengeance headquarters.

The broken timbers were covered in a fresh layer of snow, their demise a stark reminder of the aftershocks that must've shaken this plane when the Council's passage with Dualsing was severed.

"I didn't notice when I was here earlier," I replied honestly. I was too intent on racing to Eldon's side.

"Serafina," Megan asked once we were out of the boundary, "have you thought about where you're going to stay for the next few nights?"

"No, I haven't." But now that Megan mentioned it, I realized I couldn't bear the idea of staying under the same roof as my uncle, who had turned out to be a betrayer of everything I was taught. I had no idea if my own birth parents were also involved with the Greys, and I wasn't ready to find out just yet.

"Feel free to stay with me. Rosemary wouldn't mind. You remember my roommate Rosemary, right?" Megan said. Then she glanced at Eldon. "But if you prefer to be with him, my parents' house might be a better choice. Their place is bigger than mine. And I don't think they'll mind, either."

"I appreciate the offer," I told Megan. "Let me speak with Eldon first."

There was so much that needed to be said between us.

"You go ahead," Megan said with a knowing smile. "We'll wait here. I have to make a few calls about Grandma anyway. And with all the adrenaline coursing through our bodies, it's not like anyone is rushing to get home to head straight to bed."

Eldon and I split from the group and walked in silence for a few minutes. I was at a loss for how to begin the conversation, and that made me strangely self-conscious. What did one say to someone who had just said goodbye to everything he'd ever known, including his life-long ambition, his magic, and his supernatural identity? How did one comfort someone who had been betrayed on so many levels, even by his own trusted dragon, no matter how valid the reason?

I wasn't even in the position to offer him a place of my own to stay on this plane.

"Finny." Eldon finally turned to me. "I don't know what to say first."

"That makes two of us." I gave him a shy smile. When he didn't return it, my smile faltered. His gaze slid away without meeting mine, and his lips thinned into a stubborn line. He was right in front of me, yet farther away than ever, even more than when he was captured.

Noticing my hurt bewilderment, Eldon halted, catching

my wrist so I stopped as well. Then he let it go as if our touch burned him.

"Finny, I'm not handling this very well." He sighed with a mixture of sadness and frustration.

"What's the matter? At the very core of it?" I asked. There were merits in the human analogy of ripping off a band aid.

Eldon took a deep breath.

"I don't deserve you," he blurted, there was anguish in his voice now. "Because I didn't choose you."

"Go on," I encouraged Eldon to explain further. We needed to talk about this if we were to move forward.

"I didn't choose you," he repeated. "Not in the way that matters. I didn't choose you when we were at Dualsing, before you went back home. Not really. I thought I was, but wanting you got mixed up with wanting the throne. I didn't choose you for you, even when I claimed I was."

"Eldon, that's in the past." The choice he made, and the choice I made because of it, lay before us. Would I have been happier if our course was set right from the get-go? There was no use dwelling on the what-ifs.

"No, you don't understand," he emphasized. "I didn't choose you then. And I didn't give up my ambition tonight for you, either. You're not the primary reason, anyway. I did it mainly for my own people. So that's twice I put you second, and damned if I'm going to ride into the sunset with you now as if you're some kind of consolation prize."

He spit out the last two words, disgusted.

"Even if you want to? Riding into the sunset, that is." I gestured toward the last slice of the sun disappearing over the trees.

"Finny, how can you be so calm and forgiving about this?" He ran his fingers over his hair in frustration.

"Do you want me to fault you for not considering me your

primary motivator in the face of some very tough choices? You just told me you gave up the chase for power because it was the right thing to do. And that's the way it should be. You shouldn't have done it just because of me. You would've come to resent me. We're not in the land of fairy tales anymore, and we should also leave behind the unrealistic notion of their version of happily-ever-after."

"But that brings me to my next point. I'm not a creature of the fairy tales anymore. I now have no more power than a regular human. I won't be able to protect you if something happens. I might even be hunted by enterprising supernaturals who believe that my mortal status is but a cover."

I sighed. I often wished I had Megan's straight-forwardness, but now seemed like as good a time as ever to channel a bit of her practicality in the situation.

I turned on my phone and did a quick search on all the rental properties around the day care center where Gregory had placed the children we freed from Dualsing. There was an empty building nearby that used to be an indoor trampoline park. Perfect. I forwarded the link to the Advocatus family lawyer and requested that he take care of the lease for the building right away. He replied almost immediately, his text simply reading: "Consider it done."

"What are you doing?" Eldon asked, confused by my sudden obsession with my phone.

"Taking out a loan against my trust fund to set up a support center for the kids. I have a year off school. I have the time and money at my disposal to do this, and do it right. The Council might make a big fanfare out of rescuing these kids, but the actual legwork of identifying, supporting, and counseling them is not something the authorities would care about. I know what they're going through and I can help with the transition. And you're going to help me help them."

"Finny, did you hear what I said?" he demanded. "I'm no longer of magic."

"You're wrong."

He gaped at me.

"You were born a changeling," I continued. "You inherited all the traits that come with that heritage. You're not a prophesied king who was, by rare design, unselfish. But you managed to overcome your nature. *That* is your real magic. And don't you dare downplay it. I need your strength by my side."

Eldon was expressionless for the longest time, until his face opened in a slow smile. "You're a force of nature. Not the gentle and contemplative Finny I knew."

"No. I grew up," I conceded.

"I know." Eldon pulled me into his arms and pressed his lips to my forehead. "I'll be honored to help you at the support center, m'lady, and I hope we get to know each other all over again."

"As the adults we became," I said. Real life relationships took time to nurture and grow, and I wanted to get to know this new Eldon. So achingly familiar yet refreshingly new.

"As adults," he agreed.

EPILOGUE #2

BACK TO BEFORE

THE GROUND of the hospice looked the same as the last time I set foot on the property, which wasn't really that long ago, but everything had changed now.

I stared up at the window of the room where Sandra Hogan, the target from my co-op assignment, resided. I felt her life essence all the way from here, meaning it was still going pretty strong. She hadn't passed on to the next world yet, just as Gregory had promised. But she might as well because her vengeance was now utterly beyond my reach.

So was getting a degree at Demon U, for that matter.

"Megan, are you sure about this?" Gregory asked from behind me.

I took a deep breath. "Yeah."

I'd been making discreet but frantic calls to everyone and anyone who could possibly know where Grandma was—excluding her "friends" from the Council. No one had heard from her, or if they had they wouldn't tell me. I was close to the point of pulling my hair out when Esme got a call from her mom. I guess there was nothing like almost losing a daughter while climbing Mount Olympus to strengthen the mother-child bond. The renewed relationship proved fruitful as her mother had delivered a vital piece of information to us —she'd seen Grandma.

The specialist of scorned women and scorched male genitals was on her first day back from vacation, immersing her soul in the endless sea of data that was the Internet when she felt the presence of another supernatural.

A fellow vengeance demon. Weak. Substance-less. Away from her body which was shut down for healing. A soul that was part of this world still, yet not.

Esme's mother, having been Grandma's star pupil back in the days when Gran was lecturing at Demon U, recognized the essence of her former mentor—and former mother-in-law —right away.

Dammit, Grandma must be pretty desperate if she had chosen to hide out and rest on the Internet—she hated computers, no matter what a necessary evil she thought they were.

Esme was now following her mother into the Internet in search of Grandma. I couldn't even put into words how much I desperately wanted to be part of that expedition. But such a trip required someone more experienced as a guide lest the soul became lost in the vast kingdom of information. Esme's bond with her mom was of love and blood, while my only link with the lady was her ex-husband, my dad. It didn't take a genius to figure out that Esme was the better choice for the job, as much as it was killing me to wait around for news.

So instead of driving myself crazy with worry, I came to the hospice to do some detangling in my own life. Somehow, despite her status in the vengeance society, I thought Grandma would understand why I had to do what I was about to do.

Maybe that had something to do with the fact that as it turned out, her status—esteemed member of a respected governing body—had also been built on shiftier sand than expected.

Gregory faded to the background as I approached the front of the hospice. A haughty-looking vengeance demon, a TA from fourth year I knew only by face, greeted me on the doorstep. And by greeting I meant she looked me up and down as if I had dirt under my fingernails and broccoli in my teeth. I produced the vengeance file on Sandra Hogan and held it out for her, but she didn't take it. Not yet.

"Do you, Megan Aequitas, agree to hereby forego this vengeance case, and all the privileges and responsibilities that are associated with it?"

I sighed. "I called you here for this purpose, didn't I?"

I had contacted the faculty counselor after seeing Esme off and expressed my wish to withdraw from Demon U and by extension, the co-op program. I had no idea how much of the details they'd shared with the TA standing in front of me, but I was getting a strong mix of feelings from her. There was relief—likely by the fact that the university would once again be trickster-free, and anger. She was pissed that the likes of me would dare to quit the school before the school was able to quit me.

The TA still would not take the case file. "Please give me a verbal confirmation that you are indeed forsaking the full right to administer and benefit from this vengeance."

I didn't bother to point out that I'd already done almost half the work, and I'd softened up the target further by making her sweat over the remaining punishment. Didn't matter. The TA would take over the file and get the full credit for it. She probably considered it a just reward for being called here in the dead of the night, and she wasn't entirely wrong.

"Yes. It's all yours," I replied.

Without further ado, the TA yanked the file out of my

hands and walked into the hospice without as much as a backward glance.

"Are you *sure* about this?" Gregory repeated his question from earlier, revealing himself next to me.

I laughed. It sounded shrill even to my own ears. "No. But it's too late now, and I won't change it even if I can. All I know is that I can never go back to before. I can't pretend that the last few days didn't happen."

Up until then I had been the perfect student—never mind what they said about my trickster heritage. I was completely willing to do my assignments, play by the rules, and pay my dues, so that one day I would be recognized as a professional in my field. Now, knowing what I knew about the people at the very top of the vengeance food chain, I couldn't go back to being a part of the rat race anymore.

What was the point of courting a universally recognized qualification when the universe itself was hanging on such a precarious balance?

The world had earned nothing but a reprieve. I had no delusion about that. The Greys would no doubt try to get their next scheme to bring forth their master in motion. It might be a few weeks, or a few months or years, but they would strike again before I knew it. Just willing myself to calm down, or even making the ultimate sacrifice, would not be enough. They would find a new way to get to me. The "how" didn't matter, only that they would not stop. An organization that had spent centuries infiltrating the very core of the vengeance power structure would not be stopped by a few minor setbacks.

I had to actively seek a way to defeat the Greys. And I had to get creative with it.

Fir had now partnered up with the Off-Blacks, and together they planned to quietly rally the tricksters and the other lesser supernaturals—those who had the most to lose in the event of an all-out racial cleansing.

Esme, upon her return from the Internet and the search for Grandma, would work her upper class contacts, while Sui-Ling had agreed to do the same with her network of secret societies.

It would take time, patience, and stealth, as we might not be believed. It was, after all, our word against the deeply esteemed Council. And we would definitely be monitored, hence the aforementioned stealth. Fir had a few ideas about beating the traces that they would no doubt set on us, and I trusted his skills in giving us the privacy that we needed.

I would have to call a big family meeting. I considered distancing myself from my family for their own good, but then my other trickster half-brothers would have gotten the whole story from Fir anyway, and I would end up hurting my parents more in the long run if I allowed them to think the worst by dropping out without explanation and cutting them off.

Not that I wanted them involved in the whole mess, but keeping them in the dark just wasn't the grown up thing to do.

I had no idea how my parents would feel about the new direction in my career. Especially Dad. After all, I followed his footsteps by attending Demon U. But then maybe he would understand. I thought back to last fall, and the little unclaimed vengeance involving a certain terrorist that was our father-daughter secret, and smiled.

"So," I asked Gregory as we left the hospice ground, "what's our first assignment?"

"I heard there's a major jail break in Hell." Gregory smiled. "They were missing a few fugitives at the last count."

That was right—I'd partnered up with Gregory in the trade of mercenary. Part of me almost couldn't believe it, either. It was the best way for me to make new contacts and keep my ears to the ground, to fight another day against the Council. Or at the very least, stay the heck away from its clutches.

Just twenty-four hours ago I would say this was a crazy idea, that the life of a mercenary was something I would never consider. Little did I know that I had far, far less to fear from the darker side of vengeance. I knew now where the real temptation for bending to the Greys' will would come from.

My true enemy lay in my deep-seated craving for security, which was instinctive after a lifetime of fighting my trickster tendencies. I couldn't afford to get cushy and convince myself that all was fine, that continuing to be a good little vengeance girl would shield me from the Council's attention. I had to push myself out of my comfort zone and get used to having less. Fewer conveniences. Less creature comfort. Less straightforward black and white.

"This job, the money is good?" I asked Gregory.

"It's good," he assured me, though both of us were fully aware that he wasn't getting back to work this fast for the money, as the financial payoff from all the kidnapped children's families would be enough for him to buy a private dimension of his own.

"That's good then." Should I thank him for taking me on as a partner? For everything else that he'd done? Should I suggest that we go grab some shawarmas like the Avengers after the Battle of New York? Would that be, like, a dinner date? For Hades's sake, I really sucked at this male and female communication thing.

Then I felt Gregory's lips on mine, his arms wrapping themselves around me. His fresh scent filled my senses, saving me from overthinking the lot of it.

Okay, I could work with that.

THIS IS WHERE THE AUTHOR SHAMELESSLY BEGS YOU TO LEAVE A REVIEW...

Did you enjoy A GOOD VENGEANCE? If so, I would really appreciate it if you could write a review on Goodreads and/or your online retailer!

ABOUT THE AUTHOR

Louisa Lo lives in Toronto, Canada with her husband, an aristocratic cat, and more cardboard boxes than she cares to unpack. She decided to write about vigilantes, because it seems like a better life choice than trying to become one and landing herself in jail. She just has that kind of luck.

Visit Louisa's website at **www.LouisaLo.com** where you'll find her social media links.

RECOMMENDED READING SEQUENCE

Vengeance Be Mine (Vengeance Demons #1)
Before Vengeance (Vengeance Demons #0)
Vengeance Unclaimed (Vengeance Demons #2)
A Good Vengeance (Vengeance Demons #3)
Vengeance For Hire (Vengeance Demons #4)
Hell Hath No Vengeance (Vengeance Demons #5)

BLURB AND EXCERPT

VENGEANCE FOR HIRE

WHO WOULD'VE THOUGHT the dangerous life of a mercenary could be so...*normal*?

It's been a month since Megan Aequitas started her new life in the mercenary world of vengeance demons and shared a heart-pounding kiss with her infuriatingly sexy business partner, Gregory.

When Megan takes control of the 24/7 hotline for their business, she and Gregory are in for a hell of a day. The exciting stuff— kidnapped faes, secretive satyrs, and the punishment of magical creature traffickers—lasts less than an hour in total. The rest of the time is spent dealing with client interviews, service quotes, and worst of all, the relentless little old lady who harasses them with everything from jelly-bean-stealing neighbors to haunted litter boxes.

Except the old gal's seemingly trivial demands for justice might not be so trivial, after all...

Note: The events in VENGEANCE FOR HIRE take place between A GOOD VENGEANCE and HELL HATH NO VENGEANCE.

CHAPTER 1

6:03 A.M.
The Business Call

"Dôme épais le jasmine..."

I opened my eyes, startled out of a nice little dream about chocolate covered strawberries by the shrill sound of opera. I shot up from the bed. What the hell? My alarm was set to Elmer Fudd's version of *Ride of the Valkyries*, not this—

Then I remembered. It was the ring tone for the Phone. With a capital P.

I pressed the talk button on the Phone before the chorus was over. Luckily, Rosemary was already up and about. My human roommate had a habit of getting up at five thirty in the morning in order to bake. And they called *me* the supernatural.

"Hello, this is Clear Vengeance. How may I help you?" I kept my tone professional and non-groggy-like.

It'd been a month since Gregory and I started working together as mercenaries. He'd been the one who handled our business bookings. But last night, I decided that enough was enough and I grabbed the Phone off him. I wasn't stupid—whoever possessed the Phone was the one who truly controlled the business, and I desperately needed some control when it came to Gregory, even if it was only for this one aspect. I'd been feeling off-kilter ever since that kiss we'd shared, on the night I said goodbye to my life as a vengeance demon student.

Although, with the Phone linked to our 24/7 Hire-A-Vengeance-Demon hotline, this little fight for dominance might just bite me in the ass.

An old woman's raspy voice came through the receiver. "Hello, dear. I have an urgent vengeance matter that I need your help in."

"That's what we're here for." I smiled. See, this wasn't so bad.

"Can you come right away?" she asked urgently.

I glanced at my calendar. Our first appointment of the day wasn't until eight thirty, and thanks to teleportation, it wasn't like there was any time lost to commuting. We could totally fit the little old lady in before that. Besides, if I was up already, then why shouldn't Gregory be?

Geez, I sounded cranky even to myself.

After copying down her information, I hung up and called Gregory. At least there was no awkwardness in waking him up for business purposes. Being in the vengeance business was like working in the ER—people didn't always have need of us within the nine to five time frame.

"Hey, guess what? I got us some new business," I said proudly. Yes, I would focus on the positivity of the new job rather than my other, less professional feelings.

"Oh, yeah?" His voice sounded groggy, like he was talking underwater or he was still in bed. And I tried not to let myself wonder what he must look like, or whether or not he slept shirtless. I'd seen his naked chest before, so there was plenty to fuel my imagination. "What's the address?"

"53 Mango Tree Drive. Apartment 503."

Gregory groaned. "This doesn't happen to be for a Ms. Whitehall, does it?"

I frowned at his tone. "How did you know?"

"I know"—he sighed—"because Ms. Whitehall is a *TPC*."

"A what?"

"A *TPC*. Trivial Pursuit Caller. The lady in question is super paranoid and she has been calling the line every week since I started it. I don't know how the human managed to get my number, but she did and she never stops calling."

"Well, maybe she has a legitimate concern this time." I couldn't help but feel a little defensive. Ms. Whitehall might be a TPC, but she was *my* TPC.

"Last Wednesday she called about a neighbor stealing her jellybeans. But only the orange ones. The week before she thought her gluttonous cat gained weight because it was cursed by fairies."

Damn.

"I gave a code to every caller who'd ever used the line: *MVC* for Most Valued Customer, *ECFP* for Extra Charge due to Fringe Plane, etc," Gregory explained. "The code is right on the display of the Phone. Otherwise how am I supposed to tell who has an actual urgent matter?"

"Why didn't you tell me?" I complained.

"I wanted to," he said dryly, "but you grabbed the Phone and teleported away before I could say a single word."

Double damn.

"I'll cancel the appointment then." I could imagine how uncomfortable that call would be, when I had just promised the old lady that I would look into her problem less than five minutes ago. But I was the one who created this mess, so it was only fair that I was the one to fix it.

"We can't." Gregory sighed. The sound of springs creaking in the bed, footsteps, and then a running faucet came over the receiver. "By the code of mercenary, we cannot cancel an appointment without just cause once a promise to meet is given. A mercenary's word is his or her bond. Why do you think I coded the callers to begin with?"

Before I started, I would've never thought in a million years that mercenaries would have a stricter code of conduct than licensed vengeance demons from the Council, but there it was. Gone were the days when I mocked Gregory about the lack of ethics of his profession. Now it was also my profession, and it was nothing like how I'd imagined it.

CHAPTER 2

7:00 A.M.
Client Interview #1

Gregory met me in front of Ms. Whitehall's apartment door. He was dressed in his usual tight black sweatshirt and dark jeans; his hair had grown in the last month, and started to cover his chiseled cheekbones. His power signature was rich and multi-toned, and revealed none of the irritation from being jousted out of bed.

His eyes shifted away as I approached, then looked at me again and nodded. The awkwardness that had been present since that kiss was still there, though it usually subsided once I got a bit of my inner bitch going.

So exactly what happened that night in front of the hospice?

To keep the story short, while we kissed I thought I felt a spark like how they'd described what it would be like with a *solus iungere*, and I assumed Gregory felt the same way as he pulled me closer and deepened the kiss. But that obviously wasn't the case because the next thing I knew he ended the kiss rather abruptly, stepping back with an unreadable expression, and that was that.

And oh, for vengeance demons, *solus iungere* was the word for soul mate.

I rang the doorbell.

"Don't say a word," I warned. It was hard to get my inner bitch to come out when it was I who got us into this interview with a TPC.

"I wasn't going to," he replied evenly.

I gritted my teeth. It would've been better if he'd yelled at me, or mocked me. But he didn't. He'd be a perfect gentleman today.

As he had been for the past month. Damn him.

The door opened, and the combined smell of birdseed, cat litter, and dog breath assaulted my nose. I resisted the urge to gag. I'd been to the shelter that Rosemary volunteered at, and not even there was the smell of animals so pungent.

"Come on in." A woman in her sleeping robe and curlers beckoned, and I had no choice but to follow her inside. I glanced at Gregory, who shrugged resignedly.

The dark and tiny one bedroom apartment definitely had too many animals in too tight a space. As my host led me to her living room, I counted five cats, two dogs, one parrot, and a family of free-run hamsters. The gluttonous cat in question could've made off with a hamster or two and it would have never been noticed. No wonder the feline was getting fat.

So on top of paranoia, our potential client was also an animal hoarder.

"Good morning, Ms. Whitehall." Gregory bowed to her. Gotta hand it to him. His courteous tone betrayed none of his private reservations.

"Hello, Gregory." Ms. Whitehall huffed, "I haven't been

able to reach you since that one time you came here and I told you about the haunted litter box on the balcony. My Betty still gets quite a fright every time she goes in there. What do you have to say for yourself?"

Gregory pressed his lips together, in an attempt not to talk back, or to laugh, I didn't know which.

Ms. Whitehall turned to me and her demeanor warmed by several degrees. I was, after all, the one who agreed to meet her. "You must be Megan."

"Nice to meet you, ma'am." I nodded toward her.

I was rewarded with a smile.

Ms. Whitehall went to a high armchair and shooed away a napping kitten. "Sorry, Princess Penelope, Mommy has guests."

Ms. Whitehall patted at the now empty armchair and gestured at me. "Come sit over here, dear."

She didn't offer Gregory a seat.

"Can I get you a coffee or tea?" she asked me.

I doubted I wanted anything from her kitchen. From where I was I could see a sink full of dirty plates with stuck-on food. She was even a bigger slob than me. "It's alright, ma'am."

As Ms. Whitehall settled herself in a second armchair, Gregory cleared his throat. "What is it you want to see us about?"

"My neighbor," she said.

"The one you said stole your jellybeans?" Gregory asked.

She shook her head. "No, another one."

Gregory raised a single eyebrow in my direction in a look that said it all.

"Hey, if you know about the jellybeans, it means you *did* get my messages." Ms. Whitehall glared and shook her index finger at Gregory. "Shame on you for not answering an old lady's call, boy. Anyway, I'm not talking about *that* neighbor.

He's across the hallway. I'm talking about that new girl who just moved next door."

"What did this one do?" I asked.

"Why, she's an absolute slut. Slut, I tell ya. Slut!"

"Huh?"

"She's been having very loud sex all hours of the day. Moaning and screaming. More than two voices most of the time. The noise stopped just before you arrived, but it'll be back before you know it. The walls are thin here and I could hear everything. Even my neutered cats went into heat with all those god-awful sounds!"

"We're here because your neighbor is, er, having too much fun?" I had a very hard time keeping the laughter from my voice. I dared not chance a glance at Gregory. I was embarrassed, because the job turned out to be such a joke, and because we were talking about sex in the presence of a guy who'd more or less rejected me.

"Ms. Whitehall, there's no law against that," Gregory explained gently. "What people do in their home is their own business."

Ms. Whitehall snorted. "That's what the building management said, and the police, too. That's why I called you guys here to get this fixed. Boy, am I in need of some good vengeance. I'm entitled to a good night's sleep like anyone else, and my animals *not* traumatized!"

A tomcat entered, sat down on the rug in the center of the room, and promptly licked his balls for all the world to see. Yeah, he was very traumatized indeed.

"The noise has been keeping me up at night for days now," Ms. Whitehall continued. "Why do you think I called you at six in the morning?"

Gregory took a deep breath and squared his shoulders. I knew that posture. That was how he mentally steeled himself to refuse a vengeance job at the end of an initial interview. "As much as this noise is a nuisance to you, I'm afraid—"

"We'll do it," I said.

"But—" Gregory protested. I cut him off with a *we'll-talk-later* look, and rushed him out of the apartment, promising Ms. Whitehall I would be in touch soon.

"What the hell was that?" Gregory demanded once we were out in the hallway again.

"Didn't you see the dark circles under her eyes?" I asked. "She's not faking it. This is really stressing her out."

"Be that as it may, you know full well she doesn't have a leg to stand on for true vengeance."

"Who said anything about true vengeance?"

"Then what are you talking about?" Gregory frowned.

"Oh, come on, be a little more creative. There's more than one way to resolve this issue." The little trickster in me smiled. "We could put a super drying spell on the neighbor's lubricant, if she uses any. Or we could use this new charm Fir just invented called Underneath Your Clothes, which makes people appear ten times less attractive once they're in their birthday suit. Or we could scare away a would-be lover during the pre-coitus bathroom break with an illusion of mold in the toilet bowl. All this activated only after eleven at night, of course. I just want the neighbor to have fun that is a little less disruptive to others, not to stop having it altogether."

Gregory looked like he wasn't sure if he should be horrified or impressed. "You know that the name of this business is called Clear Vengeance, right? With 'vengeance' being the operative word?"

I shrugged. "I don't think the customers care, as long as the job is done. This could be like a new side business or something, with me, your partner, bringing a trickster flare to the business. I mean, it's not like you have to keep to a certain kind of services offered for tax purposes, right?"

I got him there, and he knew it.

It felt nice to give my inner trickster a chance to come out and play. It would give me something else to focus on. I refused to moon and act like a lovesick human teenager, though it was well within my rights, even socially acceptable to do so, when a vengeance demon met her *solus iungere*.

Well, I was a hybrid. My trickster heritage was all about instant hookups and getting four kids young and all with different fathers. So who knew if a real soul mate was even in the cards anyway?

Yeah, it would be my luck that I was fated to get just half a soul mate out of Gregory.

CHAPTER 3

8:30 A.M.
Mini Job #1

As mercenaries, Gregory and I took on jobs both big and small. Most assignments averaged one to three days. But big assignments that had multiple phases, or involved a lot of preparation such as vetting and recon, could span over a month. We had two of those currently on the go.

And then there were the straightforward mini jobs that were like power naps, but with money earned. They were quick, easy, and a nice way to get the cash flow going while waiting for the bigger jobs to pay off.

For our first mini job of the day, we boarded a crowded GO Train carrying human office workers from the suburbs to downtown Toronto during the morning rush hour. We headed for the Quiet Zone, a designated noise-reduced area on the upper level of the train. It was a sanctuary for the long commuters to relax and get some shuteye, to prepare for another day of keeping their noses to the grindstone.

Too bad not everyone respected that intended purpose.

"...I crunched some numbers. Sales are up this month by twenty-three percent, forty-six point four percent year-on-year," a loud voice boomed in the Quiet Zone. "We're going to have no problem hitting the EAC. And the FRS is going to hit the roof. I suggest implementing the L.A.D.D.E.R right away, and deliver some high-value, high-impact, high-functioning..."

Our target was Cameron Bell, junior account manager at a large corporation, executive-in-training. He had the habit of making long business calls in the Quiet Zone, often for the duration of the entire train ride, much to the annoyance of his fellow commuters. On top of creating the illusion to his colleagues that he was in the office already when he was still on his way there, he thrived on subjecting the whole train to accounts of his self-proclaimed success with inflated numbers and the latest buzz words, half of which he misused anyway.

Nobody liked a wannabe.

The last thing people who had to put up with the bullshit of the business world needed was to listen to more of it in their own spare time. On their way to work, people were fantasizing about time with their family, their weekend at the cottage, and their own retirement. They didn't need this endless *blah, blah, blah* in their moment of tranquility.

So a group of them banded together and hired me and Gregory.

Mr. Bell had just gotten onto another phone call. An international conference call by the sound of it. High stake. He was just launching into an overview of his achievements this quarter when the earphone of his neighbor's smart phone came loose, interrupting his speech with the sound of a military-inspired app game: thunderous footsteps, shooting, explosion, curse words, etc.

When Mr. Bell tried to talk over the noise, there came

the sound of a baby wailing, and a dog's frantic barking like it was the end of the world.

Mr. Bell looked around, but found that nobody else was hearing what he was hearing, and there were no babies or dogs anywhere on the train. "No, sir. I'm not still at home...of course this presentation is important to me. I'll call you back when I get to the office...no, I'm not still *at* home. I swear..."

I repressed a smile. The whole purpose of the noise was to stop the phone call, but the boss thinking our target was playing hooky while talking shit out of his ass was an unexpected but happy bonus.

From now on, for a year, every time the guy made such a phone call on the train, noise would ensue, may it be club music, sound of bacon sizzling, or the crying and berating of a jealous girlfriend.

Ha, try to project a sense of professionalism with *that*! He wanted to do business in public? Then he had to put up with the downside of it.

And yes, at the end of the year our clients could renew the contract at the reduced price of 20 percent off. This was, after all, a business.

Get your copy of VENGEANCE FOR HIRE today!

BE A VENGEFUL VIXEN!

I'd love to have you join my Facebook reader group! Search "Vengeful Vixens Louisa Lo" on Facebook.

Sign up for my mailing list on my website for the latest news and offers!